If I love you, what business is it of yours?

Johann Wolfgang von Goethe

Also by Stan I.S. Law

Novels
GIFT OF GAMMAN
ONE JUST MAN, Winston Trilogy Book I
[Prequel to *Elohim—Masters & Minions*)
ELOHIM—Masters & Minions, Winston Trilogy Book II
(Sequel to *One Just Man*]
THE PRINCESS [Alexander Trilogy Book I]
ALEXANDER [Alexander Trilogy Book II]
SACHA—The Way Back [Alexander Trilogy Book III]
YESHUA—Personal Memoir of the Missing Years of Jesus
ENIGMA OF THE SECOND COMING
THE AVATAR SYNDROME
[Prequel to the *Headless World—The Vatican Incident*]
HEADLESS WORLD—The Vatican Incident
[Sequel to *The Avatar Syndrome*]
THE GATE—Things My Mother Told Me
NOW—BEING & BECOMING

Short stories
THE JEWEL AND OTHER STORIES
THE CATS & DOGS SERIES

Non-fiction eBooks
by Stanislaw Kapuscinski

VISUALIZATION—Creating Your Own Universe
KEY TO IMMORTALITY—Commentary on the Gospel of Thomas
BEYOND RELIGION Volumes I, II and III
[Collections of Essays on Perception of Reality]
DICTIONARY OF BIBLICAL SYMBOLISM

Poetry in Polish
[with illustrations by Bozena Happach]
KILKA SŁÓW I TROCHĘ GLINY
WIĘCEJ SŁÓW I WIĘCEJ GLINY

To order books please contact
INHOUSEPRESS, MONTREAL, CANADA
email: info@inhousepress.ca

MARVIN CLARK
In Search of Freedom

A Love Story

A novel by

STAN I.S. LAW

INHOUSEPRESS, MONTREAL, CANADA

Published by
INHOUSEPRESS
http://www.inhousepress.ca

Design and layout
Bozena Happach
Email: info@inhousepress.ca

Library and Archives Canada Cataloguing in Publication

Law, Stan I. S.
Marvin Clark : a Love Story / Stan I.S. Law.

ISBN 978-0-9813015-8-7

I. Title.

PS8623.A92M37 2010   C813'.6   C2010-907785-7

Printed and bound in the USA

For my Wife, the Sculptor

A Word about the Author

Stan I.S. Law (*aka* Stanislaw Kapuscinski), an architect, sculptor, and prolific writer, was educated in Poland and England. Since 1965 he resides in Canada. His special interests cover a broad spectrum of arts, sciences and philosophy. His fiction and non-fiction attest to his particular passion for the scope and the development of human potential.

Autumn

Winter

Spring

Summer

Epilogue

Autumn

Autumn is a second spring when every leaf is a flower.

Albert Camus

1

Delicious Monster

The sweet smell of incense began to clear even before the last *Dominus vobiscum.* What remained was a halo suspended in a luminescent haze around the glittering monstrance.

"*Et cum spiritu tuo,*" echoed a murmur of the still sleepy voices.

Then the final dismissal: "*Ite, Missa est.*" The mass was over.

"*Deo gratias,*" Marvin affirmed automatically.

The old priest, the tall boy carrying the censer and two serving boys in short surplices left the altar. As the fragrant mists slowly dissolved, Marvin's eyes focused on a little red light guarding the *sanctum sanctorum. Ite, missa est...* Once again it was time to go. The lad who had been carrying the censer came back to put out the candles—six perfectly steady flames in the perfectly still air of the chapel. Then—only the tiny red light remained.

"Mr. Clark?"

The young lady held an open file with documents. Two letters and a memo.

"Yes, I'm coming, sister," Marvin murmured. He wanted to dally a little longer, drifting on the last vestiges of incense soon to be supplanted by the musty smell of the eternally damp stone.

"Sir?"

Marvin Clark blinked repeatedly. Then, before turning toward his secretary, his eyes focused on the red dot of the smoke detector protruding from the suspended ceiling. The musty smell, the incense, the candles were gone, hidden behind thirty years, which separated Marvin from the orphanage of the good *Soeurs Grises*. Gray Sisters in a gray convent, passing time by sauntering the long gray corridors of their monotonous lives.

Marvin took the documents, glanced over them, signed the top copy of each and returned the folder to his secretary.

"Is that all, Miss Gascon?" He was now fully in the present.

"Yes, thank you, Sir," she said as she left Marvin Clark's office with a proficient deference. It was her very first job. She wanted to make a good impression.

It was the third time this month that Marvin's thoughts had taken him back to the orphanage of *Sainte Geneviève*. He wondered why. He was sure he had put behind any morbid recollections of his youth long ago. Morbid? Perhaps just empty. There was so little to remember.

Except for the loneliness.

Marvin remembered very little, but he had the letters. The sad letters his father had written to his mother when looking for work. All over England. His mother had saved them. The letters were Marvin's only tangible link with the past. What he hadn't read, he imagined.

Marvin's parents had emigrated to Canada from a small town in the north of England. They had had little choice. The local munitions factory—the only local employer—had become obsolete, another casualty of the ravaged Empire. England found it difficult to adjust to the post-war economy. "Move a mile, move a thousand miles..." his father had written. Marvin imagined a mixture of anger and sadness on his father's resigned face. "A thousand miles?" Marvin knew his mother would rather be poor in England than rich across the ocean.

"No good would come of it," she knew. His mother had known. Women know such things. She was getting on in years. It was time to start a family, or they would be spending their old age alone. England did not seem to offer any future to her intended offspring—but a thousand miles...? The war had left them with little to pack.

Marvin was born on the first anniversary of his parents' arrival in Canada. Two weeks short of the sixth anniversary, his parents were killed in a traffic accident. Murdered, really. A youth with more beer than he could handle ran them down, ignoring the red light. Marvin celebrated his fifth birthday at the orphanage of *Sainte Geneviève* run by the *Soeurs Grises*. They gave him all the love they had to offer. Love without affection. Cool, competent, perfunctory love. Sterile. The nuns—*Soeurs*, as they preferred to be called—had never been taught how to communicate warmth.

Marvin's recollection of his early days in the orphanage was very vague. Tattered. No more than snapshots. At the time, he did not speak a word of French. What little sentiment the Sisters attempted to exude from beneath their pale-gray habits must have gotten lost somewhere in the translation. Ultimately it was thanks to the *belles soeurs* that Marvin grew up perfectly bilingual. It proved useful, expedient, living in Quebec.

It was then, in those early days, that Marvin learned to escape the perpetual gray reality of monastic life into his private imaginary worlds of light and colour. Later, years later, he found he could invoke old memories by lighting a solitary candle. Upstairs, in his attic, while staring into the flickering light, he would drift into the reclusive world of his childhood. He would feel himself kneeling, his aching knees pressing against the worn step of the hard oak pew in the austere gray chapel. He would sense, then see, the distant inaccessible shimmer of the perpetual light at the altar. Sometimes a single lingering whiff of incense would tickle his nose. Then, even as years earlier, his nostrils would flare out hungry for the shimmering warmth of the candlelight, for the forgotten fragrance, there, up front, beyond his reach. With practice, from beneath half-closed eyelids, little

Marvin could see himself at the altar's very steps, red-carpeted, soft against the hard marble... He would feel himself embraced by the reassuring flames of the six majestic candles. There, up front, and only there, he felt comforted, secure.

Marvin remembered feeling left out. Excluded from the faint heartbeat of the convent. He had never been allowed to serve at the altar, to assist in the Bloodless Sacrifice of the mass. Not that he had understood its meaning. How could he have? The mass had been celebrated in Latin. Only later in French. By the time he had learned the latter, he had been considered too old to serve. Marvin had learned early to rely on his own inner worlds for warmth, for light and colour. For escape.

Two years after he was interned at the convent, at the age of seven, he started having music lessons on the organ. All boys had been "tested" for signs of talent or ability. Marvin had been among the five deemed worthy of *Soeur* Angelica's efforts. It had meant spending more time in the chapel — the birthplace of his inner dream-world. He practiced playing the organ with a passion.

So many years ago...

On one occasion, soon after he had rented the attic apartment at Mrs. Prentis's Pension, Marvin felt the need of solace. As usual he looked for a candle to focus his attention on its flame. For some reason he felt distracted. He switched on the radio. Young falsetto voices drifted unobtrusively, then filled and saturated his ears. The Vienna Boys' Choir. The music sounded so familiar. Then Marvin remembered. The voices echoed the small boys' choir at the orphanage. The music transported him instantly to the distant brightness of the altar. From that moment on, Marvin learned to escape unwanted reality with the aid of music. In time, over successive years, the flickering candles had been replaced by the sun straining through the stained-glass windows of the east-facing chancel, by the morning rays flirting with the trembling leaves of a single aspen, by a sea of marsh-marigolds smiling in an undulating meadow... by the shimmering light caught in the ripple of a forgotten lake. Marvin's imaginary kingdom grew in richness and complexity.

He was in his teens before he realized that not all people traveled to their inner realms; that not all had found their own warm, serene domains within the prolific beauty of the rolling fields, lakes and forests; that not all could see the stars reflected in the balmy ocean of their yearning souls. Marvin felt sorry for those people. Sorry for their loneliness, for the emptiness of their lives.

At fifteen Marvin was sent to the *Conservatoire de Musique* in Montreal. The nuns had predicted a bright future for their *protégé*. He studied the piano, history of music and composition. He liked all music; he loved the piano. Successive years brought him two third and one second prize at the annual competitions. Marvin had learned fast. Until the accident. He lost the tips of his third and index fingers in a stupid mishap. He had tried to help Sister Angelica slam shut a door of an old decrepit jalopy. The hinges were rusted. Marvin had tried too hard.

His musical career was over before it began. Marvin accepted the judgment of fate with equanimity. He had learned early to expect very little of life.

The next few years he remained with the Sisters. He was their mechanic, gardener, verger, their timid contact with the outside world. At twenty-four he felt the need to venture outside the gray walls. The nuns gave him a tearful farewell party. They all seemed like his sisters, perhaps vicarious, unrequited mothers. The *Mère Supérieure* also offered him excellent references. A week after Marvin left the gray walls, he began his career as a junior clerk at the *Hôtel de Ville*. The Town Hall was the pride of St-Onge, a fairly large municipality bordering on Montreal.

"To see him is to know him..." once quipped knowingly the slouching stereotypes at the Department of Parks and Recreation. Later, when Marvin Clark inherited from his retiring predecessor his very own cubicle with a window, the same colleagues snickered behind his back: "Once you meet Mr. Clark, you'll know what to expect!" Their conspiratorial smile carried a warning not to expect a great deal.

Marvin Clark's promotion had been yet another classic case of a misjudgment perpetrated by his superiors. Marvin had impressed them as the only clerk in the department who never seemed to grow tired of shifting the voluminous sheets of paper from the IN to the OUT basket adorning his desk. The methodical indifference with which he performed his work was misconstrued as an air of quiet confidence and devotion to duty.

"You can always rely on good old Clark..." was the consensus directly responsible for Marvin's promotion over his peers.

Marvin Clark was a man of just over average height. A light stoop, however, brought him right back to the departmental mean. His dark, deep-set, invariably distant eyes never quite met his interlocutor's. His gaze seemed to travel just over the shoulder, or else waver at the tip of the nose of the man he was addressing. If eyes can be said to be the windows of the soul, then Marvin's eyes opened inward, and inward they looked. This, in turn, was misinterpreted as a sign of shyness. At 47, Marvin had been a public servant for a little over twenty-three years. In another seven years he would qualify for a full pension.

Marvin was as scrupulous about his appearance as he was fastidious about his work. The last thing he did before leaving his attic apartment, in the morning, and the first on his arrival at work, was to visit the washroom to check his appearance. He considered his demeanor a form of armour. Behind it he felt free to be himself. From childhood Marvin had been, *perforce*, an inveterate loner. The perfunctory mask of studied indifference brought him the desired results. No one ever invited Marvin for a drink after work, nor had anyone invaded his private life by undue familiarity. His studied air of quiet detachment, wrapped in a middle-of-the-way gray, immaculately pressed suit, created an invisible screen between himself and the

surrounding world. Of the dozens of people he met weekly in
the course of discharging his duties, not one could, within five
minutes of leaving Marvin's office, offer a description of his
appearance. Marvin cultivated his obsequious anonymity without
a conscious effort.

For the last seventeen years, Marvin Clark had been renting
a room at Mrs. Prentis's Pension. The solid Victorian house,
almost a mansion, fostered an air of the good old days. The
elaborate twists and curves of the red brick façade, together with
the decorative sandstone trim, had withstood the ravages of time
and industrial pollution with quiet dignity.

Mrs. Prentis rented five rooms—four on the second floor
plus Marvin's attic. The sheer size and volume of the rooms
offered by the high ceilings, the extra-large bay windows and the
splendid ornate woodwork almost qualified them to be called
apartments. All rooms had kitchenettes discreetly concealed
behind full height curtains as well as individual bathrooms with
florid Victorian showers. One additional bathroom with an
enormous bathtub, designated for common use, seemed more
reminiscent of Roman Baths than of its Victorian heritage.

All five lodgers were men. At precisely seven o'clock, each
evening, they all met for dinner, which Mrs. Prentis provided
with a reasonably tasty, if repetitive, menu. On special occasions,
such as Christmas, or one of the "boys'" birthdays, Mrs. Prentis
would say a few words and present her "boys" with a glass of
South African sherry.

The most prominent among the five lodgers was a retired
artillery officer, Colonel James Mackenzie Whittlaw. His
perfectly erect stature crowned with a generous, snow-white
mane, which he permitted, contrary to army regulations, to flow
down to his shoulders, gave him an appearance, if not quite the
air, of an early-American Civil War general. His heavily lined
forehead sloping backwards from profuse bushy eyebrows
seemed well balanced by a strong, jutting chin. This aggressive
effect was accentuated by an unwavering steady gaze, defying
anyone to question the veracity of the many stories, which the
Colonel seemed bent on imparting to any willing or unwilling

audience. By such rhetoric the Colonel assured the preservation of facts which, in his mind, were worthy of becoming part of history. And stories there were many. Anecdotal reminiscences, invariably recounted in the present tense, suggested that the Colonel must have left the army just after the Boer war. Since the retired artilleryman occupied the room directly below that of Marvin Clark's powerful stereo, the Colonel's exploits were of pertinent consequence, as they—the exploits, not the stereo—had left him practically stone-deaf.

The other three gentlemen at the dinner table shared rather a lesser rank of eccentricity. Not one of them displayed any immediately distinguishing features. Mr. Jones, Mr. Graves and Mr. Johnson blended well indeed into the post-Victorian surroundings. They seemed to be as much a part of the faded pastel wallpaper as of the musty, dark-with-age woodwork. All three men were widowers, manifestly sixty-something. By some fickle quirk of fate, all three had converged on Mrs. Prentis's mansion to quietly spend the remaining days of their lives. While the three neither contributed to nor detracted from the evening gatherings, they seemed necessary to fill the empty places at the generous dinner table, more than large enough for Mrs. Prentis and her five guests.

Marvin liked the quiet atmosphere of the house. Other than the cursory exchanges about the state of the weather, he was left to his own thoughts, while the Colonel expounded his never-ending monologues about the conduct of officers and gentlemen on the field of glory.

Upstairs in his attic apartment, Marvin was given free rein to do as he wished. The whole of the attic floor had been converted into a very large L-shaped room. Marvin was the only lodger who enjoyed a separate, enclosed kitchenette, leaving the wall space of the main living area for other uses. Over the years, these walls became progressively lined with floor-to-ceiling shelving, tightly packed with books. Later, right-angled projections with additional shelving gave the room an appearance of a selective, but well-appointed, small-town library. The only wall free of books was the Southwest side, where the mansard roof had been converted into a shallow but wide bay window. Though it gave way onto a pleasant urban townscape, Marvin seldom took advantage of the view. In the safety of his private haven, he preferred to turn his vision inward.

Directly in front of the bay window, two sturdy wooden crates were placed symmetrically on each side and in front of a deeply padded executive armchair. The crates served a dual purpose. Each housed three powerful stereophonic speakers; each also served as support for the only living entities sharing Marvin's private life. Built into the upper portions of the crates were two enormous clay pots, from which sprang countless twisted and convoluted lianas ceaselessly carrying life-giving nectar to the ever-demanding, voluptuously extravagant foliage. The two plants belonged to a family of philodendrons. This particular species was named *monstera deliciosa*.

Marvin was fascinated by the complexity of the interweaving branches which never seemed tired of reaching out still farther and giving birth to a yet greater number of heavily serrated leaves. When the liana simultaneously reached the nine-foot ceiling, Marvin began to refer to them as his Monsters. Later, so as not to offend their floral sensibilities, he added the equivalent of the Latin pronoun: Delicious. From that day on, the Delicious Monsters and Marvin entered into a secret tacit relationship. The Monsters—and only the Monsters—knew of Marvin's dreams, aspirations, of his gentle ups and his lonely downs, and most of all, of his inner, private journeys. The green delicious friends were ever available, serenely reliable, superbly quiet yet always vigilant to his needs. In this blissful state of symbiosis, the three of them shared Marvin's only remaining passion: a very selective disk, record and tape collection.

Marvin's tastes ranged from early baroque *Concerti Grossi*, through Bach and Mozart to the somber if esoteric mysteries of Beethoven. Some composers he seemed to dismiss solely because their work brought back painful memories of his final days at the *Conservatoire de Musique*. He shied away from others because they did not nourish his need for inner peace. Still others, such as Tchaikovsky, he found overly aggressive and volatile. Schubert, excessively melodramatic. In later years, Marvin grew to like Mendelssohn; and finally, though only recently, he fell deeply in love with the music of Sibelius.

Marvin listened to his beloved disks in an oversized swivel armchair. From its position in the centre of the room, between the two speakers, he savored the quiet proximity of his *monsterae deliciosae,* his Delicious Monsters, while his eyes drifted toward some dallying cloud framed by the bay window. On his left were all the paraphernalia comprising his old-fashioned stereo system, which he'd assembled himself from the very best components available on the market. On his right was a two-shelved table where his current favourite books found a temporary abode. A lamp suspended from a long, sweeping, stainless-steel arch completed his command centre.

A relatively Spartan bed hid well within an alcove at the far end of the attic. The bathroom was next to the tiny kitchen, opposite the sleeping area. It was all Marvin needed. His need for opulence did not belong to the physical world.

It was here, in this private, jealously guarded haven that Marvin spent all his free moments. Reading and rereading his favourite books while listening to music were only part of his pleasure. More particularly, the deep leather armchair served as the command module of a private spaceship, in which he not only journeyed on terrestrial exploits but defied the enormousness of space. Fired by an unbridled imagination, fuelled by hunger for adventure, Marvin ventured toward distant planets, remote galaxies, unknown universes. In his singular spaceship, Marvin traversed time, drawing a tentative isthmus between forgotten history and the mysterious future.

And the universes were endless. A single sentence from one of his books could provide the necessary impetus to launch him headlong toward a distant galaxy. Sometimes, the following day, on his return from the office, he would continue his exuberant conquests, as though no interruption had taken place.

In time, Marvin's inner world inevitably assumed the place of objective reality. His everyday activities, his work at the Parks Department, had been relegated to the level of automatic functions, no more demanding of his inner resources than eating, breathing, or maintaining his cardiovascular system in good order. Marvin did not leave the physical world; he merely placed it in the proper perspective. The mundane became the automatic. The subconscious, the subjective, the realm of his total awareness, were liberated to function without restrictions imposed by the limitations of time and space. Marvin felt free. Had for years. Until now.

The problem became apparent about six months after Marvin first noticed that the *monsterae deliciosae* had also embarked on a space conquest of their own. Starting their individual journeys atop the two loudspeakers, the Monsters ventured upwards, spanned across the ceiling, and joined forces by reaching with their aerial roots into each other's pots. This marriage of convenience, or perhaps some form of esoteric vegetal love, seemed to have mobilized both plants into a frenzy of growth. The liana already supported by an intricate latticework of bamboo sticks also spanned along the ceiling, hanging from equally spaced hooks which Marvin had anchored to the two wooden rafters traversing his room. The plants reached out sideways and downward, as if searching for new grounds to conquer, new territories to cover with their insatiable craving for space, light and air.

When the expanding Monsters reached the bookshelves, Marvin had to make a decision. He was well aware that he would never reread many of the books he had acquired over the years. His taste in literature had ripened, become more selective. He valued the book-lined walls more for the atmosphere they created than for their usefulness in housing the objects of his avid reading habits. Yet, he loved his books. By looking at the walls, he could trace his own growth, his initial attempts at allowing his consciousness to free itself from his command module. He knew that he would never need to rely on those books to provide the necessary stimulus for his travels, as in the past; yet his heart needed its own roots, even as did his Delicious

Monsters. He did not have the heart to reduce the amount of fertilizer which he administered weekly to each pot. Neither could he withhold the water ration in an attempt to stunt the voluptuous growth. Yet, something had to give.

The next day, during his lunch break, Marvin visited the local hardware store. After due deliberation, he purchased a pair of plant clippers. He could not get rid of a feeling of considerable guilt as he wrapped the implement in a brown paper bag and hid it in his raincoat pocket. He returned to the office, having skipped lunch altogether. He was just not hungry. For the first time in many years, Marvin had vague problems with his routine work. It was as if, also for the first time in years, he had become aware of what he was doing. He became aware of the physical reality of his existence.

On his return from the office, Marvin hung his coat in the wardrobe, making sure that it remained out of sight of the Monsters. On his way to the bathroom, he avoided looking at his voracious friends. As he punctiliously combed his hair, he felt at a loss as to why he was acting this way.

At seven o'clock Marvin went down to dinner. The other four gentlemen were already seated. Mrs. Prentis had just wheeled in the side table with the tureen. He was *almost* late—the first time since he had his wallet stolen and had been delayed at the police station. That had been years ago. Marvin sat down, bowing to Mrs. Prentis, nodding to the other men. He found the Colonel's droning voice boring, almost irritating! For the first time in years he was aware of the rather bland taste of the vegetables. He wondered if Mrs. Prentis always overcooked her beans and carrots. He wondered why it should matter.

Marvin lingered at the dinner table longer than usual. Normally, he would excuse himself a polite five minutes after the end of the meal. He felt uneasy, discomposed. He searched for reassurance, he knew not for what. Incongruously, Marvin noted that the cut-glass chandelier over the table could not have been cleaned since it was hung, probably toward the end of the last century. He wondered why he had never noticed it before. He wondered why he bothered to even think about the stupid chandelier. He rose from the table with the others, thanked Mrs. Prentis and, with heavy steps, climbed the four flights to his attic.

Marvin was vaguely aware of a pang of guilt as he walked past the entrance wardrobe. He shrugged. From the nearest bookshelf he picked a book at random. Without looking up, he sank into his armchair and flipped the pages. He did not feel like reading. He swiveled the chair to the left and switched off the light. Almost as an afterthought, he turned on the stereo. Beethoven's Fifth flooded the room. He turned down the volume and sank deeply into his armchair.

Music, which normally lifted him almost instantly into a different reality, this time anchored him firmly to the ground. He became aware of a pressing, esoteric weight, as Beethoven drew him into his ponderous mysteries. The chords penetrated his whole body—set up sympathetic rhythms within his bone structure. For no discernible reason he felt tired. Very, very tired. His last conscious thoughts were of a strong desire to switch off the Beethoven tape and put on Sibelius. Somehow the thought made him feel guilty.

Marvin's dream was as turbulent as his mood. He did not travel to distant worlds, nor did he enjoy the freedom which dreaming normally affords. As soon as he closed his eyes, he felt drawn, inexorably, into a thick, impenetrable jungle, a twisted maze of interwoven tendrils. Liana, pulsating coils of pungent flesh, converged on him, threatening to entangle and squeeze him into a lifeless cocoon, to suck the life force from his helpless body. He felt unable to move, unable to escape the advancing labyrinth of living, convoluted, writhing twines of green doom. With agonizing slowness, the crawling mass began to climb his legs: each fiber, each searching tendril asserting a distinct life of its own. As the first prodding finger reached his neck, he tried to scream. Too late! No sound escaped his parched throat.

He woke up just after midnight. His aching body was drenched in sweat. He felt stiff, as if he hadn't moved for countless hours. His throat hurt as though he'd been shouting at the top of his voice. When he touched his neck, it felt swollen and painful. He tried hard to dismiss the vivid dream from his memory.

Helpless, exhausted, he sat very still.

Some considerable time later, Marvin forced himself to get up. As he stumbled toward the bathroom, he was vaguely conscious of the still humming stereo. Then, as though pressed by some external command, in near total darkness, he practically tore off his clothing. His numb fingers searched for the taps. Then... then the blissful drops descended from the dark sky. The trees parted their crowns and... a warm, life-giving shower caressed his naked body. A shower from heaven. For a long time he stood, almost still, rapt in the luscious massage.

Marvin felt restored. Physically.

Still with some trepidation, he stretched out on the bed. Later, much later, just before going to sleep, a vague whimsical smile touched the corners of his mouth. It stayed there as he affirmed his resolution.

He awoke at the usual time. A breakfast of one soft-boiled egg, toast, complemented by strong black coffee tasted particularly good this morning. Better than any he could remember! Before leaving for the office, Marvin opened the window just enough to let the fresh air trickle in. At this time of the year he always kept it closed at night in case the draft would injure his Delicious Monster.

Delicious Monster. His only friend. Faithful.

He checked the thermostat, put on his coat and made his way down the stairs.

The air was brisk, an omen of an early autumn. It felt especially inviting this morning. The slight mist was bound to clear and let the sunshine flood his apartment. He crossed the street to the nearest lamppost, which had a trash can attached to its metal base. The container was quite empty. Marvin reached into his coat pocket and took out a brown paper package. As he placed it carefully at the bottom of the can, the whimsical smile playing on his lips became perceptibly more pronounced. Then, almost immediately, his thoughts turned elsewhere.

"Sibelius," he thought. "Tonight I shall visit Finland."

His eyes reached across the street to his attic window. In the slightest breeze of the open sash, moving up and down with a gently waving motion, was a five-pronged, freshly unfurled serrated leaf of his Delicious Monster.

Even as Marvin turned toward his office, he inhaled the fresh mist rising over the sleepy lakes of Finland. A little afar, he sensed a dark forest protecting the lake from the northern winds. Then he heard the music. Sibelius.

Without a conscious thought, Marvin quickened his pace so as to arrive in his office precisely at eight o'clock.

* * *

2

The Manuscript

Getting the piano to the attic was the least of Marvin's problems. Trying to convince Mrs. Prentis that he needed it, although by his own admission he hadn't played a note since the two had met, was quite another matter. On the other hand, if it weren't for Marvin's well-established, indeed cultivated, eccentricities, Mrs. Prentis would not have tolerated such an absurd idea. In fact, had she even suspected that Marvin could play the piano, she was sure to have forbidden the introduction of such a heavy and cumbersome instrument into her attic.

But then again, for the last seventeen years Marvin Clark had been an exemplary tenant. At no time had there been even a hint of scandal or a suggestion of any untoward behavior from Mr. Clark. Mrs. Prentis's knowledge, comfortable in the fact that Marvin was (indeed most probably would continue to be during her lifetime) a senior employee of the Municipal Department of Parks and Recreation, convinced her that Mr. Clark's request must have been anchored in some confidential work he was doing for the Department. At least that is what Mr. Clark hinted at, never actually saying so but neither denying that, since he had been promoted to an office with a window, there were things which he was not free to discuss outside the Municipal corridors.

Three days after Marvin received Mrs. Prentis's permission to install the piano in his apartment, four men sporting gray-green overalls of the Public Works Department emerged from a semi-van bearing municipal insignia. With efficiency presumably bred by experience, and with hardly a grunt, they lifted, lowered, carried, pushed and pulled and rolled a large crate toward, up and through the front door. Mrs. Prentis, much impressed by the efficiency of these close-mouthed deliverymen, immediately offered them a cup of tea. Had these young men been instructed to be so silent, she wondered? Was there a sinister intent behind Mr. Clark's taciturn helpers? Running a house for five extremely amenable men, Mrs. Prentis may well have been hoping for an extracurricular stimulation of her mundane routine.

Alas, Mrs. Prentis's generosity was not rewarded by any additional information. Mr. Clark's cumbersome contraption was here to stay. Surely, the young man (all men below the age of sixty-five were young in Mrs. Prentis's estimation) did not intend taking up music lessons? Not at his age, what, with those foreshortened fingers?

Some fifteen minutes later, accompanied by a crescendo of grunts, groans, ouches and hisses, the crate proceeded up the wide Victorian staircase, up, up and up to the attic. There the men settled for a well-earned rest. They were to await Mr. Clark for further instructions.

Punctually at a quarter past noon, Marvin returned home to supervise the installation. By then, all four gentlemen lodgers had left their doors ajar to partake vicariously in the excitement of a rare commotion. Marvin proceeded up the stairs, fending off quizzical eyebrows with a cryptic smile. He managed this without turning his head, as though retaining his cloak of invisibility. Mrs. Prentis had once said that Marvin hovered effortlessly where the contrasts met in a quiet, unassuming harmony; where the opposites found something in common. At least, that is what she had intended to say. What she actually said was that Mr. Clark embodied the modest, the neutral, the moderate, the intermediate, the normal. Perhaps a trifle boring, she thought, but naturally had not said so. Mrs. Prentis regarded her young man as the standard. She measured others by how they differed from Marvin Clark.

Marvin found the four carriers comfortably laid out, on their backs and sides, along the upper steps and landing. At his approach, the foreman got to his feet with a saluting grunt, whereas the others moved to one side to let Marvin pass and open the door. Marvin ignored them, his eyes riveted to the large crate. His smile broadened. Thank God it's an upright, he thought. Then his gaze wandered just to the left of the foreman's nose.

"Good morning, gentlemen. If you would be so kind?"

With that Marvin turned and walked into his apartment. The men followed, then stopped dead in their tracks. It was the ceiling. Presumably a ceiling, since whatever defined that horizontal plane of the room was completely hidden from view. All the men could see was a mass of tangled liana. Some tendrils with enormous serrated leaves were hanging down to within six or five feet off the floor. To reach the bay window, the men would have to bow and weave between the hanging branches. They decided against it.

Some weeks ago, Marvin had toyed with the idea of trimming the suspended jungle to a reasonable size. The memories of that night still made him uncomfortable. Some days later, he had begun offering individual cuttings to his colleagues at work. In his mind's eye, Marvin could see the ceilings in St-Onge—houses, apartments, offices... all ceilings, covered with the luscious, ever-creeping, crawling tentacles, until the whole town grew into a geodesic dome supported on the continuous lattice of his Delicious Monster. He thought of himself as the father of this edifice, the creator of a greenhouse wherein the building and the exhibit are one.

"This way, gentlemen, if you would?" Whatever Marvin's shortcomings, he was polite to a fault.

The men looked again at the ceiling, then at each other, one or two scratching their heads. Finally the foreman pointed to the crate. They heaved their burden in total silence, moving quickly as though wishing to escape as soon as possible. Preferably immediately. But Marvin did not make it easy for them. He insisted that first they remove and cart away all the protective crating.

"Chaque chose à sa place," he told them, with a knowing wink.

The piano was placed directly opposite the bay window. The moment the workmen left, the previous cryptic smile returned to Marvin's normally passive features. From a brown paper package he took out a three-part mirror. Folding open the half-cover at the top of the piano, Marvin hung the mirror on two hooks, directly above the music shelf. He then placed a rotating tabouret in front of the piano, adjusted its height and, almost reluctantly, sat down. Next he set the angles of the folding, adjustable rear-view mirrors to give him a panoramic vista of his beloved Monster. He was very conscious of its presence behind him. At last all was ready. Marvin rested his hands on his lap and sat very still. For a while he looked into the mirror. Then his eyelids lowered, his eyes half closed. He did nothing.

He waited...

After a considerable time, Marvin's hands rose as though guided by their own volition. His fingers twitched, momentarily hovered in an emotive, expectant silence, then gently, ever so gently, brushed the keyboard: a single, long forgotten chord... then another; then a climbing arpeggio. For the first time in twenty-eight years, his fingers caressed the smooth, cool ivory. Marvin completely forgot about the blemish of his third and index fingers. His eyes left the keyboard, wandered under and through the dangling serrated leaves, skimmed past the distant bay-window, then drifted into lands unknown, inviting, beguiling...

A beeping tattoo from his wristwatch brought Marvin back to the attic. The time was twelve forty-five. Carefully he lowered the rosewood top over the keyboard. During the next sixty seconds Marvin adjusted his tie, smoothed the lapels of his gray double-breasted jacket, combed his hair, checked with salubrious propriety the perfectly trimmed nails of both his hands, and turned toward the door. Thirteen minutes later, Marvin Clark entered the building of the Municipal Department of Parks and Recreation. At one o'clock he sat at his desk.

Even as his left hand reached out mechanically toward the IN basket, his eyes retained some of the distant, yearning luster. Marvin lowered his eyes over the printed form, made a note on the margin and, without further thought, dropped it into the OUT basket perched at the right front corner of his standard, grade-2, municipal-issue desk. Simultaneously, his left hand reached out for the next piece of bureaucratic protocol.

Exactly three hours and fifty-five minutes later, Marvin Clark washed his hands, carefully combed his hair and said goodbye to Miss Gascon.

"Au revoir, Monsieur Clark. À demain, Monsieur!" His secretary replied, rising slightly from her typing station. Her eyes followed her boss with some interest. Wasn't there a suggestion of a cryptic smile on Mr. Clark's stoic face? Perhaps a lover...?

"Non!" She shrugged. "Not *Monsieur* Clark, surely?"

Marvin Clark was returning to his spaceship.

When facing other people, Marvin took great care to maintain his invisibility. If he did harbor the remnants of vanity, then it manifested itself in his lingering pride at being able comport to his life as the antithesis of ego. He did permit himself a sufficient expression of self to support his station in life, or at least in the office. But when feeling free, when secreted within the protective walls of his private kingdom, when sitting at the console of his inter-stellar, inter-galactic, inter-universal spaceship, Marvin denied his ego, his self, almost as though he denied his own existence. He became one with his dream, his vision: one with the universe.

In the most recent past, Marvin had been escaping physical reality by invading the worlds of his secret friends. He visited private universes created by other dreamers, other travelers, who through the generosity of spirit offered to share with him their mysteries. Marvin loved his books. He loved 'his' authors. They were his family. Surely, these very same worlds were accessible to all who reached out for them. The magic kingdoms that stretched the outer reaches of Marvin's inner space.

Beyond infinity?

It took time. And effort. Marvin's ventures into the unknown began in the realm of imagination. He relaxed, he concentrated, he imagined, he witnessed. Over the years, that which he imagined solidified, became more real. At no time did he lose the distinction between the inner and the outer realities. Yet as time passed, his inner worlds grew in intensity; they acquired depth and colour. They had awakened his inner, esoteric senses.

Even as, on occasion, a single gust of wind can bring forth a distant aroma, so, too, mysterious incense first touched, then grew, then filled his private kingdoms. Later still came the sound, the harmony, the pervading vibration. The ponderous sound of trees swaying with the breath of springtime, the buzzing sound of insects hovering over some distant water... The sound of living and growing, becoming... The music of Life Eternal. In time Marvin realized that the physical, objective world is but a hazy reflection of the splendor that lies within.

There were no outer limits to Marvin's inner kingdom.

When Marvin Clark won the upright piano in the inter-departmental raffle, he knew that, as with all things in life, there must have been a reason for this turn of *kismet*. Even if reasons for any particular occurrence might not be immediately apparent, Marvin did not put much faith in accidents. Therefore, while waiting for the gods to reveal their intentions, he played his piano—sparingly but daily. Marvin had no intention of taking up music seriously. All too soon his two delinquent fingers manifested their limitations. But he enjoyed some shorter pieces, not too technically demanding. He played them cautiously, rather like meeting old friends he hadn't seen for a very long while. The memories of his studies came back as musical fragments, chords scattered across the fabric of time.

Marvin recalled other subjects at the *Conservatoire*: history of music, conducting, composition. From a library in Montreal he took out several orchestral scores. With a strange, undefined longing, he followed the partitions while listening to their interpretation on his disks. The sheets of music that were filled with black, ovoid dots, lines, quavers, crotchets, gradually began to make sense. He remembered. There was no pain in his memories. No bitterness. Just *kismet*. He became fascinated by the manuscripts. After a mere few weeks he could practically hear the music by just looking at the notes disposed on a sheet of music-paper.

Sometimes his new hobby coincided with his travels. Studying the scores while relaxed in his armchair, he would drift off to his beloved dream worlds. A touch of a button on his stereophonic console and his ship would soar, far beyond the stifling reality of his immediate surroundings. For a considerable time Jean Sibelius had seemed to impel Marvin on his journeys. Visions of gently rolling fields, of lakes and forests, of bird and beast, rapacious yet living in harmony within the wondrous scheme of nature, all seemed implicit in Sibelius's music. It had been there, within those verdant Finnish expanses, that Marvin's inner sense of smell had first experienced such great intensity, such extraordinary clarity. It had been as though each fragrance, each flower, each plant, each blade of grass presented itself individually for his sensory examination. And then each individual sensation had blended into a most exquisite aroma. Marvin's head swam for hours after he returned from that particular venture.

On one occasion, as Marvin hovered over the misty lakes of his beloved Finland, a single chord had whisked him away from the enticing regions. He found himself in a small concert hall, sitting alone, looking at the back of a man conducting a small orchestra. Marvin recalled being frozen into a state of complete immobility, of being spellbound. The conductor, with the apparent ease of a prolific genius, was transforming Marvin's visions of lakes and fields and forests into most wondrous sounds. Marvin vaguely recalled glancing at the program, half folded, lying on his lap. He remembered the words "Symphonic Poem" followed by the name Julius Christian... the rest of the name was hidden by the fold of the paper.

Julius Christian... later to be known as Jean Sibelius.

From that day on, Marvin began to examine his private, Finnish landscapes in a different light, perhaps... a different sound? And then, rather than remaining passive while being transported by the emotive power of Sibelius's masterpieces, Marvin began listening intensely to his chimerical, yet very real surroundings. Almost immediately, gentle chords—then harmonies—began to flow from an enchanted nature. Music enraptured his ears, music evocative of the diversity of forms, of the profusion of creative expression. Marvin felt drawn into the very essence of the elements, the soul of their manifestation. He sensed the vibrations that made them and infused them with quintessential substance.

One day after supper, during a lazy dusk of early autumn, Marvin drifted off on one of his emotive travels only to return, quickly, with an acute sense of longing. He felt strongly that he had left things unfinished. He felt agitated, his peace disrupted for no perceptible reason. He decided to take a brisk stroll. The gray concrete sidewalk seemed particularly anonymous tonight. The air was still warm, rather humid. Marvin's unsettled thoughts were punctuated by rows of sentinel trees holding their silent vigil on each side of the empty street. Chains of parked cars, perhaps in search of shade during the day, now resting indifferently, squeezed bumper to bumper under the elms' protective crowns. Marvin thought of his inner worlds. How different... how indifferent... He smiled at the play on words. How different from the world he'd just left—the world pulsating with life, intense with sweet enchantment. And here? How silent. How very, very silent...

He turned on his heel.

It must have been years since Marvin Clark hurried his step enough to qualify it as running. Yet at this moment he ran with all his might, his chest heaving in unaccustomed effort. He mounted the stairs two at a time. At last he stood still, his back pressed to the oak door, shutting out the obscene world of silence and derision. He was back in his own domain. Here, Marvin knew the rules; he knew how to break the silence. The silence of indifference.

The now familiar quizzical smile tugged at the corners of his mouth. He walked to the piano. His mind was already far distant. Marvin reached for a sheet of music and spread it on the inclined support. From the inside pocket of his jacket he took out an old-fashioned fountain pen. An old pen. It once belonged to his father. For a moment he caressed its shaft, as though a favourite toy; then his eyes focused on the sheet of paper. The blank staves stared back at him, inviting, nay... commanding action. He leaned forward and wrote with meticulous care two words just above the top line: *Poème Symphonique*. Then his eyes seemed drawn by the keyboard. The ivory slats appeared to shimmer...

... a white crystalline powder swelled slightly, then fell back, returned in shy, intermittent tremolos toward the blanket of oblivion. Cold, indifference. A sharp crack, a cut of a dispassionate stiletto as ice exploded in a tall, forlorn pine... Then silence. Silence but for the heedless wind howling ceaselessly, pushing and pulling, tugging at the pensive, brooding clouds. A sudden cry, pain, then... a whimper cut short by gurgle of blood, red on the white snow, death cast upon innocence, warm blood upon a sea of coldness... no animosity, neither pleading for nor granting forgiveness...

Marvin's hand wrote, then scribbled, only just able to keep up with the images swirling within him. The winter held fast yet soon gave way to spring sunshine...

... the shimmer, the whisper of bubbling brooks, a widening rill, then river, flowing, meandering, hesitant, persistent, hopeful, cascading scherzando... The lake, still frozen. Staccato cracks of

*the breaking ice... The water, oh, such wondrous water, a
sudden spark, a glimmer, a living mirror gazing up at the white
fluffy travelers on their ephemeral journey across the blue, blue
yonder...*

Marvin did not go to bed that night. He awakened fully
dressed, half lying on the unopened settee. He stood a long, long
time under the shower. It was Sunday. On weekdays Mrs. Prentis
served all five tenants their breakfast. On Saturdays and Sundays
the men were left to fend for themselves. Marvin made lots of
strong coffee, sipped it black, slowly, as though attempting to
delay the inevitable. Breakfast over, he methodically cleaned the
dishes, picked up some innocuous lint from the somewhat worn
carpet and finally, with a knotted stomach, he turned toward the
piano.

Stacked vertically on the music shelf was a handful of
double sheets of music paper. Marvin scanned the score, his face
a strange mixture of respect and amazement. He held in his
trembling hands a complete manuscript, partitioned, annotated,
complete in every detail. He searched his memory. A memory
sequestered in the deepest recesses of his mind. He thought he
remembered opening his old, cherished fountain pen, his hand
poised over the blank sheets, then moving across the paper with a
strange confidence. The ink flowing...

Sitting there, that morning, Marvin knew that even had he
been offered a million dollars, he would not be able to repeat
what his hand had done last night. Nor in a million nights.

He sank into his armchair. With a peculiar mixture of pride
and disbelief, he scanned, then studied in minute detail, the crisp
sheets of the manuscript. Moments later he heard the sound. The
notes, chords, harmonies seemed to rise from the paper, fill his
ears, head, body. The music filled his whole being—filled it to
overflowing.

Images of beauty, of all he'd ever longed for. Of suspended
limits. Of granted supplication. Marvin felt sated, blessed and...
and strangely humble.

Later, the elements of that morning remained vivid in his memory.

A month later, Marvin took the score to his office. Sending Miss Gascon on some errand, he made two complete photocopies. He made them himself. He could not allow other hands to touch the original manuscript. He then signed all the copies—not where the composer would have signed them, but on the bottom of each page, next to the page number.

During his lunch break, Marvin took a bus to Morris, Jordan and Dawson, the music publishers' office. Last week he had made an appointment with their Mr. John B. Dawson. Marvin had previously explained, on the phone, that he had come across a manuscript in old family papers. How old? Marvin wasn't sure. Marvin wondered if Mr. Dawson would kindly look at it and give him an opinion.

Marvin left a copy of the manuscript in Mr. Dawson's care.

That same evening, Mr. Dawson called Marvin at home. Mr. Dawson asked to see Marvin the next day. Mr. Dawson would not discuss the matter over the phone.

Marvin arrived at the publishers' office punctually, directly from his office. Once again, he had to forego his lunch hour. 'No matter,' he shrugged. 'I can eat every day.' The elderly secretary showed him to Mr. Dawson's office immediately. She was considerably more polite than Marvin remembered her. Her dried-up face actually broke into an evidently unfamiliar smile. Mr. Dawson actually rose to greet him.

"Would you care for a drop of old Spanish sherry?" Mr. Dawson underlined his question by attempting to jut his paradoxically weak chin at Marvin. "Perhaps something stronger? A Scotch or a cognac....?"

The jutting gentleman seemed to have shed about forty years of his considerable age as he peered at Marvin with a peculiar gleam over his *pince-nez* half-moons. Marvin accepted the first offer and sank into a well-upholstered armchair. Why, he wondered, do I feel that I am about to be swallowed? Swallowed whole, or perhaps quartered.

After the usual, if fairly succinct, exchanges about the inclement weather, Mr.—please call me J.B.—Dawson removed his gold-rimmed glasses. He walked around his flamboyant, beautifully carved antique desk and propped his antique behind on its edge. He then proceeded to scrutinize Marvin with a studiously penetrating gaze.

"It's not signed, you know," he said finally.

Mr. Dawson's face displayed a quizzical expression, while he seemed busy rubbing his thumb. The latter habit, Marvin learned later, was a sign of mild irritation.

"No...." Marvin agreed.

"Aha! Then you noticed." Mr. Dawson, for reasons known only to himself, seemed pleased. "Do you do much traveling, Mr. Clark?"

Marvin, normally an expert on poker-face expressions, could not help grinning. In fact, a deep gurgle warbled in his throat. He doubted Mr. Dawson, J.B., would give credence to his daily, inner-spatial travels.

"Not in recent years, really..." Marvin decided to remain cryptic—or at least noncommittal.

"Mr. Clark, Sir." J.B. was at his most formal. "What I am going to tell you may reach beyond your... you might not believe it." His left thumb was working overtime. "Frankly, I don't know how to put it."

J.B. did not strike Marvin as a man who often found himself at a loss for words. For the moment, Marvin decided to sit tight and observe with detachment—practically admire—Mr. Dawson's performance.

"Mr. Clark," J.B. began again. "You probably do not know this, but I have been in the music business for almost fifty years. I have handled thousands, literally thousands of manuscripts. I have examined, with meticulous care, countless scores which people believed had been long-lost treasures of a bygone era." Mr. Dawson took out a large handkerchief and gently mopped his receding forehead. "I am prepared to stake my not inconsiderable reputation that you, Mr. Clark—that you

are the owner of a heretofore unknown manuscript of Jean
Sibelius!"

Mr. Dawson delivered the last sentence standing up. Marvin
waited for any further declaration. Alas, Mr. Dawson turned,
rounded his desk again and lowered himself into his overstuffed
leather armchair. He gave signs of being on the verge of
collapse.

"Just what makes you think so, J.B.?" Marvin asked
innocently.

Mr. Dawson pressed a button in his desk. Two large sections
of a paneled wall on his left slid open, revealing a good-sized
screen. Some more manipulation of other concealed buttons in
Mr. Dawson's drawer brought two images of a manuscript to the
display area. Both projected images were about three times their
original size. Mr. Dawson rubbed his left thumb and took hold
of two handles on a portable console.

"Watch very carefully, Mr. Clark." His voice was definitely
excited. "The manuscript on the left is an authenticated copy of
Jean Sibelius's symphonic poem. The one on the right is the
Poème Symphonique which you brought here yesterday. I fed
your copy into our computer in order to trace the possible
composer. That's the way we do things, you know. We have the
very latest equipment." He stopped to mop his shining
forehead. "Now watch the copy on the right—your copy, Mr.
Clark."

Mr. Dawson manipulated the handles until the right and the
left projections overlapped in certain areas.

"There!" he almost shouted. "There!" he repeated, in a
hushed conspiratorial whisper. "Mr. Clark! Mr. Clark..."

Mr. Dawson was definitely beside himself. His feeble chin
and his left thumb were again working overtime. "This is
undoubtedly the crowning achievement of my entire, yes, Mr.
Clark, my entire career!" Once more he collapsed against the
protective comfort of his armchair.

"Did you enjoy the music?" Marvin asked quietly.

"Music? What music? Oh, yes, of course! Ha, ha." The old
man granted Marvin a look of kind, paternal indulgence. "Oh,

we don't listen to music, Mr. Clark. That's for, for..." he waved his arms, dismissing the matter as of no consequence; "that's a quite different department. Mr. Clark, you are most probably a very rich man. Why, museums in Finland would pay a small fortune for the original. You do have the original, of course, Mr. Clark?" There was a moment of suspense weighing heavily in the air.

"I shall have to look for it, Mr. Dawson."

Marvin was considerably amused by the whole affair. He made a mental note to buy tickets for the local repertory theater season. "I shall have to look for it. The moment I get a chance." He added gravely.

"Please, do bear us in mind, Mr. Clark. Do bear us in mind. We are always at your disposal. We need your permission to publish this manuscript, of course. Shall we say, ten thousand copies? We should keep them rare. To start with. Later, later..." Mr. Dawson's eyes were happily counting the mounting commissions. "We shall prepare all the papers. Have lawyers on call. Copyrights, contracts, royalties, all that sort of thing. Leave it in our hands, Mr. Clark. Leave it..."

"I'm afraid I must be going. Back to the grindstone, you know." Suddenly Marvin felt rather tired. He longed to be in his private spaceship, or at least in the relative anonymity of his office. He badly needed to be alone. Completely alone.

He shook Mr. Dawson's proffered hand and almost ran out of the plush office. He walked fast, looking straight ahead. Then he looked up. His eyes rested on an elongated, hesitant cloud. The cloud seemed familiar. Marvin smiled. He felt grateful. Could it have traveled halfway around the world just to cheer me up, he wondered? He no longer felt tired.

On the stroke of one, Marvin Clark entered his office. He was invisible again. And he was happy.

* * *

3

Fate

"It must be fate. It must be," Mrs. Prentis nodded repeatedly, affirming great conviction in her own judgment.

And well she might.

Then her attention strayed toward a full-length mirror. She smoothed her furrowed brow. It was unbecoming. She stared directly at her own reflection. Her slim and prim figure belied her fifty-seven years. Her complexion was as good as can be expected. Perhaps better. Even her hair pinned neatly under a tiny bonnet retained some of the sheen which had once turned many a head on her way back from church on Sunday mornings. She always maintained that a woman is as old as she looks, and to her own critical eye Mrs. Prentis looked very good indeed. Still. From a discreet distance. At a discreet age, one ought not to approach a mirror too closely, she knew. One ought not to tempt the demons of vanity.

As she studied her image, Mrs. Prentis scrutinized the last thirty-odd years. That's how long she had been running the Victorian boarding house. The thought of her tenants brought a thin, somewhat wistful smile to her delicately tinted lips. Through no design of her own, with the exception of Mr. Clark, all the gentlemen that she had looked after she might well have once married.

Once is such a long time...

Mrs. Prentis's supple breast heaved with a protracted sigh. It was too late now. First of all, neither of the four men had ever proposed such an arrangement and, secondly, how could she possibly choose among them? In a certain fashion, she treated all of them as her closest family, a sort of group of husbands—not the sort one kept for the first five or ten years of one's marriage, but rather the last five or ten. First her smile broadened, then her lips set in a firm resolve. She squared her narrow shoulders. Mrs. Prentis was determined that her own fate would never overtake her only niece.

It had all happened rather suddenly. Mr. Jones, from the upstairs left front room, said that he had been invited to spend the winter months in Brazil. An old buddy of his, George Gomez, had inherited a villa in Rio de Janeiro. Apparently, George simply had no inclination to go there all alone. He also wanted someone to help him decide what to do with the property. Since Bob Jones was the only old friend with whom George had maintained periodic contact these many years, he had asked Bob to join him. Imagine, all expenses paid! Admitting to sixty-seven, Mr. Jones was no aspiring globe-trotter; but when such an opportunity presented itself, he could not let it pass.

When Mr. Jones announced his intention, Mrs. Prentis knew it must have been the workings of propitious fate. Only two days prior, her niece, Jocelyn, had telephoned to say that she must vacate her apartment, which was slated to be converted into a condominium. She could not afford to take advantage of the option to buy. What little savings she had accumulated, she felt she had to keep for a rainy day. At thirty-four and single, one did that. Mrs. Prentis had invited Jocelyn to stay with her for as long as she cared to. In a two-room apartment it would be tight, but family was family. Just then Mr. Jones announced his impending departure.

Mrs. Prentis knew it just had to be fate.

She mentioned her problem to Mr. Jones, who immediately offered his own room for Mrs. Prentis's niece.

"For as long as she cares to stay. Even after I get back," he added, with a naughty wink.

The stage was set.

On the day Mr. Jones left, Jocelyn's taxi arrived. The disgruntled driver got her two medium-size valises and one trunk as far as the main hall. (Jocelyn had deposited the rest of her belongings at the General Storage, Inc., on the other side of St-Onge.) Before going upstairs, the two women spent some time in Mrs. Prentis's apartment. Though they lived little more than a half-hour's drive from each other, they seldom met. The telephone made up for the lack of physical contact. Partially. Many a hug and several more smiles and interruptions later, Jocelyn decided to take her baggage upstairs.

Here fate played her trump card.

Just as Mrs. Prentis was leading Jocelyn to the main staircase in the entrance hall, Marvin Clark entered the front door. His instant intuitive reaction to don his cloak of invisibility failed miserably when he tripped and prostrated himself at the feet of Mrs. Prentis's niece. While the trunk had been set well against the wall, one of the suitcases had fallen over onto the carpet, directly into Marvin's path. It all happened simultaneously. Marvin's vain attempt to jump over the offending object left him staring at a pair of shapely ankles, within an inch of his nose.

The hushed silence, which normally reigned in the Victorian mansion, was interrupted by a cascade of carefree laughter.

"Sir!" Jocelyn refused to budge, "you are blocking my passage!"

Having said this, Jocelyn sank to her knees, as though refusing to give way. In the process, she managed, quite unintentionally, to cover Marvin's head with her loose, pleated skirt.

There may well be many shades to Marvin's personality, but the one Jocelyn met first was distinctly red. A dark shade of crimson red. At length, Marvin extricated himself from the voluptuous pleats and raised himself to his knees.

"How do you do..." he muttered, shaking the proffered hand.

Even as Jocelyn rose to her feet, Marvin remained in a position of humble supplication. Slowly, unmercifully slowly, blood descended and found its way back to other portions of his profoundly weakened anatomy. Five minutes later, Marvin was carrying Jocelyn's baggage to Mr. Jones's room.

By the time he returned for the last suitcase, Marvin's cardiovascular system allowed him to present Jocelyn with the more usual facets of his individuality. Polite, aloof, friendly, impersonal Mr. Marvin Clark. Always at your disposal. Glad to be of help. No, really, no trouble at all.

'Oh, my God,' he sighed on the way to his attic.

The next meeting between Marvin and Jocelyn took place at the usual seven o'clock dinner. By then Mrs. Prentis had matters well in hand. When Jocelyn came down to the dining room, her Aunt performed the formal introductions. Colonel James Mackenzie Whittlaw, retired, stood his full five-foot-ramrod-eight, a good two inches taller than his usual slightly stooped self. He appeared as though he couldn't quite decide whether to salute the young lady or to shake her hand. After some huffing and puffing, though with little conviction, he chose the latter. The two remaining dining companions stared shamelessly at Jocelyn as if trying to remember something or someone they once knew very well, but had lost track of, somewhere in the haze of time past or present. Glasses of South African Sherry were raised even as Mrs. Prentis performed the introductions.

Marvin came down to dinner last, only to find himself seated next to Jocelyn, whose other flank was well protected by Mrs. Prentis. To his nibbling annoyance, Marvin found himself considerably disturbed; not by having been placed next to a rather nice-looking young lady, but by his hostess's eyes, which were definitely imbued with an unaccustomed glee. Instinctively Marvin found himself on guard.

During the next five days, Mrs. Prentis had occasion to ask Marvin for help in performing some nondescript acts of assistance—the tasks themselves having been of no consequence. Screwing in an electric bulb in too high or too inaccessible a place for Mrs. Prentis to reach, or lifting something which, for the last seventeen years, did not need lifting. No, the acts had been definitely of no consequence. But each time Marvin had been called upon to assist, the young Jocelyn was already there to hold the ladder, or just to be there in case she could help.

"To share in the experience," she once called it, with a smug smile.

Finally, after another week of this, that, and the other, Jocelyn caught him on his way to the office. She smiled with her usual warmth and sincerity, and then said out of the blue: "She's not going to give up, you know. Not my Auntie Jenny."

For a moment Marvin felt lost. Although he had spent seventeen years lodging at Mrs. Prentis's house, he had never learned his hostess's first name. She had always been Mrs. Prentis. Always. As the revelation sank in, Marvin turned his attention to the rest of Jocelyn's statement.

"Not give up...?" he asked, a circumspect eyebrow rising.

Although, even at forty-seven, Marvin had little or practically no experience with the fair sex, thanks to Mrs. Prentis's perambulations he felt almost relaxed in Jocelyn's presence. A dozen light bulbs and a stock of furniture went a long way to ease his inherent discomfort.

"That's right," she affirmed, as though talking to herself. "Either you take me out, or she'll make you remodel the whole house," Jocelyn stated as a matter of fact.

Years of studied, cherished composure deserted Marvin as if swept with a magic wand. His inner peace, his self-assurance, his long and painfully, at times hard-won imperturbability, all hovered, wavered and collapsed.

"...ah... ah... ah... out?" He hadn't stammered since he was six years old.

"Out," Jocelyn confirmed.

There was a prolonged silence. Although Marvin's innards, including his bowels, registered a state of considerable if unaccustomed agitation, he retained an outward appearance of relative calm. Years of practice must have been good for something. Gradually his visceral comportment returned to normal, or at least to that relative condition known as the calm before the storm.

While Marvin was well aware of the turmoil which had flared within him a few seconds earlier, he attempted to regard it with humor. He couldn't quite make it. He settled for a degree of detachment. He tried to look at himself and his situation as an outsider or, perhaps, through the wrong end of field glasses. The considerable influx of Mrs. Prentis's inexplicable demands for his presence suddenly made sense. The invariable withdrawal of her own presence the instant Jocelyn appeared, under some pretext, which he had never questioned, now began to fall into place.As in a cold shower in a Victorian bathtub, Marvin shuddered at his own naivety.

"I've been pretty dumb, haven't I..."

He was in control again. A good lesson, he thought. There is always a reason. For everything. Always. At least Jocelyn had been kind enough not to take advantage of the situation. Now she remained silent.

"Thank you," he said at last.

They walked in silence for two blocks. Somehow Marvin felt at ease again. In fact, he felt quite relaxed. He had weathered the storm, he skippered his ship into calm waters. For some strange reason, it had not been necessary to talk to Jocelyn. It was enough... to be. Together? Or, or am I just imagining it? I must trust my feelings, he asserted with growing confidence.

"Mustn't disappoint Auntie...?" A half-question, half-statement. He dared.

"You're serious?" What a delightful voice she had.

Suddenly the boisterous, humorous, seemingly supremely confident Jocelyn sounded genuinely surprised, amazed, and—was there not shyness in the sudden drop of her eyelids?

"I lunch at noon, precisely. We could eat together and discuss the plan of action."

Even as Marvin made the proposal, ideas began crowding into his fertile imagination. This was not altogether unlike the many "trips" he took on his own. They would have a tryst, and they would plot against the ungodly. Well, perhaps not ungodly, but the conniving. He smiled at the thought. It could be fun.

"It's a beautiful day, we could meet in the park—the North Gate?" He surprised himself at the confidence in his own voice.

For reasons of her own, Jocelyn was getting into the spirit of things. Her own mind, though a lot more at ease throughout all this than his, also needed some reassurance that she did not cross that thin, invisible line of unspoken protocol in the book of etiquette governing the realm of the birds and the bees. Yet, in all this, she sensed that it had been neither an ornithological nor lepidopteral experience. It is not that she found Marvin unattractive. Not at all. But in spite of all this, she sensed at her side the presence of a long-missed, dearly awaited elder brother. They were two children planning a scam. Poor Auntie, she probably meant for the best.

"I'll bring the sandwiches."

With that she turned on her heel, leaving Marvin standing. His heart pounded with a force quite unusual for a man his age. Perhaps for a man of any age.

At five minutes after noon, Marvin waved to Jocelyn at the North Gate. She approached him at a good yet easy gait of a woman used to long walks. In her left arm she carried a small wicker basket while her right hand fought a losing battle with a gusty breeze, which kept her hair swept back with wavy persistence. On Marvin she made an impression of a carefree spirit.

"Why, Mr. Clark, how nice to see you. Do you come here..."

"...quite often, regardless of season. This way, if you would, my lady."

Marvin took the basket from her and directed their steps toward a copse about a hundred yards away. He suddenly realized that he didn't know her name. She had been introduced to him, and apparently to all the others, as: "...my niece, Jocelyn." Marvin assumed her name to be Prentis, but it could have been otherwise.

"It is good of you to come, Miss... Miss..."

Instead of telling him she laughed. "I thought you knew. Aunt Jenny is my father's sister."

Marvin nodded gravely as though he had missed the obvious. They reached the copse in silence. Heretofore, this had been Marvin's "private" place. As a senior employee of the Department of Parks and Recreation, Marvin had access to the layout plans of all the town parks, which indicated, in reasonable detail, all the natural or landscaped features. This particular thicket contained no more than twenty or so trees, but the shrubbery had been planted so as to hide a small pump house. The walls of the small building provided adequate protection from the wind, while evergreen shrubbery afforded virtually total privacy from any prying eyes. This was his place; it was his to share. Last year Marvin had had a bench put in on the south side, although, as a rule, weather permitting, he much preferred a raincoat on the skimpy but sufficient grass.

The unusually warm day seemed to have brought out that distinct smell of autumn leaves. Marvin thought someone should bottle this strangely Canadian aroma. Now, rather than grass, the leaves provided a multi-hued carpet.

Predictably, Jocelyn ignored the bench, laying out her own light raincoat on the most inviting patch she could find. Marvin followed her in tacit submission. He enjoyed watching her sure, graceful movements. Had he thought about it, he would have found that he regarded her more as a daughter, perhaps a much younger sister—almost with pride in his eye. But he didn't think. He just watched as one watches something new, something beautiful, something that should not be touched for fear that it proved a mirage. There were moments when he was afraid to blink lest she disappear, lest he awoke and found her gone.

Marvin's eyes widened when the picnic basket revealed not only a set of neatly wrapped sandwiches, with long sticks of celery and peeled cucumber to nibble on on the side, but a half bottle of *Maçon Superieur*. Marvin never claimed to be a connoisseur of the better things in life, but again he felt a mixture of pride and pleasure at Jocelyn's obvious care and attention. Within a few minutes the food was laid out on a checkered, red and white tablecloth. The wine gathered warmth as their fingers wrapped around the small glasses. They ate in silence. When only the wine was left, Marvin held Jocelyn's glass while she quickly tidied and placed the paper plates back into the basket.

Rather than retrieving her glass of wine, Jocelyn stretched out on her coat. She stared at the sky. Marvin followed her gaze to the lazy puffs of pure white cotton wool suspended in ether, lighter than air, relaxed, carefree. Again he became conscious of a strange, tacit kinship with this delightful young woman.

"If I could paint them, I would paint them..." she uttered in a far away, almost wistful voice.

"Why don't you?"

"One cannot serve two masters. Anyway, I tried and am not very good at it," she confessed.

"And pray tell, who or what is your master?"

"I sculpt." Then her voice seemed to turn wistful. "At least, I try to..."

The next half hour they totally forgot about their planned revenge against Aunt Jenny. They talked about the beauty of the world, beauty of form, contour, silhouette as against light and colour. They expanded the subject—touched on music and harmony of time and rhythm, and all sorts of intangibles which in their words became tactile, real, solid. The subjective and the objective touched, soared, rejoiced in a higher reality of sharpened senses and returned to their private realm—accessible to all, visited by few.

By the time Marvin's watch beeped 12:55, they agreed to meet at the General Storage, Inc., this Saturday, to unravel and look at some of Jocelyn's sculptures. Almost as an afterthought, they also agreed that they needn't, at least for the present, tell Aunt Jenny of their plans. Her turn would come later.

For the next few days Marvin's esoteric spaceship took him to new places, new realms, where he witnessed fresh, hitherto unknown ways of looking at wonders of creation. He learned to regard countless elements comprising his inner universes not as objects or things, but rather as sculptures, as works of art born of Creative Spirit. There were moments when he experienced an intoxicating feeling of becoming one with the object of his attention. A strange new realm of inner exploration.

The rest of the week Marvin saw Jocelyn only at dinner. They both remained resolute not to divulge to anyone their budding kinship. Yet now and again they smiled surreptitiously, at the same moments, then quickly bit their tongues to maintain an image of serene detachment. Marvin was temporarily absolved from further bulb replacement sessions or other designs on his masculine effusion by a rare stint of overtime required by his office. His quiet disposition in no way betrayed the fact that, for four days running, he read, studied and "traveled" at the expense of sleep. By Saturday, Marvin knew more about sculpture than most people learn in a lifetime.

In the meantime, Mrs. Prentis seemed preoccupied, vaguely depressed, as though resigning herself to the drifts and rushes of cruel and adamant fortune. Had she known the truth, it probably would in no way have eased or calmed the vicarious aspirations she held for her niece.

"Alas, the fickle finger of fate..." she sighed in her kitchen, as she racked her brain to find a suitable aphrodisiac. "Ah, the fickle finger..." she mused, dipping her finger in gravy to taste its potency.

When Saturday came, Jocelyn and Marvin met outside, in the park, preferring to avoid the ravenous tongues of the lonesome tenants. Marvin took a deep breath when he finally saw Jocelyn alone. She seemed to be the first person he had ever met in whose presence he felt totally at ease. He felt no compulsion, no necessity to hide behind his cherished mask of invisibility. Her smile seemed to illuminate the world with a light akin to that he saw in his inner travels. A certain purity of spirit broke through her own outer protective armour. She seemed quite unaware of it. Marvin had long noticed that all people wore such outer layers or shields or outer bodies, as though to safeguard their subtle selves from the coarse vibrations of the world around them. Yet Jocelyn left chunks open in her own defenses, through which her inner light seemed to radiate at all who cared to notice.

Within a half-hour the bus brought them to the storage depot. After the usual paperwork, they were allowed into Jocelyn's locker. Measuring ten by eight feet, it was filled all the way up to the ceiling with a strange collection of furniture, which at first sight bore little or no relation to any particular period or style. Immediately to the left stood a large crate, packed with overflowing straw. It held and protected Jocelyn's ventures into the world of sculpture. The stacked subdivisions enabled them to examine individual pieces of work without disturbing all the others.

Jocelyn's work consisted mainly of rather deep bas-relief, almost demi-relief sculptures, about two feet or so square, all cast in a hard gypsum, which she called *gesso duro*, and stained to add richness and enhance the form and subject. Since Marvin had expected the usual free-standing statuettes or suchlike, the painting-like sculptures, some with a hint of colour, left him stunned and speechless. This had been not at all what he had expected. These were not "important" subjects or statements to invoke an emotional reaction from the unsuspecting viewer. Rather, the theme displayed a full spectrum of human form in various acts of everyday endeavour. What was more, a rare trait struck him almost at the outset: the sculptures were happy—they actually displayed joy, even humor! Not at all what one sees in museums of immortal masters. Poor masters, Marvin's mind wondered, poor immortal masters...

Jocelyn remained quiet, again shy, reticent. Inasmuch as strangers examining her sculpture had little or no effect on her, this seemed very different. She felt dissected, stripped of her

outer bodies, exposed to scrutiny as never before. The fact that
Marvin had not uttered a single word seemed to make her even
more nervous. Her usual joyful, unsuspecting smile now gave
way to nearly catatonic anxiety. She took from Marvin one piece
of her work, replaced it in the housing and passed to him the
next piece without a word or whisper. She did all this
automatically, as though passing bits of bureaucratic paper from
one basket to another.

Finally it was over. Jocelyn quietly wiped small beads of
perspiration from her forehead. "Must be the heat, not much air
in here, either," she almost whimpered as Marvin remained
silent.

After a good two minutes, which to the aspiring artist felt
like a short lifetime, Marvin cleared his throat. He had also felt
the dryness, although for different reasons. Two choices stood
before him: to express his opinion in an analytical manner, or...
or to absorb the creative spirit manifest in the sculpture at a
different level, which had nothing to do with analyses or
syntheses or any other mental gymnastics. He opted for the
latter.

"I would very much like to buy one," he said finally.

"Oh, really, Mr. Clark, Sir. Really, you don't have to,"
Jocelyn gave every sign of being acutely embarrassed. She tried
to cover it with a shield of false formality.

"Then give it to me." Marvin looked her straight in the
eye. Suddenly she realized that he really meant it. It was as
though a million tons had been lifted from her fragile shoulders.
Her special smile fought hard to replace the faint scowl on her
face.

"Do you really want one, Marvin?" She looked at him
sideways. "I do wonder, which one...?"

"The kids on the swing—with the kindred couple," he said,
without a trace of hesitation.

"*The Passage of Time?*" she asked.

"If that's what you call it," Marvin replied.

His voice carried a degree of consternation, almost
annoyance. She didn't seem to notice. With a smile she

disappeared again into the innards of the crate and re-emerged, covered with some stalks of straw, holding the bas-relief. With only a slight hesitation, she handed it to Marvin.

"You sure you don't mind parting with it?" He gave her a second chance.

"I can't imagine anyone I'd rather give it to," she said, and turned to hide an oncoming blush. She had always oozed confidence whenever she worked on a sculpture. That same confidence seemed to waver or totally evaporate the moment the sculpture was finished. When still at her old apartment, she had earned her keep at the local library with punctilious reliability. She lived, however, from one sculpture to another. Although still unwittingly, the participation in a creative act was her particular fuel, which took her to her own inner worlds. It would be quite a while, though, before she would learn to enter those worlds in full consciousness.

Marvin clutched at the *gesso duro* bas-relief firmly and with great care. He leaned against the wall, held it at arm's length and stared at it for some time. The subject matter had been rather simple. Two small children, carefree on a swing, with a vertical barrier of a wall carved out into a series of rungs, as though a ladder, dividing them from an elderly couple; the latter obviously intent on each other. Essentially that was all. Or was it?

Jocelyn closed the locker, and they made for the airy outdoors. The day was one of those rare gifts of nature that make autumn not only bearable but a joy to behold. Marvin again suggested buying some sandwiches and making to "their" place in the park. She agreed. Half an hour later, a bus deposited them at the North Gate.

This time the ground was soggy after last night's drizzle. The bench, however, filled to the brim with sunshine, presented a most inviting haven. Marvin dusted it with his oversized handkerchief and invited Jocelyn to sit while he unwrapped the present he had just received. He then leaned the sculpture against a short, sturdy bush facing the bench before sitting down himself. Instantly he was up again. The bas-relief had sunshine behind it. He wanted the light to catch it at an angle, to wash its surface with diagonal rays. He moved it; then, satisfied, he sat down again.

As during their first tryst, they once more ate in silence. This time there was no wine to raise their timid spirits, yet somehow a sense of mild intoxication permeated the tiny clearing. The conifers seemed to glisten with iridescent moisture; the smell of autumn leaves supplied the needed bouquet. They sat in Spartan comfort, content in the act of being.

"Tell me about it?" Jocelyn said at last.

Marvin took a deep halting breath. Since they came here today, most of the time he had been ignoring the gifts of nature around him. Instead, he kept looking at the sculpture. Without taking his eyes from it, he began to speak.

"It cannot be known as 'The Passage of Time' or by any other name which places it in... motion. You see, true art is the manifestation of an aspect of the divine within us. The divine is always static. Real beauty is, it must be, outside the realms of both time and space. It exists in an instant of eternity—just after the past, just before the future. It stops you in your tracks. It does not move you, nor can it move itself. It exists. It is. Your art says to me: 'Be still...' You seem to propagate that stillness within me. Within others. You don't, shouldn't, move them, even though you'll find that people cannot sustain the state of that divine stillness for long. They will move of their own accord—physically, emotionally, or through the never-ending current of their discordant thoughts. Your job is to help them sustain that moment of stillness, that moment outside time and space, for as long as possible."

Marvin stopped, sighed, and remained silent. A moment of embarrassment at his own elocution passed quickly. This was different. She was different. He turned to face Jocelyn. With a gentle smile he resumed:

"You say that the children on the swing and the elderly couple illustrate passage of time. Perhaps, at a certain level of perception. For me it is just the opposite. You, obviously guided by an inner knowingness, which you cannot translate into words but have the gift to express in an art form, in sculpture, have

shown that the joys of childhood and the peaceful acceptance of
one's older years are... contemporaneous. The children and the
elderly couple are one and the same. They have their true
existence outside the confines of time. The children on the swing
even defy, symbolically, the concept of space—while traversing
it, they remain constant, like a Foucault's pendulum."

Jocelyn looked at her own sculpture. Her eyes were filled
with wonder, as if seeing it for the first time. Slowly, ever so
slowly, she nodded. Then that wistful smile once more played at
the corners of her mouth.

"Do you think I shall ever know what I am doing?" she
asked.

Marvin didn't answer. He got up and carefully wrapped the
fragile piece of art into a sheet of wrinkled brown paper. "You
must learn to travel, if you want to know that," he smiled.
"There is no one on this big ball of clay who can answer that
question for you... But you know, when you don't know what to
do, do nothing. Just be. The rest will come by itself."

That afternoon Marvin hung his sculpture from two hooks
in the ceiling. Even as the two children enjoyed being on a
swing, so the whole sculpture mimicked their enjoyment. At
seven, as usual, he presented himself in the dining room. The
place on his right had been set, but Jocelyn was not there. The
whole dinner seemed to pass in near silence. Mrs. Prentis
mumbled something about Jocelyn being late, or about playing
with fate—Marvin didn't quite hear.

Apparently Jocelyn had gone out looking for some kind of
a studio.

"Fancy that," Mrs. Prentis added, with badly concealed
annoyance. "Fancy spending a whole day looking for a studio
when she can work perfectly well upstairs."

During the after-dinner coffee, Jocelyn burst into the dining
room as if chased by a dozen stampeding buffalo. She greeted
everyone from the door even as men rose to welcome her
presence. Then she ran to Marvin and planted a great, big kiss
on his flabbergasted lips.

"Thank you, Mr. Clark," she said. "Thank you very much. I really enjoyed our intercourse."

The invariably prim Mrs. Prentis collapsed against the back of her chair. "Salts," she called out in a tremulous voice. "Gentlemen, anyone, please get me my smelling salts!" With this she succumbed to a faltering, languid, very Victorian swoon.

* * *

4

The River

The airline tickets had arrived a full week ahead of schedule. The prospect of sharing the same flight (and presumably adjacent seats) with Mr. John B. Dawson had been more than Marvin could reasonably consider. When he had learned that on the afternoon of the performance there would be a dress rehearsal, Marvin had his tickets changed to an earlier flight. By a strange bit of luck, Marvin had completely forgotten to advise the illustrious Mr. Dawson of the change in plans. Alas, when he did finally remember, it was already too late. Marvin remembered having been so profuse in expressing his regrets to Mr. Dawson that his tongue practically bore a hole in his cheek.

Even before all that, Marvin had been torn between a desire to hear the performance of his *Poème Symphonique* and his aversion to flying. It was not the flying itself that he abhorred, or at least intensely disliked—it was the principle of seeking greener grass over the next hill. Marvin had reinforced this sentiment by other arguments, such as the loss of rhythm which had become an integral part of his studiously founded and meticulously maintained biological, emotional and mental clocks. Such interruptions would further result in a certain loss of continuity and smoothness in the currents of the languid river of his life and thus the attendant loss of serenity. But most of all, or so he argued with himself, Marvin hated the thought of the selfish imposition of horrendous amounts of environmental pollution on others. He had once read somewhere that each time a 747 lifts its enormous bulk from the airfield, a burst of pollution equivalent to that produced by a town of five thousand in a full day was dispersed over the long-suffering environs. This, of course, was a little different. Marvin did not propose to make use of the airways for the purpose of searching for greener pastures. Morris, Jordan and Dawson, the music publishers of considerable esteem and ample reputation, had sent him tickets together with a program for the concert to be given at the unveiling of a New Concert Hall in Cincinnati, Ohio. The package also included a personal invitation to the official opening ceremonies, banquet, and God knows what other variations on the theme of pompous Saturnalia. The star attraction, the *pièce de résistance*, as Mr. J. B. Dawson so proudly put it, was to be the World Premiere of *Poème Symphonique* by Jean Sibelius. A *Poème* miraculously discovered, fully authenticated by the renowned experts in the field, etc., etc. So the program affirmed at some considerable length. Mr. John B. Dawson insisted that the occasion be designated a strictly black-tie affair.

"Yes, sir." His feeble chin did its best to drive the point home. "Strictly black-tie. Or tails, of course."

Marvin decided that, after limiting his travels during the last seven years to such destinations as were accessible from his residence by bus, or preferably by bicycle, he had earned a right to attend the premiere of his work. His resolve to take advantage of the complimentary tickets, both air and the admission, had been further strengthened when he discovered, to his delicately titillated residual vanity, that he could actually wear, with comfort, the dinner jacket he had ordered when he turned twenty-eight.

Three days before the flight, Marvin had the first unsettling dream. He awoke on Thursday feeling tired, his mind holding a picture of a long, winding river. At a certain point, the river had a part of its path hidden from view—as though concealing something foreboding, something not fit for even his chimerical eyes to witness. Marvin failed to understand the symbolism of the dream. He would have discarded it altogether if it hadn't been for the nagging vitality of the images. With his usual perspicacity, Marvin drew upon his considerable knowledge of symbolism. He consulted a number of articles by Freud, Jung, and Adler. He even applied a contemplative analysis to the esoteric annals of his subconscious mind.

All to no avail. The nagging image of the river persisted.

Finally he'd been forced to conclude that not every vivid dream must necessarily be prophetic, or serve a particularly profound purpose. It could be, he reasoned, a manifestation of some disharmonies within his unconscious—resolving the unresolved. When Friday night provided him with a gratifying rest, Marvin was ready to dismiss the matter from his mind. At least, from his conscious mind.

On Saturday morning, Marvin awoke a few minutes after five. In the gloom of an overcast dawn (out of respect for the Delicious Monster Marvin never drew his curtains), his ears were filled with a thunderous roar of falling water. The dream had returned. It was virtually identical. A slight variation in the twists and turns, then the same strangely ominous oblivion followed by more peaceful meandering of the same river. Its tortuous course seemed indelibly etched on Marvin's mind. Nagging, recurring images. Marvin felt tired, edgy. But as it was already Saturday, he had little time for abortive analyses. He was to catch the 11:27 flight to Cincinnati. He made the Dorval airport with only minutes to spare.

Twenty minutes after take-off, the DC9 was cruising at 32,000 feet, well above any turbulence which might have upset Marvin's leisure. Drinks had been served, followed by a surprisingly tasty light lunch. Marvin was ready to take a nap.

In spite of the relatively short notice, Marvin had managed to book a window seat. No one would climb over his feet or reach over his lap as a result of a resolute overindulgence in the potent Martinis. Just before closing his eyes, Marvin took a last peek through the window. Even from this height, the sun-swept

land below displayed a generous blend of golds and reds
punctuated by intermittent dark greens of clumped conifers—a
phantasmagoria of resplendent autumn. Marvin loved nature not
for any profound philosophical reason but simply for its prolific
diversity. It remained unceasingly generous, regardless of our
treatment of its treasures. He looked, he absorbed, he recorded in
his private inventory memories to be drawn upon later, in his
private spaceship, in his imagination. Having left the
Adirondacks behind, he scanned the northern resolution of the
Allegheny Mountains. Perhaps not as dramatic as the
Adirondack range but surely equally as abundant in grace and
beauty.

Then his thoughts wavered.

Some thirty thousand feet below, a silver thread wound its
wary way between the hills and valleys. Some regular formations,
rather like crag and tails, caught the midday sun with such force
that it instantly brought Marvin back to his neglected dream.
The thin shimmering line continued in its winding line
southward, only to seemingly stop and reappear some
nondescript distance farther south as a broader, richer, perhaps a
more peaceful river. To anyone else, this weaving thread of light
could have been one of a dozen of relatively small rivers making
their way south to join greater waterways toward their final
destinations. To Marvin, this was a mystery that had begun last
Thursday night.

Curiously, Marvin's eyes were riveted to that part of the
river that was hidden from him. The intensity of his gaze knit his
brow. He remained motionless. He held his breath. With the
force of his vision, he tried to pierce the shadows that refused to
divulge the secret they held so dear. He dismissed the
explanation that coincidentally or propitiously placed hills cast a
deep shadow along the banks, making part of the river's course
invisible. He knew otherwise. He also knew that the dreams had
not been a product of his overactive imagination but a strong if
not adamant instruction to do—or not to do—something.
Something that remained hidden not only from his eyes, but
from his very unconscious.

Marvin felt annoyed, uneasy. After an initial reaction of profound frustration, his next resort, more typical of his makeup, was to withdraw. To become invisible to the powers that assailed his inner space, his mind, his serenity. He drew back from the window and closed his eyes, determined to dismiss the gnawing mystery. He relaxed his body, his mind...

The next instant he found himself in a canoe. He was drifting slowly, in a leisurely pace, toward the golden sun. The steep banks of the narrow, deeply contoured channel seemed to guide the pure, sparkling mountain water with assurance, as though knowing exactly where and why it was traveling. In his vision, Marvin felt perfectly relaxed, being part of the current, part of the river itself. The flow took him gently toward his destiny, revealing new beauty around each curve, each twist, each surprising turn. Sometimes, swept by the current into some deeper, more diverted bay, he seemed to drift aimlessly, in circles, only to be later released, to renew his winding journey through yet uncharted territories.

The canoe... time... life... drifted. All was peace, blissful adventure, beauty.

It was some time later that Marvin heard an ominous, sonorous pounding. A deep riveting hum, as though a thousand drums in near unison were beating a tune, a hypnotic melody. The sound took hold of his mind; it modulated his own vibrations with its commanding rhythm. It played the refrain of destiny to which he knew he would have to dance. It hinted at the unknown and thus portentous, disturbing in its apparent total inevitability, in its relentless doom.

And then Marvin recognized it. The agonizing roar of the rushing waters tore all hope from his petrified heart. The white, rippling turbulence engulfing his immediate future was but a warning of the deadly vortex further along his journey. Could he survive the onslaught of such unforgiving currents? Could he retain his sanity when drawn through such infernal anguish?

Marvin rubbed his eyelids, then blinked away the cobwebs. He was nestled in the serene safety of the humming airplane. No tossing canoe, no vicious roar of impending doom. Must have dozed off, he thought hopefully. Perhaps a passing turbulence? — he wondered. And then the images of the strange vision flooded his mind with fierce clarity.

He looked through the window. The mysterious break in the silver thread finally revealed its secret. The flight of the airplane now offered a different angle for viewing the previously hidden portion. Although the light still broke over a measured distance, the two silver strands of the river's course were now bridged by an incandescent haze, which seemed to vibrate over the cascading waters. The light catching the rising vapor shimmered like an opalescent rainbow. The terror turned to beauty, the ominous into a welcome sign of promise.

The shimmer of an opalescent rainbow? Marvin smiled a little uncertainly as the images became first symbols, then words, assuaging his tired mind.

"Please fasten your safety belts."

His reverie was cut short by a flashing sign followed by an announcement. The landing was as smooth as the flight. Within half an hour, a taxi deposited Marvin Clark at the side entrance of the New Concert Hall.

Marvin immediately assumed his best official demeanor. He donned his mask with an ease born of long practice at his office. This gray-eminence quality, mixed in with a good dose of his secret invisibility powder formula, allowed him unobstructed or at least unchallenged access to the innards of the New Concert Hall. He did flash his personal invitation card to the new, thus untrained and gullible, doorman. He did so, however, in such an offhanded manner, with such obvious signs of preoccupation with other matters of vastly greater importance, that the man at the door hardly glanced at the proffered document. He practically saluted as he held the door for Marvin to enter.

Marvin took the guard's reaction as a well-deserved bonus for his years of practice. Such blending into the occasion as to become an integral and inevitable part of the process taking place was to a great extent the secret of his invisibility. One is not surprised at seeing pigeons atop a heroic statue. One would rather sense a certain something missing, had there not been any feathered friends in punctilious attendance. Marvin could, at will, become just such a pigeon. He would sense what element was missing on any particular occasion, and then, with the ease of a proficient magician, he would fill the vacuum to the spectator's content. His real self, his individuality, would retain the cloak of total invisibility.

Marvin insinuated the body he occupied inwards.

Presently, he found himself sitting about halfway up the stalls in the darkened theatre. Thank God, he'd made it in time. He watched as Sir Arthur Bang, the conductor brought in from England for the formal opening, scanned the score. The venerable gentleman, a mop of flamboyant white hair atop his famous head, was perched on a tall stool fixed to the raised rostrum. An image of a statue with a lone pigeon flashed through Marvin's head. He smiled indulgently. Marvin knew Sir Arthur's superb interpretations. They were among the best, particularly as regards Sibelius.

Even as Marvin relaxed in the solitude of his surroundings, he sensed rather than heard the first timid tremolo of his Symphonic Poem. With hardly a sigh, Marvin leaned back, his eyes locked on the inner screen of his mind. *The snow swirled, rose in tentative rebellion, only to die down, a quiet unrelenting struggle of the long, unforgiving Finnish winter...*

The intense silence was interrupted by a strange pounding. Marvin realized that it was his temples. The musicians, the stagehands, the *cognoscenti,* and the seemingly ignorant, remained frozen, totally immobile and perfectly silent... Sir Arthur raised his arms, then lowered them slowly, and he, too, stood still, as though taking part in this silent homage. The whole *Poème* had lasted but twelve minutes... twelve minutes which wrenched all present from the rigors of time, or place, or puny self-awareness, and transported them all to a distant land of magic, where music and nature and all who visited this enchanted kingdom became one, integrated in a consummate union.

Slowly, as though with regret, people who had been stopped in their tracks by this strange experience returned to their duties. The hall had to be readied for the night's events. No one seemed quite sure what had just befallen them. Time had stopped. Now it resumed its vigil on the mundane treadmill of spurious existence.

Marvin was not exempt from this hypnotic juncture. He, too, had to find his bearings before the world around him would return into focus. He sat, motionless, not thinking, not judging, content to have heard with his ears that which his heart had already known. He was glad he had come. It was a new experience. So far in his life, he invariably listened to the music; then, later, he would recreate the sounds in the solicitude of his soul's awareness. This time the order had been reversed. He'd turned a full circle.

Even as Marvin marveled how all this could have happened, he was disturbed by a brutal noise emerging from the speakers. Apparently tonight's gala opening was to be televised. The army of workmen resumed their frantic battle with convoluting cables, lighting and reflectors, with masses of equipment which, with total ease and deftness, would still and encapsulate the seemingly intangible, impalpable, a prodigious whimsy.

With mixed feelings of wonder and apprehension, Marvin rose and walked up to an officious-looking man who obviously had the task of overseeing the installations. For the briefest of moments, Marvin ceased being the retiring, intensely private person. His shield of invisibility became totally opaque. He retreated behind a mask he reserved for very special occasions. Marvin Clark introduced himself as though he owned the place.

"I'm Clark. Marvin Clark. Would you please confirm to me the pre-concert activities, in their order of procedure?" He held his program and pen poised as though assuring conformance.

"Ah, yes, Sir." The other scratched his head. The man obviously hated these interruptions, but obediently consulted his own notebook. "Well, in order of appearance, so to speak... the... ah, what's-his-name... the mayor, the governor, a Mrs. Flint-Fitzpatrick and Sir Bang, who will introduce a guy named, ah, Dawson. That's all, I reckon." He ticked off the names as he spoke. "Why, you have any others?" he scowled.

"Not at all, you are quite in order. Thank you. You may carry on."

"Thank you, Sir."

The man sighed with obvious relief. He looked at Marvin as if ready to ask who he might be, but it was too late. His questioner was already disappearing in the shadows of the brand-new theatre. Only in the relative safety of the deeper penumbra did Marvin permit himself to wipe his forehead. Some masks were more difficult to sustain than others.

Before going to his hotel, Marvin decided to make a quick tour of the theatre. The time was already 16:20, and surely the orchestra needed time to rest, change and make ready. Marvin knew that he would not take part in all of the night's proceedings. He would have probably suffered them, had he not had a chance to hear his, Jean's, blissfully tempestuous *Poème*. A mixed metaphor, he thought, grinning; yet the words did it justice. The *Poème* glorified the inherent duality of nature. The inner worlds seemed full of paradoxes. Anyway, he had heard it, and now a herd of wild elephants could not drag him to face the black-tied elite basking in their own importance. He hoped to be proven wrong, but never in his life had he met a true music lover who could afford the first night's opening gala. On such occasions one paid not for the music, but for the event. To each his own, he smiled, to each his own pretensions.

Marvin left, as he came, by the side door. Out of curiosity, he walked around the front of the concert hall to look at its architecture. The overall pleasant façade was marred by an attempt to duplicate some elements from the work of the latest fashionable architect. Plagiarism had become the norm. He shrugged and hailed a taxi.

Since Marvin had originally intended to attend the concert, he had been booked into a nearby hotel. On a whim, he asked the driver whether he liked music. The man replied yes, but it was no good, because all they ever broadcast on the radio was noise.

"Never any music, just some guy smashin' a can against a kitchen wall. Now I ask you, buddy, do you call that music?" He would have gone on but for Marvin's next question.

"Do you own a dress suit?"

"You mean a black-tie? Sure I do, ever since I got married. We've 'ad a real formal do, the missus an' I did. So why are you askin'?" He spoke with an accent one could hardly decipher. The longer he talked, the more consonants he swallowed.

By the time they reached the hotel, Marvin had paid the man and given him his ticket for the evening's gala. He then walked up the hotel entrance before the man could comment. He registered and took the elevator to the sixth floor. A quick nap and a shower later, he went downstairs to the dining room. The room was almost empty. Marvin asked the waiter whether this was normal. He learned that most hotel guests had eaten early to watch the opening of the new concert hall. Apparently this was the big thing tonight. The city was glued to their TVs to bask, vicariously, in the glory of the formal gala.

By the time Marvin returned to his room and switched on the television, Mrs. Florence Flint-Fitzpatrick, the President of the New Concert Hall, had just concluded the introductions of Mr. J. B. Dawson. J.B. looked his grotesque best. The tails helped a little to elongate his stature but could do nothing to hide his ferret-like features. There are people who sport receding hairlines. Mr. Dawson went one better: his whole head sloped back from his eyebrows, giving him a pointed look, as if accentuating his desire to make a point. It was some time, though, before Marvin understood what point Mr. Dawson was making.

"...a rare privilege to introduce to you... (there followed a protracted list of distinguished guests) as well as you ladies and gentlemen, indeed, all citizens of the historic town of Cincinnati, nay, of our beloved country," here, presumably for the first time, he mopped his receding forehead, "to introduce to you a most rare, indeed a unique, yes, one must categorically say, unique masterpiece of one who, although never having shared with us this jewel of musical genius while gracing our world with his illustrious presence, alas, no longer with us..." the handkerchief did its round, "...it behooves us to take upon ourselves, in all humility, in all..."

Marvin switched off the television. He was all for the recognition of his favourite composer's talent, indeed genius, but there are limits to pomposity, even if directed at a noble cause. The fact that he himself had composed the piece in question was neither here nor there. If it had not been for Sibelius, the *Poème* would never have been written. In fact, having heard it today at the dress rehearsal, Marvin began to doubt whether he did actually write it. Now, in his hotel room, he would not dare to listen to the *Poème* again. The first and last performance still vibrated in his soul, still held him in that rare region halfway between the objective and the subjective reality. Marvin wanted to savor it for quite a while longer.

The night passed uneventfully. No dreams of rivers, no enigmatic messages from the archetypes or some itinerate vagabond id. By 8:30 Marvin was on his way to the airport. The same friendly smiles, the same DC9, the same taxiing along the usual bumpy runway and then breakfast at 30,000 feet. To his mild surprise, Marvin found himself actually enjoying the trip. Perhaps, he thought, it was because he was already on his way back; back to his private haven, his private spaceship and his Delicious Monster. Marvin frowned as he thought about the only living organism that had shared his life these last fifteen years. The Delicious Monster that seemed to entwine his life as much as it did his whole inner sanctum.

Breakfast over, Marvin leaned his chair back to a reclining position and closed his eyes. He wanted to play back yesterday's performance. The world around him receded, shimmered, became hazy until a field of pure white unfolded before his inner vision. Soon the strings and the French horn invaded the lonesome landscape. The steady hum of the engines seemed to assist in his hidden, enigmatic journey. Enigmatic to others, yet to him the most natural venture for anyone to master. The richness of the inner kingdoms surpassed anything he'd ever hoped for. As usual, Marvin's journey began in the realm of imagination. Began... yet soon this strange free world solidified, took substance, absorbed his senses, absorbed his soul, his being...

"My God!" Marvin raised his hands to his face. "My God, how stupid of me!"

Marvin's face registered signs of recognition, of discovery of truth beyond his outer sensibilities. The dreams, the silver thread, the forceful current of the deep-cut river, flooded his mind with clear, transparent meaning. He sat up in sheer wonder at the sudden discovery. He heaved a grateful sigh at the magnanimity of nature.

Marvin had always known that some dreams, if not all, serve as a means of communication between his higher and his lower nature. He practiced consciousness projection, or travels, as he called them, for many years. The dreams also would fall, therefore, into the same category. They all must have served to convey some hidden message—hidden until this very moment.

He looked down through the window—not searching for the long-lost river, but for any river that caught some morning sunshine. There it was! How obvious! How superbly easy!

Suddenly Marvin knew with utter conviction that past, present and future were fully accessible to any man who cared to accept the secret. As he looked down at the winding river, he saw its total passage, from start to its infusion. He could see, simultaneously, the various stages of its flow, the wherefores of its current. From his present point of view, the river's time did not really progress. It stood still, unmoving. The onset and the conclusion, regardless of subjective movement, had been predetermined, unchangeable and unchanging. Yet when he had found himself down there, in the small canoe, nothing was known about the reality around any curve or twist of the winding river. So visible from his present vantage, down there the future had been unknown, uncertain, at times intensely frightening.

The unknown lost its impact when viewed from a higher level. The roaring falls, once deadly to his mind and body, were now an opalescent rainbow when seen with a loftier vision. How well he remembered the moment when he saw that the silver thread of life had crossed the hidden chasms and emerged victorious. Marvin realized that it was up to him how he would choose to treat the perilous crossing. He could regard it as a dreadful tribulation, or see the iridescent glory of victory and serenity that follows.

Once again, Marvin's thoughts were interrupted by the landing procedures. He was anxious to get home and examine more fully his own river's currents, its twists and sudden turns and rushing, deadly maelstroms. In the light of his new understanding, Marvin knew he would get through them. Whatever their purpose, it was up to him how he'd choose to withstand them. But most of all, he knew with a clear, fateful acceptance that a great test lay at close hand before him. He did not know its nature, but he knew it was coming. Sadly, Marvin realized that there was no one with whom he could share this knowledge; no one with whom to share the burden of the impending trial. His inner peace was invaded by a sudden hunger. Not really to unburden his worries—he knew those would be transitory. What he needed most was to share his knowledge, the many years of study, the many inner discoveries, theories, conclusions. Not for the first time, Marvin sighed on this peculiar journey.

He took the bus home and walked the last mile. He wanted to walk, to breathe, to do nothing. After supposedly a vacation weekend, Marvin needed a rest. He passed by the North Gate of the park. He walked in and then to his clearing. It was gray and murky, not at all inviting. There was something missing. Marvin turned around and walked home. The house looked deserted. He let himself in and walked upstairs. The steps seemed a little higher, a little more steep than usual. He walked into his room.

On the floor, just inside the door, lay a note. It said just three words: "I missed you." It had not been signed. At this very moment, Marvin knew what had been missing from the bench at the park's clearing: it was her smile.

* * *

5

SHARING

The week preceding Marvin's trip to Cincinnati could not be recorded among the more rewarding chapters in Marvin's life. He had managed to maintain his staid, deliberately stolid exterior, but his unease had rebelled against his outward demeanor. A dozen times he had mobilized his diffident resources to confront Mrs. Prentis. After all, he had played no deliberate part in the after-dinner events of that fateful Sunday. Since Mrs. Prentis's haughty expression had completely precluded such a course of action, he could hardly have broached the subject during the daily meals. What was worse, much worse—since he had become the innocent recipient of Jocelyn's hilariously arduous if ardent behaviour—she had failed to join them at mealtimes. She, rather than Marvin, had become totally invisible.

The previously persistent demands on his time, invariably instigated by Mrs. Prentis, had ceased as though by the sleight of a magic wand. Marvin came down to breakfast, greeted other tenants with usual courtesy, occasionally contributed comments about the state of inclement fall weather, and left for the sanctuary of his attic. The same pattern was repeated at dinner. The Colonel strove to stir some belated interest in the Crimean war. Alas, to no avail. The seasonal atmosphere dominated by the gray ubiquitous fog and drizzle penetrated the dining room in spirit if not in fact.

The strange thing was that the current ambience differed very little from that which they all seemed to have enjoyed for the last ten or fifteen years. The tacit reserve, the nondescript comments about events of little or no consequence were the order of the day— indeed, of the year, even years. The meals served as occasions for placating and accommodating their gastric impulses, not for sating other, deeper hungers. Until last week, they all seemed to have sensed that any venture into the realms of intellectual or even social intercourse might, in time, lead to familiarities which they would later regret. Now, after only one week, a different presence in their midst had destroyed their undemanding amplitude in which well- contained boredom had been diligently substituted for placid serenity.

Marvin—who, for as long as he could remember, had been perfectly satisfied with his inner travels—now, one week later, seemed at a loss as to what had gone wrong; what demons had invaded his cherished, carefully nurtured world of peace and seclusion.

Or perhaps he did know, but refused to accept it?

When Marvin reached down to pick up the note lying on his doorstep, he sensed the presence that had written the three, surely innocent, words. Yet those three words released the pent-up floods long held at bay by stalwart gates of introversive shyness and... necessity. Marvin suddenly became aware of the long years of lonesome progress wherein he had no one with whom to share, nor bestow upon, the riches which swelled within his unrequited munificent nature. He held the note, his eyes fixed, his body frozen in that instant of time between the long, long past and the enticing yet so frightening future.

Yes, it must have been her smile. But also the total lack of self-imposed—physical or mental, or even invisible—barriers. The lack of pretense, the strange directness, the intractable yet so vigorous, almost lush sincerity. The total, unequivocal opposite of all that he was, had been, and seemed destined to remain forever.

Marvin closed the door to his attic. He held out the note as though a document of great consequence. He carried it to his command centre. He sat down and leaned over to finger through the many tapes and records. The note rested on his lap. He selected a short piece he had liked to rest by: the overture to the Hebrides. He pushed the disk in, pressed a button and leaned back. His lonesome room was soon flooded with relentless waves pounding the bleak, tiny Isle of Staffa, west off the hostile coast of Northern Scotland. Marvin pictured himself standing in Fingal's Cave, resolute against the sharp, biting wind. That's how he felt. That's how he chose to face this moment. He would stand alone, he would face...

"No! I will not!" he shouted at the rolling ocean. His constricted throat fought to match the howling gale. "No, I will not stand alone!"

The music swelled as though supporting him in his resolve. What magnificent seascape... Half his mind still in awe, the other already planning how to end his vigil. Vigil? Yes, Sir. Vigil of more years than he cared to count.

In less than ten minutes, the overture was over. Marvin felt washed free by the gusting breeze, by the spray of brine on his resolute features. It was now just one-thirty. He had time to do something. But what? He wasn't even sure if Jocelyn still stayed at the boarding house. So what if she didn't? Could he not find her? He who crossed oceans of time and space, would he not find one girl in the whole world who missed him?

In no more than two minutes, Marvin was out on the gloomy, damp, drizzly sidewalk. His umbrella still tightly rolled, he ran nearly the whole mile to the nearest hospital. He knew that he would find there his badly needed restitution—even on a Sunday. The flower shop was tucked around the entrance, hidden, rather as an afterthought. He smiled when he found the deep-red, long- stemmed, proud-with-beauty roses. He looked and he wondered. Then, with a surge of confidence, he selected one of quite singular beauty. A living jewel—a ruby solitaire. He refused boxes or plastic, asked for thin white tissue paper and, though quite redundant, a long red ribbon. He then remembered the drizzle. Slightly embarrassed, he requested some more wrapping paper. Satisfied, he made for the door. This time with his wide umbrella fully extended, he walked, chest well forward, a measured step of purposeful decision.

We all find props of such quaint importance. Marvin's confidence seemed firmly attached to the broad tent of his umbrella. The moment he reached home and collapsed his overhead protection, his confidence collapsed with it, stayed out, jeering, on the street behind him. The door lock seemed too sticky, the round knob spun in his grasp as though too smooth to open. Slight beads of perspiration glistened on his forehead.

Yet Marvin walked on in adamant defiance. As he climbed slowly, counting each step, he was aware of the sound of his heart pounding against his eardrums. Then he faced her door. *"Robert B. Jones, R.N. ret."* This odd fact of facing Mr. Jones's nameplate gave Marvin the needed respite. Squaring his shoulders, he knocked on the door. Three or four knocks later he gave up. Jocelyn wasn't home. My God! He whispered softly... all this just—for nothing?

Marvin removed the outer wrapping from the rose and left it. Protected only by the flimsy tissue, the jewel rested on the floor along the threshold. If she still lives here, he thought. If she still lives here. With a deep sigh, he climbed to the second floor.

His room, his refuge, his sacred sanctuary felt cold, dark, damp, deserted. Strange how he had never thought of his place as empty. The enormous *monstera* spanning over literarily the whole ceiling had always given him a feeling of his home being lived in. It waved a welcome at his every entry.

Not today. Not only did he not find haven, he felt strangely abandoned. Devoid of any feeling. Rather than return to his favourite armchair, he tossed his weary body on the settee. He felt spent and tired. Too many events in too short a time, he justified his feelings. I'll be all right tomorrow. Tomorrow—in the office...

Marvin entered his private world and shut the door firmly behind him. This is where I belong, he muttered, this is where I shall stay...

"I've been knocking for five minutes!" Jocelyn looked hurt and disappointed. "Couldn't you even say hallo when you got back from wherever? Well?" she added, hearing no answer. "If you have a naked girlfriend in there, we can talk some other time." Once more she looked hurt, almost pouting.

Marvin had dozed off. When he heard the knocking, he assumed he must have been late for dinner. Now he stood blocking the access to his attic, his mouth a little open, his eyes somewhat out of focus. Slowly he stepped to one side.

"Thank you kindly, good sir. I shall visit your kingdom."

Having said this, Jocelyn walked past him, into the apartment.

"My God! It's a jungle!" She exclaimed at the sight of the Delicious Monster. "How absolutely lovely!"

At this she clapped her hands, forgetting that she was still holding a semi-unwrapped rose. She stopped short and looked at Marvin, who still hadn't recovered from his last seizure at his own threshold.

"Look," she showed him the red petals, "isn't it absolutely lovely?"

This last was as much a question as a statement. Suddenly, as boisterous as she had been a second ago, she now seemed shy. Even to herself, her conversation sounded one-sided. Jocelyn stood without moving, her head bent toward the solitary bloom.

"Thank you..." she whispered, "...it's been quite a while...." she didn't finish her thought. Then she looked up. "Hadn't you better close the door?"

This brought Marvin out of his *rigor mortis*. His body moved, though more like a robot than a man of flesh and blood. Finally he spoke: "I'm afraid I don't have anything I can offer you..." Now he looked embarrassed. "I mean in the way of drinks..."

"I don't really drink. Except, of course, for wine." She absolved him.

"I don't have any chocolates..."

"Too fattening and ruins your complexion!"

"Or any..."

"Marvin!" she almost shouted. "This is me, remember? A sandwich in the park, cucumber and an apple? I didn't come here to..."

"I'm sorry."

This time he interrupted. His eyes rested on her face, and suddenly he felt as though a Herculean weight had slid softly from his shoulders. He took yet another deep, if still halting, breath.

"How did you know it was from me?" he asked, this time in his normal voice.

"I didn't—I was just hoping..." She turned away toward the bay window. "I have an awful lot to tell you."

He then realized his rudeness. "Oh, I'm sorry, please sit down..."

Once more he was lost. Occasionally Marvin did meet with people, but always on some neutral ground. Mostly in his office, sometimes in a restaurant, a theatre, even on a park bench. Never, never in his private haven. Finally he led Jocelyn to his console armchair and then tried to fit his tabouret from the piano in front of it. He could have suggested the settee, but he thought of it as a place for sleeping. Anyway, Jocelyn seemed content.

"It's been a whole week..." he started.

"Could I have some water? " He jumped to his feet, guilt returning to his face. "Not for me, silly!" She smiled, holding up the rose.

In the next hour each held his and her breath while the other described their exploits since the Sunday dinner. Neither of them mentioned Aunt Jenny's Victorian performance. Jocelyn started off by telling Marvin about her new studio.

"It's an attic, just like yours, only with a lot of roof lights. And it's on the ground floor." Jocelyn had her architectural terminology a trifle confused, but Marvin got the idea. She sounded exhilarated. "I couldn't possibly do my messy sculpture in Mr. Jones's room, now could I?"

"You couldn't?" The question was rhetorical.

Following their meeting in the park, Jocelyn had spent the whole afternoon looking for a studio. Essentially, she had been looking for a place to work in, but also where she might stay and live, if need be. She visited five places before finding her 'attic'.

"I haven't yet told Aunt Jenny about my plans..." she blurted, sitting up, her face flushed with excitement now frazzled with worry. "...I mean about living there," she explained.

"For fear of hurting her feelings?" Marvin offered.

Alas, these were not to be spared, even later.

Though Marvin would never admit it to himself—let alone anyone else—he was completely spellbound by Jocelyn's presence. He seemed quite unaware that only a few minutes ago his own thoughts had traveled along the same sequence, though with quite different conclusions. He listened, absorbed, noted and remembered. He did his best to ignore the turmoil that raged somewhere within some secret chambers of his psyche—chambers he hadn't visited for a very long time.

Jocelyn confessed that her search had been inspired by his words in the park. She suddenly felt a great need to return to her creative endeavour, which she had suspended when she left her old apartment. She found her studio about a half-hour before returning to Aunt Jenny's. She felt happy, exhilarated. His words still rang in her ears, her hands ready to touch clay and let them mold time into a precious instant of infinity. She tried to explain her spontaneous behavior when she had burst into the dining room. She tried, she didn't quite make it.

"I've always been like that... Quite, quite irresponsible, I'm afraid..." she finished weakly.

Since Marvin remained silent and quite motionless throughout the latter part of her lengthy narration, Jocelyn finally waved her hand in front of his eyes. "Am I boring you? I'm sorry, I was just trying to explain...."

Marvin broke out of his self-induced trance with an avalanche of protests embellished by weak excuses. Finally she believed him. "And what have you been doing?"

"First, tell me," he countered, "have you been sculpting this last week?"

"Well, of course! On Monday, after work..."

"You are working?"

"Of course I've been working! I took a week off from the library because of my moving, but I never intended to live off Aunt Jenny." She seemed surprised. "Well, on Monday I went to the storehouse and got the bare essentials for my new studio. On Tuesday, after work, I spent about five hours sketching and moulding... oh, Marvin, it was heaven..."

"You didn't let me help you move...?" There was hurt in his voice.

"Don't be silly. I have managed quite well on my own for quite a few years now. You're a friend, not a..." She seemed lost for words. "Anyway, now you tell me what you did this past week."

"So that is why you missed supper!"

"Well, of course, silly. Why else would I miss a free meal!?" When she laughed, her whole face lit up the dark day. Dark? Marvin hadn't noticed. It seemed quite filled with sunshine.

Slowly he told her about his dreams, his thoughts on them, then about the trip. He did not tell her about the *Poème Symphonique*. Not yet. For now, the trip had been—business. As a matter of fact, that is exactly how Mr. John B. Dawson had described it. "Fully deductible," he had said, "don't you worry about a thing, every penny," he had asserted, with a gleam in his eyes.

When Marvin recounted his conclusions resulting from his sudden enlightenment on his return trip, she listened very carefully. Not once did she interrupt, yet Marvin noticed signs of doubt crossing her attentive features. He couldn't exactly put his

finger on which part of his story gave her reservations. He tried
to recount the relevant events as accurately as he could. Finally
he stopped.

For quite a while they remained silent. Jocelyn leaned back
in his favourite armchair; Marvin admired her beauty with
unabashed, almost blatant openness. His habitual reserve seemed
to have left him. As he had already done once before, in the
park, it seemed as if he were again treating her as an extension of
his own being. He felt at ease in her presence because he could
not define a line where his 'space' ended and hers began. Not to
say that he would in any way invade her individuality uninvited.
Yet the permission to do so had not been given verbally.
Perhaps, he pondered, these things take place at a different level
of perception.

"I cannot quite accept it," Jocelyn said at last. "I cannot
accept the concept that our lives are predestined to such a degree
that we cannot, by an act of our will, our own free will, change or
even terminate the flow of this destiny."

"We can," Marvin said, after a while. "We can always
control, at least to a great degree, our own pace, even our place
within that flow. What we cannot change is the flow itself."

"I'm afraid you lost me...?"

"What I am trying to say is that the events in our, or in
anyone's, life—in fact, all events which could possibly take
place— have already been predetermined. It only remains, for
us, to enter the reality of those events with our consciousness. Do
you see that?"

"No more than a glimmer..."

Jocelyn looked relaxed, but her eyes were fixed on
Marvin's as though linked by some intangible yet indomitable
force. The words seemed only a part, perhaps a relatively
insignificant part, in the exchange of their ideas.

"All that we can ever experience in our life already exists.
We are not aware of the countless alternative routes that our lives
can take. The only way we can experience those pre-established
events is by becoming aware of them. By accepting them into
our consciousness. It is—as with my river. It flows, and will

continue to flow to its ultimate destiny. That destiny seems to be the joining with a higher or greater expansion of consciousness. In the case of the river, a larger river, then larger still and ultimately, the ocean. So it is with us. We cannot resist the current of the river. Sooner or later it will sweep us along... slowly, through eddies, but relentlessly toward our goal. That goal will always be a higher state of consciousness."

"Even if I accept that, what precisely did you gain from this particular insight?"

"A number of insights. First and foremost, that which I've already described. Individually, I have learned three things of extreme importance. One, that there is a challenge which I will have to face in the foreseeable future. Two, that that challenge, no matter how difficult, will not terminate or break the thread of my existence. Three, that my attitude to that challenge can become either an iridescent rainbow or a scary tribulation. It seems that, while I cannot avoid the rough waters through which my ship will travel, I do remain the captain of that ship. You must see that it is much easier to make decisions on the bridge when one knows, as an indisputable fact, that calm waters lie ahead..."

"And every person follows the current of that river?"

"The course of their particular river."

"And one day—the ocean...?" Jocelyn asked, a pensive line cutting her clear forehead. Marvin laughed.

"Oh dear, do not look so serious! You seem to have forgotten,that the streams and the rivers and the mighty oceans... they're all contemporaneous!"

"Please stop! I can only take this a bit at a time." She threw her arms up in the air in a show of despair.

Marvin did stop. He remembered only too well the first tentative steps he had taken, a good many years ago, on his particular river of life, love, and knowledge. His travels, his excursions into the inner realms grew slowly, absorbing understanding a step at a time. At no time did he imagine that he had attained any kind of wisdom. He had learned from, on occasion, painful experiences that, regardless of the knowledge acquired, today always marked the very beginning of the rest of his infinite existence. And strangely enough, even infinity seemed contemporaneous. Was it not, perforce, outside the bounds of time?

They went down to dinner together. No one said a single word about Jocelyn's absence last week. Mrs. Prentis acted as if nothing had happened, although Marvin could swear that she kept a strict eye on his every movement. He felt like a schoolboy who is told to stay after school. Contrary to his self-imposed custom, Marvin did not leave the table within five minutes of finishing the meal. After the fifth coffee, he realized he would not be able to sleep tonight. He never could after more than one cup.

And just who cares! He thought fiercely, am I not immortal? And then he saw Mrs. Prentis's stern eyes directly on his own. He rose quietly, bowed to Mrs. Prentis, and asked to be excused. She acquiesced with a regal nod.

Was there not a spark of amusement hiding behind her stern expression?

Marvin, the captain of his ship, was not about to find out.

* * *

6

The Studio

Marvin was speechless.

The studio, which Jocelyn had described as "rather like his own, only with some roof lights", looked more like one of the Municipal greenhouses which he had occasion to visit in his official capacity. The space formed a good-sized rectangle, the longer dimension running north-south. Gingerly, Marvin paced out the two cardinal directions. The area measured roughly nine paces by fifteen. In addition, a small entrance lobby gave access, on the left, to a crude but functional bathroom with all the standard fixtures and an extra large sink. Directly opposite was another room, though without a door, which contained a small range, a medium-size fridge and a tiny sink. This area seemed better fit for making coffee than a man-sized meal.

The main area, however, loomed practically empty. Some six or seven cardboard boxes and two metal five-gallon drums rested against one wall. In the middle of the enormous space stood an extra-large, massive table, looking lonely for all its size and apparent weight. The sheer height of the room, a good twelve feet, would dwarf a full set of furnishings, let alone a single table with only one folding chair for company.

In all this, Jocelyn stood, her eyes shining, her face radiant, her arms stretched out as though willing, if not able, to embrace this indoor desert. She must have seen things that other, mere mortal eyes could not see. Marvin's years of practice in maintaining a sedate expression saved him from revealing his

profound disbelief that anyone could possibly enjoy spending
even five minutes in this place without developing an acute case
of galloping agoraphobia. Assuming there was such a disease;
but if there wasn't, then this place was sure to inspire such a new
strain.

"Don't you just love it!?" Jocelyn spun on her heel,
clapped her hands and then seemed to attempt again to embrace
this vast, empty space.

Marvin swallowed hard, cleared his throat and said nothing.

"Well, don't you?" She would not let him off the hook.

"It, ah, it... it has, ah... distinct possibilities..." Marvin
practically whimpered.

Jocelyn ignored Marvin's reservations as though she had
not heard them. She danced to her lone table, removed a sheet of
plastic and some damp towels from a thick layer of irregular
clay, climbed on the only chair and gazed down on her latest
creation. Her smile froze, her pupils dilated in concentration,
then she jumped down with the lightness of a girl of twelve.

"It will be finished tomorrow!" she announced.

By this time Marvin considered his first visit to Jocelyn's
studio as a definite mistake. True, he had no idea what to expect.
Yet somehow, his orderly mind had subconsciously formed an
orderly picture of an artist's studio. He had arranged his own
life in a particularly orderly fashion. He was precise and exact.
With considerable difficulty, he had learned to be reasonably
tolerant toward others, yet continued to expect a degree of
propriety, expediency, and methodology from his subordinates
in his office. He could not abide sloppiness or disorderliness.
The one, single concession in his own life had been his *monstera
deliciosa*. It had been allowed to roam freely along his ceiling in
his own "studio"; but, after all, the Delicious Monster was a
plant, not a human being.

A studio, Marvin imagined, was a place for the performance
of a creative act. An act of participating in or with the divine.
Art! An expression of order and harmony... Art—that sublime
means of extracting sanity, order and beauty from entropy and

chaos reigning in the world around them. An act... so natural to Jocelyn, even in this vacuous desert of spatial degradation.

"I don't suppose you have another chair?" he asked weakly.

"Tomorrow!" she exclaimed. "Tomorrow they are carting over all my belongings." She ran to the far corner, next to the window facing south. "This is the seating area with all my books as divider, the sleeping over there, here we can eat or drink, and there—..."

Suddenly she stopped dead in her tracks. She realized that her statement was unwittingly presumptuous. She had no intention of suggesting where "they" might or might not eat. It seemed too late to retract her statement. She hoped he hadn't noticed. Then she threw up her arms, as though in despair, and danced toward the central table.

"And here I shall try to stop time..."

This last phrase brought Marvin back to reality. He began to realize that all that happened to Jocelyn, at least recently, had been ancillary, almost coincidental to her sculpture. She seemed quite unaware of the ludicrousness of the situation. While she must have regarded the whole chamber with an eye toward the potential inherent in the sheer size or lighting or volume of the space, to any one else not made privy to her thoughts, the oversized greenhouse was fit for growing vegetables for the local market rather than any artistic endeavour.

"You'd never believe it, but originally this gorgeous space had been designed as a space for year-round growing of vegetables for the local market!" She sounded delighted at the thought.

"Really?" Marvin maintained a perfectly straight face. "How do you know?"

"I asked, silly!" she laughed. "Two years ago there was a veritable mania for eating only those vegetables which were grown with natural products; you know, fertilizer and suchlike. No chemicals. Unfortunately, the idea turned out to be a passing fad. Too expensive. I got this place for a dime!"

"You mean you bought it!?" Marvin could hardly conceal his horror.

"Option to buy. I must see how it goes. It needs a bit of work, of course. Oh, I just love it..." She then looked up at Marvin. The sun left her face. "You don't like it," she said, her eyes turning misty.

"Whatever could possibly make you think so? Immediately after work, I shall present myself at your doorstep, ready to arrange all your furniture exactly as Mrs. Prentis would want it," he assured, with a grave expression on his face.

They both laughed.

By mid-November, Marvin was going to Jocelyn's studio directly from work. He would let himself in with his own key, sit down and wait for Jocelyn to return from the library. At quarter to seven, they would leave and walk, or on wet days take a taxi, to Mrs. Prentis's house for supper. By then Jocelyn could easily have slept in her own place, but she didn't have the heart to tell her Aunt that her generosity was no longer required.

Mrs. Prentis had noticed, however, that lately Marvin and her niece returned from work rather late. Though the kitchen where she prepared dinner faced the back of the house, she made frequent visits to her sitting room. She felt acutely responsible for her niece's welfare if not her whereabouts. Mrs. Prentis's arched eyebrows suggested that she also noticed Jocelyn and Mr. Clark entering her house practically arm in arm. Whatever thoughts Mrs. Prentis entertained on the subject, she kept them to herself. She could not resist, however, keeping a watchful eye on the young lady and the young man throughout the course of the meal. She seemed determined that they would not leave the table together and that, after dinner, Marvin would make his way directly to his apartment. If Jocelyn left the table first, Mrs. Prentis would wait until Marvin got up, walk him to the door and see him up the stairs until he was well past Mr. Jones's room. She performed these acts of chaperonage with a natural ease of one well versed in the matter of this nature. Now and again, Marvin and Jocelyn would have a bit of fun at the expense of her Aunt, but neither of them wanted to do anything to hurt the well-meaning lady.

On occasion Jocelyn would get up with her last swallow and rush to the studio to sink her long fingers into her beloved clay. Mrs. Prentis invariably waved her on from the dining room window until she disappeared around the first corner. Then and only then did Mrs. Prentis seem fully relaxed—at least for a good little while. Officially, no one knew what time Jocelyn returned; although sometime later two pairs of eyes in two darkened rooms wandered the length of the street in silent vigil. Then the eyes smiled, relieved, as Jocelyn entered the safety of the Victorian mansion. Soon the bedside lights would go out, on all three floors, and silence would embrace the boarding house until the next morning, only to repeat this same cycle again and again.

On the first Saturday of December, all the boarders at Mrs. Prentis's had been invited to a "studio warming party". When the day arrived, it turned out to be one of those particularly nasty days, saturated with fog, drizzle, and toward the end of the day with wet, chilly sleet. Marvin, assuming the role of an unofficial host, offered to escort Mrs. Prentis and the two elderly gentlemen lodgers to the studio by taxi. Colonel Mackenzie Whittlaw declined the invitation, citing an old wound as the offending culprit. The war injury invariably played up on the evenings when CBC presented Hockey Night in Canada. The remaining trio accepted the offer with gratitude and, armed with flowers and bottles of wine, arrived promptly at six o'clock at Jocelyn's new address. Marvin paid the driver and offered his arm to Mrs. Prentis. She took it with an unexpected grace. He led her to the door while the two gentlemen completed the stately procession. The door was not locked. After the perfunctory press at the doorbell, Marvin pushed the door open for Mrs. Prentis. Still holding on to his arm, she raised her long skirt over the threshold and stopped there, presumably waiting to be welcomed by the hostess.

For no justifiable reason, Marvin felt a touch of personal pride at the marvelous job Jocelyn had done with the greenhouse. While "officially" it was referred to as her studio, they, Marvin and Jocelyn, when alone, called it the Conservatory. The eighteen large pots of plants, which Marvin had managed to redirect from the municipal greenhouses, had something to do with the preferred name. Jocelyn claimed to have always dreamed of working in a conservatory. Now she did.

"And it's all thanks to you, Marvin!" She never tired of repeating.

The large room was full of people. Marvin hated crowds. He hated congested places in which one would have to raise one's voice to be heard. The room qualified on both counts to foster his distaste. He wanted to turn and run, perhaps would have, if it hadn't been for Mrs. Prentis gamely holding on to his arm. Then Jocelyn, her eyes sparkling, cheeks flushed, hair bobbing in a youthful ponytail, appeared at the door.

"Where were you?" she shouted over the noise, perilously waving her glass half full of red wine.

"And just what do you mean by that, young lady?" Mrs. Prentis was at her most prim again. No one ever argued with her under these circumstances.

"We all seem to have started a bit early...?" Jocelyn capitulated.

"You most certainly have, dear girl. You most certainly appear to have," Mrs. Prentis concurred.

"Ah, do you think we could come in?" A timid voice inquired after a few inaudible ahems and grunts. "It's a bit wet out here, you know?" Mr. Graves and Mr. Johnson still stood outside the front door.

It was easy unwittingly to ignore Messrs. Graves and Johnson. They both seemed quite used to it. Nevertheless, it prompted Mrs. Prentis to come in without any further argument. Jocelyn took her to the kitchen, which today doubled as a cloakroom. It appeared that Jocelyn's younger friends, from the library as well as from her more bohemian, artistic circles, had been invited to come a little earlier, on the assumption that after a drink or two they would disappear to their own homes for supper. In fact, Jocelyn's friends from her sculpture classes, the ones she had participated in almost nine years ago, trickled in throughout the early afternoon.

"What else could one do with such a dire December day?" they inquired, quite unabashedly, on arrival. "You don't mind, do you, Jocy?"

Jocy didn't mind. She was too happy to mind almost anything. Except, perhaps, being called Jocy.

Her friends spent their time sipping wine, nibbling on an array of strategically placed junk-food offerings, talking shop, discussing latest trends in the art world, commiserating over cost of bronze and other metal castings. The time just slipped away. By five o'clock, the library colleagues arrived. More wine, more junk food. By six no one had left, and Jocelyn had no idea what precisely was going on. Surely, she had organized it all very well, hadn't she?

"I think that they are all having a rather good time," she told Marvin after delivering Mrs. Prentis into the arms of a jovial, very elegant-looking gentleman, whom she introduced to her Aunt as Mr. James Robinson, the director of the Public Library. She explained all this to Marvin in a most peculiar blend of a whisper and a shout.

"I rather think they are!" Marvin agreed in kind.

He was beginning to recover. This was the first party of such proportions Marvin had attended in a good many years. It slowly dawned on him that a discordant crowd such as this did in fact offer a strange opportunity for melting, or perhaps merging, into a sort of blatant anonymity. He thought of himself as a swimmer within a whole school of fish—one of many, indistinguishable from any. He could watch without being seen. He could even start talking normally, as one normally does in normal circumstances, and he could be reasonably sure that no one would hear him. This hadn't been so bad, after all. At least, as long as it wouldn't last too long nor be repeated at too frequent intervals.

The real problem Marvin faced was his total inability to derive any sense of belonging. This, seemingly as nice a group of people as one could hope to meet, all appeared to be deeply involved in some sort of ritual which was totally foreign to him. He tried to eavesdrop on two or three conversations, but understood or heard nothing cohesive, nothing that would invite or motivate him to join in, to partake, to gain a sense of—belonging. If all these people were from another planet, he would feel the same degree of kinship as he did toward these friends of his friend. Or perhaps, perhaps it was he who was from a different planet. Or a galaxy, perhaps?

The music, what one could hear of it, could not be blamed. He himself put together a few tapes of Mozart, Vivaldi and some other composers to whom one could listen with pleasure yet without being offended if some conversation took place at the same time. Now, it was of no consequence whether the quality inherent in the music was agreeable or not. The only positive thing was, he supposed, that it in no way aggravated the situation. "Thank heaven for little mercies," he managed a smile.

By seven o'clock a stack of pizzas arrived. Behold a hot dinner, culinary amplitude of unparalleled distinction. Then he tasted it. Why was it, he mused, why was it that the conspicuously vulgar can be so tasteful? Or had he been sinking into an abyss of the unmitigated, gaudy tastes of *vox populi*? Then Marvin reached out for another slice. He was truly surprised that each successive morsel tasted even better—provided it was washed down with a commensurate amount of red wine.

At ten o'clock, Mrs. Prentis found him supporting one of the walls and a glass of wine. She asked if he would consider taking her home. All this must be very nice, she felt sure, but she had important things to do at home. At least that was her story.

Marvin let out a surreptitious sigh of relief. Surely, Jocelyn would let him go under these circumstances. He did, after all, deliver Mrs. Prentis, dear Auntie, to her studio at her bidding. He was bound by honor to return her, safe and sound, to her place of origin, or at least to her home. Whichever was closer.

Marvin dreamt of pizzas swimming in an ocean of red wine. There were tiny palm trees growing in the middle of the pizzas, which swayed gently in a balmy breeze. The palms, not the pizzas. With the pizzas he had another problem altogether. Each time he tried to climb on one, it buckled and sank under his weight, dumping him into the red liquid. At three in the morning he got up and got rid of as much of the red liquid as he could. The rest of the night was peaceful.

After a late breakfast Marvin went for a walk. Last night's sleet left the streets damp, though a fresh wind was turning sidewalks into a patchy skating rink. He walked over to the park and crossed the now frozen lawn to the secret spot by the pump house. It all seemed bleak and deserted. Not only the sun and the green and Jocelyn's smile, but something else was missing. Marvin could not put his finger on it. Was it something that he, himself, seemed to lack?

Marvin returned home, put on some music and picked up one of his favourite authors: Joseph Campbell. This strange man never failed to fill his mind and heart with a new, more tolerant view of the world. Never—until now. After a skimpy lunch, Marvin decided to stretch out for a while to make up for last night's chimerical digressions.

When he awoke, the shape of the window was vaguely silhouetted against a darker background. He switched on the bedside table lamp and looked at the watch. My goodness, he mused, three-thirty and it's almost dark. Suddenly Marvin sensed a surge of energy. He stepped briskly to the bathroom, washed his face, splashed on some aftershave lotion and took a long look at himself in the mirror. Gradually a certain resolve registered in his features. He put on his coat and practically ran out into the street. The air was cold. Much colder than during his morning walk. The approaching winter was determined to make its presence known.

Marvin walked fast, as though resolute to shake last night's folly out of his bones. In less than fifteen minutes he pressed the button on Jocelyn's door. Seeing the lights streaming through the roof panels, he knew that she was in. Marvin never used his own key when he suspected her presence. In fact, she had given Marvin the key when he was organizing the delivery of all the

plants. Somehow, accidentally or on purpose, he forgot to give it
up. She opened the door almost at once.

"About time!" Jocelyn greeted him with her usual smile.
"You left the women's work to a woman, I see?"

The place looked spotless. Marvin knew at once what she
meant: the clean-up after the hordes that had stampeded through
the conservatory last night.

"I plead guilty but reasonably insane." The mixed
metaphor expressed his sentiments well enough. "I would have
come earlier if it weren't for the fact that I didn't think I would
be very good company..." Marvin took a step forward and
stopped dead in his tracks. "What... ?"

"Do you like it?" She beamed.

"What... where... when...?"

"Why and who are the other two." Jocelyn completed for
him the investigative reporter's creed." Actually, this morning,
because I love it, and by a good, old friend of mine. The what
and where you can see for yourself."

And see Marvin could. In the corner of the sitting area, yet
a good six feet from either wall, there stood, on a large cast-iron
plate, an enormous wood stove. The glass doors had been left
ajar, and the joyful flames danced and flickered with the
coziness of an open fire. Marvin wondered if he would ever visit
Jocelyn without being treated to a distracting if not stunning
surprise. He seemed to love and hate it at the same time. It added
a strange spark to his routine-filled life, while at the same time
upsetting his acquired need for peace and stability.

"Do take your coat off. Surely it does give enough heat,
doesn't it?" Jocelyn mocked his flabbergasted expression.

Marvin hung up his coat and sank down in front of the
crackling fire. Jocelyn took off her shoes and also climbed on
the sofa. They sat in silence enjoying a tacit communion. After a
while, she took him by the hand and led him along the walls
which yesterday, due to the milling crowd, had remained
practically invisible.

"I cleaned out—threw out, really—over sixty glasses.
Plastic, of course."

Martin saw for the first time about twenty, perhaps thirty bas-relief sculptures hanging in groups on the walls. He looked but didn't seem to absorb. His mind today was elsewhere. Jocelyn sensed this and didn't pursue the artistic tour. Gently she took him back to the sofa. She left him there and returned a minute later with two plastic glasses and a half-full bottle of wine. She placed them on the floor rug in front of Marvin. Then she left him again. As though by magic, some gentle strains of Vivaldi, seemingly emerging from beyond the forest of mysterious plants, drifted into the large room. Jocelyn was back, at Marvin's feet, looking up into his eyes over the rim of her glass. A few seconds later, only the open fire competed for attention with the opalescent moon suspended over the large skylight in the silent game of shadow casting. The fragrance of the wine, the lingering memory of long-held-back desires...

Her skin, a pale, smooth alabaster washed gently with an enchanting sheen of mysterious moonlight, gave way in almost unexpected softness to his anxious, possessive constraint. Her eyes, filled with grotesque filigrees of dancing, charismatic shadows, submitted to the dark, compelling currents of his searching, overwhelming passion. The currents ran deep, coercing, filled with want, longing. Turbulent breakers, white crests, mounted, roared in a final glory, then collapsed... a million droplets scattered on empty, deserted beaches.

Later, he picked her up with infinite care and raised her to the sofa. The two wine glasses, red blood swirling against the dying fire, sealed their consummate union with Olympian nectar.

They were both quite late for Mrs. Prentis's supper.

* * *

Winter

"Now is the winter of our discontent..."

William Shakespeare, Richard III.

7

The Promotion

There had been occasions when incidents swelled the currents of Marvin's life as though commanded by the Force of Destiny. Occasions when insurmountable barriers had arisen, others plummeted, or when the unpredictable became the overtly natural, certainly the unavoidable.

At those pivotal junctures, Destiny employed such means as had been at Its disposal. Indifferent to personal or social demands, It did what had to be done to cajole, sway or coerce Marvin's future toward the new untested waters. Years later, upon reflection, Marvin came to realize that Destiny resolves the incalculable complexity of Its bidding, the innumerable ramifications, the perplexing twists and turns in the currents of his life with the ease of a child handling a well-worn toy. Years later...

Marvin was stunned, flabbergasted, disbelieving his eyes.

When he had first read the confidential memo about his forthcoming promotion, he had felt all of the above simultaneously, later in protracted succession. Three months had passed since his last, equally unexpected promotion—three months which Marvin had used to recapture his superfluous if wanton desire, his need for personal, social, and official obscurity. He achieved this end partially by staging a bastion at his office citadel in the form—or more aptly said, shape—of Miss Olive Gascon, his then newly acquired, fastidious, firm and forceful secretary. To Marvin she was worth her albeit diminutive weight in gold. Miss Gascon took her instructions literally and never, never allowed through his door anyone of a lesser rank than his own, without a previous appointment. This simple device of practical expediency had been introduced partially to afford Mr. Marvin Clark his much-needed privacy, and partially to allow him a little time to become acquainted with his new responsibilities. This seemingly innocuous stratagem, this innocent ploy, turned around like a well-aimed boomerang which, having grazed its prey along its circuitous route, returned to strike Marvin with an unpredictable force.

No one would have guessed that this elementary ploy would bear such capricious consequences. Mr. Clark's apparent inaccessibility had the whole Department, indeed other departments of the Municipal bureaucracy, whispering. With the efficacy of the interdepartmental gossip intercom, the news spread that Mr. Clark was performing some important, evidently confidential duty, or task, well beyond his official responsibilities. The word "official" was pronounced with a knowing wink or an indulgent tone.

The above presumption had been encouraged by those close to Marvin. They bathed in its, or Marvin's, reflected glory. It had been affirmed by others, lest they be accused of belligerent feeble-mindedness. It had been accepted and... confirmed by the departmental bigwigs who, having no idea what Marvin was doing, could not possibly admit to ignorance in matters of such ponderous importance that no one, literarily no one, knew anything about.

When the order came from above, all the way from the provincial capital, to introduce a greater element of visible or any other "type" of minorities into the higher strata of municipal government, the men (and one woman) at the helm of the City Hall faced a problem. In spite of extensive advertising in the daily press, the influx of blacks, yellows, browns or any of the more colourful members of the Canadian national matrix failed to materialize. Even more impossible was the unprecedented directive to bring such minorities into the higher levels of responsibility.

Higher levels!? Surely not *higher*... ?

Marvin was neither black, yellow, nor brown, except for the period immediately following his annual summer leave; but he did suffer from one advantage. He was not French. His fluent bilingualism bore no influence on the decision. Both Marvin, to the best of anyone's knowledge, and certainly Clark, had always been, and were likely to continue to be, English names. In Quebec that could be regarded as sufficient deviation from the norm to create a visible impression that an invisible minority had been granted a position of great visibility, ah... responsibility. If, indeed, such a responsibility, great or otherwise, could be found. Since no one, as had already been mentioned, had any idea what Marvin was doing, he could, surely, continue to do the very same thing in a larger office, with the word DIRECTEUR below his name on the solid oak doors.

That was settled, then. The City Hall of St-Onge had been saved. No possible harm could result from such a diligent choice, while the Public Relations Department was sure to rejoice in its new, fortuitous, public image. It was all settled except for one detail. Marvin had refused.

Mr. Marvin Clark had refused to accept the promotion!

Not precisely refused... but, to assure that he would be worthy of such an exalted position, Marvin had requested a precise, written definition of his new duties. This simple request had created a veritable panic at... the very top.

"*Tabernacle!* That's the trouble with those minorities. They are just a bunch of troublemakers. That's what they are. A bunch... *Ce* bloke *est un* twit!" commented the director of public relations in his *pure laine* French.

"Who the devil does he think he is?" thundered the mayor, repeatedly slamming his fist on the highly polished rosewood table. "No one else knows what the hell they are doing, and nobody else is complaining!"

The elderly mayor had to be physically restrained to save his fist from sustaining a permanent injury. Finally, the deputy mayor was commissioned to define Marvin's forthcoming duties. She begged the mayor to reconsider bestowing upon her feminine shoulders this horrendous responsibility; alas—she had to give in. The matter was of such importance that it could not possibly be delegated to anyone else.

"No one! You hear me? No one is to know about this. You are to report directly to me. Directly!" The mayor was about to smash his fist on the table again, but after a momentary massage of the offensive weapon, he decided against it.

The problem set before the deputy mayor was neither easy nor frivolous. The memo practically appointing Mr. Marvin Clark to his new office had already been issued. To rescind it would, or at least could, create another avalanche of problems, the scope of which no one could even imagine. With a cold shudder she pictured the broad, fat headlines in the English dailies: "The English slighted once again by the French bureaucracy." She saw her name mentioned quite a few times in the ensuing article. The unfortunate thing was that she truly enjoyed her English friends, sent all her children to English private schools, and had absolutely no desire to slight, injure, or offend the visible or invisible minorities in any way whatever. Marie-Claire Bourbeau had been appointed the deputy mayor because she was a woman. It really had not been her fault. And now this! There was no way out. She had to create a new position.

Two weeks later, after a considerable amount of midnight oil and the attendant, salubrious toddies, Madame Bourbeau presented the mayor with her official proposal. It had been beautifully printed on excellent-quality rice paper with the city's coat of arms impressively centered at the top of the vital document. The lower part of the document had been dignified with two seals and a space for the mayor's and her own signatures. Madame Bourbeau knew from experience that the only way to forestall procrastinating changes to any document submitted to the mayor was to present it in such a manner that it at least looked like *fait accompli.*

> *Mr. Marvin Clark is to head the new Confidential Advisory Council which, when deemed necessary, will be formed following a preparatory period of in-depth research. The said Advisory Council will initiate and oversee all proposals dealing with matters heretofore not covered by the already established departments. The thrust of the research will be directed toward establishing a closer and more intimate relationship between the existing departments, the general public, and any future initiatives which may, in time, result from the research conducted under Mr. Clark's supervision. Mr. Clark is to answer to and report directly to the Mayor and/or, in the event of the mayor's absence or indisposition, to the Deputy Mayor. Under no circumstances is Mr. Clark to announce any new initiatives prior to personal consultation with the above-mentioned duly elected representatives of the General Public.*

The mayor read the document twice, scratched his head and said: "Excellent. *C'est formidable!*" Then he added, as an afterthought, "...but what exactly is he going to be doing?" His face indicated a considerable effort on his part to fathom the document in hand.

"I rather think the same that he is doing right now, Your Worship. Only this time officially?" The deputy mayor looked a little hurt by the mayor's question. Had he not said that she had done an excellent job? Where was his gratitude?

The mayor let it ride. He was certain that no man can refuse a job which he cannot possibly understand. After all, if you are not doing anything much, you can hardly do it badly, or do much harm, for that matter. And, after all, the salary offered was excellent, too.

No more than three months ago, Marvin would have refused the "detailed" offer which, following his request, arrived on his desk just before Christmas. He was quite able to see through a farce when he saw one. He also disliked being used, particularly for an end or ends unknown to him. Unofficially Marvin had been told that he could take all the time he needed to make up his mind. A position of such sway, such range, such scope for expressing one's initiative, should not be treated lightly. He should regard it with an utmost sense of responsibility. He was to reply to the mayor, directly, not later than the week following the Christmas recess.

Excremento del toro! Marvin whispered under his breath.

Anyway, that would have been three months ago. Now, Marvin's thoughts were elsewhere. Now his mind was preoccupied with Jocelyn. How different she was from his previous tentative ventures into the domain of the other mysterious sex. Women, nearly always, scared him. Not physically, of course. It had been their apparently inherent desire to limit his freedom, to superimpose their vision of the world on his own that scared him. Marvin needed his so-called psychic space. He needed his privacy, his inner travels, his inimitable spaceship.

Strangely enough, Marvin hadn't even noticed that for the last three or four weeks he hadn't "traveled" at all. He had been preoccupied with such unaccustomed emotions that the elements which heretofore constituted his life seemed to have dissolved in a haze of uncertainty. In addition, Marvin began to feel a peculiar sense of responsibility toward Jocelyn. Physically he was attracted to her to the exclusion of any other consideration of his day-to-day existence. She invaded his mind, his heart, his wakeful thoughts, even his dreams. With a momentum acquired over the years, he continued to perform his office duties; but instead of freeing his mind to venture into the inner worlds of beauty and enchantment, his attention became firmly anchored in the physical reality of his surroundings.

Marvin's request for the definition of his duties had been almost instinctive. His inherent honesty would not allow him to act otherwise. Yet, by the time the report reputedly defining his new position arrived, Marvin had analyzed it from a different point of view. He judged whether or not it might interfere with his primary interest—Jocelyn. Marvin's concern for maintaining his inconspicuousness, his beloved invisibility, so dear to him over so many years, never even entered his mind. A new element, however, did. He began to scrutinize the offer from the point of view of financial rewards. He mused how much more money he might have to spend on enhancing his relationship with the object of his desires. He thought of a new, real studio for Jocelyn. Perhaps a new, bigger apartment? A new, different, more exciting, more prestigious address, a new...

Marvin thought of the expression on Jocelyn's face when he would announce all the possibilities which fate had thrown his way. Their way? Could he possibly refuse an offer, regardless of any other considerations, when the net gain would benefit Jocelyn? In whatever way she chose? Surely, he had no right. He thought of himself as a gentleman. A gentleman accepts his obligations with calm confidence, with a sense of responsibility.

> *"... and therefore, Mr. Mayor, I am honored to accept the position offered with a profound sense of responsibility. I further hasten to assure you, Sir, that I shall continue to exercise my duties in such a manner as to fully justify the trust which you, Mr. Mayor, have placed in me."*

Marvin added a few standard pleasantries and signed the letter. He extracted from Miss Gascon an oath of secrecy regarding the matter in hand. Before doing so, however, he had asked her if she would consider moving with him to, ah, different, ah, higher quarters...

Miss Gascon sealed the envelope in his presence, her eyes misty, her tongue tasting the glue of the envelope with amorous delight, enchanted by the recognition which her boss, the captain of her ship, had been awarded. And she would sail with him, ever upward, ever higher... My goodness, *mon Dieu, c'est incroyable!* She could hardly contain her elation. Blessed was the day when she had been chosen to serve the man whom all other girls even refused to consider. Her humility, her self-sacrifice had been rewarded. And alas, so quickly! What a magnificent present for her Christmas, she thought. I shall really pray hard, she vowed, momentarily closing her eyes. In gratitude, of course.

It was not easy for Marvin to say nothing of all this to Jocelyn over the Christmas recess. His years of solitude had taught him well. He had learned to contain his private affairs within. Marvin decided not to tempt fate by spreading the news before the official announcement. His appointment was bound to appear in the daily press. *"Monsieur Marvin Clark, Directeur."* Perhaps it did have a certain ring to it. Marvin still wasn't quite sure, in fact not sure at all, what exactly he was to direct. He decided to have faith in his superiors. After all, the whole Town of St-Onge had elected them all with an overwhelming majority. The people must have known what they were doing. His job was to serve, not to ask too many questions. Humility, my boy, he told himself, humility. All in good time. Take it easy. Relax!

At Mrs. Prentis's, Christmas was celebrated with the usual seasonal flourish. Marvin took it upon himself to supply all the wine for the Christmas dinner. A good Claret, Spanish Champagne for dessert. Jocelyn, for her part, carted in and decorated a Christmas tree three times bigger than had been usual at Mrs. Prentis's boarding house. Mr. Graves and Mr. Johnson had to walk the length of the table to get to their chairs. Yet, no one objected. After dinner, following the distribution of the minuscule *pro forma* presents, Colonel James Mackenzie Whittlaw rose, initiated, and then conducted two complete Christmas carols. Following this unaccustomed feat, the red-faced white-haired soldier, overcome with emotion, collapsed into his chair. Rather than wipe off the tears swirling in his eyes, the Colonel shook his head in disbelief at the beauty of

Christmas that had been his, once again, to partake of, to enjoy, to share in the spirit thereof.

Jocelyn got up, walked up to him, and kissed him on both cheeks. "Thank you, Colonel," she told him. "Thank you for making us all celebrate Christmas the way it should be celebrated."

At this, Colonel Whittlaw looked beside himself. He got up again, raised his hands as though acknowledging applause from a multitude of troops, perhaps his old regiment. His mouth moved, seemingly searching for the right words, or perhaps just gasping for air, and then he sat down without uttering a word. The Colonel was quite overcome.

For the second day of Christmas, Jocelyn invited all "who didn't have anything better to do" to her studio.

"Just tea or coffee, perhaps a little brandy or liqueur?" she offered. Then she looked at Colonel Whittlaw. "And for the best Christmas cake money can buy!" she added. She had already noticed that the Colonel had a sweet tooth.

With the exception of her real Aunt Jenny, and obviously of Marvin, Jocelyn seemed to have adopted all the remaining tenants. She had taken them all under her generous wings, treated them as a bunch of long lost, but dearly rediscovered uncles. Conversely, the three gentlemen would die for her, jump headfirst from their respective windows, if that was what she desired of them. Jocelyn was the one daughter they had never had, the child they had always dreamt of, the just prize for the long, honest life, finally rewarded, in genuine belief that all things come to him who waits.

Only Marvin wasn't overjoyed by Jocelyn's overt ability to show, give, and evidently receive affection, if not actual adulation, from all she came in contact with. His attitude toward her was rapidly becoming an unpalatable mixture of pride in her obvious charm and an unwitting almost subliminal jealousy at being forced to share her, or at least her qualities, with others. On a detached mental level, Marvin knew that one cannot preclude the others; emotionally, however, he would rather confine her under lock and key than allow anyone to so much as breathe the same air she did. None of this would he ever admit to her, nor to anyone else, and particularly not to... himself. Years of personal discipline enabled Marvin to retain and display an agreeable smile, a pleasant demeanor, a tolerant attitude. But it wasn't easy.

When on Boxing day the whole house migrated to Jocelyn's, Marvin assumed the duties of a perfect host with considerable success. He preferred helping with the tea, coffee, with the cutting and distribution of the Christmas cake; he preferred performing the duties of a waiter to just sitting and watching the gawking eyes of the three doting old men who made no effort whatever to restrain their open, unabashed, lecherous, satiric if saturnine admiration for his, damn it, *his* woman. Marvin continued to smile, to serve, to offer additional lumps of ice, even if such were not needed, waiting for this farce to be over.

Not the least cause for his growing bitterness was the fact that Jocelyn was evidently quite unaware of his predicament. The fact that only a few days ago they had made love seemed not to have changed her in any way, to have made no difference in her attitude to him, let alone to others. She remained her own self: free, friendly, spontaneous—beautiful beyond words. It was as if she made love to someone every day of the week. As if such an act of mutual bliss as they had shared, an act of total commitment, did not exist for her. Marvin knew that he was wrong. He knew that Jocelyn was the antithesis of the dark thoughts that seemed to invade and crowd his tortured mind. But then... why did she continue to torture him?

Finally the 'tea party' was over. Would she stay with him, at least a while longer, to share a moment's bliss? Not she. Jocelyn decided to go back with them, at once, and help Aunt Jenny with the supper. Marvin learned later that Mrs. Prentis had come to the studio only under this condition. How else was she to prepare dinner for six people if all her afternoon was taken by idle, frivolous pursuits?

"We all have our responsibilities," Mrs. Prentis admonished gravely. She took hers very seriously indeed.

The supper had always been served from a hot wagon, an arrangement Mrs. Prentis borrowed from a hotel she'd visited many years ago. The table was laid, the food prepared well in advance, placed in insulated containers on a wheeled wagon and, when all was ready, served in the dining room. The salads and other side dishes could be found at the side table. This method enabled Mrs. Prentis to partake of her culinary efforts with all her tenants, while they all took turns transferring the various dishes or dirty plates to and from the table.

Apparently this method, at least for tonight, did not satisfy Jocelyn's needs. To assure that Mrs. Prentis would have her share of Christmas, Jocelyn forced her dear Auntie to remain at the table at all times and not even to reach out for anything from the hot-plates, from the side table, or to move her feet for any other reason— notwithstanding Aunt Jenny's remarkably vocal protests.

"I am too old, young lady, too old to be told what I can or can't do in my own home, at my very own table!" Mrs. Prentis declared sternly.

"Yes, dear, of course you are," Jocelyn said, busy with her self-imposed duties. Then, seeing Mrs. Prentis's consternation, Jocelyn whimpered lamely, "I mean, of course you are not, dear Aunt Jenny..."

To seal her response to Mrs. Prentis's belated declaration of independence, Jocelyn placed a light kiss on her Aunt's rosy cheek. It helped, but her prim sternness diffused somewhat only after the third glass of Burgundy.

After dinner, the last of Marvin's hopes were shattered with an almost desperate vengeance. He was counting on seeing Jocelyn alone, at least for a while. Although he would still not tell her about his promotion, the self-imposed secrecy had built up within him a considerable nervous tension, which he could not discharge, or even compensate for, except by being in her presence. Her exclusive presence. Without having to tolerate the wandering eyes of the other tenants or the stern gaze of her dear ol' Auntie.

No such luck, Marvin found out. No peace for the guilty!

The moment the table was cleared and coffee served, Jocelyn declared that the gentlemen would now entertain Aunt Jenny, while she, and she alone, would disappear into the cavernous kitchen and tend to all that needed to be tended.

"Marvin," Jocelyn threw over her shoulder, "you will look after my Auntie, won't you? There's a dear!"

At this sad announcement, Marvin lost all hope of ever seeing his Jocelyn again.

Sleep didn't come easily.

Large bulging eyes converged on all sides. They peered intently from the otherwise blank, featureless faces. As the twin shining globules of irises came nearer, they disengaged themselves from the vacuous masks and floated in a grotesque sluggishness toward a large green crystal full of ice cubes. Marvin knew he had to hurry. He strained to find the one special face before it, too, lost its autonomous vision—but it was all in vain. As he stretched out his arms, the masks turned away in total indifference.

Marvin began the following day with a throbbing headache.

It would be four long days before Marvin would have a chance to see Jocelyn in her, in their, conservatory. By then he could finally tell her. It had been made official. The *Morning Courier* announced, on page one, the appointment of Mr. Marvin Clark to the Office of Special Works Director. Mr. Clark was to Head the New Advisory Council of Special Works. His duties were to have great influence on the future Inter-Governmental affairs as well as on Public Works and Public Relations. It was a vast field of responsibility. It was considered a major coup for the minorities, which heretofore had little if any influence on the inner workings of the city bureaucracy. Bravo! Bravo! Mr. Clark!

With the *Morning Courier* under his arm, Marvin pressed Jocelyn's doorbell. He waited the usual period of time and then used his own key. Two hours later he went back to his apartment. That night Jocelyn did not come to dinner. Mrs. Prentis said nothing. Marvin did not ask.

That night Marvin sat in his deep armchair, invoking his old trips to the lands where magic, beauty and serene happiness ruled supreme. He tried his old favourite fuel, the never-failing Sibelius, the poignant Mendelssohn, the lighter-than-air Mozart. But his heart was heavy. Too heavy in this moment of his greatest glory.

* * *

8

Waiting

"Three weeks and a day..."

Jocelyn's smile wavered on the verge of uncertainty at the thought of the last twenty-two days. She counted them almost subconsciously. Three weeks and a day had passed since...

She looked at the large sheepskin stretched in front of the wood stove. She could still see that fire... dancing brightly, filigree shadows on the tall walls. And then... and then gently, with infinite care, he raised her onto the settee. Three weeks had passed since he had filled her glass with the red, poignant wine, since he covered her moon-swept alabaster shoulders with a soft angora blanket, and held her. And held her close until the embers died, one by one, slowly, as though ominous of that which had flared in a short burst, a wanton spasm of glory, only to die a death protracted by desire, by hope, by memories.

Jocelyn knew that with Marvin's apparent shyness it had been up to her to create conditions, an atmosphere conducive, propitious, to his dropping his guard, forsaking his need to hide his inner, true self from the world, from all people, even from her. Yet she also knew, as only a woman who loves a man can know, that beneath that mask of self-imposed, taciturn, obstinate armour hid a strange being rich in surprising, unpredictable gifts, growing, maturing, though perhaps not ripe yet to cross the narrow, precarious isthmus between his inner oceans of beauty and serenity and the objective reality of the outer, turbulent waters.

Jocelyn decided to wait.

Unless he, Marvin, was ready to take a chance, to risk losing his secure, proven, formidable defenses, to venture out into the open, often dangerous, unforgiving world... neither she nor anyone could help him. She knew of but one way to gain love. It had failed her once already in her dim, youthful, innocent past. Yet she had not lost her faith. Jocelyn knew that the only way anyone can gain love is by giving love. Love attracts love, even as hatred attracts hatred. An ancient esoteric tenet—yet ever a risky proposition. There were no guarantees; never an assurance that love can conquer all. That adage was no more than romantic nonsense, the stuff of gothic novels rich in emotion, poor on fact and substance.

There was no other, no alternate, safer, easier way. To gain all, she gave all. In her heart, there were no half measures. Jocelyn felt that heaven was reserved for the brave, not the saintly. Since her troubled childhood, her journey had not been easy. Many a time she had tripped and fallen. She had lost ground, felt swept by the turbulent waters of her own exacting river. She had been left with some bruises, but not for want of courage. The radiant smile she shared, even with strangers, was not an empty grimace well worn by habitual disposition. It was an open challenge to take her at her values. A challenge to risk all, to give love, and thus become richer.

The day after that Sunday evening, Jocelyn had waited for a flower, a token of his caring. She had waited as a wife awaits her distant warrior lover, but also as a mother awaits her hapless, wandering children. How much Marvin had need of her was abundantly obvious. His eyes, his touch, even in moments of his perceived weakness—his words bespoke his need to trust one, just one, single person in this forbidding world, which he rejected as deprived of whatever he searched and longed for.

Jocelyn waited for a flower...

...a tiny thing of beauty, a kind word, a poem, perhaps a short confession, a sign of a crack or fissure in his impervious

armour. Yet from the day after their fleeting bliss of sharing,
Marvin had withdrawn into a cocoon so tightly woven, so sealed
to any outside contact that Jocelyn didn't dare to broach his
lonely, stalwart prison. She had no choice but to wait and
continue waiting. Even if she did venture to enter his seclusion,
what could she accomplish? Rather than help him, she, too,
might well succumb to the safety of donning her own protective
armour. They would spend the rest of their lives hoping for the
other to take the next step, to open the floodgates of the rushing
waters. Rushing? Or just pent up to smash the gates of heaven.
Alas, there was no one to knock on the forbidding portals.

During the weeks preceding Christmas, Jocelyn had
sporadically tried to sculpt, with none too good results. The clay
formed its own shapes, often distorted, whimsical or angry,
refusing to comply or obey her kneading fingers. Yet she
continued, knowing full well that her heart was also not at peace
in this passage of time. She knew that the best way to free herself
from the darker side of her withdrawn soul was to continue her
efforts. Sooner or later, her inner self would triumph; she would
emerge victorious, with... or without Marvin.

Their physical contact, so wonderful (at least so it seemed at
the time), rather than bringing them closer, evidently tore them
further apart. Day after day, at breakfast and at dinner, she had
given him ample opportunity to break the artificial barrier
which, surely not by her making, had suddenly grown between
them. Marvin acted as though he were embarrassed by her very
presence, as if by having dropped his guard in a moment of
unaccustomed weakness, he now felt unprotected, naked,
exposed to her judgment, her penetrating if not demeaning
scrutiny. Finally, on the second day of Christmas, she had hoped
that by placing Marvin among people who were all well known
to him, in whose company he would surely feel free and relaxed,
and sitting by the very same warm, open fire, he might begin to
feel less constrained and come out of his protective shell. Her
efforts had misfired. Marvin would not or could not sit still, not
even for a moment; he had seemed overanxious to please

everyone, seemingly attempting to divert everyone's attention from what he was—to what he was doing.

Oh, how she missed her former, invisible hero.

Later, when she announced that they would all return home for dinner together, his normally rugged if sensitive mouth actually appeared to pout. She could not believe her eyes. A grown man—pouting! Jocelyn admitted to herself that she had decided to clean up after the Boxing Day dinner herself, just to teach him a lesson. Although, undoubtedly, she was also almost as glad that Aunt Jenny was the beneficiary of Marvin's puerile comportment!

Four heavy, drawn days—and as many nights—later, just after she'd arrived at the library, Jocelyn received a telephone call from her friend Marion. They had renewed their friendship at Jocelyn's studio-warming party. They had sworn, then, not to lose touch as they had once done, following the sculpture course they had taken together ages ago. Apparently, Marion was vacationing all alone in West Palm Beach, Florida. Hearing Marion's voice was a magic panacea for the temporary eclipse in Jocelyn's usual smile. Her mind stepped into overdrive.

Jocelyn's hopes for Marvin's return to sanity were fading fast. With the muse of her sculpture evidently rebellious and, on top of it all, Marvin's limiting his romantic courtship to a formal, gilt-edged card to wish her Godspeed in the coming New Year, Jocelyn got angry. She asked her friend if she could, right now, join her. Marion was elated. The two-bedroom condo her friends had lent her would easily accommodate a lot more than just two people.

"Why don't you bring with you your latest beau—what did you say his name was...?" Marion was fishing.

"His name is Blithering Idiot, and he is not invited!"

Jocelyn didn't get angry often. On the occasions she did, she compensated well for the lack of frequency. Wisely, Marion did not ask any more questions. She gave Jocelyn her address

and told her to take a cab from the WPB airport. With that she
hung up.

Jocelyn had one week left from her last year's leave still
owing. She went to see Mr. Robinson, her director. For years
now he had treated Jocelyn practically as his own daughter. He
agreed to her vacation immediately.

"One week? No one will even notice—although I shall miss
you..." He waved her goodbye.

Next, she telephoned Aunt Jenny. She told her of the
invitation she received a minute ago. For reasons she could not
fathom, Aunt Jenny didn't seem pleased. Jocelyn pretended that
she didn't notice.

"I'm just calling to tell you, I won't be home for supper.
I'm sorry, Aunt Jenny, I couldn't give you more notice. It all
happened at once!"

Quite unexpectedly, in spite of all that had transpired,
Jocelyn sounded like her old, joyful self. If Marvin could have
heard her, he would never have forgiven her. Just as well he
didn't, she mused, a little sadly.

In twenty more minutes, Jocelyn was "booked" on a
standby for the two o'clock flight. Her one and only hand
baggage contained the bare essentials for a subtropical vacation.
Bare was a lot more accurately descriptive than Marvin would
have ever imagined. Just as well, her thoughts echoed her
previous contention, a touch of wickedness in the smile playing
at the corners of her full, inviting mouth. Just as well...

Ah, to hell with Marvin!

The just shall be rewarded. Jocelyn didn't have to die to
reap her rewards. Her standby booking was smoothly converted
to a boarding ticket. The flight was picture-perfect. By seven and
some minutes she landed in eighty degrees of humid, soupy
weather. She carried her hand baggage; no waiting for her at the
never-ending baggage carousels! The taxi driver delivered her to
Marion's doorstep within twenty minutes. Within twenty-five
minutes, Jocelyn was stripped of a lot more, or perhaps a lot

less—depending on one's point of view—than the proverbial half-naked. Moments later she relaxed, a tall glass of ice-cold, beautifully crisp Bloody Caesar nudging her elbow, her friend Marion rejoicing at her sudden company. Both women reclined in luxurious, padded lounge chairs, squinting their eyes to catch the last rays of the blood-red sunset as it washed, at a steep angle, the large, beautifully landscaped terrace. And then, without any warning, Jocelyn's eyes filled with great, big, disconsolate tears.

Marion was much too mature to rush forward with a box of Kleenex. From their telephone conversation earlier that same day, she had guessed that Jocelyn's sudden desire to fly south had not been precipitated merely by her need for hot weather. She waited calmly, neither saying nor asking anything, until Jocelyn was ready to unburden her evidently heavy heart. It took only five minutes, but those minutes had been necessary. Younger people often think that withholding, or bottling up, one's emotions is a mature thing to do. Jocelyn was old enough to know better. Surely, she had no intention of wearing her heart on her sleeve or burdening all her friends with her troubles. Yet she also knew that there were times when a release of emotions brings a great comfort and restores a better judgment. This was such a time. Finally, Jocelyn raised her glass.

"Goodness, how I needed that. I feel like a new woman!" She took a deep swig from her tall glass and, for the first time, looked around her. "But, Marion, this is lovely! Why, you never told me you had such rich and obliging friends. Here's to their good health, and to yours, old friend!" She raised her glass again, perhaps on purpose in such quick succession.

Marion uttered some inconsequential welcome and waited for Jocelyn to gather her wits. There was no rush. Down south, as the Canadians called it, time traveled at a different pace. Perhaps being closer to the equator, one covered a greater distance around the earth's axis, and thus dilated one's time, or at least one's perception of it, emotionally if not physically. Marion thought that Einstein had something to say on that subject. For now, she just waited.

Suddenly, without warning, a cluster of clouds formed and stayed suspended on invisible strings, static, in a rapidly darkening sky. The leading west edges of the fluffy whipped cream abruptly turned red, while retaining a pinkish white, soft underbelly. The other fringes, those facing the mysterious east, assumed an almost solid definition, pensive, perhaps a mite lugubrious portends of the dying daylight. Indeed, this was yet a spell of aimless indecision, of casual, noncommittal waiting. Then time slowed down even more. Hovering in fragile abeyance, it seemed destined to stop in its weary progress, and then—with the suddenness reserved for subtropical magic—there was night.

The two women remained immobile, refusing to take part in this charade. They lingered on as part of the timeless moment, as though attached to the group of fading, gradually dissolving clouds, now but mere shadows of their former, nearly opalescent delight. A sigh or two escaped Jocelyn's ostensibly relaxed bosom, deep, halting sighs, unsure of their source, unsure of the future, lost in the moping present. When the moon rose over the picture-postcard palm trees, she bit hard on her lip. The colour of her body took her back three weeks and a day, to that ephemeral moment when her body was swept by the very same moonbeam, by the cold, indifferent rays of borrowed, reflected sunlight.

Marion rose quietly and disappeared inside the apartment. Soon she was back, with two fresh drinks on a small tray accompanied by two bowls filled to overflowing with a variety of mixed, ready-to-eat nuts. She put one drink and a bowl by Jocelyn's lounge chair, taking the rest to her own seat. Jocelyn smiled her gratitude, then again raised her glass in a silent salute.

"Did you have any lunch?" Marion suddenly remembered.

"Lunch? I had a sandwich at the airport. Am not really hungry." Jocelyn dug into the nut bowl, belying her assertion. "I could do with a shower." In two days she would acclimatize; right now she felt sticky.

"Will you come with me, or shall I get the hose...?" Marion was ready to make good on either offer. "You'd better come with me. I'll show you the apartment."

Jocelyn got up, filled her mouth to overflowing with nuts, picked up her glass, gave a second look to the lonely bowl left behind. Her eyebrows came together in abject concentration. She then bent down, took the bowl of nuts in her left hand and turned to Marion.

"I think I am ready."

They both grinned but didn't leave the terrace until Marion emulated her friend's good example.

About an hour later they left for the beachfront snack bar, ready for a more substantial meal. The two Bloody Caesars, purposely mixed by Marion with a generous potion of salutary vodka, had the desired effect. Whatever churned at Jocelyn's heart seemed to have subsided. She looked and sounded full of life, enjoying the warm night air after the torturous Canadian winter. Jocelyn decided, and said so, that to any warm-blooded being, human race included, such climatic injections were of compelling necessity.

"There always was a reason why I chose to live in Canada," she declared. "It is simply that unless one does, one cannot possibly appreciate being here in the middle of winter. The middle of our winter!"

"For the same reason I like to hit my head against the wall—it's..."

"...so nice when you stop. No. It's not the same. If I had to choose, as indeed I have done, I'd choose Canadian climate. Not for the love of winter, although even it can be beautiful if you get out of town, but for the extravagant variety, the creative diversity which Mother Nature throws at us with such prodigious generosity. That's what I find so exciting. Every spring, year after year, without ever getting tired, the avalanche of gifts to all, without exception... It makes me wonder if it isn't the creative act itself that is so important, not the end result. If nature wanted to sit on her laurels, she would give up after the first winter, the grass would stop growing after two or three spats with a gnawing lawn mower, the rose would stop blooming when you cut its..."

"...tongue! Jocelyn, are you trying to tell me something?" Marion shook her head at Jocelyn's oratory. "Eat your steak; it's much better when warm."

Two bites later Jocelyn returned to what apparently was her favourite subject. It was evident that when she wasn't actually sculpting, she was readying herself for the creative acts to come. She described some of the premises she had developed during the last embattled week she had spent at home. She tried to explain that if she was to partake in the causative flow of the creative spirit, then her job was essentially limited to that of an instrument, which the unmanifested energy could use to become manifest or visible. Her fingers, hands, even her eyes and mind, were all relegated to a subservient function. The moment this act was accomplished, the next step would be to discipline herself to translate the creative act into a physical form. To a degree this could be accomplished with the subconscious, perhaps even the unconscious, guiding her hands in molding the clay, in shaping the intangible into that which is discernible to and by our limited senses.

"You know, to hear you talk like that makes me sorry I did not keep up with my sculpting since that course we took together..."

There was a wistful look in Marion's eyes as she listened to Jocelyn. She no longer pulled Jocelyn's leg about her obvious obsession or perhaps great love affair with the creative process.

Jocelyn ate for a while in silence, sipped a little of the Californian house wine, then leaned back with relish.

"Would you believe," she said, "this is the first steak I have had in... probably a year? There is something to be said for the primitive custom of the sanguine carnivores masticating on bloody carrion. The tenderizing process is called, I believe, seasoning. We haven't progressed that far in the last few thousand years, have we?" It was a rhetorical question.

"You know, I really listened to what you have been saying." Now it was Marion who couldn't let go of the subject.

"It sounds as if this creative act you were going on about really takes place before you even touch the clay... is that what you're implying?"

"Yes, it does, but it doesn't stop there." Jocelyn was delighted that she had finally drawn her friend into her life's passion. "Basically, the process can be broken down into a sequence. First, you need the so-called inspiration. Nobody quite knows what this word means, but we can assume that it is the primary cause or the initiator. The mystics will refer to it as the silent whisper of the soul; the more down-to-earth will relegate it to the unconscious mind. If you accept the latter, then you are stuck with the problem as to where the unconscious gets the idea? Therefore, we must *perforce* agree that the primary creative impulse must precede the mind. Conscious, sub- or the unconscious. Next, however, the mind does enter. Usually the sculpture grows in, what I can only refer to as, my unconscious and subconscious for quite a while, before it is real enough in my... mind, for me to get excited about it. This excitement, this emotional involvement is the next imperative component of the process. It is a sort of mild form of obsession. I must sculpt the subject matter—even if often I don't quite yet know what exact form it is going to take. I am still at the stage of a 'feel'. This feeling, however, must be strong enough to motivate me into action. Real, physical action. The clay must be purchased, the table must be swept and ready, I must find time. Finally my fingers touch the undefined, lumpy, incoherent chaos. For a while I try to be the creator. Nothing happens. I can't get started. Then, not without a battle, I relax. I almost watch my hands begin to do the work. I start intuitively, then, gradually, if I am lucky, I become part of the process. If I can make it to this stage... Ah, Marion, this is the trade of the gods... You feel one with the flow, the... oh, there are no words for it."

Jocelyn sat back, as if she had emptied her heart of what lay there, unshared for a long, long time. For a while, each woman lost somewhere in her own thoughts, they listened to the surf washing the sandy shore.

"The trouble is that he knows all this. And... and I don't even know how." Jocelyn's eyes seemed to cross a dark ocean to some distant, inaccessible shore.

"Who...?" Marion looked back from the ocean.

"Who? Marvin. The Blithering Idiot, remember?"

"Oh," was the cryptic comment of an old, wise friend. "Oh..." Marion repeated. And then they went back to the apartment. It was quite a long walk on a balmy, serene night. They talked about the weather. And about the sea.

And they talked about nothing.

Nothing at all.

* * *

9

Wilderness

It stretched as far as the eye could see.

For the first time in over a month, Marvin experienced what grudgingly had to be termed a success in his inner travel. The old, well-tested mode of travel. Strapped by a self-imposed trance to his intergalactic, intra-universal controls, at the helm of his dependable ship, Marvin resumed gallivanting through the oceans of time and space, through the waters of pure intellect fired by burning emotions.

Well... almost.

On this particular occasion, Marvin had little or, to be honest, no control over his unruly traveling machine. Time and space, which normally contracted to whisk him instantaneously into the lands of enchantment, lands of beauty and serenity, now deposited him on a vast, totally boundless plane, vast beyond imagination: a plane with no beginning, no end, no visible or perceptible horizons; a realm which offered no point of reference to mark his position within this white, featureless expanse.

Marvin waited, he knew not for what. He felt suspended, weightless, in an ethereal body—if such a term could apply to an altered state of consciousness, which manifested a total absence of the crude, the gross, the physical. Yet in this strange realm, Marvin did possess a body—not tangible, not subject to the laws of the puny universe of coarse, physical dimensions, but a body nonetheless—capable of seeing, or perceiving directly, the object of its attention. If so commanded, this inner, more refined container for his consciousness could experience all the senses. He, or it, could see and hear, and detect a most refined texture with far more sensitive fingers than those that served him in the outer, objective world.

A dream world?

Marvin had often wondered if *this* weren't the *real* world—the world of fluid matter. Only time would tell which of the universes lay nearer to the heart of true reality. The time encapsulating lives of travel, of constant vigilance and study, and most of all of living the life of the Living—not the vegetal state of those not even as yet awakened, or worse, much worse, of those who shed their mortal bodies never having become conscious of the Life within them. There had been moments when Marvin felt acutely conscious of those churning insipid legions who shed their mortal shells only to wait their turn to step once more onto the dull, perennial treadmill—the Wheel of Awagawan, of Life, to start again the long climb to reach out, to grasp, perchance to hold the awareness of their own true state of being.

Perhaps this was the nearest Marvin ever came to defining his need for these ventures into the intangible worlds of pure, or nearly pure, existence. He felt the need to find, to conquer, or at least to observe, the essence of Life. Until his very recent experiences with Jocelyn, experiences over which he had little and lately no control, Marvin had retreated into the inner worlds—not to escape the physical state of consciousness, but rather to find the substance which motivated and thus controlled the mode of his existence. It may have all begun as an escape—once, in the hard pews of the musty gray chapel—but it had long matured into a persistent discipline: into a way of life.

Marvin had long refused to accept that the seemingly aimless carousel of life was indeed so aimless. He observed that recorded history attested to gradual degradation, to symptoms of regression rather than the proclaimed and acclaimed evolvement. Events which to others, the learned, the erudite, the respected others, indicated evolutionary advances, to Marvin were but signs of decadence and failure.

It was late afternoon. The darkening attic fed the shadows of Marvin's despondency. The Monster's tendrils reaching down from the ceiling, the loops, sinister nooses, hung ready, waiting... Snow, driven by a sobbing wind, clung to the panes cutting him off from the world, from the future. He felt trapped by the white, seamless, ubiquitous winter.

Seated at his controls, his back pressed deeply into the absorbing cushions, Marvin appeared relaxed. Yet hidden behind the mask of indifference, his dark thoughts searched for culprits, for scapegoats, for those he could blame for the hollow, bitter emptiness of his soul. While the darkest recesses of his heart screamed for help, his brooding mind churned in anger at those who dared to tell others how to act and not act, what to think and how often.

Marvin shrugged. It will pass, he told himself. He made an effort to divert his thoughts into calmer waters. He pictured his office. Then his superiors.

The image of the rotund mayor drew his thoughts toward the high and the mighty who usurped and diverted the harvest of other peoples' labors to their own conspicuous comfort; those puffed-up public pillars of petty prominence who dragged down the long-faithful, trusting masses into their own quagmire, their own moral depravation—and the countries they ruled to economic ruin. Marvin's mouth involuntarily contorted into a wry grin when he thought of men who bolstered their exulted egos with self-proclaimed titles of mutual admiration while they continued to line their greedy pockets with the bloody sweat of

their subordinates. Our noble rulers, thought Marvin, the
prominent examples of the world fast tumbling into an eternal
abyss.

(Yet she seemed above it all...)

He shook his head. It ached with vague, persistent dullness.
A streetlamp cut luminescent shapes across the bay window. It
was quite dark outside.

A good many years had passed since Marvin allowed such
dark reflections to disturb his serenity. To do so more often, he
would have to give up living, if for no other reason than to stop
the members of the ruling classes from adding their own mind
and body to those multitudes already held in the throes of
protracted anguish, death and dissolution. The ruling classes!
The ever-growing barnacles on humanity's posterior whose lives
seemed motivated by an inherent need for taking—never, never
by an unconditional act of sharing.

(Had my sharing been unconditional?)

Taking to gain power, he mused. If power corrupts, then so
does the imposition of one's will on another. Not just in terms of
power to control their lives, but much, much more so by
suppressing their spirit.

(How could I tell her what to do?)

It was from these reflections that Marvin escaped into the
worlds of magic. Within his inner realm, all beings were destined
to be givers. Not just the wondrous sages clad in their
shimmering robes, but all that vibrated with life, with the
quintessential joy of living, shared that very joy with every
wandering traveler. Every? For that he could not vouch; he was
still too new to those inner explorations. But whenever he
ventured into the realms of freedom, he came face to face with
beauty; with a generous outpouring of abundant nature;
bestowing yet requited; serene, undemanding.

Until today.

This plane of pale gray, not quite snowy whiteness seemed
to deny him access to the enchanted dreamland. The reality so
needed by his tired senses was not to be attained by nor given to
the guilty. Not guilty of commitment of error or omission, of a

crime or misdeed, or any such partaking. No. The very first time he stood at the gates, he had learned that the world within was open only to those who bore no ill will in their hearts for others. The exacting entry to the inner kingdom was so simple, so easy as to be missed by most wandering, straying, lost, vagabond people. Small children experienced no problem crossing the elusive barriers. Yet their all-knowing parents, forever teaching, tedious with instruction, forever holding some concord with dissatisfaction... were barred from the gates by their own undoing.

And now, it was his lot. Lost, hapless in this apostate desert. His mind could function, reason; but his heart denied commitment. Marvin half sat, half reclined in his favourite armchair, desolate and lonely, the unrequited feelings not fully experienced, nor defined fully—at odds with his own heart's disconsolate condition. The unrealized absence of that inner peace denied him access to his worlds of travel.

(Surely, surely I tried to see her.)

The winter of his anguish, of desolate contention.

Later that evening, after dinner, Marvin dallied at the table. He toyed, as though preoccupied, with his seasonally incongruous ice cream, lingered over his coffee, until finally, unnerved and strangely bashful, he was alone. Mrs. Prentis had already cleared the table. Marvin heard the tinkle of glass and porcelain in the kitchen—stuffing the dishwasher? At length, Mrs. Prentis returned to fetch his cup and saucer. It was then that Marvin again cleared his throat, perhaps for the fifth time. Mrs. Prentis regarded him sternly, without her usual, benevolent smile.

"Well, she isn't coming," Mrs. Prentis ventured, uninvited.

Marvin had waited to hear from Mrs. Prentis for some days now. He had rehearsed what he would say, how he would inquire. He was taken aback. He had expected to employ some well-chosen words before an opportunity presented itself to breach the subject directly. Now, here it was, in the open.

"N-n-not coming?" he stammered, waving his head from side to side.

"That's right, young man. Not coming. And what can you tell me about it?"

Mrs. Prentis looked as though she were about to tie him down firmly to a straight-backed steel chair nailed to the floor in a soundproof room and extract from him, under a penalty far worse than death, a full confession. Instinctively he sat up, drawing himself farther away by pressing his spine into the back of his present, more accommodating and forgiving armchair. The fact that in spite of his forty-seven years Mrs. Prentis continued to refer to him as a "young man" had an additionally unnerving effect.

"How could I possibly know anything about it? Why, I waited... I waited to ask you..."

Mrs. Prentis decided not to make it any easier for him. She continued to stare at Marvin, looking no less overbearing in her kitchen apron. While Marvin remained seated, she took full advantage of her standing position in order to, so to speak, tower over him from her five-foot four-inch frame.

"Well?"

Ignoring Marvin's inane excuses, Mrs. Prentis continued to glare down at him. She seemed to transfix him with her unblinking eyes. "Well?" she repeated, her tone a notch higher.

"Mrs. Prentis, I'm as anxious to find out what happened to Jocelyn as you are. You must believe me. You really must!" By now his voice was pleading.

"What happened to Jocelyn? What happened...? Young man, I know very well what happened to Jocelyn. I am her aunt. I expect to know what happened to my niece." Mrs. Prentis took a deep breath. "What I want to know from you, young man, is why?!"

"Why? Why, Mrs. Prentis? W-w-why... what?" Belatedly, Marvin wished he had left with the other tenants immediately after dinner.

"Why did she go to Florida. On a moment's notice." Then Mrs. Prentis reverted to her question-and-answer game: "Well?" she demanded, "WELL?"

"Jocelyn went to Florida? When? Why didn't she tell me?"

The last was not a question directed at Mrs. Prentis. "She didn't even tell me..." Marvin repeated slowly, his eyes losing any apprehension he may have felt toward Mrs. Prentis. In its place there was sadness. Great, resigned sadness.

This sudden change was not lost on Mrs. Prentis. She picked up his cup and saucer and said: "Sit here until I get back."

No "please", no "if you would". This was an order. Then the churning sound of the dishwasher reached him through the kitchen door. Another minute later, her apron gone, a touch of delicate perfume to eliminate the culinary smells lingering about her, Mrs. Prentis was back. She didn't come toward Marvin but made for the liquor cabinet. Her tenants were of such discipline that the cabinet was never under lock and key. She took out two oversized snifters. A bottle of Rémi Martin provided generous quantities of the rich, golden nectar in each glass. She swirled them slowly in her hands as she came toward Marvin. She put one glass in front of him, then took a sip from her own. Marvin didn't move. He never drank anything stronger than wine. Mrs. Prentis picked up his glass and placed it in his hand.

"Now lift it up, put it to your mouth, tilt your head backwards and drink it."

There was neither humor nor any form of sarcasm in her steady voice. She gave her instructions as she would have told him how she wanted him to water her plants.

Marvin did precisely as he was told. He raised his glass, tilted his head backwards and emptied the glass into his throat. There followed a long spasm of coughing. When it was over, Mrs. Prentis asked coyly: "Would you like some more cognac, Mr. Clark?"

Marvin only stared at her with wide-open, incredulous eyes. A tiny recess of his tired mind wondered whatever had happened to the 'young man'. Slowly he shook, or rather nodded, his head from side to side.

"Very well." Mrs. Prentis was ready to resume the painful extraction of a full confession. "Now that you are relaxed, tell me all about it?"

Marvin remained silent for quite a while. This time, Mrs. Prentis did not prod him. She sat straight yet relaxed, warming her glass, taking occasional tiny sips of her favourite cognac. At long last, Marvin seemed ready.

"Something happened which I cannot understand. You see, Mrs. Prentis, your niece is most... she's just the most... To tell you the truth, Mrs. Prentis, I believe that I'm in love with her."

This last he blurted out as a young boy would admit to having been naughty and having been caught at it. Yet he was glad that it was out, at last. No more of this masquerade, this tortuous game of holding back his secret, disconsolate emotions. Mrs. Prentis took another tiny sip. There was plenty of cognac left in her glass. She had given them both quite generous portions. She offered no comment. Apart from anything else, she knew full well that her own hands were not clean in all this delusory trapping.

Marvin began to fidget, as though trying to decide how to approach the subject. He also didn't know how much he should tell Mrs. Prentis, in order not to aggravate the already rather difficult situation. As before, Mrs. Prentis was of no help. On the other hand, the overly large gulp of the burning cognac he had swallowed at the beginning of this discomfiting discussion began to find its way into his cardiovascular system. The first messengers of the powerful stimulant began to arrive at their destination. They reached his brain cells. Marvin, cautiously if unwittingly, began relaxing. He also felt a sudden emergence of badly needed Dutch courage.

"It all really started, well, almost like a game..." He spoke as though thinking out loud. "She was a mere child... a girl, a younger sister. I truly have no idea what happened later... I never had any idea... She is so very open, so sincere, so very, very trusting." He looked at his own hands. "And when she touches her sculpture, she changes even more into, well, into a sort of angel..."

Marvin's voice trailed off, his inner eye seeing Jocelyn sitting at her large, heavy table, while he sat on the sofa, pretending not to watch her. Suddenly he turned to face Mrs.

Prentis. His face, normally a pleasant mask of well-concealed indifference, now showed unbidden anguish, a deep concern for Jocelyn. Mrs. Prentis took pity.

"She's all right. Least, I hope so. Her friend called from down south and invited Jocelyn to join her. She'll be back on Sunday. The end of this week."

The tension left Marvin's face, though only for a minute. Suddenly it came to him that he had opened his heart to an almost total stranger. During the seventeen years of living under the same roof, Mrs. Prentis and he had never spoken of any such matters, not even of matters a lot less intimate than those raised tonight. His mind whirled in belated realization that he lived in a world where everyone was a stranger. He knew of no one with whom he could discuss his problems. He never seemed to have had any. And now... now, in the midst of winter, no heart would beat faster at his pain, his misfortune. There had been one warm, caring heart... but now? Now he had lost her.

"Would you like a little more cognac?" Mrs. Prentis's voice was no more than a whisper. Marvin didn't move, as though he had not heard her.

Once more his time appeared to slow down. Although his eyes remained open, his inner eye, perhaps his imagination, created a picture of great, pale gray, almost white desolation. He did not try to fight it. He sat still, only half aware of where he was or what he was doing. He stared into this featureless landscape, unfeeling, unthinking, hardly aware of his own existence. In a state of strange, altered time and consciousness, he saw white crests, as if some turbulent water were boiling in the middle of this bleak and lonesome desert. Then, forming as suddenly as a tropical storm, the pearly whiteness took on a third dimension. It grew till it engulfed him from all sides. It fumed as it fizzled, a mad turbulence of insane, cosmic proportions. And then came the noise. At first approaching slowly, then accelerating until the decibels multiplied into a sinister, maddening, apocalyptic roar. A continuous thunder, a vicious onslaught on his trembling nerves, on his already weakened powers of resistance. And then, quite suddenly, without the slightest notice, the roar stopped. And there was total, blissful, undemanding blackness.

"Mr. Clark, young man, look at me, Marvin..." Mrs. Prentis was tugging at his sleeve, then actually shook him by the shoulders.

Marvin opened his eyes. At some propitious moment they must have closed of their own volition. He thought he must have fainted, although he remained sitting in the high-backed chair. The latter had evidently saved him from falling or collapsing. If he had lost his awareness, it could have been only for a briefest instant. For a fleeting moment, Marvin remembered that he had hardly slept for well over a week. An hour or two nightly, a short nap when in his room, before supper, was hardly enough to sustain the functions of his exhausted body.

As his eyes focused, Marvin saw Mrs. Prentis, her face close to his own. She looked concerned, a question in her raised eyebrows. He tried a weak smile of friendly reassurance. It suddenly dawned on him that this woman, the woman whom he, in spite of the years of acquaintance, just minutes ago had considered a relatively indifferent stranger, was truly concerned about his welfare.

"Ah, there you are, young man. There now. You just take it easy. There's no need to rush things."

With fingers as light as a duckling's feather, Mrs. Prentis stroked his face. Marvin once more closed his eyes, trying to recall a touch of such concern. He reached back to his early youth, yet still drew an empty, unrewarding blank. Of the orphanage there were few memories to draw from. And before...? Before remained a dark question mark. His eyes closed, he retained the smile. Then, filling his lungs deeply, he sat up somewhat straighter.

"I am sorry, Mrs. Prentis. I don't think this sort of thing had ever... never before happened." His grammar was forgiven, the reassurance accepted.

"I should really hope not! Why, you young people overdo things nowadays. Whatever have you been doing, young man, to reach such great exhaustion?" There was scolding concern in her voice, rather than curiosity.

"I guess I forgot to sleep lately..." Marvin confessed, lamely.

"Off you go then. And get plenty of it." Then Mrs. Prentis gave him a long look, that nondescript, or perhaps just unspecified concern returning to her eyes. "And I'll have you know, young man, the next time you have a problem, and I don't care of what nature, you come to me, you hear? Come to me at once!" With that she shook her finger at him.

Marvin had no choice but to smile. He got up slowly and did what he thought he would never have the courage to do. He gently yet firmly took hold of the shaking finger, drew the whole hand toward him, bent down and kissed Mrs. Prentis's hand.

"Thank you, Mrs. Prentis." His voice was shaking slightly. "Thank you, Aunt Jenny," he added in a quiet, hardly audible whisper.

"Off you go now, young man." Mrs. Prentis bit her lower lip to stop it from trembling. "We shall talk tomorrow."

The latter, even more than the former, was firm if polite; nevertheless it was an order. And then Mrs. Prentis turned toward the kitchen to hide a deep blush of pleasure rising in her cheeks. She really liked this silly, silly boy. This man of boyish shyness, of immature emotions. Seventeen years... she shook her head sadly. Seventeen years had been wasted. Then she squared her slender shoulders as though determined not to make a similar mistake again.

"Not in seventeen years, not in a million years. I've learned my lesson," she muttered, in a self-addressed bland anger.

"Did you say something, Mrs. Prentis?" Marvin asked, his hand already pressing the old-fashioned door handle.

Mrs. Prentis spun as if bitten by a hive of bees in her nether quarters.

"I thought I'd sent you to bed!" she practically shouted.

"Yes, Madam. Yes, at once, Mrs. Prentis!"

Marvin closed the door firmly but quietly. For the first time in years he knew he had an ally. For the first time in weeks he could and did afford a great, big, open, hopeful, unreserved smile.

* * *

10

The Chambers

After twenty-three years, Marvin was well used to working in large open areas. The vast wilderness, officially referred to as General Office, had long been set aside as the natural habitat for the lethargic army of anthropoid inmates, who, over many generations, had invaded and were now well established in every nook and cranny of this paper-churning wasteland.

The bureaucratic jungle.

The spacious vistas of Marvin's particular jungle were strategically punctuated by a series of well-placed tree-columns, which supported, or so it seemed, a convoluted lattice of modular ceiling. Stretching in all directions as far as his eye could see, the off-white overhead foliage was enhanced by fluorescent fixtures, shimmering at regular intervals, reminiscent of sunlight filtering down, finding its way to the lower strata of the jungle. Some cold, indifferent light actually reached the nondescript, dirt-concealing soil, which in turn reminded Marvin of a green-brown, slightly speckled carpet. Between these intermittent, rather bland light sources hung tiny bright-red berries, inverted, protected by silvery, delicately fluted cups, ready to rain at the slightest provocation of danger. Their cousins, also red but more crimson, spent most of their lives in serene silence. But when threatened by smoke, the tiny kernels came to life with a vengeance, emitting screams of horror in wild, ear-shattering falsettos. Still farther apart, attached to the underside of the foliage, lived the inverted heads of *boleti* mushrooms, their large cups punctured with many tiny pores devised to let through the noise of departmental speakers. The rest of the flora which graced the upper reaches included lesser fungi of intercom outlets, some cute little posies masking security detectors, and the great, white-petaled blooms of air-conditioning rosebuds, all living and breathing life into the perpetual jungle.

At an intermediate level, the underbrush was masquerading as the standard, often curved, upholstered, mid-height and free-standing, colourful partitions. This well-placed shrubbery afforded the inhabitants a degree of privacy when in a slumbering, sometimes referred to as working, position, while allowing a relatively distant view when the indigent life forms rose on their hind legs. And they did rise to feed, mostly tea or coffee, to visit running waters when encouraged by nature, or sometimes to assist a client, a poor misguided taxpayer in need of some so-called expert assistance.

After many years of peaceful habitation, Marvin had grown accustomed to this restful jungle. It offered him comfort, a needed sense of belonging, perhaps—security.

Little more than three months ago he had suffered his first promotion. The penalty for the acceptance of his new position had been instant incarceration within a minuscule prison. Marvin had to give up the extensive vistas. The steel walls of his cell rose all the way to the ceiling; a steel door kept him under lock and key. The doors were intended to admit wardens on the days of special import. And his secretary—more often. Marvin had been sentenced to perform his duties within this cell. Having risen halfway to the mighty Olympus, he was expected to give a tacit and reserved example to the lesser mortals, slumbering all around in their comfortable burrows. Example of what, he knew not.

Marvin had enjoyed his long stint in the outer jungle. For many years he had been left in peace, free to dream, to travel, to stretch out his youthful esoteric wings above and beyond the underbrush partitions. Gradually his imagination had gained more power. When ultimately Marvin had learned to perform his duties without having to withdraw his attention from the inner worlds, he saw no reason to strive for promotion.

But fate ruled otherwise.

Marvin's original promotion had destroyed his many needed points of reference so diligently acquired over years of practice. The trees and the bushes, the latticework above him with the lighting matrix, all had played their part in his intrepid travels. Marvin had been cut off from his beloved jungle.

But he did not give up.

The day after he was installed in his cell, Marvin set out to master his new surroundings. In three short months, before the wardens saw fit to commute his sentence, Marvin learned a great deal. Most of all he learned that the process of acclimatization is taxing and disturbing, and that such moves, such promotions, should be avoided if at all possible.

Once more fickle fate chose to interfere.

This time, Marvin was determined. He swore on all that's holy, on all he had ever held sacred, that wherever the gods chose to place him in their indiscriminate bidding, there he would stay forever, perhaps even longer... or at least until his retirement.

Alas, the stars turned against him...

On his return from the Christmas recess, following the announcement in the local press, Marvin knew he would suffer the onslaught of the curious. To his abject horror, he was told to linger one more week in his present office before being transferred to the yet undefined, secret place of glory. A place of glory? Onward and upward he would climb the exalted steps of the Holy Mountain and abide in the exalted Chambers!

"If I must..." he sighed, resignedly.

In spite of Marvin's many, many years at the Municipal Department of Parks and Recreation, he had never learned the true significance of those 'exalted' areas. He had heard, on occasion, about the 'Chambers' where the gods resided—the gods who had chosen, out of love for mankind, to assume the bodies of mortal human beings. But the Great Ones fooled no one. Their presence was always blatantly announced; red carpets came a-rolling, the media closed in to catch a word, a smile, or at least to share the same space as the High and Mighty.

Marvin had kept his distance.

By far the most equal among equals, St-Onge's illustrious mayor reigned as the most articulate spokesman. Right behind him, basking in his reflected glory, stood his staunchest supporter: the mayor's lady-deputy. These high among the highest seldom left their Olympian Chambers. And never, never had they directed their steps to Marvin's teeming jungle.

Little wonder.

Even the subservient gods of little or no repute seldom soiled their feet at the lower levels. Why should they? Were not the inner Chambers their rightful place of worship? Did they not, on special even if rare occasions, allow men to enter the outer, plebeian Chambers?

Marvin had always managed to avoid them. Yet now, such vain thoughts, such lonesome reminiscences lingered on Marvin's mind. He felt lost. He realized that, although his lifelong ambition had been to find seclusion, to stay invisible in his private burrow, now that he came close to a potentially greater isolation, he wasn't quite sure whether he really yearned for it. Yet the die had been cast; Lady Fate had taken over. Not only had he risen to Olympian status, albeit lesser than some though greater than most, but he could now claim access to the highest levels. He would answer directly to the Pontius Mayor, the exquisite being on the throne of power.

"Will you take with you, Sir, all the present files?" Miss Gascon faced Marvin, a worried look on her face. "I am sorry, Sir, really, I did knock for quite a while." She was visibly flustered.

"Files, ah, what files?" Marvin's mind was still far away.

"The last three months' files, Mr. Clark. There is quite a stack, Sir; in fact, we've got over three hundred jackets."

Marvin had no idea that he had been so prolific in the execution of his duties. Contrary to popular belief brought about by the directives he had given Miss Gascon regarding his appointments, Marvin had actually been working—quickly and efficiently. He had fought his way through hundreds if not thousands of his predecessor's letters, entangled reports, badly written minutes, disjointed pieces of information lost in the so-called general files, without allocation, without rhyme or reason. In his quiet, methodical way, Marvin had sifted through those stacks of unrelated data, arranged them in some form of coherence, allotted them new files. In a mere three months, he had managed, to his own surprise, to rectify the obvious shortcomings of Mr. Jean-Paul St-Pierre who, during twenty-odd years of municipal service, had failed to develop any methodology in his staunchly bureaucratic madness.

Marvin had not minded inheriting this vaguely disagreeable condition. In fact, arranging things in order, endeavoring to wrench order if not harmony out of chaos, was practically his unspoken avocation. He performed such tasks without passion, with complete detachment, virtually without thinking. Marvin felt a little unnerved at having achieved the desirable condition within the scope of his brief reign. He would now have to forsake it. He would give it up to someone who would destroy it. They all destroyed order: with a little help from indomitable time and a lot more from mental abnegation—a condition inherent in the type of mind capable of doing the job he had just vacated. Marvin had no bloated illusions about his own acumen.

His musings were in no way derisive toward his past or future colleagues. He simply noted the observable data, facts to be neatly filed in his memory. Marvin was a keen observer of the universe he lived in.

"Please make copies of the general cross-referencing files and the catalogues only, Miss Gascon. I doubt that we shall have need of any other files."

Marvin smiled. Miss Gascon needed reassurance. She had been rather nervous, these last few days. Evidently she, too, was affected by Mr. Clark's and her own forthcoming transfer to the elusive Chambers.

"Oh, but Mr. Clark! But, Sir... but, all this work...?"

She looked shocked if not flabbergasted. For a moment Marvin had forgotten that while he did the actual checking,

commenting and decision-making regarding the mess which
they both had inherited, Olive, the long-suffering Olive Gascon,
did the actual arranging, re-filing, re-allotment of the masses of
documents.

"I am sorry, Miss Gascon. But don't worry. In the
Chambers we shall have rather nice filing cabinets to fill with
masses of documents to our content."

Marvin said this as a joke. He had no idea what, if any,
filing cabinets had been allotted to the lesser gods. He wanted to
relax her. Instead, at the mention of the Chambers, Miss Gascon
stiffened while her cheeks took on a wan tinge. She left his
office with no further comment. Marvin had no idea that a single
word could precipitate such a powerful effect.

In fact, Marvin Clark also felt lost.

He dared not stick his nose outside his office for fear of
being besieged by his ex-colleagues, ex-assistants, ex-cohabitants
of the perennial jungle. Strange. For years, when Marvin had sat
amongst them, his one ambition had been to remain invisible.
Now that he could escape from their heretofore undesirable
presence, he... almost missed them. The marching thousands.

Marching workers—unite!

Except that his ex-colleagues had no need to march; the
union took care of all that. As for 'united', that they were. The
only problem was that, in all the years Marvin had spent in their
midst, he had never, never discovered for what purpose. 'Must
stick together!' claimed the old adage. Together?

No one had ever told him, nor had he ever asked: 'Why?'

The next day was Thursday. Three more days till Jocelyn's
return. Would she want to see him, he pondered? Was her rapid
departure indeed, in some intangible or, perhaps, tangible way,
precipitated by him? In some way? What way? Mrs. Prentis had
implied as much. I'll have to speak to her, he decided. Auntie
Jenny. Marvin smiled at the thought. He also felt a slight shiver.

Since Monday, Marvin had had nothing to do in his present
office. Miss Gascon had been taking care of all that had to be

taken care of. She was truly amazing. They say that, given time, every one will rise to their personal level of optimum inefficiency. Given time! Well, Miss Gascon had not been given this derisive opportunity. Three months ago she had been a young member of the general typing pool. The women sat around, polished their nails, applied additional lipstick to enlarge their already well-smeared lips, combed their hair—in fact, kept busy with their little pocket mirrors which seemed to oscillate in a regular pendulous fashion between their handbags and the palms of their heavily manicured, crimson-tipped hands. When tired of these undoubtedly fascinating pursuits, the women would make a phone call or two; during office hours they were allowed a maximum of four private calls per day. When all else failed or when compelled by an unbearable fit of boredom, the typists might actually type a letter, a report, or even tackle the badly written, hardly legible hand-scribbled minutes of some inconsequential meeting. Why inconsequential? Because any meeting which might possibly have been of any value in advancing the cause of the local denizens in the course of eventually enhancing the quality of their parks, or the scope of their recreation, would invariably be attended by a departmental head who would bring his or her private secretary with him or her. The typing pool provided a service that only taxes could buy.

Only three months ago, Olive Gascon, a petite woman of no less than twenty, no more than twenty-something, had joined this pool. She did not know her way around the municipal departments, even less so the 'ins and outs' of the unwritten, parochial laws which guided the behaviour of the employees. The first and foremost rule, one never to be broken, was, and forever will remain, to avoid any and all work, at all possible pretexts. The second on the list of fundamental axioms was the abiding rule forbidding volunteering. When Marvin's initial promotion, the one last autumn, had been announced, the official statement on the departmental notice board said that Mr. Marvin Clark would be interviewing the prospective secretaries on a particular day. It turned out that Olive Gascon was the only one waiting outside Marvin's office. Marvin, slightly embarrassed, asked her if she really wanted the job.

Marvin remembered that day. Miss Gascon, looking tiny in her simple gray frock, stood at the door of his office. He asked her to sit down. She closed the door quietly, then sat very straight in front of his standard-issue desk. She reminded him of the way the nuns had sat in the visiting room: on the edge of the chair, head held up yet the eyelashes pointed to the floor. He had wondered what colour her eyes were.

Green and lively, once she looked up.

She was quite pretty but with no pretensions to beauty. Perhaps a little too much lipstick, but that was the norm these days. Fairly high cheekbones framing her small, slightly upturned nose gave her a pert appearance. She looked nice. Marvin had been pleased by her appearance, without any desire to linger on her face.

"Working for me might not be as exciting as you might imagine, Miss Gascon," Marvin had prodded, looking directly into her eyes.

She had assured him that she would do her best to serve him in every way she possibly could. Evidently, Miss Gascon had not had enough time to learn from the indigent species of the typing pool that Mr. Marvin Clark enjoyed a departmental reputation of being the pinnacle of dullness, embodiment of boredom. Mr. Clark reputedly never joked; never indulged in juicy or even mundane kind of gossip; he did not partake of Friday night, or even Friday noon, beer binges; in fact, he was a total loss.

Last Tuesday, the day after Marvin Clark's most recent promotion had been made public, Olive Gascon strolled through the typing pool on her way to somewhere. The moment she put her foot inside the old, familiar area, she was enveloped in a sudden, hushed, alienating silence. The women who had initially quite liked her, who later pulled her leg about her taciturn superior, now seemed to have lost their wagging, seldom-restrained tongues in their flapping, busy, red-rimmed muzzles. Miss Gascon did not mind the sudden stop to the tiresome, invective sarcasm; but when she tried to exchange a few words with her closest girlfriend, she realized to her chagrin that now there was a barrier. A departmental head, a group or section leader, all such people stood firm on the edges of the common jungle. They were the higher apes but still remained kindred—of the same, known species. But she, Olive Gascon, had lost her status, her herd affiliation. She had lost her friends in transit to the strange world of the upper Chambers.

Now both she and Marvin dangled in abeyance.

The sad thing was that neither Miss Gascon nor her already illustrious Director-in-waiting had any idea what those wondrous Chambers were. Her lack of experience in bureaucratic protocol, her ignorance of know-how, of procedural decorum, prompted her to utter the almost unspeakable.

"Mr. Clark," she declared with innocence and candor, "should we not now visit our future quarters? Surely we must make sure that we are ready for them?" She did not specify whether 'them' was a 'who' or a 'what'.

Marvin regarded his secretary with surprise. Now, why had he not thought of it himself? After all, it was one thing to wait for his Chambers to be made fit for his arrival, quite another to move in without even a short preview.

"You must come there with me, Miss Gascon. Are you free this minute?" He smiled at his own imperious decision.

"I'm always at your service, *Monsieur le Directeur!*" The word 'service' sounded more like 'orders'. The title 'Director' demanded instant obedience.

Marvin had to restrain himself from looking over his shoulders to find out whom was she addressing.

There was an underground passage from the Department of Parks and Recreation to the Town Hall proper. Since Marvin had joined the municipal service, he had used the underground passage twice. On each occasion he had delivered a file from his departmental head to the secretary of the deputy mayor. Another time, another world, he mused. The recollection made him smile.

The indoor passage relieved Marvin and Miss Gascon of the necessity of dressing for the bitter outdoors of the Canadian winter. This in itself was a major blessing. They left at once. Marvin led the way; Miss Gascon followed three paces behind him. There seemed an added deference granted Marvin since she had read his name in the paper. In all her twenty years, this was the very first time that she actually knew someone, personally, whose name had been printed on the first page. The first page! All this was just incredible.

At the other end of the passage dallied a uniformed man. He was impressively large in girth if not in stature. His bleak eyes seemed moist, or perhaps just bored to tears. On their arrival, the man moved his bulk to face Marvin, then, in a grotesquely slow motion, 'sprang' to attention. As Marvin came closer, the guard straightened out to his full height. Marvin was quite unaccustomed to such a show of respect. When the man actually saluted, Marvin was lost. His hands dangled uncertainly at his sides. He tried to hide his discomfort behind a nondescript smile. Was that why the Big Fish invariably sported such inane smiles?

"Good morning, Mr. Clark, Sir. It's very nice to see you!" The guard remained stretched out in his full regalia. He addressed Marvin in English.

"Good morning, ah..."

"John Brampton, always at your service!" The man remained quite rigid.

How come everyone's at my service? Marvin wondered.

"Good morning, John. I am glad to meet you. But you know, if we are to be friends, you must learn to relax."

Marvin had no idea why he said what he had just said. He was never a very friendly person. Not because of any animosity toward his fellow men, but strictly as a result of his nearly pathological shyness. Now, for reasons unknown to him, the years of studied invisibility seemed destined to fall in ruins. The moment Marvin uttered the congenial greeting, he felt quite embarrassed. If it weren't for Miss Gascon standing right behind him, Marvin would have made a hasty retreat. He had no way of knowing that the repercussions of the simple statement he had just uttered were to follow him, in a strangely gratifying fashion, for years to come.

"Thank you, Sir," the man smiled. "Is there any way I can help you?"

Marvin suddenly realized that he had no idea where he was going. He knew that his new office, his exalted Chambers, were in the main building, but that's all he knew. For once, his orderly mind had failed him. He forgot to inquire where the high and mighty had decided to place him. The Town Hall was quite a large building. A labyrinth of corridors devised to mislead the guilty. The innocent? He was guilty of profound ignorance. If it weren't for the stark embarrassment of the situation, Marvin would have found it funny. He decided he had little to lose.

"Tell me, John, my good man. Have you any idea where I am now going?" he tried to sound jovial.

"I'll be honored to escort you to your Chambers, Sir."

John Brampton beamed as though a great privilege had just befallen him. Once more his chest fought a losing battle with his waist, though the latter appeared to contract, if marginally, or perhaps shrivel. To Marvin's disbelief, the man actually spun on his heel to face the guard sitting in a kiosk behind him.

"Look after this end, *François!*" he admonished. Then, as if afraid that Marvin might relieve him of the bestowed honor, John Brampton marched briskly forward. Marvin and Miss Gascon closed ranks and followed.

Marvin could not believe his good luck. This highly undesirable situation had resolved itself in a most rewarding fashion. For a brief moment he wondered how on earth John knew who he was. Then it all rushed back to him in a flood of recent, not at all pleasant memories. He had been sitting in Jocelyn's studio, awaiting her arrival. A tightly rolled copy of the *St-Onge Herald* was under his arm. The newspaper he intended to accidentally drop on the sofa, after she came in. His photograph was prominently displayed on the front page. Marvin had never been particularly photogenic. But it did not matter. Jocelyn never came in.

"Will there be anything else, Sir?" John sounded like a well-trained butler.

"No, thank you, John. That will be all." Marvin smiled at the man. "For now!" he added, almost as an afterthought.

"Yes, Sir! Thank you, Sir." The man again saluted.

So such is Olympus, Marvin thought with a wry smile. John Brampton had left them facing enormous oak-paneled doors, about ten feet high. A discreet brass plate on the central panel announced in elegant, deeply engraved letters:

MARVIN CLARK
Directeur

Marvin Clark, Director.

Miss Gascon stepped in front of him and pressed down on the highly polished, ornate doorknob. The right-hand door gave way. There was no need for keys in the upper Chambers. No mere mortal would ever dare to enter uninvited.

Miss Gascon stepped aside to let Marvin come in. He took the first step into his new surroundings. The thick carpet gave way under his feet. Then it seemed to rise and press gently against the soles of his shoes. This was the anteroom of his deeper, inner, private Chambers. Marvin filled his lungs with the clear, no longer stagnant air of the lower classes. He stood still, listening for any noise, for anything that might disturb him in his future travels. He heard nothing. He decided he might learn to like this. He turned toward Miss Gascon.

"Thank you," he said belatedly. Then Marvin raised his chin and added in as formal, as officious a voice as he could make it: "Welcome, Miss Gascon. Welcome to my Chambers."

And then, for no reason that he could possibly imagine, Director Clark tilted his head back, closed his eyes, and let out — quite contrary to his timid nature — a great, rolling, protracted bellow of uncontrolled laughter.

* * *

11

Moving

'To every thing there is a season, and a time to every purpose under the heaven. ...A time to kill, and a time to heal...' "...and a time to heal," Jocelyn repeated out loud, then she murmured under her breath: "...and a time to move." Fragments of old memories flitted through her mind as she looked at the closely written pages.

It was her last day in the lands of perennial warmth.

Jocelyn had already decided that the lap of luxury had its merits. The six days she had spent with Marion in West Palm Beach went a long way toward healing. A long way, though she knew that deep wounds never really healed. There may come a time when they no longer presented a disturbing hardship, when the pain which had caused them would subside. By an act of will they may be relegated to secondary sensitivity, and almost, almost, forgotten. But the scars remained.

Jocelyn did her best not to dwell on the subject; but now that it was time to leave, the pain returned with renewed vigour. The scars, she whispered, the scars...

Sometimes they seemed minor; they could hardly be noticed. Sometimes they remained hidden, incised so deeply that only very particular circumstances brought them to the surface, to the forefront of better-forgotten, unwanted memories. But on such occasions even the deepest, the most denied vestiges of those cruel, sad mementos itched painfully with a fresh life of their own. The old injuries churned and blistered, became inflamed, painful, renewed sores.

At such times it was best to move. Not to escape the cause of the initial abrasion, but to allow time, needed time, for healing.

On her last day in Florida, Jocelyn picked up, quite unwittingly, an old, obviously well-read copy of the King James Holy Bible. It perched on the bookshelves, wedged between the Koran and Bhagavad-Gita. She glanced at all three. Her eyebrows rose to unprecedented heights when she discovered that the Koran was printed in Arabic, the Bhagavad-Gita in what looked like Sanskrit. For quite obvious reasons, she selected the Bible.

Years had passed since Jocelyn's hands had held the holy book. Not that she was averse to the Judeo-Christian teaching. Just the opposite. It was because she had conducted a scholarly, if private, study of the scriptures that she had set them aside. At the time, Jocelyn had tried to trace their influence over the last two millennia. All too quickly, she had reached the conclusion that the authors of the inspired Word had been born two thousand years too early. People were not ready. Jocelyn had analyzed the efficacy of the Word in terms of the countless millions who had been, and continued to be, exploited, brutalized and murdered in the name of the many gods (ostensibly but One) and idols supposedly depicted in the poetic scriptures. She had listened to and reflected on many a teacher, many a pseudo-philanthropic guru who had claimed, with utter dogmatic assurance, that his and only his interpretation of the Word was of the righteous, if not of the divine, uniquely divine, inspiration.

Once there was a time when Jocelyn had needed someone, something, to lean on. Someone more permanent. Someone who would not let her down. She had searched for a strong shoulder, a spiritual haven. She had found a quagmire.

She had found that few cults had not dipped their long, parsimonious hands into blood—up to their elbows. She had shivered at the thought of the countless holier-than-thou religious leaders who did little more than amass riches. Those

self-proclaimed exponents, purveyors of subjects totally
unknown to them, never indulged in the deleterious folly of
practicing what they preached. They were too busy damning
others to hell and eternal fire. Few pompous sermonizers,
preachers, clerics, ministers, parsons, evangelists, chaplains,
curates, pastors, missionaries—the titles seemed
unending—would accept the notion that Whatever had inspired
the many, many scriptures in the distant, veiled, evanescent past
might still be resonant, alive today. Fewer still would consider
that, to find the divine, one had to look within Self—not without,
to others, to their insidious gods of greed and hostile contention.

Jocelyn had searched for someone who taught and
manifested just... kindness, tolerance, friendship with one's
neighbour, and most of all the perception of the divine spark
which seemed so deeply hidden, yet surely always extant, within
all creation.

In a way, she did find them, though they were not teachers.

Though often perilously close to those cesspools of
religious fervour, she had come across many innocent
bystanders who manifested a kind, joyful smile of friendly
contentment. Those unassuming innocents seemed to rejoice in
the riches of their inner resources. They seemed to practice the
essence of the perdurable Wisdom. Jocelyn discovered that those
extraordinarily ordinary people were the true and the only
messengers of the long-lost yet immortal tenets.

They were the source of Jocelyn's quite unintentionally
enigmatic smile.

She had learned that the reality, the essence, the truth of all
the ages is not a single tenet of some long-past Master. She had
discovered that truth couldn't be held, constrained in one's
unwieldy fingers. Her own Truth was feather-light, ephemeral; It
could only be touched gently, rediscovered daily, often in the
most unlikely places.

Though mostly in her heart.

Jocelyn did not pick up the Holy Bible with any notion of
renewing an old acquaintance. She opened it at random. The

Ecclesiastes passage about the 'rightful season' stared her in the face, commanding by its presence to take score, to balance the sheet of her recent exploits, if that was the right term for her emotional digressions. Rather than take stock at that very moment, Jocelyn replaced the book on the crowded shelves. Instead, she took a long walk.

As far as the eye could see, the ocean washed the shore with its incessant rolling breath. The ebbing surf, quiet and resigned, retreated from a troupe of terns performing their evening dance. A single white pelican, perched atop a wooden post, presumably a remnant of an old breakwater, supervised the performance. Jocelyn felt a deep sensual pleasure as her bare feet touched the cool, wet sand. It was in direct contrast to the still-hot trade winds blowing steadily since her arrival. The contrast made her think of her mixed emotions, of the adverse forces, gratuitously contemporaneous within her troubled consciousness. Her needs and her desires, at opposite poles of her personality, the dictates of her heart as against her mind, created a fermenting dichotomy not easy to resolve.

As Jocelyn approached, the pecking terns took to the air, only to return the instant she had passed. The pelican ignored her. Long diagonal shadows cut sharply across the deserted sand. The reddening sun cast a final glance at the beach, then withdrew in cool indifference. The wind held its breath. Apart from the whisper of the balmy ocean, there was silence. Jocelyn was alone on the beach. She was very alone.

It was a long walk.

Jocelyn landed in Canada in the middle of a snowstorm.

"Home sweet home," she murmured resignedly to the yawning customs officer. He nodded his understanding.

As the taxi made its way through the blinding white, ubiquitous melee, Jocelyn could only smile at the sturdy fortitude of her relaxed, long-suffering compatriots. In London or in Paris, even Washington or Boston, the city traffic would have long stopped in horror and resentment. Here the taxi driver was full of pep and vigour. He passed the time by asking about her short, southern diversion.

"We should buy Florida. Cheaper in the long run," was the man's caustic judgment. "It's good economics."

In the long run, he was probably right. After all, who needed escape from the wiles of winter more than Canadians? There is nothing like a taxi driver to set one straight on the fundamentals of life. Jocelyn once heard that in the old days the same function had been fulfilled by the barbershop arbiters. But that had been a service for men only. Nowadays, loving wives and even willing girlfriends performed, when needed, the tonsorial functions. Alas, Jocelyn doubted that the womenfolk delivered to their dear menfolk the vital, necessary eco-political briefing. For women it was always the taxi. No other choice existed.

Jocelyn drove directly to Mrs. Prentis's. The red Victorian mansion wore a puffy white hat, which the wind threatened to raise at a gust's notice. The sills supported a two-foot-high wedge of snow. The snow on the front steps swallowed her left shoe. Jocelyn had left Quebec in a hurry. She hadn't prepared for the Canadian homecoming.

She deposited her spurious baggage in Mr. Jones's quarters, dropped off her other shoe, and ran downstairs to be welcomed by her dear ol' Auntie. And welcomed she was dearly. Mrs. Prentis, concerned for her niece's welfare, hugged Jocelyn to within an inch of her life.

"Aunt Jenny," she panted, "I've been away for less than a week!"

"That you have, my dear, but I've been very worried. You left us in a panic. As though something had been on fire?" Mrs. Prentis, still not satisfied with the hugs and squeezes, embraced her yet again.

"Well, there was some fire, well under control now," Jocelyn assured her.

Jocelyn spent the next hour telling Aunt Jenny about her friend Marion, about the luscious condo, about the sun and ocean, the balmy, glorious weather. She told her that the latter was unseasonably gracious, considering the time was early January. Even in Palm Beach, the eighties had been rare at this time of the year.

"I guess I'm just born lucky!" Jocelyn concluded.

At this, for no reason at all, Aunt Jenny's eyes suddenly filled with moisture. The self-inflicted tension, which she suffered during Jocelyn's absence, gave way to a hopeful relief. She managed a weak smile, a fortitude of comfort.

"I missed you, dear girl." Mrs. Prentis studied Jocelyn's face. "Are you sure all's well now?"

"As well as can be, in the stew of my making. But..." Jocelyn hesitated.

"There are always some buts..." concern returned to Mrs. Prentis's eyes.

"Aunt Jenny..." Jocelyn started. She decided that postponing the announcement of her decision would only make things worse later. "Aunt Jenny," she repeated, "I want you to know that you were awfully nice to have me..."

"...but you decided to move now to your own studio," Aunt Jenny concluded.

The two women embraced again. No more words were needed. After a while, they sat down and, as though on command, both smiled. There was a certain relief in those pensive smiles; there was also great love and concern for each other. Mrs. Prentis had known Jocelyn since her mother died. Little Jo had been only eleven, precocious at the time. Mrs. Prentis had taken care of her, helping her widowed father. He, Mr. John Prentis, had been the first of her onetime 'lodgers'. A sort of paying guest, to help out with the finances. John Prentis had stayed at the mansion, with Jo, for some years. Later, when Jocelyn turned seventeen, she decided to live on her own. Mr. Prentis, by then semi-retired, also moved out to live in the country. He had always loved the wild outdoors. He could finally satisfy his long-held-back desire. A week after Jocelyn and John Prentis moved out, Marvin Clark found an ad in a local paper. He celebrated his thirtieth birthday at Mrs. Prentis's table.

"I shall miss you a little..." Mrs. Prentis admitted, mostly to herself.

She knew she would miss Jocelyn; she always had—from the day she last moved out. Jocelyn had always been much more than a niece to her. They were as close as perhaps only a mother and daughter can be. Mrs. Prentis understood Jocelyn's problems before they were even spoken. Now her knowledge that she had been the instigator of a closer contact between Jocelyn and Marvin weighed heavily on her shoulders, more so on her heart. An additional problem she had to face was that, many years ago, she had also adopted Marvin. Not in any legalistic way, of course. She had adopted him as one adopts a forlorn, lost child—even a child of... thirty. Marvin had always aroused within her some undefined, unspoken, yet deep, maternal instincts. The fact that Mrs. Prentis was no more than some ten years older than "her young man," did not seem to make any difference. He seemed lost—she was secure. Or perhaps, years ago, she had needed someone to look after.

After Jocelyn had moved out.

It seemed, it felt, like a sort of tacit, reciprocal arrangement.

The last seventeen years, Mrs. Prentis had woven tales about the two youngsters—young only to her maternal instincts. She wove tales about an innocent, chance meeting. A meeting that would result in a deep and lasting friendship. Maybe, maybe more... Yet, never, never would she dare to even think of creating any artificial conditions in which such a meeting could or would take place. She had too much respect for other people's privacy: physical, mental and certainly emotional. Yet when fate knocked on her very own doorstep, when the tide of events swept the conditions into her patiently waiting, able, caring and, oh yes, truly willing hands...?

God knows that Jocelyn badly needed someone of a steadier, more sedate disposition. Someone who was more inclined to spend more than one or two weeks in one place, at least—in one country. When Jocelyn had first left Mrs. Prentis's protective wings, she had somehow found time and money to

travel, practically the world over. Not in any regular or
organized fashion, certainly not as a young lady ought to travel.
From time to time, she simply disappeared. Hardly a word of
goodbye, hardly a word... It was as if she had needed not only to
spread her own wings beyond the geographic boundaries of her
own mother country, but to reach out beyond the mores and
customs of the familiar world. It was as if she had been searching
for something elusive, unspoken, undefined, yet to her,
apparently, very vital, perhaps even real.

Jocelyn's departures invariably happened with the same
spontaneous rapidity as her last flight to Florida. By now, Mrs.
Prentis was well used to her niece's unruly, unconventional
behaviour. Under normal circumstances she would not have
worried. It was because she had influenced the present events,
because she had dared to dip her hands in the affairs of fate, that
she was troubled. She did not feel guilty. Guilt she reserved for
people who lacked the strength of their own convictions. Mrs.
Prentis knew very well what she had been doing. She would have
again acted in the same fashion if the circumstances had
repeated themselves. No. She was worried because she cared
deeply about her niece. She also cared deeply, even if
unbeknownst to a single human being, about Marvin. Yes,
Marvin. This somewhat peculiar, seemingly lonely, often
enigmatic, pathologically reserved, until a few days ago never
once truly sincere... her dear, unique Marvin.

To her mind, Marvin needed exactly what Jocelyn had to
offer. She was endowed with exactly that which he lacked. With
that which would bring more vibrant, more virile blood into his
veins. Mrs. Prentis believed that Marvin, within his own
parameters, did achieve a degree of personal, secure, if a little
dull, happiness. She also believed that by cutting himself off
from the world, Marvin had put a ceiling on the very happiness
that he strove so hard to protect and preserve. One cannot make
an omelet without breaking eggs, she reasoned.

Even as Jocelyn searched for her elusive heaven in some
distant lands, Marvin seemingly refused to admit the very

existence of the physical universe. Could it be that she was wrong? Had she misjudged him?

"Does not truth lie in the paradigmatic middle?" she'd once asked him. It had been on her birthday after a third sherry. Marvin had said nothing.

Surely, whatever one may think about the world we live in, we can escape from it neither by traveling to some distant place nor by hiding inside one's own inner, introverted, all-exclusive existence. Whatever she had done, Mrs. Prentis did not regret, though she did regret the outcome. At least for the present. Fate will do its own bidding in its own good time. Whatever it might be. All she needed, right now, was patience—a lot of patience. And—humility.

"If ever you have need..."

"I know, Aunt Jenny. I always knew that." Jocelyn smiled a little sadly.

Mrs. Prentis swallowed hard. Lately she had difficulty hiding her emotions.

"There are things which we must all face, do, even conquer alone. The hills, the tall peaks, and..." Jocelyn looked at the snow-shrouded window, "sometimes the long, uneventful planes of desolate, wintery wilderness... It's all part of growing up, I suppose." Her eyes drifted over some distant ocean, some uncharted, wondrous, as yet unreachable shore. "But, you know, Aunt Jenny, somehow I feel glad. Almost as though I've been singled out—sort of, privileged. It seems to me that behind all this, this melodramatic nonsense, there hide some enticing, compelling reasons. Sometimes I feel that I can reach out and grasp their meaning, almost. Then... it's gone again. It's strangely compelling."

For a few minutes the two women were lost, each in her own thoughts. They knew each other so well that they felt comfortable in sharing their silence. Jocelyn always regarded this as the highest degree of friendship.

"When will you go?" Mrs. Prentis asked after a while.

"Right now." She couldn't quite meet her Aunt's eyes. "It's best that way."

"But the snow storm..."

"It's already subsiding. Anyway, I've all I need already in the studio. I didn't want to tell you, but I moved all my things two weeks ago. I can carry what's left in a shoulder bag."

"I know. I've been cleaning your room." Mrs. Prentis smiled forgiveness.

"I never could hide anything from you, Auntie, could I?"

"I most certainly hope not." Mrs. Prentis made her decision. "Now, off you go. It's getting dark outside. My goodness! Now look what you made me do. I forgot all about the supper for my boys!"

"Shall I stay and help you?"

"My dear young lady. The day when I cannot rustle up a dinner for three men in under an hour, I shall call you and you will help me, and I have a lot longer than an hour to do it. Now, be off with you."

Jocelyn gave her Aunt a friendly kiss on the proffered cheek and ran upstairs. She decided against a taxi. She wanted to walk, to feel the snow on her face, to feel the biting wind welcome her in her own home. Her country. It may not be the most inviting of the world's climates, but it did make you tough. Tough as hell. Or was it nails?

With one bag slung over her left shoulder, her Florida traveling pouch swinging on the other, Jocelyn gave a last glance at Mr. Jones's lodgings. She could not imagine spending her life in such confined quarters. If she could not afford a larger, more spacious apartment, she would move south, where one can spend a lot of time outdoors. To each his own, she shrugged. Perhaps, if Mr. Jones had been so happy here, he also would not have agreed to spend the winter in Rio. Then, a wistful smile appeared and stayed on her suntanned features.

"...and I would not have moved in with Aunt Jenny, Marvin would not have rearranged half the furniture in the house, nor changed practically all the light bulbs, I would not have met him, would not have rented, practically bought, my studio, would not have installed the wood stove, would not..."

Indeed, there is a tide in the affairs of men... and women. Jocelyn wondered to what extend we humans really were the proud possessors of that cryptic quality called free will. In her own life, whatever she did, wherever she had run, she seemed to have returned to some predestined place, in which, overtly by a set of totally unrelated circumstances, she had been placed in a position of challenge not of her own planning. This happened when she had lost her mother; later when her father had wanted to move to the country, leaving her to chose between spending the rest of her life in a bush or starting on her own at seventeen. The sculpture course she took had happened quite by accident. She wondered... "But if we did not really exercise our own free will, as we so presumptuously imagined; if we were not truly the skippers of our ships, then—who was?"

She had to go.

Were the turbulences, the eddies, the sudden unexpected cataracts or the invective doldrums of our own making? Do we only face problems that we have ourselves created, or are these same problems merely the sign of our opposition, a free-will opposition, to the tide, the current, the direction, which we have been destined to take—to start with. Could we avoid them by submitting to some invisible, perhaps untenable, impalpable fate? A destiny which, sooner or later, would have its own way with us, anyway? Were our efforts to control our lives no more than juvenile assertions, puerile pranks or tantrums of a good, perhaps willing, but still completely ignorant child facing the vastly superior will, knowledge, experience of its parents?

"And am I ever going to stop arguing with myself and get out of here before I lose my courage and resolution to face the blistering wind and snowstorm outside?"

With a broad grin, Jocelyn hopped and skipped down the staircase, landing, to her own surprise, on her two feet. Mrs. Prentis was standing by the front door.

"I thought you would never leave!" she admonished, in a studiously stern voice.

"I shan't. I shall always be with you, Aunt Jenny!" Jocelyn replied as she ran out through the door.

"Be careful down those steps..."

Mrs. Prentis tried to put some brakes on her niece's sudden boisterous spirits. Then she shrugged her narrow shoulders, smiled, then shrugged again and murmured to herself: "To be sure, whatever must happen, it most certainly, most certainly," she repeated as if needing confirmation of her own thoughts, "it most certainly—will."

* * *

12

The Key

A lot easier said than done.

Sitting in his room, Marvin had spent the whole day arranging his words, his vocal tone, even his facial expression, into a sort of simulated concerned indifference. He was sure that the first impression he was going to make on Jocelyn, when meeting her at dinner this Sunday, would be of utmost importance.

Marvin had repeatedly called the airport to find out what time the flight from West Palm Beach was scheduled to come in. He had been told, on three separate occasions, that they weren't sure, that due to a heavy snowstorm all the flights from New York and Boston had been cancelled. Would he please call later—perhaps the conditions would improve; it was quite impossible to give any firm assurance.

Could he please call later?

The last time Marvin had called, at about four-thirty, he had been told that, yes, a flight from West Palm Beach had in fact landed as scheduled, at 1405 hours, perhaps a few minutes later. Marvin had been stunned, speechless, by this contradictory information, so much so that before he had a chance to strangle the telephone operator by breathing malignant life into the wire, she had hung up.

Marvin's first reaction had been to rush downstairs, to see, to welcome. His hands were slightly trembling, he started to perspire, his palms felt as if he had just washed them and forgotten where he'd left the towel. He looked again at his watch. It was now almost five. If Jocelyn had landed at two in the afternoon, she must have arrived at the mansion not later than three-thirty. Unless the buses were not running, nor taxis operating. Marvin stepped up to his frosted bay window. The powdery snow outside had been swirling in a mad, ludicrous abandon, falling and rising, coming and going, to and from all directions, obliterating or equalizing everything in its path. He could not see if any cars or buses moved on the street below. As a matter of fact, he could not see the street. The dinner would be in just over two hours. He had to sit down and wait. Just try to relax. Read a book, listen to some music, just try to relax. Relax. He sighed deeply.

A lot easier said than done.

The last ten minutes before seven, Marvin had paced the floor checking his watch every ten or twenty seconds. Time had obviously decided to slow down to a snail's slithering crawl; it usually did on such occasions. At last it was five minutes to seven. For the hundredth time Marvin confronted the mirror, readjusted the perfectly tied Windsor knot on his tie, again ran a comb through his perfectly groomed hair, checked his pocket handkerchief. He then took three deep breaths. He held each inhalation as long as he could, then let the air out slowly. When he was through, he presented a fair facsimile of his usual, semi-detached, semi-indifferent, semi... himself.

He arrived at the dinner table on the stroke of seven. He was the last. Last of the gentlemen. Mrs. Prentis was just wheeling in the cart with the tureen and the main course on hot plates.

Jocelyn was nowhere to be seen.

Marvin took another deep breath. It had only just turned seven o'clock. She was either late, not for the first time, or stuck at the airport. Or—Marvin practically gasped in sudden relief—they must have heard about the snowstorm in Florida and she had decided to stay another day. The tension, which Marvin managed to build up to a near frenzy, began to fizzle out like air from a punctured tire. Suddenly his knees felt weak. He crossed the few steps to his chair and sat down heavily. He took great care to breathe regularly, surreptitiously yet deeply, to quiet his pounding heartbeat.

It was only then that Marvin noticed that no place had been set for Jocelyn. How could he have missed that before? "I must go back to my deep relaxation exercises," he admonished himself. "I'm becoming a wreck..."

"I had been under the impression that Miss Jocelyn, your niece, Mrs. Prentis, would be joining us for dinner tonight, what?" Colonel Mackenzie Whittlaw not only asked a perfectly innocent question but, at the same time, took the opportunity to enlighten Mrs. Prentis about her family colligations.

For some strange reason, Marvin found the first totally unnerving and the latter profoundly annoying. What business did the old man have in asking what was, after all, exclusively his—ah, and... of course, Mrs. Prentis's business? If anyone had asked such a question, it should have been he. If he chose not to ask, then... Marvin wasn't quite sure what 'then'. At any rate, it was definitely not the Colonel's business. So why, in all blazes, did Mrs. Prentis not answer?

"Indeed she had intended to, Colonel. It is good of you to ask." Mrs. Prentis smiled her very best, noncommittal smile.

"Well???" Marvin almost screamed, though his mouth remained firmly shut.

It was very probable that Mrs. Prentis had not heard the Colonel's full question. As the plates were passed to her, she carefully filled them with steamy, thickly rich, homemade soup. Mrs. Prentis always said that a soup is an absolute must on cold, wintry days.

"There," she finished filling to the brim the last plate with her extra large, sterling silver ladle, "a rich, homemade soup is a must on cold, wintry days such as this. Don't you think so, gentlemen?" There was an instant chorus of polite, murmured agreement. "There is more where that came from," she assured them, with obvious pleasure.

Marvin ate his soup with calm, measured strokes of his right, hardly-at-all-shaking, hand. He forced himself to think about the obvious benefits such a soup would bring to his constitution. The soup was definitely very good. It was very beneficial to everyone at this table, to anyone who tasted...

Why didn't Mrs. Prentis answer Colonel Whittlaw's question?

It may not have been the old goat's business to inquire, but a question had been asked. Surely, one shouldn't ignore one's dinner companions. Even if they were nosy.

The soup. The rich, filling, warming soup.

"Would anyone care for a second helping?" Mrs. Prentis was her usual caring, motherly self. Three plates were raised almost in unison. The Colonel being the oldest got his seconds first, followed in quick succession by Mr. Graves and Mr. Johnson. Mr. Graves had actually been licking his lips rather as a cat does after a good feeding.

My God! Who the hell cares about the stupid soup!

Everyone seemed to have forgotten about Colonel Whittlaw's question. Obviously Jocelyn must have been detained in West Palm Beach. One would have to be crazy to travel in such weather. Jocelyn was not crazy. She was, my God, she is a very sane, well-balanced, perfectly reasonable girl. Woman. My goodness, was she ever a woman! I could learn to hate soup!

An hour later they were finishing the dessert. By then, Marvin managed to swallow today's offerings with a degree of comportment; with as much grace and detachment as could be expected of him. Periodically he glanced at Mrs. Prentis. She, too, seemed preoccupied, maybe just a touch pensive. She did not give any outward signs of her well-guarded concern about something. No. It was more a total absence of such a sign, the exemplary correctness of her speech and actions, the absence of her usual spontaneity. That was what gave her away. Naturally, to no one but Marvin. Marvin was on the lookout for some such telltales.

It was only when Marvin found himself alone upstairs in his reclusive kingdom that he suddenly remembered that he could have inquired about Jocelyn himself. The dinner had taken over an hour. During all that time, he could do little more than control his hands from shaking, his face from showing signs of stress, his words, which he kept to the strictest, polite minimum, from sounding over- concerned, or perturbed, or giving indication of being unable to sustain his usual self-control, his usual courteous, affable detachment.

"So why should that have stopped me from showing polite concern for a member of the household, who failed to come to dinner? Would I not have expressed just such concern if it had been the Colonel, or Mr. Graves, or Johnson, who were absent?"

The silent questions poured and piled up waiting to be answered, to be dissected, to be somehow analyzed and conquered.

"But how? Whatever is it that makes me the way I am?"

Marvin wondered why he found it so necessary to build these walls that now seemed to stand in his way, which now barred his progress to his own happiness. When he had been busy constructing these formidable barriers, he had rejoiced in his evident, compounded success. He wanted anonymity, he wanted seclusion; he had been convinced that the direction he had devised for himself was the right direction. Surely, if one is truly detached from all the external influences, is one then not safe from any pain, any disenchantment, from the tearing anguish of yet more disappointment? If one expects nothing, one cannot be hurt by being given nothing. So what was his, surely, fundamental error? What was the missing ingredient in the thick, rich, winter soup of his own so-patient, so-consistent making?

It was a painful night. A night of deep confessions.

Not to some lenient and benign priest who, with a kindly smile, would grant him absolution—an absolution that would cure the outward symptoms while retaining all sickness in the deep crevices of his subconscious. It was a full confession, the first in many years, the first since his 'last confession'; a self-directed rhetoric—prodding, questioning, relentless; a re-examination of the basic tenets on which he had built his very life's foundations. Some hours he spent pacing, then sitting and reclining, changing his positions to remain alert. At some point he collapsed, exhausted yet still quite unsated, with half his mind enforcing its will on the other to resume this tractate, this punishing endeavor, until his soul would grant him the desired resolution.

It was not absolution at all that he was seeking. Such implied a feeling of guilt, or intentional wrongdoing. Neither had ever been his professed objective. Marvin had searched to find his river, the current of his destiny. He thought that he had found it, he thought he knew the eddies. Marvin thought... until merciful Morpheus claimed him to his chimerical kingdom.

...thunderous, roaring waters filled Marvin's ears. Had he been dreaming already? Even as he regarded those cataclysmic surges, Marvin recalled this very same image from some previous nightmare. A pounding, rushing water; a pounding and relentless, terrifying...

With the last vestiges of his departing consciousness, Marvin thought he saw, perhaps merely dreamt of, a far distant, a far... far... distant... rainbow.

On Monday, Marvin reported directly to his Chambers. Reported to whom, he wondered? Surely not to the mayor!? Miss Gascon was already waiting, fresh flowers on the receptionist's desk, a broad, almost defiant smile on her fresh young face. Apparently the receptionist still had to be hired. Marvin handed Miss Gascon his coat after she refused to allow him to hang it

himself. Just as well—he had no idea behind which panel the
wall concealed a wardrobe. Then, for the first time, Marvin
regarded his own office.

The fully paneled room measured about twenty feet by
twenty. A heavy-looking, highly polished mahogany desk had
been placed directly opposite the double doors. Directly in front
of this oversized altar there stood four upholstered chairs, two on
either side, reminiscent of some, unknown to him, French-
Provincial style. When closed, the tall double doors differed
from the rest of the paneling only by an architrave which, having
surrounded the hardwood door frame, continued in repetitive
pattern all around the room. Any one panel could well have
concealed some, as yet secret, unexplored compartments. Marvin
wondered who had occupied this opulent room before him.
Since there had been only a week's delay in his move to these
Chambers, the room had obviously not been prepared for his
specific taste; particularly, since no one had taken the trouble to
inquire as to what his preferences were. Marvin smiled at the
thought. Had he been asked, he would have had great difficulty
in expressing his singular, distinct, particular desires.

"This is your private *salle de toilette, Monsieur.*"

Miss Gascon pointed it out to him with obvious pride. She
had never imagined she would ever work for someone who had a
private washroom.

"And if you walk through here, Sir, you are in your
conference room," she continued to beam.

The conference room's size and proportions were more
logical: about twelve feet in width, by eighteen, maybe twenty.
Again a mahogany table. It was framed at the head by a richly
carved, high-backed, stuffed-beyond-the-call-of-duty armchair,
evidently destined for his exalted posterior, and six armchairs of
more modest proportions. Four additional twins of these lesser
armchairs stood at ease at the side board, awaiting call to action.

"And just where is your office, Miss Gascon?"

"Why, you just passed through it, Sir..."

Olive Gascon's face, so refulgent in all this splendor,
showed a slight disappointment. And rightly so. When they had

crossed from Marvin's office to the conference room, they had
passed through another compartment. It was her office. A bank
of filing cabinets screened her desk from the passage. The
cabinets themselves were fully seven feet high, within two or
three feet of the lofty ceiling, with a hardwood frame casing on
three sides, a full-length mirror on the other. Although Marvin
had passed by this very mirror on his way to the boardroom, he
had failed to notice it. This time he did stop. He did not like
what he saw. His face was drawn and sallow, his deep-set eyes
bespoke of some recent night's disorders. His cheekbones
looked even more angular than usual, accentuating his slightly
too prominent nose. The dark hair to which he had always paid
so much attention now appeared dull, the gray at the temples
more pronounced.

Marvin grimaced in considerable distaste. "Just as well she
didn't see me," his mind drifted to last evening and supper.
Even as he turned away from the chastising mirror, he looked
straight into the admiring eyes of Miss Gascon. "The poor girl
must be myopic," he murmured under his breath.

Marvin returned to his office. He had to decide what to do.
He had been given no direct instructions. He also had to keep
Miss Gascon occupied. Marvin was well aware that few things in
life were more debilitating than sitting in one's office, not being
allowed to leave, yet having nothing to gainfully fill one's time.
This very condition had been, at one time, co-responsible for his
inner travels. His mind had been too rich for doing simply
nothing.

Marvin wondered why so few, if any, of the so-called
'superiors' ever thought about the pain they caused by
abdicating their responsibility of not just paying the
commensurate wages, but of providing a sense of human,
personal worth to the employees. No honest person can feel
fulfilled or happy if they take even a low salary for nothing.
Marvin was convinced that those self-aggrandizing despots with
overblown egos would one day face the echo of their past
shortcomings. They would retire, probably in Florida, to spend
their lonesome, redundant years in idle expectation of

someone's expressing interest in their fate. Divorced from the stream of action, they would seek to gain comfort—not the mundane comfort of financial security, but that of compassion and of simple caring. Yet, no one would come to give comfort. No one would care or remember, even as they once forgot about their basic responsibilities.

Marvin pressed one of a dozen buttons on his private telephone exchange. In idle speculation, he continued to press others, in succession, until a voice answered:

"Yes, Mr. Clark?" Thank heaven it was Miss Gascon.

"Would you please come and join me? And bring your pad... as usual," he added, unnecessarily. During the first three months, Miss Gascon had never forgotten the essentials.

By the time his secretary came in, Marvin had sat down in his high-backed, plush, swiveling, rotating, probably self-propelling armchair. He immediately spun it around to face the window. The view was very different from his previous office. Not much to see in the winter, but he remembered the large grove of freshly planted red oaks. It had been his department which implemented this promising landscaping. Isn't it marvelous when your past catches up with you?

"Mr. Clark? Where are you...?"

"I am out in the oak grove," he didn't move. "You wouldn't care to join me?"

A smile flickered in Marvin's eyes when he imagined the expression on Miss Gascon's face. He hoped that in time she would get used to his harmless eccentricities. Alternately, he hoped that in time his eccentricities would become harmless.

Marvin gave Miss Gascon enough instructions to keep her busy for a week. He wanted a comprehensive list of all the City departments, the names of departmental heads with their personal telephones, home and office, not those published for the outside public; same regarding their deputies ('you also ought to know the names of all their secretaries'). Finally, he requested a full set of plans of the various buildings, the City Hall and the ancillary, interspersed departments.

"Oh, and one other thing." To hide his facetious grin, Marvin spun his armchair again to face the window. "I would like you to find out where *les Directeurs* take their luncheon, within the premises or outside (*vide* secretaries), what time they usually come into the office, on weekdays, on the weekends—and any other such items of personal interest would be appreciated."

He spun back to face Miss Gascon. She was busy with her pad, her face a picture of rapt attention. He waited until she looked up.

"I needn't tell you, all this is confidential." Marvin regarded her from his impressive stuffed throne.

"Oh, but *Monsieur*, Sir, I would never..." Miss Gascon seemed near tears.

"Oh, but of course you wouldn't," he hastened to reassure her.

So much for the present. Marvin hoped that the expeditious concern he had shown for Miss Gascon's morale would one day be counted, when it became his turn to dutifully report to Florida to await his demise. Now he had to occupy himself with his own, heretofore nonexistent, as yet undefined problems. He opened his black briefcase and extracted a file. As he opened it, a single sheet of paper floated onto the shining mahogany mirror of his desk. He let it lie there for a moment, then reached out and placed it within reading distance. The official, officious, pompous document seemed to belong on the oversized, otherwise empty desk, in front of an oversized, overstuffed armchair. Below the regal-looking coat of arms of the city letterhead, Marvin read the definition of his forthcoming duties:

"...head of a new, advisory council, which, when deemed necessary, will be formed, following a preparatory period of in-depth research. The said advisory council would initiate and oversee all proposals dealing with matters heretofore not covered by the already established departments. The thrust of the research..."

Marvin read the document twice, then reached into the right- hand drawer in his new desk. To his delight (bravo, Miss Gascon) he found a full set of highlighting markers. He selected a couple and proceeded to try to make heads or tails of his future. He underlined such words as *initiate*, and *oversee*, and, lower down, *more intimate relationship*, and finally *general public* and *future initiatives*. Then he reached for the other marker, this time a red one, and made a large circle around the word: *initiate*. This had to be his catch phrase. INITIATE. One way or another, he had to forego his dear, cherished invisibility and... initiate action. He would have to make waves.

God, how he hated the very thought of making waves.

Marvin left his office at five o'clock, precisely. He asked the uniformed guard at the door to call him a taxi. It arrived almost immediately. The stand was just around the corner. He gave the man an address. They got there in five minutes. He asked the driver to wait. He got out, spent a few minutes inside, and emerged with a large package. He walked to the taxi quickly, as if trying to protect something from the penetrating wind. The man drove him to another address. Marvin paid the driver and got out. He walked to the door and pushed a small button. Nothing happened. He knocked lightly, then more sharply. He reached into his vest pocket and took out a small key. He opened the door. With a pounding heart he called out. He was greeted by silence.

Marvin left his galoshes at the door but kept his coat on. He walked into the kitchen. There he found a large glass container. He filled it with water and unwrapped the large package he had brought with him. He took out the flowers and very carefully arranged them in the vase. He carried the bouquet into the living-room area. He then took out the small key, again, and placed it softly under the overhanging bloom. The flowers looked wrong, perhaps out of season. Too bad. He stood for a short while looking down. Perhaps at the flowers, perhaps at the key. It did not really matter. There were things he had to do on his own. Without any bouquets, without even the small key.

Marvin turned and slowly walked to the door. His feet felt peculiarly heavy. He put on his rubbers and pulled the door shut. He raised his collar against the biting wind. How come it always blew into his face? Marvin's eyes reached out beyond the hard, slippery, partially snow-covered sidewalk. He quickened his pace. It was time to start again. Somehow. To end this season of disconsolate oblivion.

To end this winter of his discontent.

* * *

Spring

*Sitting quietly, doing nothing, spring comes,
and the grass grows by itself.*

Zen Proverb

13

Retracing His Steps

You just had to be there.

Marvin was deeply convinced that no one who had not experienced firsthand the bleak, protracted term of a Canadian winter could possibly imagine the inner warmth, the tacit, intimate joy which touched every surviving individual at the arrival of spring. He had seen avid skiers, who had once conducted marches avowing to stamp out summer, undergo a sudden metamorphosis. At the first sign of warmer, more forgiving weather, those impassioned snow-lovers stripped down to ridiculous shorts, exposing their winter-bleached calves, knees, thighs to the still persistent risk of freezing.

Some years ago, on the slope of Mount Royal, Marvin had noted even more vivacious youngsters, who had bared their pale, sun-starved chests in the perennial celebration of the sacrosanct rites of spring skiing. Reigning over all these were the nymphs, the ephemeral spring-bunnies, often referred to as snow-bunnies, who, by a mystical aptitude known only to themselves, arrived on the slopes ready-tanned, exposing their golden, divine, voluptuous profiles not so much to the sunshine as to the sun worshipers, since of the sun they themselves were the sublime vestal, if on occasion slightly tarnished, virgins.

Marvin was content to join the ranks of the saner, perhaps the more mature survivors, who flooded the public parks of St-Onge and the neighboring Montreal in search of a drooping snowdrop, a premature shy bluebell or some fragile yet courageous, blue or white or yellow crocuses. If he failed to find them in the public parks or gardens, he would stroll along the sunny, wind-protected sidewalks and surreptitiously peek over the fences to spot an early bloom adorning the porches.

Many such rites proclaimed the arrival of spring. Yet all the rituals shared one quality above all others: they filled all hearts with gladness. They all shared in the rebirth. They drank of the wellspring of exultant glory. They hummed in unison with the fresh flowing juices, with the bustling trees, forests, with the budding branches eager to break loose from the spell of slumber. They danced the dance of sunshine trapped in exuberant forsythias; they stared in awe at the bloom of fresh magnolias.

They all paid homage.

Marvin's old Department of Parks and Recreation took part in the preparations for the official spring season. Many thousands of flowers of varied species had been grown in the municipal greenhouses. They all had to be made ready on time to fill the countless baskets suspended from the lampposts, ready to overflow from the large metal containers lining city sidewalks, to enrich the built-in, permanent granite boxes.

To enchant the pedestrians.

While Marvin's greenhouses buzzed with feverish activity, armies of municipal trucks invaded the city highways, streets, roads, lanes, avenues and pathways, filling in the cracks, gashes and pernicious potholes, washing and hosing down the salt and sandy pebbles, tending to the wounds of many wintry battles. Others dusted park benches, added new seats in strategic places, gave the bronze statues their annual touch-up.

He remembered it well....

Marvin missed the frantic pre-spring period. Swiveling his armchair away from his desk, he regarded wistfully the water maintenance trucks performing their annual ablutions. Not that Marvin had ever actually driven one. But, somehow, he had once felt part of this frenzy, part of this regeneration. Now he seemed no longer part of anything. Resolute destiny had selected him to take the next step on his own cognizance. No person would now tell him where or how to do things. At least, not for the present. He did not seek limelight, or fame, or superfluous titles.

How cruel were the dispositions of chance, he mused sadly at his Olympian window.

About two weeks after Marvin was transferred to the City Hall, he received a telephone call directly from the mayor.

"Would you drop in and see me? When you can find a minute?" The mayor's voice was laced with golden honey.

Marvin peered deeply into his leather-bound diary. He decided that he could fit the mayor in somewhere between right now and infinity. In fact, at any time at all. That was not, however, what he had said to the mayor. Twenty years in the municipal service imparts some fundamental precepts. Discretion is e'er the password when dealing with those still higher.

"I shall make myself available at Your Worship's convenience," he assured.

"Jean-Paul to you, Marvin—we are, surely, now playing on the same side of the net, *n'est ce pas?*" (Marvin's jaw fell. So there are people who still used such expressions?) "How about later this afternoon, say around fourish?"

"I shall be there, your, ah... Jean-Paul."

It made no difference. The mayor's receiver had been replaced before Marvin had a chance to confirm the time. The question had been rhetorical. A matter of politeness. One does not question the dispositions of the gods.

Marvin reflected that addressing 'The Right Honorable Jean-Paul LeGrand His Worship the Mayor' by the two intermediate, rather insignificant portions of the full appellation would not come easily to him for some time. He blamed years of conditioning. He had already heard by the Gascon grapevine that the mayor cultivated a habit of informal relationships. To remain *dans bonnes grâces* of *Monsieur le Maire*, one had to respond in kind. But beware! Marvin extrapolated from Miss Gascon's reports that at the least sign of opposition, the mayor roared thunder and lightning at the offending party. Such would sting with the sheer force of contrast from the previously lax, bogus benevolence.

At four o'clock precisely, Marvin presented himself in the mayor's anteroom. A blond maiden, whose skin-tight dress waged a losing battle with her apparent appetite, waded to greet him. She had to wade or, had she been less voluptuous, to float. One cannot walk on a knee-deep carpet.

Marvin was immediately recognized. This instant recognition had a particularly unnerving effect on him. He was forced to conclude that his steadfast portrayal of a nondescript, average, melting-into-the-crowd, middle-aged man would no longer pay dividends. Had his new position put something into his stride, his posture or something intangible into his facial expression? Marvin continued to speak in a low voice, with polite if laconic economy. It wasn't enough.

"The mayor will see you now, Sir."

The overfed sylph spirited him toward the interior. She opened the doors for him. Marvin, who was ready to, figuratively speaking, fall on his knees, came face to face with the mayor's secretary. The tall, even more epicurean woman granted him a perfunctory smile and led him toward yet another set of doors in the wall ahead. She knocked and, without waiting for an answer, pushed the doors open. As Marvin stepped in, the door shut silently behind him.

He was facing His Worship.

The mayor had been busy talking on one of the three telephones on his desk. None of these modern, fangle-dangle multi-buttoned telephone exchanges on his bridge. The telephones, a bouquet of fresh-cut flowers, a jug of water with two glasses on a silver tray, and a single file were all that cluttered the expanse of polished rosewood. The rest of the shining, deep burgundy skating rink remained empty. It gave a shimmering interplay of light and shadow. To anyone standing where Marvin now stood, it also offered a slightly distorted reflection of a full-size portrait hanging behind the mayor. A portrait of His Worship in full regalia. Before the mayor got fat. Before the mayor's face assumed the shape of a baboon's backside or, to be more kindly, of a rosy full moon. The moonscape was animated by the ever-mobile mouth, rather than by two tiny craters masquerading as eyes. Marvin remained standing. He admired the reflection.

The mayor laughed very loudly. Immediately afterwards, with equal force and producing paramount amounts of noise, he slammed the receiver down.

"*Bâtard!!!*" he shouted, turning his head toward Marvin. "My dear, dear fellow, how nice finally to meet you. Do sit down. Are you happy? Can we do anything for you?"

The mayor's broad, inscrutable smile wrapped around Marvin, raised him up and transported him into one of the copious armchairs. All this time his pudgy hands and arms were inscribing great, obviating circles in the air, as if directing a symphony orchestra, or perhaps just instructing the evil spirits to leave him and Marvin in peace. All this was certainly in stark contrast to the French expletive with which His Worship had concluded his telephone conversation with the fatherless gentleman.

"You have asked to see me, Sir?" Marvin came back to earth quickly.

"Jean-Paul, please, Jean-Paul. Now that is an order, ha, ha, ha! *Mon vieux.* Yes, I did ask to see you, to make sure you are happy. Were your Chambers quite ready, fit for your arrival?"

Except for his accent, the mayor spoke practically flawless English. Marvin could have sworn that the mayor really cared about his welfare. He could have sworn, but he wouldn't believe it. Throughout this tirade, whenever the mayor switched to French, he addressed Marvin by the familiar French *tu* rather than the formal *vous*. Marvin had not been quite ready for this.

"Yes, Sir, ah, Jean-Paul. More than satisfactory. I'm indeed delighted."

Marvin wondered if he hadn't said too much already. Perhaps he had been called here to give a report on his work to date. He kept himself quite busy, but so far he had no results to show for it.

"Good, good... would you care for some coffee?"

Without waiting for an answer, the mayor pressed a button on his desk and a girl walked in with a silver tray bearing beautiful, see-through china. Two cups and saucers, a medium-size matching jug of coffee, cream, cubed sugar with an oversized pair of tweezers, dainty silver spoons and some attractive biscuits on a filigree silver platter. There had been no time lapse between the mayor's invitation and the arrival of the coffee. Indeed, there was magic in His Worship's presence.

The polite buffoonery lasted another ten minutes. Marvin had no idea what could have been the reasons for the extended pleasantries, unless the mayor thought that he could somehow extract some sort of information about himself, about his potential, reliability or whatever. If the mayor had been playing at being a psychologist, then Marvin had no inkling whether he had passed the test or not. When the ten minutes were up, the mayor picked up the single file lying on his desk as if it were a distasteful, offending object. Abruptly changing the subject, he gave it to Marvin.

"On some rare occasions, we have some little problems, little spats, between the various departments, or some, ah... devious taxpayer. I rather thought that you might care to look into this, ah, little, ah... the file will explain it all. I am sure you can handle it quietly. Wouldn't want to rock the boat, make any unnecessary waves, break any eggs..."

Marvin's ability to shut himself off from inane drivel had long been his mainstay. Hiding behind this fundamental bastion of his hopefully still well-preserved sanity, Marvin did not think that this was the appropriate moment to ignore the lord and master of his immediate survival. He tried to listen without showing on his face that the mayor was a total, unadulterated moron. On closer examination Marvin might have thought otherwise, but at that particular time it would have been extremely difficult to draw any other conclusion.

"... the same side of the net, if we let the tree bend a little more—just, just maybe, some of the branches will fall into place. All by themselves. Do I make myself clear?"

To his horror, his utter amazement, Marvin recognized in the mayor's prattle a monologue he had heard many years ago. A man called Freberg or Freeburg, or some such American wit, had once cut a satirical record using the same or very similar expressions. Mr. Freberg had been, perhaps still was, a very funny comic. But there was a fundamental difference between his and the present performance. The mayor repeated the recorded witticisms with a perfectly straight face, without a single suggestion of satire or even veiled humor. It was at this point that Marvin suddenly remembered why so many of the mayor's past speeches had sounded so familiar. They had been, all too often, interspersed with lengthy, verbatim quotations borrowed from His Worship's favourite stage personalities.

The mayor misunderstood Marvin's smile of sudden comprehension as a sign of acquiescence to or for his question.

"That will be all, my boy, ah.... ah, Marvin. Ha, ha, Marvin. An unusual name, *n'est-ce pas, mon vieux?*"

With that question still hanging in the air, the Right Honorable and Worshipful mayor performed another of his amazing faster-than-eye tricks. Simultaneously, he handed Marvin the offending file, pressed a button on his desk and picked up one of his telephones into which he barked: "Get Gervais!" Without losing a breath in the process, His rotund Worship rolled around the desk, took Marvin by the elbow, and had him halfway to the door, even as his secretary opened the portals from the outside.

"I am sure you can handle it, my boy. Come and see me. My doors are always open!" With this final assurance, his secretary firmly closed the door behind Marvin.

If Director Marvin Clark had learned anything during the years of faithful service in the municipal menagerie, he had learned one dictum thoroughly: *Never open a new file after four-thirty.* With this tenet firmly in mind, Marvin walked down to his Chambers, gave the file to Miss Gascon and asked her to make a working copy for him for tomorrow. He had no difficulties in not quenching his curiosity about the file's content. In his life, he had seen just too many files. Far too many.

Marvin continued into his own office, sat down, and tried to make heads or tails of the ridiculous interview (or had it been a meeting?) with the mayor. In these new circumstances, his past experience was virtually useless. Marvin's brow remained furrowed for some twenty minutes. Then he shrugged. It was time to prepare for departure, to visit his private washroom. He faced the mirror. His features were distorted by a wry smile.

"Surely," he asked his pensive image, "surely the old goat must have some redeeming features?" Then he shrugged again. "Mustn't he?"

From that day on, Director Clark's Chambers became the dumping ground for strife and argument, not of his own making but his to deal with. Marvin became the internal arbitrator, the oil on the turbid waters, the Solomon of the municipal pyramidal bureaucracy. Marvin had been called upon to bisect many a contentious infant, his sword invariably stayed by the pleas of the presumably more deserving party. Surprisingly, Marvin performed these operations with the ease of an experienced surgeon. He became the buffer, the moat surrounding the highest of the high, the most equal of all, His Worshipful Innocence Jean-Paul LeGrand the First.

Not even in his wildest dreams had Marvin imagined that he would become the Arbiter General of the many difficulties which, even with the best of intentions, did and would arise in inter-human relations. The ability to erect moats and ramparts, which Marvin had gathered with such conscientious care over the many years, no longer served his own interests. By yet another capricious wave of a magic wand, those very same skills had been reassigned for the benefit of others. By the time spring arrived, Marvin Clark had already been cited as the wise man of the City, as a man to be respected, and particularly to be trusted. The winners in the controversial cases he had helped to resolve loved him for his fair-minded judgments. The losers did not hate him but, though on occasion grudgingly, attested to his open and direct impartiality. The City Hall had saved millions of dollars by avoiding formal litigation.

The very first case the mayor had given Marvin had threatened the City Hall with adverse publicity. Marvin, rather than attempting to cover the City's tracks, took upon himself to admit an error inadvertently committed by a City official. The following day the press gave the City Hall of St-Onge front-page laudatory coverage. They praised the fair play: "...*so rare these days, when the little man has no chance against the big boys, the big and powerful city officials.*" As of that newspaper article, Marvin's reputation had preceded him, making his work easier, though not actually more pleasant. Each bone of contention had been accompanied by at least two barking dogs that had to be placated, stabilized, emotionally disarmed, before any hope of intellectual or mental exercise could come into play. Marvin was learning to manipulate people. He did not like doing it, even if it was, surely, for their own good.

At home, spring had little effect on the three amenable senior citizens. Regardless of season, Mrs. Prentis enveloped them with her usual maternal care. To partake in the Rites of Spring, one had to get out of the musty walls. Marvin's work forced him to do so. He walked to work, regardless of weather. Mrs. Prentis had her shopping, her daily constitutionals. But the three retirees seldom left their Victorian enclave. By all appearances, they regarded the outdoors as a foreign country. The bright light which Jocelyn radiated on the old walls came and went like a transient comet, amazing in its beauty, yet short-lived, esoteric, ephemeral, shining and then disappearing for years, centuries—to live on in memories of all those who had seen it. Marvin tried hard to dismiss his memories. He tried very hard.

As for his inner life, Marvin had to retrace his steps. A strict discipline necessary to restore his ability to travel became his priority. He felt convinced that his failure to enter the alpha state at will was at the root of his difficulties. He began, once again, spending regular time at the console of his esoteric starship, examining and adapting his old fuel, searching for the lost, attempting to find the new. Seven weeks had passed in a most uneventful fashion. It was a lonesome endeavor.

One evening toward the end of February, after work and before supper, Marvin sat at his usual command post. For no particular reason he felt unsettled, a little frustrated. Lately he enjoyed some success in his ventures, but... the inner world seemed almost bland. It did not sate him. Something, some element was missing. Marvin toyed with the disks, unsure which music to use as his fuel. He felt very ambivalent. Finally he gave up. It had been a long struggle. He stopped trying.

The room was very silent. The street must have been deserted. There was still enough light in the attic for Marvin's indifferent gaze to linger over the convoluted shapes of his Delicious Monster. The one faithful friend. Such a long time, so many memories.

And then he heard fragments of a distant melody.

Marvin did not attempt to analyze the state of his consciousness. It seemed immaterial whether the music reached him through the open window or from one of the lodgers. It simply did not matter. As he continued to listen, the sound increasingly absorbed his attention. It seemed strangely familiar. Like an old song that had been hidden in his memory—familiar, yet elusive. It was the sound of a recorder: a warm, caressing, strangely round tone, mostly a single note, variable in intensity rather than pitch. In all this, the sound remained haunting, engaging, different yet evocative of times and places he had visited in some distant past. It had one other peculiar quality. It did not seem to originate from anywhere. It just was. It lingered. It... enfolded. Slowly Marvin's attention drifted to an unknown seashore. Perhaps the sound had come from the ocean. From the endless, serene, seemingly eternal, seemingly at peace.

Ubiquitous peace.

The image changed. The swelling tone drew him to other vistas, other unexpected places. The images Marvin witnessed were not as real as some he had enjoyed in his previous travels. Before, he had been a spectator. Now, rather than being observed, the oceans or the landscapes seemed in some strange way part of him. Or rather he part of the landscapes.... It was as though the observer and the observed had intermingled. They were not one and the same, but he had the ability of blending at will, of melting or of merging, his self into the other.

After a while he became the skipper.

For the first time since Marvin had started his travels, he felt a tentative linkage with the power, with the energy that not just controlled his mind or body or physical senses—in a way this power seemed to flow with the single tone from the core of his being. From the substance of his uniqueness?

Facing this mystery, he became inexplicably humble. He knew instantly that he must relinquish the title to his spaceship. He was not yet ready for command. But he'd tasted the waters. A time would come... the music seemed to be saying. A time will come...

A tentative promise of an inner kingdom. As before, yet quite different.

Shyly, as once at the chapel's altar, he set his sails.

* * *

14

Frenzy

It was by far the most difficult thing to do. To do nothing.

To bide her time while staring at the most beautiful, the most magnificent, by far the largest bouquet she had ever received. Ever. Nothing in Jocelyn's memories matched such splendor, such exquisite filigree delicacy as the more than a dozen exotic orchids which gazed at her—tempting, inviting, invoking gratitude and forgiveness.

What right had she to sit in judgment of another human being? Perhaps he had excellent reasons for his previous behaviour. Perhaps he simply did not know how, perhaps he...

Perhaps...?

Perhaps she had been wrong to expect a mode of behaviour from him, as she would from anyone else? Whatever Marvin had been, was, my God, whatever he is this very moment, he is anything but 'anyone' else. If ever the word 'different' applied to any man, it most surely applied to Marvin. If nothing else, his mask, which he obviously cultivated with such determination, had made him different. The mask that had not fooled her for more than a few seconds, even as he lay prone at her feet during their very first meeting.

If nothing else?

If nothing else, he had opened her eyes to the knowledge of pure art, knowledge of the essence behind her work, her efforts, her studies. Had he not shown her the illusion of time? Did he not hint that space itself, the very essence of her medium, had but a transient existence? He had treated the whole world almost like an illusion, like an ephemeral component of time itself. On his lips such words had rung true. Could such concepts be uttered by an ordinary man? Whatever his other failings, whatever the shades and shadows to his curious character, Marvin, this mind-wrenching man, was unique. He had left her flabbergasted, discombobulated. He had left her utterly lost! He had also left her astonished, astounded, dumbfounded, and bloody, yes, bloody annoyed. Irked. Steaming, screaming mad!!!

Figuratively speaking, of course.

All that and more had been true, pertinent, before Jocelyn's trip to West Palm Beach. Marion, with her discreet yet always willing and available ear, had provided precisely what Jocelyn had needed at that particular time. Now, while the concepts remained, the heat and the hurt had abated to a tolerable level. On her return to St-Onge, Jocelyn regained her usual, perfect, or at least perfectly erratic, self-control.

"Perfect, damn it, bloody perfect..." She made a face at the full-length mirror.

Except for occasional moments of weakness. After all, were not all artists supposed to have a wild temper? Was this not something to do with an artistic temperament? Well, wasn't it?

"Or should I simply learn to relax," she hissed through clenched teeth, crossing her arms over her panting, heaving breast.

How beautiful is an orchid?

Some deep, some painful, some more inconsequential thoughts churned through Jocelyn's high-spirited, emotional head for almost three months. Now, in the middle of March, the spring had caught up with her. Jocelyn started rising earlier to have time to walk to work. She needed to inhale the invigorating, fresh scents emanating from anything that grew or bloomed or was about to flower. Springtime aromas lingered, seemingly trapped within some air pockets, sometimes drifting from across the Saint Lawrence River, ever ready to share and apportion the joys of the annual awakening.

Jocelyn loved all four seasons. She loved the pristine, cleansing purity of winter. She let her mind and body absorb the mellow ripeness of summer. She immersed herself in the plethora of mature smells and colours of the Canadian autumn; rich smells like oak wine-casks she once inhaled in the green hills of Catalonia. Yet she held a furtive, particular affection for nature's favourite daughter. Perhaps more so since the spring in St-Onge was such a shortchanged child. With four months of winter, a fair autumn and summer, the short-lived spring seemed unfairly treated. Under Mars's bellicose command, winter continued undaunted, ignoring the equinox as though of no importance. Yet by the time gentle Juno came forth to administer her domain, sprightly daughter of Mars was forced to relinquish her bursting energies. A short yet glorious season. A season of feverish frenzy.

Each day of springtime brought Jocelyn new inspiration, new ideas for her sculptures. Before meeting Marvin, she had treated her creative work as a pleasant, relaxing hobby. On rare occasions, she would shyly offer one of her reliefs to someone who expressed some interest in it, or give it as a token of gratitude for favours received. Although some latent artistic ambitions may have hibernated in the deep recesses of her heart, they never really surfaced. Her aspirations had never been sufficiently defined to reach her full awareness. The thought of becoming a professional sculptor had never entered her head. Not until very recently.

"A professional sculptor," she once uttered, regarding her face in a mirror. "Good God, how marvelous it sounds!"

She repeated the words with euphoric delight.

And then she blushed. Not at the idea of becoming a professional sculptor, but at her growing habit of speaking out loud—to herself. Living alone for quite a few years relaxed her vigilance.

"I am becoming an eccentric old maid."

She made sure she did not verbalize her thoughts. Yet such personal chats had always been part of her spontaneity. The studio was her domain. There she felt free to be herself.

"If that be eccentric, let it so be! I am a mistress of my own castle!"

She once admitted to Aunt Jenny that on occasion she was apt to conduct long, often exhaustive discussions with herself as the sole interlocutor. She never imagined that any harm could possibly result from such behaviour. After all, as long as she remained well aware as to who were the participants in any argument, what harm was there?

"None, as long as you don't expect an answer to any of your questions," offered Mrs. Prentis.

"But, Aunt Jenny, I always expect an answer. Or at least a good argument!" Jocelyn watched as Aunt Jenny's brow furrowed in consternation.

"Well, I think it's unhealthy," Mrs. Prentis declared sternly.

Jocelyn had other habits that Aunt Jenny regarded with considerable anguish. When alone in her studio, her niece thought nothing of walking about quite naked. She never considered that the human body had any stigma of shame attached to it. Not unless it had been ruined by ravages of abuse such as gluttony, or such an aberration as a total disregard of physical exercise. Her own nakedness provided her with an instant model, reflected in four mirrors strategically positioned around her working table. Naked or otherwise, Jocelyn talked and danced and sang to her heart's content, although the latter she reserved for moments of assured solitude. Those unfortunate few who had heard Jocelyn sing would certainly approve of her magnanimous restraint.

After returning from Florida, Jocelyn spent a regularly allotted time at her large, portentous table, moulding and re-moulding, working till her arms and fingers hurt with exhaustion. Her sculptures grew in size, in symbolic meaning, also in depth of expression and complexity. Not so much in complexity of form as in the range of emotions frozen into that interspatial, untenable instant of time.

Not all her new efforts were equally good. For the first time since she started sculpting, Jocelyn learned to pass judgment on the end product of her own efforts. An attempt at impartial, objective opinion was often painful, emotionally taxing. As she examined her creations with more mature eyes, she relegated about a quarter of her collection to "promising experience". With hardly a crocodile tear, she discarded many of her early attempts into the basket. The "I can do a lot better than that!" basket. The next minute she was working again, validating her stringent decision.

Then came the next step on her creative ladder. She bought a shoulder-hung portfolio, selected three of her best efforts and carried them with her to the library. From there, at the expense of eating, she spent her lunch hours peddling her wares to the established art galleries. Having exhausted St-Onge, she ventured out to the elegance of Sherbrooke Street in Montreal. It hadn't been easy. She had to face professional gallery owners, present her work, and hear the few, repetitive, well-chosen words of refusal.

"Very, very promising... Miss, ah, Prentis?" The tone was invariably reserved, contained, perhaps just a trifle bored. "Do you have anything else to show us?"

She handed over a folder of some twenty transparencies.

"Now, where is our projector...?" The art peddler peered through the window at the busy lunchtime crowd milling along the street. "Do you think you could come by some other time? When we're a little less busy?"

Jocelyn wondered why the artistically garbed gallery owners found it necessary to make use of the royal 'we'. Never had she seen more than one person making any decision regarding the sale or purchase of any works of art.

The vast majority of the galleries catered exclusively to painting. The days of Rodin, Moore, Manzu, Brancusi, Giacometti and, surely, a number of other gifted, uncompromising sculptors were over. Dead. Those glorious days when one could chance upon a work of art, be it in a museum, a gallery, a park, or even forgotten on a sidewalk... a work of art which would slow one's step, cause one to reflect, absorb, to share with the creator that ephemeral moment of infinity....

Those days were over, buried in the decadence fueled by the chase after the uncompromising, jealous god: the sacred, all-powerful, divine Dollar.

Jocelyn doubted if a contemporary artist could or would ask himself: "Am I faithful to the spirit which guides me? To the creative energy which selected me to act as its chosen instrument?" And she did not blame them. Today the great houses of the world were no longer run by farseeing, philanthropic Patrons of the Arts, but by the myopic greed of hard-fisted accountants. Today's artist bowed deeply and asked the powerful art peddler: "What is most likely to feed my wife and children?"

"Perhaps you have something in bronze, or in some, ah... precious metals?" The accountant owner asked Jocelyn with knowing candor. He or she knew what would sell and, certainly, what didn't.

"Well, Sir (Mister High 'n' Mighty), I really do not think that my particular art form lends itself to such a hard, cold medium. And furthermore, I'd like to make my art accessible to a larger market, to all those who can't afford the bronze or precious metals...?"

The expert held up his hand.

"Miss, ah... Prentis!" This time the jovial, paternalistic owner made Jocelyn's name sound like 'my dear, dear, slightly backward child.' "Art is not bought by people who can ill afford it. Art is an investment! A gateway to the future! A means, Miss Prentis," (he got her name right!) "...a means of growing richer by doing well, by... ah, by doing good!"

By now the eyes of the speaker clouded over with dreams of glory measured in fat percentages of a vendor's fat commissions.

"Investment, Miss Prentis. Always remember, *investment!*"

The story repeated itself with predictable regularity. Jocelyn assumed that gallery owners also might well have had to support their own wives and children. All needed to eat, to survive in a world of this new, financially disseminated, global, green religion.

"Funny," she mused, toting her heavy bag along Sherbrooke. "I always thought that green had something to do with ecology?"

Jocelyn would return from such lunchtime outings with a growing sense of impotence, practically of depression. Two factors remained in her favour. The first she owed to her Aunt Jenny. Over the years Mrs. Prentis had taught her that everything had a reason. That no honest effort is ever truly wasted. That if she continued her work without demanding instant recognition, her work would either fail, because it was not very good to start with, or it would prevail, regardless of untoward circumstances. Aunt Jenny also taught her that patience is a divine virtue, not to be wasted on undeserving causes, but to rejoice at any opportunity which demanded its manifestation.

The second advantage Jocelyn enjoyed was the conspicuous absence of any wife or children—or husband, for that matter. She was free to do with her free time as she chose, particularly since the library job catered to all her basic necessities. It even left her with a little bit over.

Then came the Idea!

In the middle of March, Jocelyn was struck by a strange if frightening thought. The experience she had acquired during her noon visits to the various galleries had suddenly caught up with her. The idea came with the force and rapidity of a bolt of lightning—she practically reeled under its compelling impact.

She finally realized that, regardless of the many faults which the gallery owners may have demonstrated, there must have been a reason why a vast preponderance of their stock was given to painting. The buyers wanted to hang their artwork on their walls rather than have it cluttering their tables, floors or other useful spaces. The public also wanted a dash of colour. They wanted to brighten their gray, dull lives. If she wanted to reach people, she had to, at least to start with, give those art-starved clients something of what they wanted. Or at least to give them what they thought they wanted.

This idea mobilized Jocelyn into action.

The next Saturday she got up with the sun. She didn't walk, she ran. She wouldn't sit for a moment of rest. She seemed in a state of frenzy. She began by extracting old moulds from storage crates. She proceeded to make new castings. For the last two years, Jocelyn had been experimenting with rubberoid moulds. This synthetic material enabled her to produce as many new castings as she wanted.

Jocelyn started a production of multiple editions!

She simplified the process while improving the quality. She added variety as well as depth to some of her original forms. The original low relief, the *basso-relievo*, seemed to swell into a middle and even high relief. The latter, the *alto-relievo*, added drama and contrast to her early work. The *mezzo-relievo* furnished a depth of expression previously possible only with single, non-reproducible castings. The synthetic rubber also enabled Jocelyn to interlock convex with deeply concave shapes, to work at right or acute angles to the sculpture's background. She worked feverishly, tackling three or four sculptures simultaneously, adding, subtracting, scraping and moulding, then covering her still-drying creations with the wet goo of the rubberoid compound.

Sometimes, with seemingly inexhaustible energy, she whirled back or jumped on a chair, regarded her latest effort from a greater distance, then jumped down and smashed her fist on the sculpture in abject denial: the clay had failed to convey her inspired vision.

Jocelyn had become her own sternest critic.

Next came the final phase of her newborn idea. While the many new castings had to be left for drying, Jocelyn walked—no, once again she ran—to her local art shop. Fifteen minutes later, she dumped a pile of watercolour, acrylic and a batch of other paints of mixed chemical bases on the counter.

"Just in case!" She panted to the flabbergasted salesman. "I'm in the middle of an experiment!" she added, when the man took a step back.

"Just in case..." the man half-muttered. His face gave every indication that Jocelyn's experiment dealt with high explosives. "Will that be all, *Mademoiselle*?"

The man seemed quite relieved when Jocelyn exploded from his shop.

She jogged back to her studio and collapsed on the settee. Only then did Jocelyn remember that she had had no breakfast. Sighing, as though lumbered with a punitive chore, she struggled to the kitchenette, broke two fresh eggs into a blender, squirted in salt and pepper, added a large banana, then drank the concoction in four large gulps. She shook her head with relief that that chore was over and returned to her worktable.

The gypsum castings were ready to be extricated from their moulds. The synthetic rubbers had to be washed and replaced in their rigid supports. She then prepared wire reinforcing and arranged it carefully in the waiting forms. She was now ready to prepare and pour in a fresh mixture of gypsum for her next multiple editions.

It was hard, backbreaking work. Jocelyn loved it.

The first two castings reached the stage of dryness necessary to start her experiments. She brought some water, opened the newly acquired box of watercolours, and very gingerly began to apply dabs of paint onto selected areas of her sculpture. She did not paint them. She allowed the drying gypsum to absorb the moisture from the brush together with the attendant paint, rather as blotting paper absorbs any water-based liquid. To complete the experiment would take from three days to a week. Various surfaces absorbed the aquarelle at a different rate. The work required patience and good judgment; neither was among Jocelyn's more noticeable traits of character.

She was attempting to replace the evaporating moisture with new, coloured liquid. This way she was not just applying the colour to the surface but feeding it much deeper, and thus instilling the colour permanently into the fabric of the gypsum itself.

It worked! Jocelyn carefully replaced her brushes, then jumped up, performed a quick whirling dervish fantasy, and collapsed on the sofa.

To her utter amazement, even her first attempts presented interesting new effects. She knew that it would be very easy to overdo the colour application. She had to be a little less spontaneous, a mite more premeditating and analytical, in this aspect of her work. Help came from quite unexpected quarters.

Jocelyn hardly ever used makeup. She reserved lipstick or eye shadow for very rare occasions, and rouge for days when she did not want to scare people with her pallor. When she did use makeup, she never did it to really change her appearance, but rather to restore her face to a normal, healthy, summery appearance—to underline and emphasize her natural features. Now, although reaching beyond the skin-deep application, she was adding makeup to the faces of her sculptures. She emphasized their features, she strengthened their inherent strength, she reinforced the expression which they were already invoking.

Time passed at a maddening rate.

By late evening, in a single day, Jocelyn had poured, cast and enhanced with delicate tones five *mezzo-relievo* sculptures. She felt drained, exhausted and, for the first time in a long time, exuberantly happy. She felt that she had spent the whole day in an intense frenzy of giving. A conspicuous absence of a long cue of admirers, avidly waiting for her to shower her gifts upon them, was neither here nor there.

A time would come...

Jocelyn slept like a log. Her father had once told her that she was most beautiful when sleeping. It must have been her relaxed features. He had said that her mouth widened, as though sharing in some secret joke. Jocelyn was awakened by a moonbeam. She knew she had been dreaming but could not recall the substance of the dream. She just remembered a smile. Just a hovering, rather shy, questioning smile. Not a mouth or lips—just a smile. She was reminded of Lewis Carroll's Cheshire cat: "...and only a smile was left behind."

Perhaps the smile was the substance of her dream.

The following day was Sunday.

She took things a little easier; at least until about eleven, when the next idea hit her like a ton of paintings. *People wanted paintings.* Paintings have frames. Within minutes, Jocelyn was jogging merrily along the sidewalk. It was a fresh, sunny morning. She caught a bus in the nick of time; she nearly missed it. On Sunday that could mean a long wait. Twenty minutes later she got out on *Notre Dame*, an older, rather dilapidated street in Montreal. Many merchants here specialized in antiques. They always stayed open, even on a Sunday.

The word "antiques" was a euphemism. Anything that was either decrepit, falling apart, or more than some thirty years old, had been classified as an antique. Jocelyn wondered if she qualified. On the grounds of age only.

She came to *rue Notre Dame* on a very specific quest. In their unobtrusive basements, the older stores often kept old, rejected picture frames.

"Paintings have frames," Jocelyn asserted, staring at the antique dealer. "I want the ones you don't want."

She needed frames. For six hours, in over a dozen stores, she sifted through literally hundreds of frames. Many were falling apart, many more had chipped sides or corners, many were just too expensive. Jocelyn extracted twenty-two frames. Some were gilt-edged, some covered in real gold leaf, most needed a little work. All were of about the right size, for about the right price.

Staggering under her load, Jocelyn hailed a taxi. Not a mean feat in that part of town. It was a long ride. By the time they got to her studio, Jocelyn had described her plans to her driver. She had to. She was bursting. Practically frantic. The driver was so impressed with Jocelyn's enthusiasm that he carried all the frames into her studio. And then refused her tip.

"Miss, if you wanna do what you said you's gonna do, you need all'da help you can get!" The driver commented with a big grin. "And you know somtin', miss, I gota feelin' you's gonna do it!"

"You can bet on it!" Jocelyn assured her benefactor with a grave face.

She dialed for a pizza. She had decided to celebrate. She opened a bottle of good Chilean Merlot. By the time the pizza arrived, half the wine had reached room temperature. The other half was even warmer in her stomach. She raised a toast to Jocelyn Prentis, the sculptor. She felt that there was something still missing. But she was a little too tired to think. Something to do with paintings. She shrugged.

"Tomorrow is another day," she muttered, raising her glass again.

Jocelyn really liked the Merlot. She wondered if she would also like Chile. Then she frowned with a smile as dry as her wine. She ate only half of her pizza. She had run out of wine. The settee felt very comfortable. Her eyes closed of their own accord. A gentle, almost elusive smile widened her mouth.

Perhaps it was her essence.

* * *

15

A Dream

"To sleep, perchance to dream..."

There were moments in Marvin's life when he could not truly define his state of consciousness. He could swear that he had merely dreamt of a particular event. He felt sure that he had dreamt of it at night in his bed, or as he traveled—in the transcendent capsule of his unbridled imagination. The problem was that while he could not pinpoint the event in his waking hours, he witnessed the results of his dreams, or imagery, or travels, in the very solid world of objective matter. The effects of an intangible dream-event manifested themselves in tangible, objective reality.

Marvin wondered which phenomena could be defined as objective. He thought that the definition had to be *perforce* limited to such events, incidents, or experiences as could be shared with or perceived by other people—or at least one other person. Yet what of the creative process? What of the scientists, of the great masters of canvas, of the immortal composers? The results of their labours had been and continue to be shared by millions. But at the time of conception, at the actual moment of creation of their later famous efforts, they could not share their image. They could not share the sublime essence, which only later became translated into an objective existence. Must the creative act therefore remain forever subjective? If so, then, by analogy, all objective reality has its birth in an individual subjective state of consciousness.

"We are gods!"

A frightening postulate, yet the only logical conclusion. Or at least the only practical working premise. Marvin wiped his forehead.

The next question that bugged him concerned the generally established concepts of reality itself. Is reality only that which could be perceived by our senses? Or, to turn the scales, is that which is perceived by our senses—real? By such definition all the creative processes were destined to remain *unreal*. On the other hand, a mirage perceived by a desirous pair of eyes—is.

So much for the established concepts!

Now dreams, Marvin accepted, were obviously subjective. Were they therefore unreal? Certainly! Provided reality is only that which not merely can be, but actually is, perceived by another person. Dreams unreal?

"Nuts! On occasion they've given me headaches. Very, very *real* headaches!"

Marvin's logic rebelled against such stringent definitions. Could there not be a sort of latent objective reality in all our thoughts, our emotions... perhaps a mixture of the two in clearly prescribed proportions? And by that token, did the dreams have any substance? Or was it just that the substance, the essence of dreams, was from a realm where objectivity is measured by a different set of postulates, judged by totally different rules? Are all the dreams, of all people, perhaps even those of the 'lower' forms of life, measured by those same, different, yet consistent standards? Can one share a dream with another, willing person?

To sleep, perchance to dream...

Marvin adjusted the angle of his command chair. As he leaned farther back, his angle of vision became limited to the convoluted realm of the Delicious Monster. What of his, or is it her, reality? he wondered.

The prophets of old had been proficient observers of dreams. Reputedly, they could interpret the potential or intended reality of those ancient ventures into the subconscious.

Marvin smiled. Over the years he had become a truly doubting Thomas.

In that sense dreams were, or at the very least could become, objective, rather like the music first heard on a subjective plane of an attuned composer. Then what were the rules? Why were the dreams, at least in the old days, invariably cloaked in some incomprehensible, symbolic jargon? What good were dreams to us if we could neither understand them nor control their passage, evolvement, or outcome? Or could we? Could we at least all learn to understand them without the dubious aid of the long-departed and extremely dead prophets? Carl Jung had intimated as much. So had others....

Marvin rejected the imposition of such limitations.

He adjusted his armchair again. The stream of ideas flashed through his mind at such a rate that he could hardly attach symbols, words, to the whirling concepts. He sat up and closed his eyes.

To understand the dreams was just one thing. But it wasn't enough. Not nearly enough. We spend a third of our life in bed, a lot of that time in dreaming and, on top of that, we seem to dream most of our waking hours. We dream of a car, we dream of a house, a wife, a dozen children, money, success, position and possessions. Some strange (judging by the majority rule) deranged individuals even dream of giving!

None of us—we never, never stop dreaming.

Yet only some dreams come true, only some become solidified, set in an objective reality. Set, like Jocelyn's sculptures, in a physical reality. Concepts reduced to fragments of space and time. The other dreams go by the wayside...

Why? What are the rules? Surely, there are always rules.

Or could it be that the True Reality would forever remain subjective? Could it be that the eastern sages had been right? Could it be that all objective events, things, material trappings, physical manifestations were no more than transient, ephemeral illusions? Mere reflections of True Reality, forever destined to remain subjective?

Perchance to dream....

Some four hundred years ago, the bard of Avon dreamed of nearly forty plays. He dreamed and he slept, perhaps in a reverse order, and that which had been born of his subjective reality had become—for our sake—objective. Could that be the coveted, ever shrouded secret? For *our* sake? For the sake of another?

"But surely," Marvin shrugged, "dear ol' Willy retired with a modest fortune..." Then he looked at his watch. "And if I do not go down to dinner, I shall retire with an empty stomach!"

During the last week or so, Mrs. Prentis had given an impression of being slightly agitated. She had also favored Marvin with a little extra attention. She had given him furtive glances, paid close attention to anything he uttered. She appeared unduly interested in Marvin's state of mind. This vague, almost secretive departure from her normal behaviour did not go unnoticed.

During the last few months, Marvin's office work had been directed at resolving problems caused by other people. Constant professional involvement served to vastly sharpen his powers of observation. Dealing with professional sharks, he needed such perspicacity. The slightest nuance, a fleeting grimace, a faint Freudian slip going unnoticed, could well have spelled the difference between success and failure. And failure, His Worship had not taken to kindly. As a professional Shylock, Jean-Paul LeGrand would be bound to exact his pound of flesh.

As it was now becoming his nature, Marvin returned Mrs. Prentis's tacit compliment by granting her his own surreptitious attention. He did not spy on her. There was nothing particular he desired to learn about dear Mrs. Prentis, save to find out what was her extracurricular interest in his own behaviour.

Since that fateful evening when Marvin, following an ungainly amount of cognac, had made an absolute ass of himself, Mrs. Prentis and he had twice enjoyed a friendly *tête-à-tête*. Those succeeding chats had been a little more restrained, more reserved, less so than they would have been a year ago, but not yet in an atmosphere of total openness and trust. Evidently, on the first occasion, the Rémi Martin had been conducive to the weakening of Marvin's defenses.

The later chats had been concerned, principally, with Marvin's exploits, his promotion, his new unexpected duties. On the last occasion, Marvin had gone so far as to tell Mrs. Prentis about his reservations, his profound doubt, whether he had it in him to carry out what was expected of him. To his surprise, Mrs. Prentis agreed with him.

"Can't say I blame you. A city arbitrator doesn't sound like your cup of tea."

Marvin had expected Mrs. Prentis to support his ego, to help him to overcome his qualms. Her contrary position had forced him into the opposing corner—that of defending his own ability to do whatever had been, or could be, thrown at him. He had developed quite an argument supporting this new thesis, his own ability, his strength. For once Mrs. Prentis had listened without any comments or even mildly bullying remarks; in fact, without a single interruption. Too late Marvin had realized that she had drawn him out, had forced him into a state of self-realization, an evaluation of his own worth. He had stopped in mid-sentence.

"There, now," had been Mrs. Prentis's mild comment. " I couldn't have put it better myself."

Days later, Marvin still blushed when he remembered that evening. He also developed a new, even higher respect for Mrs. Prentis. She had taught him to keep his guard up—though not in his old, defensive, ostrich-like manner. This new guard was a more confident, more purposeful guard. He had learned to jockey for a better position, to develop a strategy, rather as in a game of chess. This single chat with Mrs. Prentis had helped him enormously in his present work at the City Hall.

And now, Mrs. Prentis was watching him. In a way Marvin felt almost flattered. Mrs. Prentis had categorically proven her friendship; but in a certain way, she was also an admirable adversary.

Marvin was definitely quite curious.

After a full week of this cat-and-mouse game, he decided to take the bull by the horns. Not his preferred method of perfunctory procedure. After dinner, Marvin lingered until the three gentlemen had left the room. He himself then rose and helped Mrs. Prentis clear the table. In all his years at the Victorian mansion, Marvin had never helped with the dishes. At least, not voluntarily. Finally, when the familiar sounds of incessant waves breaking on a distant seashore emerged from the dishwasher, Marvin sat down and waited for Mrs. Prentis to join him. She did almost at once, her reserved smile a little uncertain—possibly disturbed by some mixed feelings. Without sitting down, she made straight for the liquor cabinet.

"Not for me, Mrs. Prentis," Marvin affirmed, seeing her raised eyebrow.

His refusal neither stopped nor slowed down her committed stride. Mrs. Prentis poured herself a generous measure of Rémi Martin and left the cabinet door open.

"In case you change your mind?"

She sat down very straight, very prim, took a tiny sip of her much-loved cognac, and waited for Marvin to start the conversation. Even without the aid of the fiery liquid, Marvin was growing bolder.

"Is there anything I can do for you, Mrs. Prentis?"

"Yes."

She regarded Marvin with a pensive, perhaps skeptical expression. To Marvin, Mrs. Prentis's features indicated that she was weighing, perhaps juggling, a number of ideas. She seemed none too sure which of them should be given precedence.

"You know, you have changed," she said at last. Her hands, usually in perfect repose on her lap, now seemed agitated as they massaged warmth into the snifter. "You have changed so much that I hardly... I hardly seem to know you..."

To his surprise, Marvin detected both sadness and pleasure in the tone of her voice. Mrs. Prentis took another sip and continued to rub the glass—almost anxiously.

"Was I so bad? Really?" Marvin kept his voice detached, as though wondering aloud.

"Yes." The moment Mrs. Prentis uttered the syllable, she wanted to withdraw her harsh judgment. "In some ways, dear boy, just in some ways..." Her attempt to lessen her previous assertion made things even worse. "Oh, I didn't mean it."

"Well, you should have meant it." Marvin had done a lot of thinking since their last discussion. "I've spent forty-seven years of my life thinking of myself, Mrs. Prentis. Forty-seven years. That must be something of a record!" There was a strange hollowness to his wry, demeaning laughter.

Mrs. Prentis remained silent.

"Yes, you should have meant it..." he repeated softly. This time his voice trailed off into silence.

"So you knew?"

"No, I didn't!" He sat up. "Not for all the years, I didn't. These are things, I suppose, one learns when one's very young. And I... and I just didn't, Mrs. Prentis."

The silence stretched as the grandfather clock patiently counted off the seconds. Mrs. Prentis continued to sit very straight. Her hands found their resting place in her lap. The snifter shimmering with golden light seemed forgotten. Marvin, in his belated insight, had expressed all that either one of them could have said. Some things one learns on one's mother's lap. Early. Very early. Marvin hadn't. There had been no lap to bestow the essence of giving to that forlorn baby. And even if there had been some early lessons, the later events had been so traumatic that Marvin contrived to virtually obliterate most memories of his childhood. Furthermore, there had been no one to consolidate any such lessons in his later years. As far back as Marvin could reach, he had always felt alone. Totally alone. He had grown up in full knowledge that if he did not look after his own wellbeing, no one else would, either. The first law of survival.

"And now?" Mrs. Prentis did not look up. She wasn't yet quite ready to meet his eyes.

"And now, I shall probably need a lot of your help."

Two lone, lugubrious tears formed, then rolled in a ludicrously slow motion down Mrs. Prentis's cheeks. She made no effort to hide them. She looked distant, detached, as though reaching into some other time altogether. After a long, pensive moment, she looked up.

"I have always been here." There was great concern in her gentle smile. There was also a sorrow. A sorrow of the long years wasted?

"It was I who was far away. Will you ever forgive me?"

"I? Forgive you?" Mrs. Prentis was visibly shaken.

"It is as you just said, Mrs. Prentis. You have always been here."

This time it was too much. Mrs. Prentis no longer remained the cool, prim, Victorian lady. She reached for her glass, and with total absence of restraint she emptied it in one sweeping motion. Almost instantly her cheeks took on a rosy glow. Whether her colour was due to the sudden inflow of cognac or to a sudden release of some heretofore-restrained emotions was of no consequence. She now looked much more her solid, reliable self.

"Are you sure you won't have one?" she asked, before she put her glass down.

"Perhaps a little port, or some dry sherry."

Marvin got up and searched inside the cabinet. He found an old-looking bottle. He was about to put it back, but Mrs. Prentis stopped him.

"That's what it's for. It has been preserved for drinking." She smiled her usual confident smile. "You know, Marvin, this is the first time in all these years that you are actually pouring a drink for yourself?"

"Another of my failings!" He looked contrite.

"May all your problems be as big and taxing!" She looked very pleased—either with herself or with her new perception of Marvin.

"Mrs. Prentis, I sense that you wanted to talk to me about something. You seemed to have kept your eye on me just a little bit more than usual." Marvin returned to the business at hand. He suspected there was still something unsaid.

"In some ways you have answered me; you told me all I really needed to know." Mrs. Prentis hesitated before continuing. "May I ask you, though, a very personal question?"

Once again the prim lady lost some of her poise. Marvin had never seen Mrs. Prentis quite so nervous.

"Surely, you needn't ask for permission, Mrs. Prentis. You are like a... " He couldn't quite say it. The word 'mother' had not crossed his lips in over forty years. "... y-you need n-never ask," he fumbled.

Mrs. Prentis' hazel eyes assumed a strangely penetrating strength. Marvin found the stare quite disturbing. She then asked in a flat, impersonal voice: "Is it your intention to see Jocelyn again?"

The glass of rich ruby port shook in Marvin's hand. Whatever question he had expected, this was not it. His sallow face paled even more. He felt as though a cold breeze just brushed his forehead.

Marvin sat up, then fell back against the back of the chair. He needed time. Not a single day had passed in the last, God knows how many, days, without his thinking about Jocelyn. How could he avoid it? Her sculpture hung in front of the armchair on which he had spent at least three hours every single day. He spent hours staring at the joyful children, at the elderly couple enjoying the intimate comfort of the touch of their frazzled hands... He saw himself as the stooping old man, Jocelyn as the wondrous, supportive, ever-present woman. He had spent hours thinking of the hands that molded this strange, enigmatic balance. The balance of the children frozen on a swing, a balance which united their springtime with the serenity of autumn. Yet there was implicit happiness radiating from both couples. Perhaps it came from the enchanted sculptor?

"Not if I am likely to hurt her again..." His voice was hardly louder than a whisper.

"Are you likely to do so?" Mrs. Prentis continued to regard him sternly.

"How can I see into the distant future?" His eyes followed his words, drifting into the corridors of time not yet charted. " I must be... I just must be more certain."

"You will never be certain." Mrs. Prentis lowered her own voice to match his.

They sat facing each other, hardly a pace apart; yet, in some ways, there seemed oceans between them. There was a hint of doubt in Mrs. Prentis's eyes. She must have wondered if she would ever bridge the abyss which Marvin had dug over so many years. Then she shook her head as though denying access to her negative thoughts.

"You must, however," she said slowly, "be quite, quite certain of your feelings toward her. If your motivation to see her is to satisfy your needs, then you are not ready. If..."

"Why do you suppose that she would want to see me?" There was unexpected hope in the tone of Marvin's voice.

"I have no idea. I do not know if Jocelyn would ever want to see you. But I do know that there is only one way to find out."

An artificial silence interrupted their conversation. The dishwashing machine's cycle had abruptly finished. Marvin got up. For a moment it seemed that he was going to say something, then he shook his head.

"Thank you, Mrs. Prentis. I'll examine carefully everything you told me." He walked to the door. He stopped again. "I cannot, I simply cannot hurt her... again," he whispered, the last word almost inaudible.

For a while Mrs. Prentis sat alone. There are moments when silence is so intense that one can hear one's own heartbeat. She seemed to savor that elusive silence. Then she looked at the clock. Perhaps it had been she who had shut out even the grandfather's shadow. By the time Mrs. Prentis got up, she had made her decision. Her trim stature was again upright, her head set straight, leading with her purposeful if delicate chin. On her lips there appeared a slight, whimsical smile. Then the smile widened. She looked at the door through which Marvin left.

"You won't, my dear boy," she muttered. "Not if I can help it."

Marvin did not try to think about the conversation downstairs. He had long ago learned that to see well into the substance of anything, of any concept, he needed to give it time. What a marvelous invention. Time, surely man's creation, had the capacity to arrange things in new perspectives, new angles of perception. It did not mean that he really didn't think about the matter so dear to him. It simply meant that he had delegated the resolution of the problem to his subconscious mind. In time, he would return to the puzzle and make a conscious judgment. Coolly, efficiently, less influenced by his emotional desires.

Marvin sank back in his deep armchair. He listened to some music, read a little more Campbell. In about twenty minutes, the book descended to his lap, his eyes closed. When they opened again, he directed them upwards, to the suspended sculpture. By an effort of will, he emptied his mind of any and every thought. He breathed deeply. He saw himself on the swing, going to and fro, to and fro...

...ubiquitous spring ...scent of the flowers, a carpet of grass, euphoria of buds bursting on the cherry tree above. The swing—an effortless pendulum... marking off segments of time... effortless: to and fro, to and fro.... A carefree smile solidifies into a girl's face, close beside him. So close.... She extends her small legs, points her toes to add more momentum. To and fro....

....*now he stands looking at her face. Her features—so familiar.... So very, very familiar? Surely he would know them, if only he could release...? What? Release what? Something to do with individuality. The woman's face turns up at him, trusting, an unspoken question hanging on her parted lips. What happened to the little girl? Can I inhale understanding from a woman's face? The meaning of time, a flow, a current... children*

merging into an older couple—both pairs contemporaneous. An
act of becoming merging into being? The two are inseparable.
They are one and the same. The two what?
    They are one and the same.
    "One day, one day..." a tiny upturned face. It has Jocelyn's
eyes. "One day?" ...a joyous smile. "Yes!" The eyes strain to
convey their emotive meaning. "Yes! The two are one. The two
are one."
    The two are one?

Marvin dreamed on and continued dreaming. Later he
sailed the great and mighty oceans, he soared above the crags of
some forgotten ranges, he extended his arms along the pointed
wings of a swooping swallow and grazed the dales filled with the
rites of springtime....
    The two are one?

The observer and the observed joined in ephemeral
oneness. Joined beyond the limits of contrived reality. Even in
his dream, Marvin's lips parted in a smile of pleasure. Great
joyous pleasure of the Idea.... of the enormous consequences of
his new perception. He felt the reassurance of the small, strong
fingers holding his own chimerical hand. He looked down at her
face. This time he recognized it fully.
    And he just smiled.

* * *

16

Meeting

Jocelyn stepped back, sighed deeply, and regarded her work. Forty-seven of her creations were all ready for hanging. All the sculptures had been appended to coloured baseboards that provided the necessary *passe par touts*. Twenty-four of them had been framed. But the baseboards were *the* missing link.

With paintings it would have been easier. The sizes of canvases were standardized. Not so with her sculptures. Jocelyn had spent hours, days, trying to find a way to fit her different, irregularly shaped sculptures into the various frames. Finally she found the means. The missing link. It was an easy matter to trim baseboards to fit the frames. In addition, the baseboards not only contributed the enriching accent colour, but supplied the means of transferring the weight of the sculpture onto the frame. And *vice versa*. Work related to the weight transfer had been much more time-consuming. The back of each relief had to be drilled, nuts and bolts inserted, then the gypsum carefully repaired with an admix of some resin for extra strength. Finally, the reliefs had been carefully bolted, at precisely the right angle of inclination, to the prepainted baseboards. Jocelyn's later sculptures would have their hanging reinforcement built in.

Jocelyn hardly believed her own eyes. It was all done!

The colour of the background invariably echoed the dominant accent colour of the sculpture itself. It strengthened it, complemented the other colours and, most of all, it gave Jocelyn full control over the immediate environment surrounding the relief. There was no need of such treatment for the larger creations. Their size alone produced powerful enough statements to dominate their surroundings. With smaller works, the wrong background—for example, flamboyant or floral wallpaper—might well have destroyed any value the delicate sculpture may have created.

Jocelyn had two more days.

Two days in which to arrange all her works in a reasonably professional manner on the extensive studio walls and on the two stands she had borrowed from the library. She had to suspend them diligently on thin but strong wires least they descended at great speeds, at inappropriately embarrassing moments, on the unsuspecting heads of her customers. Jocelyn giggled at the thought. She was rapidly approaching the point of exhaustion. She had two days in which to calm her nerves, get enough sleep, buy a few gallons of wine and prepare some kind of cheese and cracker semblance of a not too amateurish-looking preview. Her very first *vernissage*.

Bless dear, tireless Marion. She had refused to allow Jocelyn to do anything with which she could help, or that she could do herself. She was a true friend.

"If it hadn't been for you, I would be lying in tears on my still dirty floor, desperately trying to think of a way of cancelling my already announced exhibition," Jocelyn confessed as Marion finished scrubbing the floor on which her host sloppily spattered gypsum powder, splashes of wet paste and blotches of colour.

"I plead guilty but insane," Marion admitted. "But I couldn't let you opt out that easily."

In a way, it was all Marion's fault. When about a month ago Jocelyn had told her that she had been getting absolutely nowhere with the art galleries, Marion had questioned Jocelyn's need for any sales agents.

"Don't they take forty or even fifty percent right off the top from any poor novice?" Frankly, Marion had had no idea. "I wouldn't be at all surprised!"

"Surely not fifty...?" Jocelyn was impressed. She had never gotten far enough with them to find out.

"And furthermore," Marion pressed her point home, "aren't they obliged to add another small fortune in the various sales taxes to boost the price sky-high?"

So far the Federal, Provincial and the St-Onge governments had not contributed a single penny to Jocelyn's years of effort. Now, they were all ready to dip their fetid, rapacious fingers into her regal banquet; to gobble up her exhausted, at this stage very nervous, pounds of flesh.

"I suppose so...?" Jocelyn voice sounded crestfallen. She had enough trouble without Marion's stabbing her in the back.

"Listen!"

There followed a long tirade, which sounded as though Marion had thought of nothing else during the last few months. She had convinced Jocelyn that her studio was a nearly ideal place for holding an exhibition.

"What could be more attractive to a prospective buyer than the opportunity to meet the artist in her very own studio? Would you not like to visit other artists to see the environment in which they worked? Not just sculptors, but painters, and composers, even authors and poets and aspiring designers?" Marion sounded triumphant.

The next day the two friends had spent the evening designing the announcements. The posters were restricted to the maximum size that could be printed on Marion's computer: fourteen inches by any length desired. More than enough. The following day Marion had brought sample copies. That evening it had been settled. The posters suggested: *"...what you should buy yourself for Easter that all your friends might also enjoy."* A self-centered sales pitch, which Jocelyn had picked up and adapted from the knowledgeable accountants of the professional galleries. It implied that you might do well by doing good. Or something to that effect. Then came the punch line that read:

"You do your own evaluation!"

Within two days, the posters had decorated the walls all over St-Onge as well as in four of Montreal's major office towers. Marion had also squeezed them into five shopping centers, four church halls, and a dozen other assorted places.

The dice had been cast!

Jocelyn had worked like a destitute immigrant on an expiring temporary visa. She had lost over five pounds by the sheer intensity of her labour. She had not only prepared all sculptures for the exhibition, but had added four new ones, apparently an inner compulsion that would not be denied. On evenings and on weekends, Marion practically moved in with her. She prepared Jocelyn gallons of black coffee, made sure she ate properly, forced her to take some rest.

Now, with two days left, the job was almost finished.

At 5:30 p.m., Marion arrived with two medium-size pizzas—an unenviable staple, a compromise for the moment. She set herself immediately to the job of wiring and hanging. In the meantime Jocelyn, in her own handwriting, added little notes, suggestions of a title for each and every sculpture. The note also stated the number of hours it had taken her to complete every single exhibit. There was no mention of money. The prospective customers would be told how long it took Jocelyn to buy the materials, to prepare the original clay sculpture, to make a complex rubberoid molding, to prepare and make the wire reinforcing, pour the final casting, add the final touches to the sculpture, add colour and patina staining, prepare the colour background, the frames and the... hanging.

It was up to the customer to propose the price.

There had been an additional small note added to the major sculptures. If the buyer were to insist on the original mold or casting's being destroyed, he had to pay double for whatever price he or she deemed fair and equitable.

By ten-thirty at night the work was finished. The framed sculptures were all hanging; the others were disposed in an interesting manner on the black-painted stands. The stickers were all pinned or glued under every exhibit. One whole day, the Thursday, albeit only after work, had been reserved for rest. A rest and the preparation of cheese and crackers. The two weary friends were delighted. They opened a bottle of wine, sang an off-key duet from Madama Butterfly, and giggled with or without any reason.

They were in a state of imminent collapse.

Right at the beginning of this horrendous effort, Marion had decided to launch the *vernissage* on a Friday. During summer or winter, this would not have been a good idea. Too many people would have left for their country cottages. This time of the year, however, it was already too late for skiing, and much, much too early for a dip in the Laurentian waters. Hopefully, people were looking for an intelligent diversion.

And a free drink.

On the big day, Jocelyn left the library at noon. She felt she had to be home to perform the final touches, to cross all the T's, to water her numerous plants, sweep the floor (again). At three-thirty, completely out of the blue, her father, Mr. John Prentis, arrived. There was some very emotional sniffling. Jocelyn had no idea that he would come all the way from his beloved cottage on the Georgian Bay. She had had no intention of even telling him about her attempt at an exhibition.

Somewhat to her nervous surprise, John Prentis made some knowledgeable comments about her reliefs. At sixty-seven, without ever letting her know, her father had started painting. That was some three years ago, after he'd moved to the Georgian Bay. He (and another widower, for company) had been fed up. John Prentis was among the many thousands who were fed up with the constant strife and bickering of Quebec's politicians. He referred to them as "the pompous parasites", who fostered a permanent state of dissatisfaction—first with the language issues, then with the purported exploitation of the 'poor' *Québecois* by the Rest of Canada, by anyone who ever spoke any English, by the whole world. According to Jocelyn's father, those at the helm *created* the general atmosphere of discontent. He had once said that he was too old to live among people who only asked what they could get—not give to the rest of the country. Mr. Prentis was born and raised in Quebec. It was home for his family for four generations. In recent years, he had been made to feel like an intruder.

One day he packed his bags and quietly moved out.

At seventy, John Prentis looked great. Not the proverbial 'half' his age, but a goodly portion of years less than his completely gray hair implied. Evidently, there was something in the combination of country living, fresh air, pristine beauty of nature, and creative endeavour that agreed with him. His features beamed health, contentment, a feeling of profound, relaxed serenity. The traits which, until quite recently, Jocelyn had radiated herself. Now his presence made her remember, made her relax. Those virtues, if virtues they be, seemed inherent in him. Inborn, rather than acquired. He had always considered himself a very lucky man. Without saying a word on the subject, he imparted a feeling of contentment, of being lucky. Jocelyn breathed easier. Her father's inner peace was contagious.

John Prentis, with Jocelyn's permission, made some subtle adjustments to the lighting; and he lent his hand in a few, seemingly peripheral details of Jocelyn's concern. He even filled sixty plastic glasses with red and white wine.

He made himself useful.

And then came that peculiar, seemingly impossible moment. Almost to Jocelyn's consternation, the preview, the long-awaited *vernissage*, was ready.

John Prentis took Jocelyn by the arm and led her to the settee. He practically had to push her down. She sat fidgeting like a schoolgirl waiting for her first date. Her father then walked to the other end of the room, picked up two glasses of white wine and brought them to the debutante nervously twiddling her thumbs.

"You will stay here until I tell you to get up. Is that understood?"

Mr. Prentis stuck out his meager chest in a show of commanding masculinity.

"Yes, Daddy."

Mr. Prentis seemed genuinely taken aback by his daughter's evidently rare show of equanimity. They both laughed. It helped. It released some of the built-up tension. Nor for long, though.

After two hectic months, *there was nothing to do!*

Father proudly regarded his daughter's handiwork. He asked her a few innocent questions, but Jocelyn was too nervous to indulge in any intelligent conversation. John Prentis left her on the settee, walked up to the small table where Jocelyn had placed the sheets listing her works, some biographical notes about herself, and an open book in which she hoped the guests would contribute their comments. He picked up a ball pen and wrote:

"This is my daughter's work and I am very, very proud of her. She is also a great sculptor."

He signed, very legibly: John Prentis, father. He then picked up two self-adhesive red stars, walked to the south wall and pinned them on two of the framed sculptures. He then wrote his initials on each star. They were Jocelyn's first sales. They were also her first tears of joy in quite some time. She wiped them on her father's lapels.

At 5:30 Marion arrived with two extra gallons of wine.

"Just thought I would play it safe."

She had never met Mr. Prentis. He took to her immediately. Within ten minutes she was invited to visit him in the Georgian Bay.

"I'll have you know, young lady, that you are the first maiden to ever have been invited to our den of iniquity. You are very lucky that you'll have a chaperon in the person of George, my buddy, and a dirty old man in his own right." Mr. Prentis gave Marion as lecherous a look as his kindly, benevolent features permitted.

Punctually at six o'clock, all six employees of Jocelyn's library filed, one after the other, into the studio. They were led by their director, Mr. James Robinson. That made nine people present. The place continued to look completely empty. Only then did Jocelyn realize the size of her workshop. She had already forgotten the milling hordes who had invaded her domain at the housewarming party.

About fifteen minutes later, people began to trickle in. In groups and in couples, all happily reaching for the glasses of wine, then moving toward the walls and around the stands, looking, drinking, admiring, and most of all—talking. Seemingly, all at once. By seven, a continuous, steady hum filled the studio. About forty people were actively passing their comments on the exhibits, on the studio, on the state of the economy, politics and the weather. At 7:30 Marvin came in.

As might well have been expected, Marvin had Mrs. Prentis firmly attached to his left arm. They were followed by Colonel Mackenzie Whittlaw and the inseparable Messrs. Graves and Johnson. Mr. Jones, the intrepid globetrotter, had already returned from Rio, but the rigors of travel and the attendant climatic changes had left him feeling a bit under the weather.

Apparently guided by a sixth sense, John Prentis came immediately to take possession of his sister. Marion inserted her arm under the Colonel's elbow and led him to the wine table. Mr. Graves and Mr. Johnson had already disappeared into the crowd. In the midst of some forty-odd people, Jocelyn had been left alone, facing Marvin. Completely alone. Their eyes met and held. No words were spoken. They stood, looked, studied, inquired. All without a word.

"Could I offer you a glass of wine?"

To Jocelyn's surprise, it was Marvin who spoke first. Instinctively she smiled.

"White or red?" he asked. He seemed in perfect control of his vocal cords.

"How are you, Marvin?" she asked, still looking into his eyes.

There was another brief moment of silence. A few seconds, a century or two. No matter. It had been three whole months. Long winter months.

"I missed you," Marvin's eyes said it all; he only confirmed.

Then, some of his newly acquired poise was gone. He looked more like his old self—shy, a little lost, invisible.

"I'm so glad you let me come," he said, very quietly.

"Why wouldn't I?" Was there a shade of anger in her voice? "It's an open house, you know?"

"I brought you these..."

Only then did Jocelyn notice a large package hanging down from Marvin's left hand. Curiosity prevailed. She opened the package and caught her breath. It was a bunch of those incredible orchids she had found in her studio on her return from Florida. This was too much. Her vision blurred. She spun on her heel and ran out to the kitchen. Marvin remained riveted to the floor. She found him standing there some five minutes later.

"They are very beautiful."

She was in control again. She faced him, holding the same vase he had once used for the orchids himself. Her face was framed by the delicate, exotic blooms, her eyes still misty but smiling. She looked incredibly radiant.

"So are you." Hardly more than a whisper.

Jocelyn smiled her old smile. Old? Ageless. Her father's smile.

"Come, I have a surprise for you."

In a matter-of-fact manner Jocelyn took Marvin by the arm and led him toward the sitting area. She carefully placed the vase on the low table. Then she turned to her father.

"Dad, I want you to meet a friend of mine. Marvin Clark. Marvin, this is my father."

The men shook hands—John Prentis with a relaxed, firm but easy handshake, Marvin with just a touch of tension. He wondered whether Mr. Prentis had noticed.

"You are not responsible for these, are you, Sir?" Mr. Prentis asked, pointing at the orchids, looking at Marvin.

"I'm afraid I am," Marvin confessed.

"Afraid?" The older man squinted. "Afraid???" His voice rose with the question mark in utter disbelief.

Mr. Prentis watched Jocelyn from the corner of his eye. There was a subtle change in her. Was it happiness? He faced Marvin again and cleared his throat:

"So you are Marvin Clark, are you?"

At this, Mrs. Prentis, who had remained sitting throughout all this interchange, spoke for the first time in a level, no-nonsense voice:

"Sit down, John!"

Mr. Prentis sat down. As far as Mrs. Prentis knew, John Prentis had absolutely no idea who Marvin Clark was. He certainly had not learned it from her, and she doubted very much Jocelyn had had a chance or inclination to say anything.

"Would you get me some more wine, please, Marvin?" Mrs. Prentis's glass on the low table, still quite full, was ignored by all.

Jocelyn looked flustered. "Oh, dear, Marvin hasn't had any himself, yet. Come, let me serve you. After all, I am the hostess."

They left together, her arm interlaced under his. Mrs. Prentis's eyes followed them until the milling crowd swallowed them from view. She nodded very slowly, perhaps in silent affirmation. Her smile held a touch of whimsy, then grew in quiet confidence.

"Who is this Marvin?" John Prentis broke into her thoughts.

"You would be surprised..."

Mrs. Prentis answered before she was aware that she had spoken aloud. For a moment John appeared lost, though he soon recovered. He waved his finger at his sister.

"You're up to your little games?" He peered intensely into Mrs. Prentis's steady eyes. "Well? Are you?"

Once, a long time ago, he and his sister had played games of love and marriage. Jenny was thirteen years younger than he, yet he felt sure she had had something to do with his marrying Jocelyn's mother. John had never told his sister how grateful he was for the part Jenny had played in his life.

"I beg your pardon? Really, John, you should know better!" Mrs. Prentis was at her most prim and proper.

"Granted. Now, Jenny, tell me about Marvin." Back to square one.

There was a moment of silence. John did not push. If there was anything between his daughter and the young, relatively young, man, he wanted to know. He was prepared to wait.

"It's rather a long story." Mrs. Prentis felt uneasy. "Could we leave it till later?"

Mrs. Prentis had never imagined that one day she might have to give an account of her actions concerning this young couple. For, in her mind, they were categorically a couple, even if they didn't know it themselves. Yet. Now she was called upon to report on the two people closest to her heart. John had a right to know. She had no idea how to tell him.

"How long will you stay with us?" she asked.

"How long will you have me?"

"You can sleep in my living room. The settee is quite comfortable. I have slept there myself," she offered.

"Thank you, sister. And thank you for letting me know about this." He made a large circle with his arms, embracing the whole studio.

The time passed quickly. New people came in, some had already left. The wine flowed, the little red stars appeared next to about fifteen sculptures. Marvin asked Jocelyn to give him a guided tour. He had seen most of the sculptures before, but then they had been neither mounted nor framed. Marvin's first reaction to Jocelyn's presentation was not very favourable. He kept it to himself. Then the idea grew on him. By the time they finished the tour, he was sold on the colour and on the idea of framing.

"Mind if I say something?" he asked, almost shyly.

"I'd never forgive you if you didn't!" Jocelyn was herself again.

Marvin looked again at some of the framed sculptures from a distance, his brow a little furrowed, his dark eyes smoldering dots of concentration. Then he nodded to himself.

"Is one allowed to reframe them?" he asked.

"Only if you buy them first!"

"Then I'll take the rest of them."

There was not a trace of humour in his voice. Jocelyn looked up at him, still expecting some sort of a joke to follow. None did.

"I would expect a small discount, of course. I believe it is customary in such cases." Marvin continued to look at the sculptures lined up on the walls and on the two stands.

"That's not very funny, Marvin." Jocelyn sounded hurt. "Why do you think that I won't sell them tomorrow or on Sunday?"

"Oh, I am quite sure that you will. That is why I made my offer today."

"I believe you are serious..." Jocelyn was studying his face.

"I am."

"But why?" She looked and felt quite flabbergasted.

"I have never invested any capital in anything in my life. If you already sold, and I counted, sixteen sculptures in—he looked at his watch—just over two hours, on your first exhibition, then you are probably the best investment going. I shall keep the best works for myself, and wait until the others rise in price. Do you mind?"

Suddenly, Marvin looked concerned. Whatever happened, he did not want to hurt her feelings. My God, never, never again!

Jocelyn continued to study his face as he was talking. Then she shook her head.

"I am sorry, Marvin. That wouldn't be fair to people who have been told that the studio will be open throughout the weekend. Assuming, of course, that anyone will come!" She smiled, but her face did not register excessive confidence.

"I understand." The matter was finished. "What about the reframing?"

"I already answered that," she said coyly.

Marvin asked Jocelyn to excuse him for a moment and directed himself to the small reception table. There he picked up

four red stars. He knew exactly what he wanted. There wasn't a
trace of hesitation in his step or in the selection of the sculptures
of his choice. He initialed the four stars. Jocelyn;s eyes followed
his movements through the milling crowd. About fifty people,
right now. He returned to her side.

"You didn't have to do that," she said, her voice both
pleased and uncertain.

"Of course I didn't. You are not going to refuse me the
sales, are you?"

"No. On one condition, though. On the condition that you
will tell me why you selected those particular reliefs." She
looked stern, but her voice was almost pleading.

"Tomorrow, about lunchtime?"

"That would be very nice."

Suddenly the whole exhibition became less important. The
weeks, months of work seemed forgotten, insignificant. Jocelyn
looked at the milling people. So many nameless faces. Some, if
not most, here merely to pass the time. It did not seem to matter.
She looked up at Marvin, still trying to read his eyes. She gave
him yet another disarming smile.

Old habits die hard. Marvin did his best to look detached.
He felt as though waves of hot air rose from his heart and rushed
upwards to his ears, his face, his head.

"Yes, that could be rather nice," he agreed.

And then he needed to sit down.

* * *

17

Becoming

To be or—*what* to be, that was the pressing question.

No outrageous fortune had been accumulated, but a tidy little profit she had made. Out of forty-seven sculptures, Jocelyn had sold thirty-two. Of the fifteen reliefs left behind, eleven seemed a little sad in subject matter. They were good sculptures, but she could not really blame her customers for not wanting to look, day in and day out, at something sad. Four reliefs were either too large, or would have proven too expensive for private collectors. She had learned her lesson. The prices had been related directly to the earnings of any one buyer. If you earned ten dollars an hour, you paid ten dollars for every hour Jocelyn had spent on your selected sculpture. If you earned twenty, you paid her twenty. Time plus expenses. The latter have been kept down to a minimum. Jocelyn had also limited her compensation to a maximum twenty-five dollars per hour.

"I believe it's only fair," she had told Marvin. "Otherwise, judging by your meteoric rise to fame, soon you would not be able to afford me!"

All calculations had been based on mutual trust.

What now? According to Marvin, she ought to have a short and snappy farewell party at the library, and start doing what she was always, according to him, supposed to have been doing for years. According to herself, she ought to collapse on a soft bed and sleep for about ten or twenty years. In peace. Alone.

To be—or not to be... a sculptor?

Not a question of life and death, but of living and dying. To continue in her present, pleasant semi-vegetative state of relative ease and comfort, or to become a channel for the Creative Spirit? Did her success merely reward her efforts or did it demand a commitment? Could it be that the Vibrant Force she felt flowing through her fingers found her a useful outlet for Its ends? Or had she already served the useful purpose for which she had been intended and now she ought to go back to the kitchen... oops, to the library, where she belonged.

What was that question?

Last week, Jocelyn had asked Marvin what had led him, at her *vernissage*, to select the particular four sculptures. The next day, on Saturday, they couldn't talk. Marvin had come as promised, but there had not been a sufficient number of people to create their own momentum. Jocelyn had been obliged to act as a dutiful hostess. She had chatted to the prospective customers, to those merely curious, to others who had stupid questions to ask.

"Why were the sculptures not painted completely, all over?" One gracious lady inquired. "Was it an indigent scarcity of paint, or... artistic license?"

Coming from her lips, the word license sounded, at best, like some contagious, malignant idiosyncrasy. Jocelyn had only just managed to restrain herself from commenting that, contrary to her sculptures, the lady's face suffered not from a scarcity but rather from a pretentious plethora of paint.

Marvin had passed the time with John Prentis, who had been glad of the company. Mr. Prentis gave an impression of being a little flustered at having learned virtually nothing about Marvin. He had found Marvin ostensibly pleasant, well-spoken, knowledgeable on a diversity of subjects, erudite if a trifle pedantic, even communicative. Marvin, according to Mr. Prentis, had expressed many an original viewpoint, some quite contrary to popular, accepted trends or opinions. Yet throughout their chat, Marvin hadn't said a single word about himself. So far, Mr. Prentis had learned from Jocelyn that Marvin worked at the City Hall. Marvin had not denied it, but had failed to tell Mr Prentis what precisely was his function.

"To be honest, Mr. Prentis, I couldn't really say...?"

The question had been posed like a subject not worthy of discussion. When prodded, Marvin repeated that he did not precisely know. To this day, John Prentis was not sure whether Marvin had been joking or not.

By Sunday, Jocelyn was exhausted. Not so much physically, although long hours on her feet had been taxing. She was debilitated emotionally. On top of the customers trying her patience with an avalanche of quite inane questions, there was the sudden appearance of her father. Mr. Prentis hadn't left her for more than six or seven hours a day, or rather night, to catch some sleep at Aunt Jenny's. Jocelyn loved her father very much. She had also grown used to solitude. Having lived alone since she was seventeen did entrench certain habits—little things, not noticeable under normal circumstances, but missed dearly when suddenly taken away.

And then, there was Marvin.

Although Jocelyn could not define it in any precise way, Marvin seemed a different man. Hardly possible after only three months, she mused. Different, yet the same. It was rather like looking at a familiar tree in your garden, but from a different side, from a different angle. So many branches, leaves, nuances of reflection. Could it be that it was she who had changed? If Marvin was the same, then there seemed so much more of him. Was it a new depth, new confidence, new... maturity? Surely, not in three months! All his new traits must have been present in him before. Perhaps the protective screens he had erected around himself had kept facets of his personality hidden, not only from her but from himself? Perhaps he had forgotten himself that they existed within him.

Jocelyn had seen so little of Marvin, she didn't even know whether she liked what she saw. Marvin had been an enigma when she met him, an enigma he remained. Only a different one. All this Jocelyn found emotionally draining. Why did he continue to invade her thoughts?

Jocelyn's father left on Tuesday morning. He needed a full day to drive home. The hugs and promises to keep in touch more often, by letter or by phone, lasted only a few minutes. John Prentis appeared suddenly—he left almost as fast. He loved his daughter but was well aware that she needed and deserved her privacy. Her own time and space. He drove back in his battered old Plymouth, loaded with sandwiches, a thermos full of black coffee and two of his daughter's sculptures.

There was another unexpected problem. Although up to the time of the exhibition most of her sculptures had been kept in crates, Jocelyn found parting with them unnerving. The fact that she had retained the negative molds of most of them didn't help. The moulds were like coffins. Unless she breathed new life into them, Lazarus would remain a shell devoid of spirit.

Her sculptures were her children. She had once given them birth. Often protracted, painful. She had watched them mature—and now, leave home. She knew they had to. The children deserved to have a home of their own. Yet, somehow...

Jocelyn had said a furtive goodbye to each and every one of them. On some she had shed a silent tear. They were her memories.

Why were goodbyes always so difficult?

By the time Jocelyn returned from work on Tuesday, her father, the ever-helpful Marion, and thirty-two sculptures were gone. She sat alone, unable to work, unable or unwilling to read. Even television failed to provide any diversion. She felt like going out, like being away from her studio. She had spent too much time there lately. The place had become emotionally supercharged. It needed a sort of psychic airing. And then the telephone rang. She wanted to let it ring. She did not want any more clients. Not tonight. In five minutes it rang again. With resignation she picked it up. It was Marvin.

"Have you rested any, yet?" he asked.

"Take me out," she replied.

"Any preferences?"

"Yes, somewhere where I will not see any sculptures."

"I'll be there at six." He hung up.

Marvin showered, shaved again, then ran down to Mrs. Prentis to tell her, belatedly, that he would not be able to make it to supper. He was sorry to give her so little notice. It had been quite unavoidable, he assured.

" 'bout time," Mrs. Prentis muttered, over her shoulder.

"Boat time, Mrs. Prentis?"

"Have a good time," Mrs. Prentis admonished with a grave voice.

Marvin didn't pursue the subject, but he couldn't imagine how Mrs. Prentis knew that he was in a position to have a good time. He went back upstairs, finished dressing. A gray Harris Tweed jacket with freshly pressed pants, a white shirt with slightly starched collar, and a matching tie and breast-pocket hankie. Pretty old-fashioned. He then applied a liberal amount of *eau de cologne*. He knew that three-quarters of the scent would be gone by the time he arrived at Jocelyn's studio. The mirror gave him a grudging approval.

"Wish me luck, Monster!"

Marvin ran all the way down the stairs, two steps at a time. A thought crossed his mind that the last time he risked his neck in this manner was when he was seventeen, or thereabouts. He had very nearly lost his balance on the penultimate step. This, in turn, reminded him of their first meeting. Marvin felt young, fresh. He felt like taking a risk—a hitherto unknown feeling. Quite unknown. He hailed a taxi, whistled an old tune on the way, and asked the driver to wait at her door. At six, he pressed Jocelyn's doorbell.

"Look, no flowers. Not enough notice." Marvin raised both hands, exposing his empty palms. "I've kept the cab waiting."

"Forgiven."

As always, Jocelyn greeted him with a smile. The same mouth, teeth... eyes? Not the same sparkle. Jocelyn was tired. It showed in her eyes, in the lack of bounce in her step as she retreated to don her light spring coat. She was out in seconds. Marvin studied her along the few steps from her door to the waiting taxi. She wore no makeup, at least none that he could see. He wondered for the thousandth time what it was that made her so attractive. Olive Gascon had good features and made twice the effort to look her best; presumably, at least in part, to please him. But Jocelyn was Jocelyn. She was what she was. And whatever that was seemed infinitely more than any woman he had ever met. She embodied the traits which he, over the years, had found attractive in a dozen different women. Both physical and otherwise. It was just that those other women were given those traits one at a time. Jocelyn combined, harmonized, integrated them into a single, cohesive whole. Individually they were attractive as qualities. In Jocelyn they blossomed into an entity where the whole seemed so much greater than the sum of all the parts. An old adage embodied.

"Any preference?" Marvin asked when they reached the taxi.

"You decide." She leaned back in the seat and half-closed her eyes. "Take me away from all this!" she added in a serious voice.

Marvin had no previous experience of taking anyone away from anything.

"Driver, would you take us to *Les Pêcheurs* restaurant in *Jacques Cartier*?"

"*A Montréal, monsieur?*" That would be quite a drive.

Marvin had read a write-up about that particular restaurant only last Saturday. It had been given more stars than seemed possible. Five. Marvin did not recall eating in any *fruits de mer* establishment that sported more stars than others had courses. He was glad his last promotion carried a considerable increment in his income. He was even more glad of the latter after he saw the gilt- edged menu. The edges must have been cast in twenty-four carat gold. Four months ago Marvin would have collapsed from shock.

Jocelyn refused to participate in any decision-making.

They sipped *Kir* while waiting for *hors d'oeuvres*. Smoked salmon salad was followed by Alaskan Crab. To further titillate their respective palates, Marvin ordered a bottle of *Puilly-Fuissé*. The wine was chilled to perfection. At least, Marvin thought so. He seldom drank wine costing a quarter of the price. Tonight, he simply didn't care. If he didn't like it, he would simply send it back.

The food was superb. Already after the delicious pink, tangy salmon, Jocelyn's eyes were beginning to recover a little of their glitter. The Alaskan Crab finished, the delicate bouquet of the pale golden wine teasing her nose, Jocelyn recovered completely. Evidently her weariness had not been physical. At the time, Marvin did not know that no woman ever feels tired in the best restaurant in town. Not after a delicate and superb dinner served between high flickering flames, statuesque in silver candelabras. In the background, a discreet pianist flirted with the ivory keys in a most seductive manner. Jocelyn took it all in stride, as if she did this sort of thing daily, for more years than she cared to remember.

Jocelyn was definitely a woman.

The *maître d'* came and offered Marvin an oversized, evidently choice cigar from a richly encrusted silver box. Marvin declined but asked for coffee, *Cointreau* and Peach Melba. For both. The *maître d'hôtel* passed the order to the attending waiters and promptly withdrew.

Jocelyn again said nothing.

Throughout dinner they spoke about practically nothing. A precious little about the zest of springtime, about the warming weather, a little about the English-language by-laws, about the purported drain of money from Quebec caused by the chauvinistic restrictions. It did not matter. The words they had both spoken had been no more than pawns in a game of waiting. Then Jocelyn reminded Marvin of his promise to tell her what had motivated his choice of her sculptures.

"There is little to say. I simply looked and listened. That's all," he said.

"And?" she insisted.

"That's about all." He sipped his *Cointreau.* "Every work of art has a certain resonance. When that resonance strikes your own, that resonance or vibration which is within you, a bond is established. Then, if you can, or want to, you buy it."

Marvin's tone suggested that he had been talking about the most obvious, most evident matter. He sounded a little surprised that Jocelyn had asked. There followed the first short silence since they had come in. That only happens when people start listening to each other. Not just talking.

"Is that true of all the arts...?" Jocelyn mused aloud. " I mean, regardless of quality?"

Marvin didn't answer at once. Years had passed since he had read James Joyce. Originally, not all Marvin's opinions on art had been his own. Some he had borrowed, adopted from others. It took years of reading and thinking to establish his own views. Yet even now he recalled some of his more favourite authors.

"Yes and no. Every work of art which is the result of a creative endeavor does, or at least can, strike a chord with the recipient. The question is what chord. It, the work, may motivate you to action, to love or hate, may stir or invoke emotions within you that will galvanize you to do things you wouldn't otherwise do. There are different forms of artistic expression affecting, obviously, different people in different ways." Marvin studied the flickering candle flame reflected in his glass.

"And what were you motivated to do by my art?" Jocelyn's eyes were drawn to the same flicker dancing in Marvin's pupils.

"Nothing." He continued to study the flame.

"Nothing? Then you do not classify my efforts as art."

Jocelyn sounded offended and hurt. She loved listening to him when he opened his mind and heart to her. In such moments, all the old barriers seemed to retreat, become nonexistent. Marvin smiled. He looked away from the candle. He gazed into her eyes.

"If they did motivate me into action, I would not have bought any," he asserted.

"Then..."

"Then, perhaps I look for things different from what most people do. My whole life is an expression of action. Not so much physical as mental. Essentially mental. Lately," he momentarily lowered his eyes, "also emotional."

Then, even as moths are drawn to a moving flame, Marvin's eyes drifted again to the candle. He seemed to be organizing his thoughts. Jocelyn waited until he was ready.

"Of all these," he resumed, "the mental activity, the mental inner noise is the hardest to still. Yet one must do so in order to hear the... the inner voice. What does your sculpture do for me? It helps me to still that mental commotion, that... constant, unrelenting turmoil. To stop thinking, to still my mind, is by far the most difficult thing I ever attempted to do."

The silence lasted again a few moments. Jocelyn played with the corner of her napkin. Then, without looking up, she said quietly: "Thank you."

"Would you care for some more coffee?"

The sterling silver jug was standing all alone on their table. The question was superfluous. The waiter responded to Jocelyn's smile and Marvin's nod. He left quietly. Then the haze of candlelight, or perhaps of shadow, enclosed them once more. The other Epicureans dissolved, their voices merging into a single, monotonous hum. They were alone again.

"What do you want to be?" she asked.

"That is the question. I do not know." There was no humor in Marvin's voice. "After years of apostate, vacuous existence, so many things happened in my life, in relatively quick succession, that I feel a little at sea. I need time to sort myself out. You understand?"

Even as he asked, he classified his question as redundant. She reached out across the table and covered his hand with hers. Neither he nor she needed words to expand on this gesture.

"To be or—what to be," she murmured.

"*Who* to be. What is relatively easy. I have few ambitions in that area."

Anyone watching them would probably imagine that they were bored with each other. Every few moments, they would stop talking and look into the flame or some distant, unreachable shores, listening to the rote of the incessant surf. To Jocelyn and to Marvin, those very same moments were the closest; the silent communion which welded strange, invisible strands of unconditional, undemanding golden threads between them.

"You know... I spent years trying to escape life. I was convinced that by stepping within my own inner consciousness I would be relieved of any responsibility for whatever happens in the mundane, the prosaic, the worldly. I completely forgot that, inasmuch as ultimately one is responsible solely for one's own development, one can only develop oneself by interaction with others. In fact, it is only when the barriers of one's ego drop that we can experience the foreshadow of that portentous mystery. A hint of that sublime merging of the micro- and the macrocosm..."

Marvin looked at Jocelyn as if seeing her for the first time.

"I wouldn't be at all surprised if you and I did not constitute fragments of a larger, as yet incomprehensible organism. What else could possibly explain the irresistible drawing, the magnetic..." he suddenly stopped and reached for his coffee.

Jocelyn did not interrupt. She listened as much to his words as to the things he'd left unsaid. She had never really been troubled by the stream of thoughts that seemed to be churning in Marvin's mind or heart. Whenever she felt frustrated by the twists and turns of her fortune, she bought an airline ticket in an unspecified direction and would come back refreshed, or at least having forgotten the reason for her departure. Then she had met Marvin. Now she, too, asked herself: "What do I want to be, or, as he said—who?" Somehow, such questions had never bothered her before. She was a very practical woman. She had the intuitive heart of an artist, but her thoughts were more down to earth.

"Is it enough to decide that I will, or will not, become a sculptor?" she asked.

"That will decide what you are, not who," he answered.

"What then? Why do I feel, ah... unsettled?"

"The problem is, whether you make an actual, conscious decision or not, you already are a sculptor. The 'what' die has been cast. Now, to find inner peace, to sate that certain hunger, you must decide on the 'who'."

"I am not even sure I understand what you mean."

Jocelyn looked at Marvin, her eyes oceans of hope—vast, unexplored oceans, asking for help. He smiled his understanding.

"This is a case of the blind leading the blind. But let me try to explain. Every human being is an absolutely unique creation. If there are no two identical blades of grass on this verdant earth of ours, how much more unique are we, countless millions of swirling atoms held together by forces we cannot even begin to understand. The scientists may have even developed names for them, for these energies or forces. But they are just about as ignorant as we are. Our job, it seems to me, is to at least attempt to discover who we are. We can achieve this by trying to find out what makes us unique, different and therefore indispensable in this vast cosmos. It is an ongoing process of self-discovery. I always thought that we could find this out by going within, by stepping into our subconscious mind and shutting the door. Well, we have to do that, too, but only for the purpose of finding out how to apply what we have learned within to the outer, the so-called objective world."

"Why would that be so very important? Can we not just be?" Jocelyn's voice sounded disarmingly innocent.

"Of course! That is the ultimate secret."

"What is?"

"How to *just be*."

It could have been the wine, or the *Kir*, or both, but Jocelyn thought that what Marvin was saying began to sound much too esoteric. What is so difficult about 'just being'? Is that not what everyone does? Are we not all just being? And then Marvin ruined it all again with a single question:

"If it's so easy to 'just be', why do so many of us try to stop others from just being?"

"Or from being just."

"Or even from becoming?" Marvin added.

"Take me home," she said.

The previous fatigue began to catch up with her. Jocelyn decided to save the world some other time. The dinner was over, as were all the arguments. Their mutual becoming had only just began.

* * *

18

The Rainbow

Mr. John B. Dawson, of Morris, Jordan and Dawson, Inc., the renowned music publishers and manuscript antiquarians of the highest repute, was extremely agitated. Nervous, to say the least, for a whole week. His last contact with Marvin Clark had been eminently embarrassing. Mr. Dawson, at his own expense, had invited Marvin to attend the world premiere of the *Poème Symphonique*, in Cincinnati, Ohio, and his generosity had landed him in a very confounding situation. Mr. Dawson recalled the incident as though it had happened only yesterday.

After the introductory speeches celebrating not only the world premiere of his newly discovered manuscript (attributed, through his unerring expertise, to Jean Sibelius) but also the opening gala of a brand-new concert hall, Mr. Dawson had returned to his front-row seat. There, in the adjacent stall, which he had personally reserved for Mr. Clark, Mr. Dawson had found an uncouth-looking stranger sitting, or rather sprawling, all over the elegant, prestigious seat. *In the Front Row.* Imagine!

Mr. Dawson had always known exactly what to do with such gate crashers.

He hailed an usher and, quietly but firmly, with appropriate dignity, demanded that the offensive presence be removed from his vicinity. There were only minutes left before Sir Arthur Bang would bid the orchestra to rise for the historic, first bow. Luckily, the ominous creature must have known his station. The man rose quietly and left with the usher. Mr. Dawson breathed a contented sigh of relief. He had done his duty.

To Mr. Dawson's unimaginable chagrin, the aberrant individual returned within seconds and prostrated himself, again, in the adjacent seat. This time Mr. Dawson took matters into his own hands. He raised himself to his full five foot five stature, pointed his ferret features at the derelict individual, and advised him in unmistakable terms that, unless he made himself very scarce within the next ten seconds, he would have him thrown out of the theatre.

Mr. Dawson's controlled voice was well used to giving orders. Thus, at the precise moment when the auditorium lights dimmed with the attendant hush, Mr. Dawson's precisely enunciated command was heard by not less than three to four hundred people. What followed, Mr. Dawson recalled as an ignominious agony.

He, John Benjamin Dawson, had been hushed!

Mr. Dawson had sat down, his blood boiling, his pride at an all-time low. During the first intermission he learned that the individual on his immediate right was the possessor of the requisite ticket to occupy the adjacent stall with impunity. Mr. Dawson resigned himself to put it squarely on the shoulders of the inexperienced staff, whose teething problems would take some time to overcome. Rather than pursue the matter, Mr. Dawson preferred to withhold the incident from Marvin, who may well have been given the wrong ticket by the inept sales agents.

The incident, however, resulted in a permanent scar on Mr. Dawson's modest self-esteem. He developed a pathological apprehension, bordering on acute anxiety, at the very idea of Marvin's presence. The fact that it had not been Marvin's presence, but rather his absence, which had precipitated the Cincinnati fiasco, was neither here nor there. Pathological phobias are not supposed to be logical. Mr. Dawson could write to Mr. Clark, treat him with all due decorum, engage in complex business negotiations with him, but—at a goodly distance.

And there lay the problem.

Mr. Dawson could either advise Mr. Clark about the forthcoming recording session at which the *Poème Symphonique* was to be electronically immortalized, or he could go to Toronto himself to deliver the fascinating story, which would be imprinted on the jacket of the CD. The fascinating story would be passed on to the deserving world, the saga of Mr. Dawson's discovery of the elusive manuscript to the utter, incredulous surprise of its ignorant possessor, and of Mr. Dawson's resultant, generous gift to the world of music. Nay, to humanity. He also needed to sign some documents relating to the royalties of which he was to receive the usual percentage.

To invite or not to invite Mr. Clark. That was the question. A week of anxiety, of agitation, of nerve-racking quandary.

Mr. Dawson felt well justified in choosing the latter course. In due time, Mr. Clark would receive the complimentary CD, with the accompanying royalty cheque. That was bound to suffice for Mr. Clark. After all, under normal circumstances, it would even satisfy Mr. Dawson himself.

In due course, Marvin did receive the compact disk of the first recording of the *Poème Symphonique*. The cheque he deposited in his bank with hardly a glance. His present position at the City Hall removed any residual interest he might have entertained in financial matters. Over the years, regardless of his income, Marvin always forgot to spend the money he had earned. The disk was quite another matter. He immediately made a copy, placed the original in his storage compartments, inserted the copy into his player and fell back into his command chair.

Marvin was pleased. Very pleased.

The events of the last few months affected his ability to lose himself even in his most favourite music. He had listened to his revered composers more to relax than to be motivated to any particular course of action, within or without the objective world. While still enjoying his daily esoteric exercises, Marvin had discovered a more vibrant mode of existence in his conscious hours. It was as though he now lived in a state of greater, more intense awareness. He was more awake. He actually felt sharper, more perceptive.

The *Poème Symphonique* brought back the depth, the richness of musical appreciation that he had enjoyed up to a few months ago. Marvin was instantly transported to the images that had precipitated the composition. There was a difference, however. The sharper senses, which more recently appeared to serve him in the physical world, also became more acute in his subjective consciousness. The effects were quite staggering. The snow was 'snowier', the wind 'windier', the winter—more wintery.

Marvin's perceptions had become, in some subtle manner, more intense. He analyzed his impressions after the first hearing of the CD. The nearest he could come to describing his experiences would be to say that he had increased his involvement in what had transpired. Marvin not only saw and felt the snow, but, in some intangible way, for an ephemeral instant, he *was* the snow. He became, at least to a degree, the object of his attention.

The next day in the office, Marvin spent his whole time in meetings with lawyers. They briefed him on hundreds of disjointed facts, which might or might not prove useful to him in his forthcoming arbitrations. Marvin absorbed like a sponge the masses of data, while retaining the ability to dismiss them from his memory, or at least to bury them in the deeper recesses of his overtaxed mind, when no longer required. His recall was generally regarded as fantastic. After not quite six months, Marvin was treated as a human computer with an oversized memory, making himself not only indispensable to the present administration, but positively dangerous, should he wish to make use of the confidential information for his own ends. Marvin remained completely unaware that he could, to all intents and purpose, write his own ticket—or, for that matter, his own cheque.

Last week, a clerk newly assigned to his chambers put together a document which, more or less, proved that Marvin, to date, had saved the administration something on the order of thirty-two million dollars. Even with the megalomaniacal magnitude of the City's ever-growing budget, this was a serious amount.

As the clerk so aptly described it, "It sure ain't no chicken feed!"

In spite of all this, Marvin did not find satisfaction in his present work. Well, perhaps there was a degree of satisfaction, but not fulfillment. Marvin knew that pouring oil on stormy waters of human emotions had been, and would continue to be, a positive contribution to the pulse of the community, but... somehow it just wasn't enough. It dealt with the repairs to, and the maintenance of, the *status quo*, rather than in breaching new horizons, helping to channel the community into uncharted waters to enrich its fabric, its scope, its ultimate potential.

A year, nay, a few months ago, no such ambitions (if ambitions they be) would have invaded Marvin's insular consciousness. Now, something had happened. He seemed to have crossed a narrow isthmus, reached, perhaps uninvited, the point of no return. He felt a deep conviction that the white waters which pummeled his fragile canoe along his own personal precarious river had now been put behind him, that the time had come to set sail on the new, more promising waters, toward the distant, perhaps unlimited, horizons.

When Marvin returned home, he played his *Poème* again. When the CD stopped, he remained motionless. He tried to go back in time. He managed to visualize the river, which he had learned to associate with this musical jewel. He saw the canyon, the winding waters, then the no longer threatening, once onerous cataracts, and the wider, broader, calmer river beyond.

He searched for the rainbow.

The repeated attempts to scan his memory bore no results. When he finally succeeded in visualizing a beacon of light over the previously abysmal darkness, it did not resemble the old joyful iridescent arches. Instead, the light beam held firm, whitish gold, pure and perfectly static in its uncompromising wholeness. Marvin had no idea what had happened, what had seemingly lessened the richness of his visual recollection. He gave up trying, knowing from past experience that things are made clear only to those who have grown ready for the unveiling of knowledge.

A whole week passed since Marvin had last seen Jocelyn. They spoke daily on the telephone, but he had learned to respect the fact that she could work on her sculpture only after she returned from the library. Her evenings were hers to grow in her becoming. Since the force of destiny had seemingly removed Marvin's myopic goggles, he also needed time to learn and to consolidate his own learning. He studied and he waited. He hoped. He was rewarded. On the first glorious Saturday of May, Jocelyn called him early in the morning to propose an outing.

"We are both living downtown. We've long since given up breathing. Shall we try to taste air, the real thing, in the country?" She sounded very enthusiastic.

"What time shall..." They were always laconic in their telephone discussions.

"You stay where you are now. I'll do the up-picking!" Her voice sounded more excited than usual. "Well, when will you be ready?"

Was she anxious or nervous? Marvin knew something had happened.

"I can be downstairs in about five minutes," he assured her.

"Be there in... twenty."

Marvin held the receiver farther away from his ear. He looked puzzled. Had Jocelyn giggled? A very un-Jocelyn-like behaviour. He shrugged.

"I'll be there." Marvin replied into the dead mouthpiece.

The twenty minutes seemed much too long. In ten minutes Marvin had changed into his best country-squire regalia—or, to put it more precisely, into jeans and a sweater. He had no idea what else to take with him. Jocelyn had given him no chance to ask. Her spontaneous whims may have abated slightly, but Jocelyn remained Jocelyn. "And I'll be darn glad of it!" he implicitly assured himself, peering into the mirror.

With still ten minutes to go, Marvin ran downstairs. "Control yourself, man, you are pushing fifty!" he murmured under his breath. He seldom listened to his own advice. He would hate to twist an ankle and have to forego Jocelyn's invitation.

"Will you be back for supper?" The diminutive figure of Mrs. Prentis blocked his access to the front door.

"Oh, ah, Mrs. Prentis. Good morning. I really couldn't say, Ma'am. I suppose so?" How am I supposed to know, Marvin wondered.

"Be careful how you get there," Mrs. Prentis admonished, and disappeared into her parlor.

Mrs. Prentis had failed to enlighten Marvin as to where "there" might be. As so often in his dealings with women, Marvin had no idea what Mrs. Prentis had been talking about. Thank God, he thought suddenly, thank God there are so few women involved in arbitration. If there were—I'd just have to resign.

TOO -TOOT.

A most ghastly, obscene, blaring foghorn shook him out of his reverie. Marvin looked through the glass panel of the front door. Sitting next to an open window of a prehistoric automobile was Jocelyn. The cacophonous foghorn apparently belonged to the bright-red wreck that she was driving.

Marvin opened the front door. He took an instinctive step back before taking one forward. Then he stood still. There had been nothing wrong with his instinct for self-preservation. Jocelyn doubled with laughter.

"You look positively petrified."

"Nonsense," he replied. "It's just that I am positively petrified!"

His chin thrust forward, Marvin ran down the steps.

"Is this thing legal?" he asked, his voice very serious.

"Get in and keep quiet," she admonished.

Twenty minutes later they left St-Onge and other suburban municipalities behind them. The dilapidated Ford, which Jocelyn had borrowed from a girl who, according to Jocelyn, would remain nameless (probably to protect her from being arrested on grounds of criminal, misanthropic insanity), behaved almost like a real car. Its very soft suspension contrived to hide the strange, squeaky, bumpy sounds the car made on sharper turns. Apart from that, the ride was unexpectedly smooth. By eleven Jocelyn found her planned destination: a deserted spot overlooking a relatively small, pristine, Laurentian lake. The pristine aspect was a phantasmagoric impression due this time of the year. Two or three weeks from now, the lake would look like a speedway for odious, squealing speedboats driven by people determined to pollute the countryside with noise, smell, gasoline and oil. Marvin often wondered why the Canadians so hated their own country.

For over an hour they took a leisurely cross-country walk. On return to their selected spot, Marvin apologized and took off his socks. He had to dry them in the sun, after crossing a number of small run-offs. On northern slopes, protected by the thick, tightly spaced tree trunks, or secreted under projecting rocks and sharp crevices, they found many rills carrying off the still-melting snows. By contrast, the slopes facing south, those protected from the northerly winds, were in the full swing of springtime. Directly in front, Marvin saw delicate green sails stretched on the white spars of slim birches reflected in the mirror-still water.

The air was full of strange smells never encountered in the midst of a city. Buzzing insects, the infamous black flies, seemed busy all around them. Marvin hoped it would take a while for the blood-sucking monsters to discover their presence.

On the protected glade the snacks, which Jocelyn had prepared, tasted like a regal banquet. In addition to sandwiches, they shared two roasted legs of an oversized chicken. They finished the meal with ripe Camembert. A bottle of Chilean Cabernet Sauvignon provided the finishing touches. Marvin felt embarrassed for having come empty-handed. He said so.

"I was under the impression that you treated me royally at *Les Pêcheurs* not so long ago?" Jocelyn absolved him.

"Are you keeping accounts?"

"Only when I do the inviting."

Marvin knew he had lost the argument. He should have been the instigator. He certainly wanted to be one. Did he really still need more time? Each day brought him fresh knowledge, fresh confidence. He apologized.

"What for?" She dismissed his qualms with a wave of her hand. "We are all free to do and act in the manner suited to our needs. I just happen to be a little more impulsive. If we were identical, we might bore each other to death."

"Would we?"

Marvin loved hearing her open, uninhibited views. She must have embodied the true meaning of sophistication. Wherever she was, whatever she did, she seemed relaxed and 'at home'.

Jocelyn ignored his last question. She stretched out on the blanket, her hair spread like a delicate golden halo around her head. She stared at the pure, intensely blue sky, interrupted here and there by lazy, seemingly motionless puffs of whipped cream.

"So many..." she mused, "I have so many hopes. I wonder if it's healthy to live so much in the future."

"Only at the risk of sacrificing the present."

Marvin's eyes following hers to the few listless clouds. Then, propped up on his elbow, he looked down at Jocelyn's radiant face. "You don't, do you?"

"Sacrifice the present or have too many hopes?" She was only half serious.

"Either."

"So it's unhealthy?"

There was a moment's total silence. Not even a whisper of the slightest breeze invaded their privacy. The chirping birds held their tiny breaths. It lasted only a moment. Then a lone fly, the first of countless armies of the forthcoming kamikaze pilots, alit on Marvin's hand. The magic was broken.

"Some say that hope is the mother of invention," Marvin offered.

"And you? What do you say, Marvin?" She kept her eyes on the clouds.

"I say, and I don't mean to be patronizing, that hope is an emotional escape designed for weaklings."

Marvin wondered if he had said too much. When he thought out his views, he did it in the privacy of his attic. He never minced words when arriving at a conclusion. He was not used to sharing his soul's secrets.

"Explain."

Jocelyn turned her eyes to face Marvin. She didn't sound offended.

"Ten thousand destitute Mexicans come daily to Mexico City, hoping for a better future. They spend the rest of their lives exploring the gargantuan garbage heaps and breeding—still hoping for a better future." He took a sip of wine. "While I sip wine from their southern neighbour..."

A half bitter, half sardonic smile twisted his mouth.

"The world's principal religions teach you to hope for a better future, doing little to improve your present. The politicians tax you to improve your future, not to mention their own, naturally, at your expense—that is, at the expense of your dissipated present. And we allow them to rob us, hoping for that elusive rainbow—forgetting that a rainbow is no more than pure light after it's been refracted. It is for the pure light we must search, not its refracted image. All these trends, all these factors, are the direct result of a misused and abused concept of hope. Hope teaches you to procrastinate your efforts."

"Isn't that a rather harsh judgment?" Jocelyn wasn't convinced.

"We must live in the present," Marvin insisted. "If you live to the full, you don't mind dying tomorrow. And when you lose all your fears—you have little to hope for."

"Do you?"

"Live to the full or have I lost all my fears?"

He laughed for some time. He laughed, releasing some deep-rooted tensions.

"Neither!" he confessed, still laughing. Then he added: "But I am learning daily. I am growing daily. And I make sure I do not do so at anyone's expense!" And then his voice dropped to a low whisper. "Not any more..."

"Whatever happened then to faith, hope and charity? Was St. Paul just kidding?"

"That's a mistake people continue to make. What may well have been true two thousand years ago may no longer apply. Truth, contrary to popular belief, is not a static, dead set of archaic rules. The truth is always living—and change is the very essence, the prerequisite of life."

"So he was right, then...?"

"How do I know? I wasn't there. I wouldn't presume to sit in judgment over other people's beliefs. Arbitration is bad enough!" he added, with a wry smile.

And then Marvin's voice became serious. "Hope is what you need when you are devoid of faith. Faith you need only when you have not conquered knowledge. And as for love, that is a different thing altogether, nothing to do with any of the others."

At this Jocelyn sat up. "Nothing to do with any of the others?"

"I see you've been listening," he grinned.

"Marvin, don't be flippant. What you're saying is serious."

"Yes, I suppose, it is rather serious." He sighed and collected his thoughts. "We all still need faith, because it is the dynamic for procuring knowledge. However, once you know, faith becomes redundant. If you are a car mechanic, you do not have faith that the car will function—you know that it will; the others, the ignorant drivers, must defer to an act of faith that it will perform adequately. If you know you're immortal, you do not have to have faith that you are. But faith should never be used as an excuse for *not* gathering knowledge. That would be one of the greatest sins... if sins are those acts which withhold us from the experience of our ultimate destiny."

"And love?" Jocelyn's eyes seemed as distant as the suspended clouds.

"And love is the essence. It is not an emotion. It is the essence of life itself. Without this secret and sacred force, not one of us would be alive! Why would we bother? Can you conceive of a life without love? Isn't that what hell is? Whatever you love, you must love something. A thing, a person, an idea! Or an ideal. Love is the dynamic, the motivating force for all our actions. I said force, not energy, because love itself is static—being omnipresent. It causes us to be. It is life itself."

Marvin expelled his thoughts in a staccato manner, as though freeing himself of some long-held secrets. He now leaned back again, as though he had nothing more to say. For a moment strange embers continued to smoulder in his dark eyes.

Jocelyn regarded Marvin's face. She made no comment. Was there a trace of doubt in her steady gaze? After a while, Marvin propped himself again on one elbow.

"Can a man reach an Olympic standard without loving his chosen, all-consuming sport? Can a man write a good book, good from any standpoint, unless he loves writing? Can a woman create a sculpture unless she submits to the love within her and lets its force fill her until ultimate fulfillment? That and only that is true love. The very act of real living. The act of being one with the creative force. Or, as I said before, it is life itself."

Now Jocelyn also sat up.

"So that is what you meant that evening. Becoming and then, as you or I said, of just being. I mean, being one with the object or with the act engaging our attention... So that is the oneness, the love's manifestation..." Jocelyn was thinking aloud.

"We were given hints of it throughout ancient history. Socrates, Plato, Aristotle, on and on, the procession of searchers for truth, unrelenting... Later the affirmation, perhaps the most misunderstood of all: 'I and my Father are one,'—remember? The joining, the oneness, the congruent, sublime, contemporaneous union between the infinite and the individuation. That is the aim. The love made incarnate. The ultimate goal... at least, until we think of a new one..." His last statement sounded like a question.

Marvin lay down next to Jocelyn. The blue of the heavens hadn't changed. Through the clear, brilliant ether, his inner eye saw creation at its most ebullient moment—the instant of conception. The birth of universes... Images of beauty, beyond time, eternal... Nothing, nothing but pure love could have brought the universes into being. Pure and unlimited. The galaxies, the stars, the planets effervescent... Marvin no longer just believed. He knew. He knew that he and Jocelyn and all the worlds about them, the seen and the unseen, the known and the as yet hidden, were no more than an exuberant manifestation of the Infinite. Of the infinite, inexhaustible current creating, permeating and sustaining the universes—with love.

He raised himself on one elbow, leaned over Jocelyn and gently, perhaps timidly, brushed her lips with his own. Once again he was in awe of her beauty.

"Could it be that that which joins us is the very same force which holds the universes together?" he mused aloud. And then he gazed into her eyes and wondered no more. He no longer needed an act of faith to fuel or sate his desire.

He knew.

* * *

Summer

A single sunbeam is enough to drive away many shadows.

St. Francis of Assisi

19

The Lilacs

There had been four more picnics.

As summer approached, the black flies, the mosquitoes, and particularly the human infestation had invaded the wilds. It was difficult to find a quiet spot for a one-day excursion. Marvin and Jocelyn no longer risked their lives by driving derelicts discarded by Jocelyn's bohemian friends. When in need, Marvin quietly mentioned in the office that he needed a car. The rest was up to Miss Gascon. She always knew what to do. At a prescribed time, an elegant limousine would be waiting at the City Hall garage. Or at his home. With or without a driver.

Fringe benefits notwithstanding, Marvin thought seriously about investing in a country cottage. Jocelyn had opened his eyes to nature's little treasures. Real, physical, down-to-earth treasures. He once needed great oceans, crags piercing the infinite blue yonder, the hypnotic power trapped in the heart of a spiral galaxy. He needed to travel. Jocelyn made him aware of the red and yellow and orange universes also trapped in the smile of a wild marigold. He was virtually blind until he saw nature through her eyes. As his responsibilities grew, Marvin began to rely on Jocelyn's inspired picnics to escape the humdrum of the week-long carousel.

Yet, all in all, there was still a problem.

Marvin was not quite ready to take the next step with Jocelyn. His viewpoint changed each time his intrepid canoe turned the next corner. Marvin was sure enough of his feelings toward her. He wasn't yet sure he had it in him to give Jocelyn's personality the full range of freedom she deserved. He was still afraid that somehow he might hurt her. Hurt her feelings, restrain her latitude, put chains on her wondrous free spirit.

He assumed that whatever form 'the next step' would take, it would be acceptable to her. The word marriage had never been mentioned between them, although he sensed that even this institution carried different connotations for each of them. Different also from those accepted in a civilized society.

Jocelyn was a free spirit; Marvin—a free thinker.

He imagined that if one married at twenty or thirty, one concocted images of children, of a house full of joyful patter—never of agonizing, incomprehensible night-long whimpering. One marveled at the blissful innocence in a child's smile—not at the endless, exhausting and nerve-wracking tantrums. One assumed years of bubbling, youthful, inexhaustible health—not of the heart-wrenching worry and fear, and the long silent prayers to avert some sudden, unexpected illness or, God forbid, life-threatening accident.

When, on the other hand, a half-century was knocking on your doorstep, when the dust at your temples reminded you daily of your growing past and ever shrinking future, you thought of substantial changes in your life in a less impulsive, more premeditated fashion. Would Jocelyn still want children? Would she, perhaps, insist? Would he adapt well to a life of intensive sharing? Are the paternal or maternal instincts reawakened by the presumed bliss of wedlock? Or was such an awakening a natural outcome of the power of love linking with invisible threads the animus and the anima in a vain attempt to join forces, to become one, in a supreme act of sharing one's very existence?

For Marvin, the four picnics had been followed by four nights of portentous heartwrenching. Four evenings of unquenched desire; four eyes invoking, lamenting in an unrequited hunger for that which his lips could not yet, not quite yet, utter.

Even before they had met again at Jocelyn's exhibition, Marvin was well aware that it would be up to him to take the last few, strangely tremulous steps. The agonies he went through were completely incomprehensible to him. He knew he loved Jocelyn, loved her by any definition of the word known to him. What were then the grating, abrasive reservations? If they had nothing to do with Jocelyn, then they must reside within his own psyche— his own unreliable, immature psyche. How could he overcome this strangely masochistic, self-inflicted misery?

"The answer is within me," Marvin repeated, pressing his back into his command chair. His head was throbbing from intense concentration.

And it was.

As long as Marvin relied on analyses followed by systematic synthesis of his real or imaginary problems, he trod the same, spurious water on the treadmill. The water, like his thoughts, obeyed its own rules, sinking to the lowest possible depression.

"I must be on the wrong track...." he mused more and more often.

New precarious tenets had to be formulated. Now. Immediately. The questions in Marvin's life had always addressed his desires. His needs, his contentions, his likes, his own ego. The new track called for total sublimation of his previous premises.

Marvin's new realization gave him an undefined sense of freedom. He felt a strange elation, a sudden release from old, acquired dogmas. His lips moved tentatively, forming an unaccustomed carefree smile. Could her smile be contagious? For the briefest moment, Marvin hated himself for being so obtuse for such a long time.

"What a waste! How could I, a grown man, for so long have been so stupid?"

The self-condemnation came and passed in an instant. Whatever would happen, whatever Jocelyn's answer to his titanic question, the world would continue to unfold. And so would he. So would Marvin Clark.

They met one evening in early June.

Spring came late this year, curtailed further by a mid-May freak snowstorm. Officially summer had not yet started, but the evening was warm, inviting. Serene stillness in the air was saturated with the aroma of lilacs. The park was virtually deserted. Here and there a young couple strolled slowly, hand in hand, blind to all but each other. Marvin, perhaps three times older than most aspiring springtime lovers, seemed to fit well with their myopic vision. Should his attention wander, even momentarily, it returned quickly, drawn to Jocelyn's eyes, sparkling, demure, seemingly contented. Only his nose digressed from his concentric senses. The intoxicating fragrance followed their every footstep. If they both lived to be a hundred, neither would forget this evening of overpowering aroma...

Lilacs in full bloom.

They walked arm in arm, fingers interlaced, like two secretive students, smiling, without talking. Now and again Jocelyn would point at something—a fluffy-tailed squirrel or elegantly striped chipmunk, busy with last year's acorn. Marvin would stop, smile recognition, then continue walking. Later they sat down by the pump house, the place of their first encounter. It seemed as though years had passed, years of unspoken longing, a season better left forgotten lest it encroached on this magic moment. Here also the omnipresent lilacs shielded them from the park's walkways. Hardly necessary. Yet, behind this plethora of the ebullient indigo clusters, they felt gratifyingly protected.

"How do I love thee...?"

Marvin, never a poet, felt that, should Jocelyn command him, he could write a sonnet. He was in great danger of starting to act like an adolescent. He breathed deeply, as though trying to capture and hold this moment forever.

"I don't know how to put it—didn't have much practice..." he started.

"Yes?" she asked gently.

"But, from the moment I met you..."

"Yes?" she encouraged.

"I really wanted to ask you..."

"Yes?" she nodded her head.

"But I was afraid to ask..."

"Yes," she agreed gently.

"Must you keep interrupting?"

"Yes," she affirmed tersely.

"Then what would be your answer?"

"Yes." She didn't argue.

"Then you mean..."

"Must you always keep talking?"

"Yes," he affirmed meekly.

And then she leaned on his shoulder and they sat and said nothing. After a long while, Jocelyn tilted her head backwards and with half-closed eyes she searched for his mouth. He kissed her lips gently as though afraid to hurt a precious possession. Perhaps even more afraid to lose reins on his hunger. Again there was silence.

"You must do this more often," she admonished.

"Yes, my dear, my darling. Yes, yes, my lovely..."

"Oh, do shut up and kiss me!" And he obeyed, this time much less gently.

"Marvin! I must do some breathing," she gasped, near exhaustion.

As they came up for air, the lilacs filled their starved lungs with such potency as to make their heads swim. The sweet, overpowering, intoxicating scent permeated everything. It was truly omnipresent.

And in their hearts it became eternal.

They met the next day, after work, in Jocelyn's studio. Marvin found it hard to believe that this was the first time they met there, alone, since that moonlit night so many eons ago. This was very, very different. The days were much longer now. The late afternoon sun cut sharply through the slanting roof lights. The light and its reflections filled the conservatory with a warm, pinkish-rosy glow.

They met as lovers meet.

They embraced and they kissed, then sank to the same old settee and held each other close. Later, a prosaic drink of bottled spring water in their hands, they forced themselves to remember that they came to talk business. That was how Jocelyn insisted on calling this session. She had good reason to talk serious business. Marvin had spent almost twenty years at Aunty Jenny's. Jocelyn finally had a studio in which she was very productive. Marvin had his... *monstera!*

After the pain of winter, after all that had befallen them.... After the nights of anguish, of emotional turmoil, Marvin's bone of contention became his big, sprawling, monstrous *deliciosa.* Jocelyn had to swear that nothing untoward would happen to his unwieldy baby. Then, decisively, she led the discussion into calmer waters.

"What made you ask me, finally?" She couldn't resist the question.

Up to this moment, at Jocelyn's instigation, Marvin had been totally preoccupied with practical, mundane subjects. After all, they were here to discuss their future. Whether to move quickly and, if so, where and wherefore? What to do about dear ol' Auntie Jenny? How would all these changes affect his, her, and their joint future? How big an apartment or house would they need now? In which area of town? Would Jocelyn want to continue working? In the library, or elsewhere? Did she or perhaps did he, did they both together, how soon and how often, if so when, what and wherefore...???

"What did you say, dear?"

It seemed Marvin hadn't heard her. Jocelyn grinned coyly and repeated the question, adding: "...at that particular moment?"

A sweet scent of lilacs wavered on the last, sharply slanting rays of the setting sunlight. Marvin knew Jocelyn had not referred to the 'when' of last evening. This was a deeper, much, much more important question.

"I had to have a reason," he answered enigmatically.

"So your question was not precipitated by your fervent, all-consuming passion?"

Jocelyn enunciated the words, scanning individual syllables. Simultaneously her eyebrows rose, her lips pouted. Marvin had never seen her so absurdly disenchanted. He could not hold back laughter. Whatever the future had in store for them, he knew they would never, never be bored with each other. By the time they both recovered, he ignored her last question.

"It took me quite a while..."

Marvin's eyes once more assumed that distant look Jocelyn had learned to love. Whenever he talked, she never had an impression that Marvin was attempting to convince her. About anything. He simply shared with her that which was close to him. From within the now hesitant, partially collapsing ramparts of his once impervious stronghold, the real, the true Marvin allowed her to enter his secret place, the inner recesses of his mind, the very heart of his consciousness. In such moments Jocelyn felt privileged; she had no doubt that Marvin was not in the habit of opening his heart to many people—to any people at all.

"The real problem was not my present, but my past. That may be the case, of course, with many if not all people. We seem to handcuff ourselves to old concepts, to ideas which either our parents or life have bred into us. We become slaves to them, being convinced that we shall not only die, but incur some form of eternal damnation, should we let go of any of those old tenets. At the very least, we are afraid to let go for fear of the unknown."

He smiled a little sadly. He leaned down and planted a gentle kiss on her lips.

"How much easier would life be if we could, sort of, die daily and start again with a fresh slate each and every morning? We can see, all around us, staggering changes in technology, mind-boggling advances in many branches of science... yet, our myopic views, our ethics, remain at a standstill!"

Marvin sighed deeply, then with a single motion drained his glass of spring water. Jocelyn thought this symbolic. She thought of finishing the old before one could successfully start on the new.

"But surely, the old truths hold true today, as they will forever. One cannot change ethics with the times—for convenience," she insisted.

"True. There are ethics that were and remain true throughout the ages. But aren't you forgetting that ethic is but an empty word unless put into action? What is the prime purpose of any, *any* ethic?"

There ensued a long silence. Surely, she thought, everyone just knew that. We were told that ethics, or our system of ethics, was the highest set of rules to live by. They controlled our morality. Ethics separated us from primitive people. Or did our distant forefathers also live by some, unknown to us, rules of conduct?

"To sustain morality? To create some order...? To..." Jocelyn was thinking aloud. How come I never thought this one out, she wondered.

"Please. Don't confuse the issue!" Marvin admonished sharply. "Morals are no more than rules created by the ruling classes for the explicit purpose of controlling their serfs. By introducing some rules and regulations defining morality, their subjects—or, more accurately, taxpayers—became reduced to a common denominator. Thus, they became predictable and therefore manageable. Every ecclesiastical and lay controlling body invariably insisted on the morality of their servile, submissive and very obliging subjects. They seldom, if ever, subscribed to those same rules themselves. Just look at history..." There was no merriment in his dry, sardonic laughter.

Jocelyn did not feel comfortable. Marvin had been steadily destroying most, if not all, of her buttresses. She had less and less to lean on. Slowly, very slowly, she began to understand how Marvin felt in a world which, apparently, was becoming transparent to his vision. She began to understand his need for some degree of protection. And now, the ramparts were falling. Did she partake in this risky, unilateral disarmament? Did she hope for it? Had she in some way encouraged....

"The purpose of any ethic is one—and one only. The purpose is survival!"

Marvin raised his empty glass and put it back on the table. Jocelyn brought a fresh bottle from the fridge and set it in front of him. Marvin drank almost a full glass before resuming.

"Be they professional organizations, powerful nations or established churches or religions, they all usurped the very concept of ethics, to assure their collective survival. Yet this is a total perversion of the truth. Periodically, great men visit our primitive societies and, through divine inspiration, introduce and reintroduce the basic tenets. These transcendent avatars tell us, quite explicitly, that what matters is not the survival of some self-serving organization but the survival of an individual. As a matter of fact, they even tell us *how* we can assure our survival as individual units of consciousness. This basic tenet is repeated *ad nauseam*. Alas, to no avail."

"But, surely, no individual is greater than the whole," she insisted.

"The Whole is not whole with even one component missing."

Marvin smiled an odd smile. Perhaps he shared his humor with the faceless many who failed to be recognized as more than disposable governmental statistics. He then spoke as one of the many.

"Every single one of us, famous or obscure, is a complete whole. Every single one of us is a unique micro-universe. True, we are part of a greater Body, but such a Body would be lacking with even a single limb, a finger or an atom missing. It would be incomplete, imperfect. The macro and the micro are interdependent. Unto the image and likeness... The Father and the Son... Indivisible, ever coalescing yet contemporaneous, concentric, omnipresent."

It was that time, just before sunset, that was the precursor of an approaching darkness. Jocelyn reached over and across Marvin. She picked up the telephone.

"Aunt Jenny? This is me. He'll be late again. It's my fault, of course. What? ...as punishment? Well, I am very tempted.

Thank you, I will tell him." She waved her head in disbelief, even as she laughed.

"I've done it again, haven't I? I could almost make it if I ran all the way." Marvin completely forgot that supper was served at seven. At least—for the last seventeen years.

"We shall run together," Jocelyn announced.

"What was that you were saying about some, ah... punishment? I couldn't help overhearing." He was boyishly curious.

"It's twofold. One, I must attend the supper. That is my punishment." Then, once again, she giggled: "...and two, you owe Aunt Jenny a full bottle of your favourite sherry."

Marvin grinned with relief. Then his brow furrowed in an apparent lack of understanding. Something was not kosher. He raised his brow at Jocelyn.

"Auntie Jenny must find an excuse for our tardiness. She decided to make a celebration. I have a sneaky suspicion what it might be." Jocelyn refused to say any more.

In a mad, childish scramble they raced for the door. Who said that only fools and drunkards are lucky? This sentiment must surely be extended to irrepressible lovers. Even as they pushed the door shut, a wanton taxi crawled along the sidewalk. In less than ten minutes they were at Mrs. Prentis's table. As they passed the hall, they winked at each other. They both recognized the sweet, intoxicating scent of lilacs.

"Does that mean I am absolved from having to buy the bottle?" Marvin whispered in Jocelyn's ear.

She kicked his ankle and threw her arms around Aunt Jenny. After extricating herself from Jocelyn's embrace, Mrs. Prentis looked at her niece at arm's length; then, she regarded Marvin. Without so much as a 'good evening', she started with a scolding.

"Well?" She threw the question about halfway between them.

"Ah, yes, we are sorry, Mrs. Prentis." Marvin sounded very contrite.

"Why? What have you done?" Now Aunt Jenny sounded pugnacious.

"Why, I thought, ah, that you thought, that we were late?" he wondered.

"You were here at seven," Mrs. Prentis said flatly and turned away toward the kitchen. Jocelyn nodded her understanding.

"You didn't tell her, did you?" she asked, knowing the answer.

"I didn't have a chance yet."

"If you value your life, you'd better do it now," Jocelyn advised gravely.

"Why me?" Marvin wanted to run to his room. This was no arbitration regarding a few million dollars. Here, he had to face Mrs. Prentis.

Only at this moment did they notice that the four gentlemen were already in the dining room. They must have arrived together in the last few seconds. Or they were already here when Jocelyn and Marvin arrived. The senior citizens smiled at Jocelyn, with hardly a nod to Marvin. Colonel Mackenzie Whittlaw was about to speak when Mrs. Prentis joined them from the kitchen. Rather than pushing the food wagon, she walked to the bar.

Jocelyn leaned toward Marvin and murmured: "I warned you..."

The death threat worked. Marvin crossed the three paces to the liquor cabinet and said to Mrs. Prentis:

"Allow me?"

With that he took out the requisite number of glasses and filled them with a dry Spanish Sherry. He then carried the tray to Mrs. Prentis, to Jocelyn and each of the gentlemen. He then turned to face all present.

"Gentlemen! Mrs. Prentis has a little announcement to make." With that he raised his glass toward Mrs. Prentis.

"I do?" Mrs. Prentis' eyes grew larger by the second.

"You certainly do, Mrs. Prentis." And as she continued to
look lost in the stew of her making, he added in a half tone:
"Oh, yes, you do, Aunt Jenny."

Marvin never thought he would live to see Aunt Jenny
blush. Yet, her normally pale, gently powdered cheeks assumed a
hue of such pleasure that she seemed ready to burst some
overtaxed blood vessels. Then, raising her glass with one arm,
she placed her other hand against her pounding heart.

"Gentlemen, my dear friends. I am pleased to announce
my niece's engagement to Mr. Marvin Clark. I give you a toast
to their health and happiness."

Having taken no more than the tiniest sip of her sherry,
Aunt Jenny staggered, tears filled her eyes, and she run out,
sobbing, into the safety of her kitchen.

* * *

20

A Question of Balance

The evening was hot.

"You never really answered my question, you know?"

Jocelyn's head nestled on Marvin's shoulder, her eyes misty, her features in blissful repose. After a week of hard labour, during which Jocelyn created two new sculptures while Marvin attempted to resolve amicably three different disputes, they met in the park in an attempt to replenish their lost energies. The patch of grass, still damp from an early afternoon drizzle, did not look or feel inviting. The bench at the pump house, which would forever be known to them as *the* bench, offered a dry and protected haven.

The lilacs were gone. Instead, the trees, bushes, and lawns, washed by the refreshing shower, offered a richness of delicate greens, of subtle verdant permutations, which were in evidence only in the early part of summer.

"You asked me a question? Let me count the ways..."

Jocelyn bit his earlobe. "Answer my question," she insisted. Then, seeing that Marvin really was lost, she reminded him: "I asked you last week whatever made you ask me at that particular moment. Remember?"

"Remember what?" Marvin's innocent question was followed by a loud: "Ouch! Yeeesss!"

"Ah, so you do remember..."

A smile of victory.

During the whole of last week they had telephoned each other at least twice daily. As was usual on such occasions, they talked about things of little or no consequence. It was a matter of hearing each other's voices, rather than of solving the world's latest problems. Also, Jocelyn's need to see Marvin was becoming great and growing. She knew instinctively, as did Marvin, that fate arranged the flow of events at its own pace. The secret was to live today in such a manner as not to regret it tomorrow. That way she would always have something new to offer. She would neither incur nor accumulate any superfluous debts. She would retain her freedom.

"I asked you because I was ready," Marvin offered.

"You are ready to have the rest of your ear bitten off!"

Jocelyn's voice was deadly serious, even as her playful eyes continued to search his face.

"Well, in a way, I did answer. I could have asked you only after my mind caught up with my emotions. I always wanted you. I don't mean just physically. I had a strange desire to make you my own. To turn you into my possession. Practically my property. I have never owned anything, not to mention anyone, of any consequence. I could not ask you until I got rid of this inherent desire. If I hadn't, we wouldn't have lasted together for more than a week..." He smiled down at her, kissed her possessively, and contradicted his words by reaffirming his hold on her with his right arm. "Like this!" he added.

"It doesn't feel that bad..." she teased.

"It would after a week," he said.

"Try me," she insisted.

Marvin ignored the tempting invitation. Instead, he tried to arrange his thoughts to be able to tell Jocelyn what went on in his mind a week or two ago. His insights into his own behaviour, the workings of his own psyche, were seldom totally conscious. More often than not, the understanding came at a subliminal level long before it percolated by a strange process akin to osmosis into his waking awareness.

"Well, there was another problem." Marvin grimaced, remembering the ordeal. "You see, some time ago I had discovered that there are all sorts of laws governing our lives. Most of us appear to traverse the short span between birth and death without ever uncovering many, if, indeed, any of them. I am referring to one particular law, the law of balance."

Marvin sat up. He was still in the process of collecting his thoughts. He had never actually arranged his conclusions in an orderly fashion. Finally he gave up, deciding to muddle his way through as best he could.

"In the most direct way, as affecting your question, the law demanded that, whatever I desired in relation to you, I had no choice but to assume that you would harbour similar, or at least comparable appetites toward me. I do not mean that I had actually imagined a word-for-word reflection of all my aspirations. Not at all. Just sufficient to restore, in this case, a negative balance. The effects were horrendous. Mostly because our—or at least my— consciousness seemed to be very much like an iceberg. About one tenth is clear—conscious awareness; the rest is subliminal."

He turned to Jocelyn and kissed her. "I love both your parts, all of the above and the part below the water," he interrupted himself.

"Later, Marvin, later..."

Jocelyn would not forget her promise.

"Normally," he resumed, "that which we can verbalize is the tip of our mental consciousness. That which is emotional, instinctive and particularly intuitive, is the rest of the iceberg. So it was with me. I never actually imagined that you would usurp, or assume possession of, any specific portion of the wholeness I refer to as myself. No. The law of balance had created subliminal conditions within which I had been scared silly, scared stiff— petrified is not too strong a word—of losing myself, my personality—for all that it's worth, my freedom. Men, the atavistic or archetypal conquerors, the 'doers' as against the 'be-ers', are inherently more possessive than women. That is why so often men who are desperately in love with their chosen mates still hold back from the final step of commitment for fear of being subjected to their own imagery of possession. A regrettable by-product of the above is that the innate desire to restore the balance causes men to lose interest in their quarry as soon as possible. After the conquest, of course."

"And you worked out all this yourself?" Jocelyn was quite impressed.

Marvin started laughing. He couldn't stop. After a while she joined, not quite knowing why. She admitted as much.

"You see, whenever I might be in any danger, whatever, of my profound thoughts' going to my head, you are likely to bring me down to earth in a hurry!"

Marvin's laughter changed into a series of convulsive chuckles. This time Jocelyn joined him with renewed vigor.

"What is it?" he asked.

"I just liked the part about your thoughts going *to* your head," now she couldn't stop laughing. "Isn't that the general area from where they are supposed to originate?"

The evening lingered, suspended in the stillness of warm, already humid air.

Not even a whisper stirred the fresh foliage. The sun crawled imperceptibly from one reddening cloud to another, flirted with the opalescent edges, then dove gently behind a taller building. Time drifted at an easy, relaxed pace. It was too hot to hurry. They got up and spent the next hour ambling along and around the park's main lanes. They played a game. Jocelyn tried to spot couples who were still in love. Marvin counted those pairs who had been married longer and continued by the sheer force of the initial momentum. Together they judged the chances of younger couples' finding a fraction of what they had found between themselves.

Since Marvin's days at the Department of Parks and Recreation, he had retained his interest in public parks. His knowledge about trees, even forestry, with a particular interest in preservation, was quite impressive.

"Just look at that!" Marvin pointed to a particularly commanding oak. "If the taxpayers' money be the blood racing in the city's veins, then parks, surely, are the lungs which sustain the humanity of its citizens."

"Humanity?" Jocelyn shared Marvin's interest, but for purely aesthetic reasons.

Marvin smiled.

"You don't drive cars in the public parks. You don't rush through after a quick buck, nor pay public homage to the almighty dollar. You meet people, here, at a human scale, eye-to-eye, smile matching a smile. Whatever happens outside the park's protective boundaries, here people are essentially equal, not flaunting their positions or possessions. They are relaxed, basically contented. A rare haven, indeed."

"And so are you, dear," Jocelyn said.

"Rare haven?"

"I thought you said raven," she stroked his hair. "Well? You are certainly a large bird, you do have lustrous black hair, a rather pointed beak, and you inhabit the temperate zones of the northern hemisphere. You are intelligent and articulate. Lately, you also crow quite a lot."

"My lips are sealed." Marvin tried hard to look hurt.

"Let me part them for you." She pressed herself against him.

They stopped at a cafe for a cup of anything. A half-hour, two hot dogs, and a coffee later, each brandishing a triple-cone ice cream, they directed their steps, almost without thinking, back to their private harbour.

As ever, their secret spot was deserted. Marvin sat down at one end of the bench, Jocelyn stretched out, her head on his lap. He made some comment about not being able to kiss her when in that position, the old bones being stiff and weary, but to no avail. Jocelyn liked the view of the sky, which, Marvin had already discovered, was her favourite vista. Again, they felt no need for words. Marvin leaned his head against the wall behind

him. The humid heat of the summer's day made them both
drowsy. They both closed their eyes, suspended in a no-man's
land. They both hovered on the edge of consciousness, halfway
between a dream and a waking state.

"Would you like to come with me?" Marvin whispered.

"Hmmm...." Jocelyn agreed, without opening her eyes.

Marvin released the tenuous hold on his substantial
awareness. He drifted into a vision of his previous making. In his
mind's eye he held Jocelyn's hand and...

*...soared up and up, over a far, far distant horizon... out of
nowhere came sounds, fragments of chords, then more
substantial harmonies, congruent images... a vague memory of
summer gave way to swirling, snowy, ubiquitous whiteness... a
lone sigh swelling to a howl... a wolf, perhaps just vacuous
wind... a bleak, featureless plane, forgotten frozen desert...*

*...whiteness solidified, compacted into resonant paleness
above... it stirred, churned... congested into staggered vapors...
the white, gilt-edged clouds fomented a warmer melodious
concordance... snow now lying heavy, placid... then a prevalent
humming, growing, spawning a bubbling brook, then more and
more rushing water, cool, refreshing, swelling into rivers
opening to lustrous lakes shimmering in sunshine's caress with
resplendent glory...*

*...a warm breath... the clouds scatter, drifting... sweet
lassitude of hot, humid languor... a hot, humid breath mounting
in slow, rhythmic waves, oceans of florid grassland... the
wilderness now teeming with life, buzzing and cooing, stamping
and snorting and....*

"You'd never believe it... I dreamed it was still winter. At
least to begin with..." Jocelyn sat up, rubbing her eyes. "What a
strange dream. It all seemed so real..."

"Did you meet anyone there?" Marvin asked, his voice
hopeful.

"In the dream? No, I don't think so. I think it was just nature... I am not very good at remembering dreams. Have I been away long?"

Marvin looked at his watch. "About two or three minutes?"

"What!?" At this she sat up. "B-but... it seems to have lasted much longer." She sounded unconvinced. "Are you quite sure?"

"Time is a relative factor in all the inner travels," Marvin assured her.

"Travels? What travels, oh, you mean in my dreams..."

"Well, yes. In a manner of speaking."

A rubber ball struck the wall above Marvin's head and bounced into the bushes. Two youngsters chased after it without paying Jocelyn or Marvin the slightest attention. The younger, perhaps a twelve-year-old, managed to get to the ball first. He let out a shriek of joy. In another two seconds the boys disappeared.

"You see, I told you," Marvin said.

"Of course I did see, but what have you told me?"

"Their time travels at a different rate from ours. In about ten seconds, they managed to cover more ground, make more noise, express more emotion than we would in an hour!"

"Speak for yourself. I am not as old as you look," she countered.

Jocelyn stretched as if she had slept for an hour.

"You know, all this is great fun, but the last time we met to discuss our future, we didn't get anywhere. Any ideas?"

Marvin hated this moment. No point delaying the inevitable. He imagined he was in his office, chairing a table of people, none of them knowing where they were going nor, appropriately, how to get there.

"We can both stay in my attic. We can attempt to buy Mrs. Prentis out, throw everyone save Aunt Jenny out, and convert the mansion into a Taj Mahal. We can both move to your studio. We can buy a house. We can buy a condominium. We can rent one of the last two." As he talked, he counted them off on his fingers. "I make that seven options. Let's see if we can apply a process of elimination."

Jocelyn nodded vigorously.

"Two people are not enough to fill a house," she decided. "I cannot make the noise I make sculpting in any condominium. When I remove forms from some moulds, I often use a hammer for an hour—usually after work, late at night..."

"...when other people are trying to rest in peace, amen. A charming neighbour you would make!" Marvin made faces commiserating with her poor victims.

"Funny!"

"You know, by a stroke of genius you have eliminated just about all the options. The house, new or Aunt Jenny's, is too large; the rented or bought apartments are out, on the grounds of noise. That leaves your studio."

"We could, of course, live in one place, and I could continue working in my studio nearby?" She did not sound at all happy at the prospect.

"From six p.m. till eleven, plus weekends. The rest of the time we could spend together. Ah, for the joys of marital bliss!" Marvin, too, did not sound particularly impressed. "You wouldn't want to give up working in the library?"

"Eventually. I would need a lot more assurance that my sculpture is of a sufficient standard before I'd want to do that. But you know, there is more to it than that. You seem happy to enter your inner world and close the door behind you. I still need people. I love my sculpture, but it is the contact with people that, in some strange way, provides me with inspiration, with the anatomical form, or expression, which I incorporate later in my reliefs. Does that make sense?"

"Artists are messengers of gods and goddesses. They are not supposed to make sense." Nevertheless, Marvin nodded his understanding. "Why don't you leave it with me. I have one or two ideas. Will you trust me?"

"With my life, oh lord and master of my miserable existence!"

"Who said that messengers of gods cannot clown around?"

"I am perfectly serious," Jocelyn corrected.

Jocelyn was certainly perfect—even if not very serious, Marvin thought. He dreamed of the day when she would acquire sufficient confidence to take up sculpture full time. He thought that the rather convoluted talk about her need of people was principally apprehension of a total commitment. How well he knew that feeling. It had tortured him for the last six months. We all needed to do things on our own time track. We are all unique, he repeated to himself. He had learned his lesson.

That evening they ate supper together at Aunt Jenny's. Mrs. Prentis approved. She insisted that Jocelyn had not been eating properly since she moved to her studio. She may well have been right. Jocelyn had lost about five pounds. Contrary to her Auntie's conclusions, however, it rather pleased her. Marvin refused to get involved in the argument. After dinner, Marvin walked Jocelyn home and left her at the door. They both knew that if he were to put his foot over the threshold, she would not get any work done. No work at all.

The next day in the office, Marvin sent Miss Gascon out to the archives to get plans of a certain nondescript building in the less fashionable area of town. Miss Gascon assumed that her mission was, as usual, to assist Mr. Clark in his confidential work. She had learned not to ask questions, not to talk about nor ever repeat anything which had taken place in Director Clark's office. Olive Gascon was as loyal as loyal can be.

During the next two days Marvin spent every free moment poring over the plans, sections, elevations and even structural drawings of a small building. His years at the Department of Parks & Recreation had taught him how to read technical drawings. He had acquired the knowledge of the basic principles underlying construction. At two o'clock on Tuesday, Marvin asked to see an architect and a structural engineer from the Construction Permits department. Both reported immediately. Marvin knew them both by their first names. Now, the engineer addressed him as *Monsieur le Directeur*. He let it ride.

The two professionals left two hours later. They were back on Thursday with a stack of schematics. Marvin made a few minor adjustments and smiled his satisfaction. Thanks to the efficacy of computers, the final drawings would be ready for construction in another three or four days. Next, Marvin called Mr. G. Gagnan, B.A., B.C.L., an old acquaintance from the Municipal Registry office. They talked for a few minutes. At four, Mr. Gagnan crossed over to Marvin's office. An hour later, the documents were ready. One does not keep *Monsieur le Directeur* waiting. Another colleague, also a lawyer, joined them at five. The documents were checked and signed.

Marvin sat back. He felt tired but excited. He felt as though he had been playing a game of poker for high stakes. He grinned. He had never played poker in his life.

"Now... how am I going to get rid of her?" he pondered, concentration reappearing in his eyes. "This part might prove the hardest."

Construction holidays were due in two weeks. That was the period when all the construction projects would stop. It would also be the time when one could arrange to have some personal or, to put it another way, some clandestine work done without the big unions raising hell. The union bosses were all too busy playing golf.

One other thing remained. He had to get Jocelyn to come with him on his holidays. After all, they had hardly seen anything of each other lately. They both needed a rest. Marvin broached the subject that evening during dinner. He counted on Aunt Jenny's support.

"... and after all, we hardly see anything of each other," he concluded, his head down, his mouth on the verge of pouting, his features dejected.

"Well?" Aunt Jenny wanted to know.

"For how long?" Jocelyn asked.

"I made a provisional booking for three weeks. The last two of July and the first of August. It is a wonderful place. You'll love it. Swimming, golf, tennis, horseback riding, windsurfing—you name it. I've been there before." Marvin tried to sound as enthusiastic as he could. It wasn't that difficult.

"Well?" Auntie Jenny's voice took on a threatening tone.

"I must see the director," Jocelyn said.

"First thing tomorrow morning?" Aunt Jenny wanted to know.

"Yes, Auntie dear. First thing," Jocelyn complied.

Marvin took a surreptitious deep breath. So far so good. Must keep my fingers crossed, he mused. He had done all he could. The rest was out of his hands. So far, fate had been kind to him. At least, he thought so. He was convinced that he was doing the right thing. If not, what the hell, you can only die once!

After dinner, only the second time since they met, Jocelyn visited Marvin in his attic. Mrs. Prentis contrived to look studiously the other way.

"How things have changed since my younger days...?" Aunt Jenny muttered as she disappeared into the kitchen.

Jocelyn was again overcome by the monstrous *monstera*. It seemed even more incredible. It totally dominated the room. Yet, Jocelyn had to admit that the plant, the jungle, had a certain charm of its own. She just wasn't quite sure what it was.

Marvin had invited Jocelyn up to show her his records, CDs, and books. Those three collections and his inimitable Delicious Monster were Marvin's sole possessions. He owned little else. No tidbits accumulated over the years of travel—he seldom traveled farther than his office. No family mementos cluttering his shelving. No useless echoes of an exciting past. Marvin's past was his books and his music. With one exception—his freshly acquired art collection. On either side of his control chair there now hung, from the ceiling, four of Jocelyn's sculptures. The fifth was leaning against the wall over the piano. Jocelyn greeted the sculptures as members of her family. She examined each from close by, made some faces and smiled her approval.

"You have a strange taste, *Monsieur le Connoisseur*," she said finally.

"I picked *you*, didn't I?" Marvin countered.

Jocelyn could have expressed her reservations as to who had picked whom, but she let it pass.

"Do I cause time to stop for you, too?" she asked instead.

"Indubitably!" He assured her.

"Duba-dooba-doo..." Jocelyn intoned but stopped, seeing the painful expression on Marvin's face. "Pig!"

Marvin led her past the shelves, slowly, where stacks upon stacks of books told their own story of Marvin's life. About an hour later, he brought from the kitchen a bottle of Dry Fly sherry. He poured it over a tall glassful of semi-crushed ice cubes and added a twist of fresh lemon. As on the previous occasion, Marvin insisted that Jocelyn take the commander's armchair, with himself perched on the piano stool in front of her. They sipped the dry, almost tart drinks while Jocelyn's eyes continued to rove over the countless book jackets. Marvin leaned over the console and inserted a CD of one of Mozart's piano concertos. He owned all twenty-five of them.

"I am glad you answered my question this morning," Jocelyn said, nodding her head in rhythm with the music. "I, sort of, needed to know."

"The question of balance?" Marvin asked.

"Sort of..."

"Few people seem to realize that we live in a dualistic world. They know it, they just don't realize it. If we upset the balance..."

"Dualistic...?" Jocelyn interrupted.

"No black without white, no mountain without a valley, no low without high, no light without a shadow... Some well-meaning sociologists try to make this valley of death into a perfect world. But it cannot be done. How would we know it was perfect if we had nothing to compare it to?"

"Tears," Jocelyn declared. "Valley of tears."

"Suit yourself."

They both smiled and remained exuberantly alive.

When the Mozart piano concerto was over, Marvin inserted the CD of *Poème Symphonique*. He said nothing about it. The music started with such a delicate pianissimo that one could hardly tell when it began.

Jocelyn sank deeper into the embracing armchair. She relaxed, releasing the stream of thoughts flittering across her mind. She listened. In minutes her brow contracted, her features assumed an expression of surprise, then disbelief. That expression of attention, almost of consternation, remained on her face until the end of the performance. Marvin said nothing. He waited patiently for her reaction. None came. He was unwilling to invade her private world. Finally his curiosity prevailed.

"Well?"

Jocelyn's face relaxed on hearing his voice. She looked at him with a very peculiar expression in her eyes.

"I just... cannot f-figure it out," she practically stammered.

"What is it, dear?"

"I've seen this music before!" she said.

"Oh? Just where have you heard it?"

Marvin knew that she couldn't have. Not yet. The tapes and records were not yet on general sale.

"I didn't say I heard it. I said... I have seen it?" She looked as though she did not believe the sound of her own voice.

"Oh. Oh, I see." Marvin smiled his very best enigmatic smile. "Would you care for a little more sherry?"

* * *

21

A Chicken Omelet

"I shall sleep on the balcony, of course," Marvin said.

He felt Jocelyn needed reassurance as they entered one of the best suites Blue Rocks had to offer. Having said that, he slid open the panoramic balcony doors, inviting Jocelyn to join him. She stayed put, her face a picture of surprise and consternation.

"You do mean, Sir, that you are not going to carry me over the threshold into your, aaah... den of iniquity?"

At the prolonged 'aaah', Jocelyn lowered her eyelashes, raised her hand to her palpitating breast, and inclined her head, sidewise and downwards, in a grotesque show of offended innocence. Marvin spun round, covered the three steps separating them in a single leap, picked her up as though she were a feather and, emitting a grunt of pain, carried her over the pertinent step.

"Ah, Sir, I do believe, I shall swoon..." Jocelyn whimpered.

"For God's sake, do it quickly!" Marvin begged her, panting.

"Pig!" Jocelyn shouted, trying to disengage herself from him.

"I love you, too, darling," Marvin answered.

Marvin had spent most of his annual vacations at the Blue Rocks. Not being a skier, he preferred to splurge on his summer holidays. Over many years, it had been the only luxury he had allowed himself. Such frugality had been motivated neither by a sense of greed nor by undue concern for solvency during his later years. He simply had no need for most things that most people found indispensable. Normally, Marvin booked his room well in advance. This year things got a bit out of hand, but since by then Marvin enjoyed a "preferred customer" status, he managed to secure this gorgeous suite even on very short notice. Probably a late cancellation. He also let it slip, without actually saying so, that he was there on his honeymoon.

Having crossed the troublesome threshold, and after paying the porter for his efforts with her lips, Jocelyn absorbed the breathtaking panorama. They were in the penthouse of an eight-storey building. The view gave onto twin rounded peaks, about four thousand feet in elevation. The twosome was reflected in the bluish mirror of the perfectly flat surface of a beautifully scenic lake. By some quirk of nature, the reflections of the twin peaks in the still water were perfectly blue—darker than the sky, yet distinctly and unmistakably blue. The famed Blue Rocks. Jocelyn stood very still. She seemed to breathe slowly, as if afraid that the fabulous vision might disappear. When she turned away, it was to throw both arms around Marvin's neck.

"Thank you, darling."

"Do not mention it," he answered. "I had them painted only this morning..."

"Oh, do shut up... isn't it gorgeous? Just simply, simply gorgeous?" Judging by the radiance of her eyes, Jocelyn had just arrived in seventh heaven.

"I couldn't put it better myself," Marvin admitted.

"You will not tell Aunt Jenny?" she needed reassurance.

"About the simply gorgeous...?"

"About sleeping on the balcony." She looked a little worried.

"Does she have something against fresh air?"

Marvin was a cautious man. Having posed his last question, he spun on his heel and ran for his life. Not too fast. She did catch him, and he was lucky: in the resulting tumble he came up the loser. It was a new experience. He rather liked being the loser.

Marvin's last week in the office was hell.

He had had to advance, reschedule and/or delegate the mounting work related to arbitration. He had also met with eleven building material suppliers, eight installers, two prospective contract managers (in preference to a general contractor) and, having made a selection out of this bunch, he had signed on a half-dozen subcontractors. The principal contract for structural steel—in the interest of time Marvin had been forced to use only standard sections—had been signed and awarded, the delivery assured for the day of his departure to Blue Rocks.

It had meant cutting it thin, but he had had to. Frankly, having had some experience with the building trade, Marvin knew he was counting on miracles. For his plans to succeed, there had to be no snags. The delivery of all the materials, fittings and fixtures, the availability of all the suppliers, tradesmen, and professionals had to be pre-coordinated with the architect, whom Marvin had hired on a *per diem* basis.

Then Marvin had had a masterful idea. A touch of genius. He had appointed Miss Olive Gascon as the plenipotentiary for the overall coordination and general, on-the-spot decision-making. The inscrutable girl had not even raised an eyebrow. She had taken it all in her high-heeled stride, with poise and sagacity, as though she'd been used to doing the impossible in half the time, half her life. She must have started when she was ten!

Olive Gascon now held the keys to Marvin's kingdom.

The first day at the Blue Rocks hotel passed at a leisurely pace. They looked around, they examined the possibilities, they stretched their overly stagnant wings. On the second day, they entered the full swing of activities. A pre-breakfast swim, a nine o'clock lesson on the golf range, a ten-thirty game of tennis followed by another swim, a light buffet luncheon at noon, with the digestive process taking place atop two mares that followed a prearranged, two-hour trail amid the most beautiful countryside. Another swim, a basket of balls on the golf range, and dinner.

The next day they both experienced considerable difficulties trying to get out of bed. They hurt in places they refused to admit were parts of their own bodies. They cancelled most of the activities assigned for the day and spent most of the time under a shady elm. Periodically they gingerly ambled down to the lake for a gentle soak in the tepid water, then negotiated the return trip to the deckchairs with a minimum amount of pain.

Marvin was saddled with an additional, confidential chore. He had to maintain telephone contact with the irrepressible Miss Gascon. On day two, after three calls during a single morning, Miss Gascon told him in her brisk, to-the-point-no-nonsense manner that she would greatly appreciate it if he would get on with his holidays and let her get on with her work. Marvin expressed appropriate contrition and managed to stay away from the telephone until the following day. It wasn't easy.

"Can't they give you peace even once a year?" Jocelyn complained about his first two days' telephone interruptions.

"It goes with the territory." Marvin managed his glib lies with a perfectly straight face. "Ah... the duties of Office."

On the fourth day they cautiously returned to more active pastimes, but thought it safer to stay close to the water. It turned out that Jocelyn was a near-expert windsurfer. She gave Marvin innumerable pointers, which succeeded, with great regularity and even greater conviction, in landing him in the water. After an hour of constant climbing onto the surfboard rather than standing on it, Marvin opted for a sitting-astride position, his legs dangling on either side. From the safety of this undignified stance, Marvin watched Jocelyn maneuver her colourful six-meter sail across the width of the lake with effortless ease. To Marvin, till the last day of the holidays, Jocelyn's dexterity remained a total enigma.

But he loved to watch her.

In fact, he could not take his eyes away from her. Her slim, lithe figure seemed even more beautiful when silhouetted against the twin peaks. She zigzagged the wind-ruffled water like an ethereal butterfly. Like a slice of a rainbow. She was his rainbow. She was the promise of things yet to come.

When Jocelyn did finally return to the shore, Marvin paddled back the few yards to join her. On coming out of the water, he noticed an irregular, broad, blood-red stripe across the white surfboard. It was obvious that he had cut himself. Since for some time he had been sitting astride with his feet in the water, he must have sustained his injury some time ago. He could have been losing blood at a reasonably good clip for at least an hour. Marvin felt a touch of weakness when he reasoned it all out. Within seconds of coming out of the water, the four-inch diagonal gash in his left calf began to itch like the blazes. He felt weak, frustrated, and angry. Mostly at himself.

"How could you just sit there bleeding?" Jocelyn's concern was mixed with annoyance.

"I didn't feel a damn thing!" he complained. "Not even the slightest bit of pain."

Marvin bit his lip. Why the hell does it throb like that now? Jocelyn was concerned, but she suspected that Marvin was not going to die. He looked more annoyed than hurt. It could have been quite another matter had he continued to lose blood for another hour.

"It didn't hurt, because you didn't know you had it," she explained.

"What has that got to do with it?"

"Just about everything," Jocelyn smiled reassurance.

Marvin shrugged. He was still boiling at his own stupidity.

"I must have cut myself at one of the instances I was climbing back onto the stupid surfboard. Windsurfer. Whatever!" He continued sulking. "At my age, I should have known better."

He should have been more diligent. A person with a different set of principles might well have considered suing the hotel. Marvin felt more like suing himself.

The consequences following turned out to be exactly what the doctor ordered. The wounded man remained prostrated on a well-padded deckchair, on their private penthouse terrace. He no longer sulked but took his medicine in the form of a succession of well-diluted Bloody Caesars. He gazed assiduously at the multi-hued greens of the fairways, the roughs and the billiard-table putting areas of the golf course flanking the three sides of the lake. Jocelyn left him periodically to get some more ice for their drinks, to fall into the lake for a quick swim, or to find out about the other activities, which might be suitable for her injured, afflicted, incapacitated, suffering man. Marvin used those occasions to jump from his deck chair, grab the telephone and get the latest news from Miss Gascon. Placated, satisfied, he returned to the self-imposed inactivity, only then being aware of any discomfort in his bandaged calf.

During the afternoon, clouds had gathered. Marvin insisted they had been organized by the hotel management for the explicit purpose of spraying the golf course. Jocelyn bought some magazines at the main lobby boutique and slumped down next to Marvin. She had not read for long before Marvin, by now thoroughly bored with his idleness, engaged her in the dissection of a statement she'd made yesterday.

"Just what did you mean it didn't hurt because I didn't know I had it?" he asked. He expected Jocelyn to read his thoughts even before they formed clearly in his own mind.

"Did I?"

A beautifully feminine answer, he thought. He waited patiently. Jocelyn sighed, put down her journal, and let her eyes wander over the breathtaking view. By some trick known only to herself, she knew exactly what he meant. The reason was that exactly the same thing had happened to her once in Florida, and that had been in salt water. In spite of the salt, Jocelyn hadn't felt a thing until she returned to the shore. And even then, initially, it took other people to point out to her the bloody sand under her feet.

"Well, I simply meant that it appears that unless you are aware of something, you are not aware of it."

This was very probably the most precisely inane answer she had ever given in her life. It wasn't her fault that her answer was also precisely correct.

"A state of consciousness...?" Marvin mused.

"I suppose so."

Jocelyn was much too relaxed to get involved in heavy thinking.

For a while they both seemed lost in their own thoughts: Marvin—in concepts leading to the evolution of consciousness; Jocelyn—absorbing the hypnotic beauty before her. When Marvin interrupted the silence, he sounded as though he were going off on a completely different tack.

"The Universe is reputed to be between ten and twenty billion years old. The earth is given between four-and-a-half and a maximum of five billion years. Most of that time it was a gaseous, then fiery ball. After a big little while, it evolved into a barren rocky desert interspersed with disgusting steaming wet cauldrons bubbling with foul-smelling soup reminiscent of rotten eggs. Am I boring you?" Marvin paused and sipped a little of his latest Bloody Caesar.

"My goodness, of course not! I just love rotten eggs. Preferably soft-boiled." Jocelyn got into the spirit of Marvin's eggs.

"To continue." Marvin did not take offence easily. "I heard recently that, somewhere in Italy, some paleontologist discovered some mollusks which had been petrified in some sort of rock, reputedly for five million years. Apparently, there was little or no discernible difference between the five-million-year-old shell and its present-day great-great-great-to-the-nth grandson. Conclusion of the commentator, regarding all this, was that evolution seems to progress at a pace somewhere between dead slow and dead slow."

"That seems to be about the pace at which you are advancing your argument, whatever it might be," Jocelyn affirmed gravely.

"Bear with me," said he, with his usual stoicism.

"What? In the middle of the day?" Jocelyn sounded very surprised. Marvin ignored the remark.

"When the smelly soup got tired of farting the hot gases into the practically nonexistent atmosphere, in time, a looong, looong eonesque time, macromolecules began to develop. Probably for no reason at all. Now man, the so-called *homo sapiens*, is given at best several million years. Somewhere in-between, for no reason that anyone can even venture to guess, the macromolecules evolved into human beings. That function being intermittently slowed down by periods of repetitive ice ages, the last of which occurred only some ten or twelve thousand years ago. We do know that one tends to be a trifle lethargic in cold temperatures, particularly when covered by a few thousand tons of ice. Are you with me, so far?"

Jocelyn gave up on the view and looked at Marvin. She still had no idea what he was driving at. She gave him the benefit of the doubt.

"So far," she temporized.

Then, presumably influenced by the sanguinary potency of the Bloody Caesar, Marvin appeared to have changed the subject again.

"So, which is first—the chicken or the egg?" he asked, his face perfectly serious.

"I vote for a chicken omelet!" Jocelyn volunteered.

Marvin looked at Jocelyn with admiration mixed with considerable surprise. He put down his glass, leaned over and stared into her eyes.

"You know, you're probably right!"

"I could have told you that to start with," she beamed.

"You see, we are always trying to decide whether the egg produced the chicken or the other way round. In other words, did evolution spawn intelligence, or was intelligence the necessary precursor of evolution. Well?" he asked.

"Quite well, thank you, and you?"

"If we assume that intelligence is antecedent to or of the evolutionary process, then it, the intelligence, exists outside the confines of physical environment. We can then explain evolution in terms of the intelligence evolving a matrix, a model, through which it can find a means of self-expression. The reverse thesis I had described before and, frankly, it tends to insult my intelligence." Marvin looked pensive.

"And the chicken omelet?" she asked.

"That's the whole point, don't you see?" He sipped a little more of the Clamato juice laced with vodka.

Jocelyn waved her head from side to side. That usually meant 'no', or, if directed principally to one side, her desire to go to bed.

"As the creative process advances in complexity, it begins to, sort of, take part in the so-called evolution. The chicken and the egg become contemporaneous: a chicken omelet." Marvin smiled. "Darwin was right. At least partially. There is a process of natural selection. But it advances at a pace far, far slower than it would have to have been in order to explain the arrival of man on this planet in the time it did, in fact, occur."

Marvin collapsed on his deck chair, his expression confident that his argument was irrefutable. Or at least ironclad.

"Charles would be happy to hear that," Jocelyn contributed. Then she gave Marvin's ideas a little serious thought. "Well, it all started with our agreeing, even if not in as many words, that we are a state of consciousness. Right? Now you tie all this together."

This time Marvin needed more time. He agreed with Jocelyn's statement. It was quite another story to put it into words. He wished he had taken it a little easier with the Bloody Caesars.

"We are what we think we are. A penniless man counts his blessings while counting the stars or regarding the bloom of an open pasture. A multimillionaire commits suicide out of perennial boredom. Who is—or in this case, was—the richer of the two? Obviously he whose consciousness was abundant. This parallel can be drawn into all sorts of examples. But, and here is the omelet, if a man is so destitute that his permanently growling stomach prevents his consciousness from enjoying freedom, the inherent richness cannot become manifest."

Marvin looked for affirmation. Jocelyn liked what she heard. She decided to continue the argument herself.

"For as long as we, the-states-of-consciousness, are attached to our demanding bodies, we have no choice but to maintain them in a condition through which our consciousness can become manifest." Then she sat up. "But, Marvin, this is almost exactly what you said before!"

"The chicken omelet," he agreed. "The problem starts when we forget about either side of the equation. As independent states of consciousness, we need our—what I can only describe as, our— physical consciousness in order to function. In this material world, so to speak, there are rules. There are always rules. Don't you ever wonder—who, what, created these rules?"

"This reminds me of what you said about ethic. None of this is any good to us unless we can survive. So the survival is the highest ethic." She still seemed to wonder.

"Ah, yes. However, the real question is, for which consciousness are we to assure survival..."

"Both?"

"That would make us immortal physically." Marvin grimaced. "That's a little bit hard to swallow."

"Well, that just leaves us with one other... Marvin, can we really become totally aware of this other, this free consciousness?"

Jocelyn's eyes drifted to the distant peaks. She and Marvin sat in paradise, discussing whether paradise existed. Progressive silence was slowly descending over the retiring nature. The mostly overcast sky to the east became scattered as it reached out toward the west, leaving a horizontal gap directly over the undulating horizon. A few piercing rays of liquid gold seemed to bounce off the mountains and paint, from beneath, the ponderous clouds with a pinkish softness. As the wind, as almost always at sunset, died down, someone stretched out the water on the now lustrous lake. The majestic twin peaks solidified, their smoothly rounded, perfectly symmetrical contours clearly etched in the enchanted mirror. The Blue Rocks were truly blue again.

Marvin completely forgot that he was supposed to be an invalid. He rose lightly from the deck chair and sat next to Jocelyn. "You know, darling, those twin peaks seem to remind me of something."

Later they went down to dinner.

The day, thanks to Marvin's slightly exaggerated injury, helped to restore them to their previous condition. The condition they were in, before the joys of holidays converted them into bundles of twitching pain. They felt rested, relaxed, and very much in love. It was quite immaterial what they did. The only important thing was that they did it together. During the last fifteen years, Marvin had visited the Blue Rocks annually. He always found the famous view surprising, even interesting. Yet never had he been moved deeply by its unfolding beauty.

After an early dinner, they took a leisurely stroll. How lucky can you get, Marvin wondered. Two and a half weeks to go. Two and a half weeks of heaven. Jocelyn seemed to agree.

Then they were back on the terrace. A moonbeam spread a narrow, unwavering cone of light across the lake. It cut the dark surface directly toward them.

"Who on earth did it, Marvin? Who was the sculptor?" She leaned her head on his shoulder. "Is it real? If order and harmony, blending, maturing into beauty is the product of an evolved intelligence, then, pray tell me, Sir, who has designed this breathtaking illusion? Blind evolution on a pilgrim snail's progress?"

Jocelyn did not expect Marvin to provide an answer. Yet to her disbelieving ears, he did. He said very softly,

"In a way, you did, darling."

* * *

22

Surprise

On Tuesday, the third of August, Marvin went back to the city. The drive took about two hours each way; the business he had to attend to, no more than four hours. A little after three in the afternoon he was back.

Marvin had invited Jocelyn to come with him, though he had left it up to her.

"My first meeting is at eight-thirty, so we should leave around six. Bit earlier, I suppose, to beat the traffic. If we get up at four-thirty, that should do it."

"And just what time are you seeing the hotel psychiatrist?" Jocelyn had been appalled.

"Can't be sure they have one..." Marvin had mused, with a straight face.

"With people like you around, they darn well should!" Jocelyn just wasn't amused. After all, this was a holiday, wasn't it?

Jocelyn had decided to make do without Marvin.

In the meantime, Marvin was rubbing his hands in tacit self-congratulations. He had decided to leave at dawn, gambling that Jocelyn would be disinclined to break the unwritten law that one gets up at six only in case of a wailing fire alarm. Perhaps, in very exceptional circumstances, for the first tee-off. But there was nothing in the PGA rulebook about getting up at five, even for golf. The gamble worked.

Marvin returned from St-Onge with mixed feelings. The work he had organized was on schedule, but there was no way it could be finished, in time, to the level of his expectations. Not in three weeks. Marvin had managed to extract a promise from the construction manager and the various trades to work the coming weekend. The fourth working weekend in a row. Marvin had to sweeten the pot considerably. The workmen were already on the verge of collapse. Still, it had to be done; the men needed more time. For his part, Marvin had to keep Jocelyn at Blue Rocks till Sunday afternoon. Presently, they had scheduled their return for Friday evening.

In spite of considerable pressure, Olive Gascon remained perfectly relaxed. She had no idea why Director Clark took the trouble to drive all the way from Blue Rocks in the middle of his holidays. Had he not left her in charge? Had not all been organized for the explicit purpose of avoiding just such a necessity? Did she not have the keys to his apartment or the plans for the exact disposition of his furniture?

"Really, *Monsieur* Clark. I really thought that you trusted me. Surely a simple phone call would have sufficed?" There was a pouting hurt on her youthful face.

Aaah, the youthful, the young... Marvin mused with a twinge of jealousy. The young never got tired. Marvin glanced at the construction workers. They really did look half-dead, meaning: 'have-been-dead-for-quite-some-time-now-but-have-continued-by-force-of-habit'. The young had another advantage. They had no idea that at least a hundred million things could go wrong. Things which they never even imagined existed.

Ignorance was their bliss!

"Miss Gascon! Not only is progress better than I had expected, but you might as well know that, without your involvement, I would not have even attempted such a venture."

Director Clark's assurance pleased Miss Gascon fiercely. In fact, his compliment disturbed her cardiovascular system to the extent of increasing an upward surge of blood toward her already rosy cheeks. For a moment she was speechless.

"Thank you, Mr. Clark, Sir." She remained formal but couldn't hide a smile tugging at her still pouting mouth.

On his way back to Blue Rocks, Marvin reflected that he, the reputedly phlegmatic, sedate, unruffled individual, who for those very qualities had been entrusted with the protection of millions of dollars percolating in and out of the City coffers... he was the only one acting like a bundle of nerves. He had to regain his composure before facing Jocelyn. Actually, Miss Gascon had been right. The work had progressed better than he had any right to expect. The extra time was more in the nature of a safety margin than of dire necessity.

Back at Blue Rocks, Marvin needed a drink. Until this holiday, he had never indulged in cocktails. Evidently his present City Hall duties, coupled with the construction work, took a lot out of him. Marvin had changed in more ways than he himself imagined.

As previously agreed, he found Jocelyn on the terrace overlooking the golf practice range. She looked contented, sipping *Kir* from an extra tall glass full of ice cubes. A demurely refreshing way to pass the time. Marvin felt like drinking something stronger but managed to restrain himself. He signaled a waiter for another round and sat next to her. He managed to avoid discussing his trip by passing comments about the men and women practicing their golf shots. Basket after basket of balls, swinging the driver in a long smooth motion.

"I understand their drive for perfection, but surely, isn't that overdoing it?" Marvin pointed to a man going after a third basket of practice balls.

Jocelyn doubled up with laughter.

"What's the joke?" Marvin looked surprised.

"It's your drive for perfection... they also use their short irons, you know!"

Jocelyn couldn't believe he missed his own golf joke. She guessed that Marvin was tired, but she couldn't resist pulling his leg.

"I see I have to *drive* my point home!" When Marvin still didn't respond, she smirked knowingly: "That's what comes of getting up at four-thirty!"

She let it go. Marvin drained his *Kir* and asked for another.

"Please, don't laugh," Jocelyn said a good while later, "but I have a little problem with this drive-for-perfection business." It was evident from her tone that she was not referring to Marvin's unfortunate pun. "Whenever I work on my sculpture, I really have no idea what, if anything, I can do to improve myself. Other, perhaps, than to stop interfering."

"With the process itself?" Marvin asked.

"Just interfering. The more I want to do something particular, the less it seems to work out... I must have an idea, I must think out its development. But once it is clearly formed in my mind, I don't seem to be allowed to change it. It's a very strange feeling."

"And what if you disobey your intuition?"

"I invariably pay for it. Sometimes I manage to get back on track. Usually, I give up and start on something new. Concepts come, concepts go. I have to jump aboard the train while it's moving, do what I have to, and get off. The train doesn't wait."

Jocelyn looked puzzled. It seemed that her own observations were surprising her.

"Not much like hitting a golf ball..." Marvin mused.

"... and yet, the golfer and I, we both strive for perfection. Funny, isn't it?"

"It might have something to do with motivation," Marvin offered.

"What do you mean?" She looked up.

"The golfer does his practice solely to improve himself. That is his sole motivation. Don't you go beyond that?"

"I really don't know. Do I? Perhaps my own perfection *per se* does not matter to me that much. I am what I am. I am more concerned—I said it before—with not interfering with the process. Could that be it?"

Jocelyn looked at Marvin, expecting an answer. He had none. He leaned back in the heavy club armchair and tried to clear his mind. Watching a dozen people spending their time hitting balls was not the most inspiring sight; nor was it conducive to finding a solution to a philosophical problem. Marvin had no idea what had started Jocelyn's train of thought. Then he remembered his 'drive for perfection'.

"Altruism?" he tried again.

"What has altruism got to do with any of this?"

"There is none in the case of the golfer," he said.

The *Kir* was finished. They sat gazing at the distant hills, each trying to fathom the question—or the answer. Marvin sensed that if Jocelyn's quandary had been shallow, it would not have attracted their thoughts. He was beginning to relax.

"I read about it some weeks ago. Altruism comes from Latin *altro*—meaning other. In Italian, I believe *altrui* is something like to or of another. I do not know who originated the word, but to me it implies an attitude. A golfer wishes to improve himself for his own sake. You, or I suppose any creative person, may have a different motivation. Your desire is directed to or toward another. Perhaps for the benefit of another?"

Marvin sounded as though he had been thinking aloud, accentuating the various references with the tone of his voice.

"And the—what I call, non-interference?"

"That's all part of it. Aren't you striving, at least at the subliminal level, to be an instrument or a channel for the creative force?" Marvin asked.

"That may be true. But does it work even if I am not aware of this fact?"

"You tell me... does it?"

She smiled broadly. "Of course! Ignorance of the law is no excuse for breaking it, but no one is punished for obeying it. In fact, isn't the fulfillment of the law supposed to be a reward in itself? Assuming, of course, that what I am trying to do is the fulfillment of some esoteric law!"

"The laws are not really esoteric; rather, we are myopic. The laws are there for everyone to see, if we would only open our eyes. Shouldn't we?"

"Shouldn't we what?"

"Open our eyes! And that goes for your ears."

He laughed a little too loudly. Some people in the club turned around. A year ago, Marvin would have shriveled into an invisible ball. Today, he hardly noticed.

"But it all depends on your point of view. Or on your attitude. Once we learn to care, we are apt to concentrate on finding ways of saving the world rather than ourselves."

"By what we just said, that would seem like a good thing."

"Not really. The golfer cannot impart his knowledge to someone else until he first acquires it himself, can he?" As he talked, Jocelyn's face was becoming cloudy. He laughed again. "It's as I said. It is a question of attitudes."

"Intentions?" Jocelyn offered, still having a problem with the concept.

"No. The intentions are immaterial," he said, sounding very sure.

"What!? You are kidding!"

The other guests again looked over their shoulders.

"I'm afraid not. The intentions must *perforce* be immaterial if you wish to be an instrument, a channel for a force, power, whatever, outside your own control. Agree?"

"Go on..." But rather than letting Marvin continue, she did so herself: "And therefore, the only thing that matters is the attitude toward the process itself. And if the intentions are immaterial, the end product is also, basically, of no consequence." She looked triumphant.

"I wouldn't say of no consequence. There is always a reason. It's just that it is not really our responsibility. We abdicate it the moment we, by an act of free will, agree to be a channel. Right?" This time he spoke very softly.

"But this would give us wonderful relaxed serenity, a tremendous sense of peace..."

Jocelyn's eyes drifted toward a narrow valley cutting in half the western horizon. Marvin loved that look in her eyes.

"...a peace beyond human understanding... I am told."

Incongruous in the midst of people drinking beer, oblivious to outbursts of hilarious laughter. Incongruous with their own musings drifting away, far, alone yet also close, together not only with each other but feeling, sensing and enjoying strange, invisible ties with all life, all life forms. Incongruous with the search—for the feeling of having discovered; incongruous yet belonging, close to an ancestral home.

Their hands touched, their sunburned fingers interlocked in a silent embrace.

"You know," Marvin whispered, "a very wise man once said that altruism is not an attribute or a trait of character. It is an act of self-preservation."

It required surprisingly little effort to persuade Jocelyn to remain another two days at the Blue Rocks, as long as she was assured of returning to the library by nine o'clock on Monday. She said that she would have been very unlikely to dip her fingers in clay, had they returned as initially scheduled; what, with her head full of glorious vistas of prodigious nature? Jocelyn had often found nature a source of inspiration, but it would be months before the impressions of the last three weeks would translate themselves into tangible forms that she could capture in her sculptures.

They left on Sunday, after an early lunch.

The drive back was smooth. Sadly, the product of man's civilization slowly displaced the panoramic vistas.

"What a pity..." Jocelyn remarked.

"Agreed. It is hard to believe, let alone accept, that man is part of nature!" Marvin commented wryly.

Driving at a leisurely pace, they arrived in St-Onge by four in the afternoon. Marvin was in no hurry. He had no more than a vague idea what they were likely to find on arrival. Infinitely more unnerving was the fact that, all along, he had treated this escapade as a surprise. He had no idea what Jocelyn's reaction would be. When she had said, some two months ago, that she trusted him 'with her life,' Marvin took her at her word. He may well have upset all her dreams, may have destroyed her aspirations. Now that the moment of truth was near, Marvin had no clear idea what on earth had possessed him to barge into her life in such an overpowering fashion.

He was never a spontaneous man. To be sure, this venture had been well premeditated, required a great deal of thought, work, coordination and sheer guts. Yet, when all was said and done, the concept itself was spontaneous. A spur of a moment. A figment of his imagination. Now that they were approaching this figment, Marvin was scared. Nervous. Becoming irritable; laconic in his answers. He wished he had discussed the whole inane idea with Jocelyn.

"Too late. My God, it's too late now..." He felt like crying aloud. "Stay here, darling, I'll open the door, then I'll fetch the baggage," he said instead.

He didn't move. He was delaying the inevitable.

Marvin had parked his rented car directly in front of Jocelyn's studio. Thank God it was Sunday. At least he could park anywhere. Almost. The stupid parking meters didn't operate on Sunday. So who cares?

"Nonsense. You stay here and I'll open the door."

She was out of the car and running before Marvin could unhinge his jaws.

God, I am nervous. What if they haven't finished? What if the whole place is an unholy mess? What if...?

Jocelyn disappeared inside. Marvin sat in the car, his hands sweating, a prickly sensation at the back of his neck. She must have gone in without looking up. So far so good. Why wasn't she coming out? Marvin was afraid to follow her. Four, five minutes, six...

Marvin wiped his palms, got out of the car and opened the trunk. With a measured step he carried two suitcases to the front door. Jocelyn had left it ajar. He walked in. Jocelyn was sitting at her working chair. She seemed very still.

Marvin cleared his throat.

When Jocelyn had first come in, she had almost missed a circular staircase on her left. It was tucked in around the corner like a delicate metal sculpture. She must have seen it from the corner of her eye. She stopped, looked behind, blinked, then looked up. The sloping roof lights were more or less where they used to be, but seemed about three feet higher, perhaps even larger, and closer to the outside wall. Well set back from their sill was a sort of gallery or mezzanine, running the full length of the main studio. It terminated about twenty feet short of the west wall, where it extended at right angles in both directions, creating a loft over the sitting area. A wall extending to the ceiling cut off part of the upstairs area.

Jocelyn turned around.

Over the existing entry with the adjacent small rooms was another mezzanine, also enclosed, hiding some mysterious compartments. The main studio area, about twenty-five feet long, remained a two-storey space, with the bridge spanning across it eccentrically, evidently to avoid blocking the natural light from the roof lights. It was apparent that the main roof had been raised. There was now almost twenty feet of unobstructed headroom. The effect was dramatic. By contrast, the sitting area, which previously had seemed lost under a fourteen-foot ceiling, now had shrunk to a more domestic scale, making it cozy and inviting.

Jocelyn heard Marvin come in. Her mouth remained slightly open, her eyes very round, the rest of her body in a peculiar kind of stupor. Only her irises moved, in quick, jerky movements, from time to time pulling her neck behind them.

"Would you like to see the rest of it?" Marvin asked lamely. His palms were sweating again.

Jocelyn looked at him as if he were some strange entity recently arrived from an alien planet. Then her eyes narrowed— there was a sign of recognition. Her head, in a seemingly involuntary movement, nodded acquiescence.

"Please don't say anything until you've seen it all..." Marvin's voice was pleading.

He needn't have worried. The possibility that Jocelyn had already regained control over her vocal chords was remote indeed.

Marvin took her by the hand and led her, unresisting, toward the circular staircase. It was just wide enough for them to walk up side by side. On the top Marvin stopped at the black, wrought-iron railing. The full length of the studio was laid out below them. Next he pulled Jocelyn's hand toward a closed door. He turned the knob and stepped aside. Inside was a large room, taking up the full area over the vestibule, the entrance hall and the kitchen below. It was sparsely furnished with office furniture. The walls were lined with bookshelves. Marvin pulled Jocelyn back and pointed to another door.

"An extra bathroom."

Jocelyn looked at him, ignoring the second door.

"Above the one below. To keep the plumbing together," he explained, pushing the doors open.

White fixtures were set in deep blue marble wall and floor tiling. Overhead the roof lights continued. The room looked like an underwater showroom.

By now Jocelyn's breathing returned to reasonably normal. Only now and again, she seemed to inhale in a strange, halting manner. Otherwise she remained silent. Once more, Marvin led her by the hand, this time to the other end of the mezzanine bridge. The mystery compartment over the sitting area still waited to be discovered. He pushed the door open and remained outside. Jocelyn, as though drawn by mysterious forces, went inside. She seemed off balance. Stepping back on the bridge, she took off her shoes and barefoot continued inwards. She pressed her feet into the deep, sensual pile. She'd never walked barefoot on a carpet that thick. With the exception of a small brother of the wood stove below, the room was quite empty.

Jocelyn reached the middle of the chamber and stopped. She must have swallowed hard at least a dozen times. Later, still speechless, she followed Marvin down the spiral staircase. She moved like a small girl; as though knowing full well that should she lose touch with her mother's hand, for even a second, she would wake up, the dream would be over, the magic spell would simply shrivel, depart, disappear.

Marvin led her to the sitting area.

"Wait for me here...?" There was a slight tremor in his voice.

Jocelyn waved her head from side to side. She refused to have this dream die. She refused to let go of his hand.

They went to the kitchen together. All new fittings and, according to Miss Gascon, the latest labour-saving gadgetry. It all made even this space look strangely different, as though wearing a suit of polished, shining armour, or at least its Sunday best. Marvin peeked into the new fridge. "Bless you, Miss Gascon," he muttered. A bottle of *Moèt & Chandon Brut* and two slim champagne glasses were waiting. Marvin, his nerves stretched raw by Jocelyn's inconsiderate silence, removed the wire, twisted the cork out with fingers on the verge of shaking, and filled two glasses with the effervescent nectar.

"Welcome home, Mrs. Prentis-Clark," he said very softly, handing one crystal flute to Jocelyn.

Jocelyn took the glass but did not raise it to her lips. After a brief moment, she put it on the counter. Then, as though still not trusting her senses, she put her arms around Marvin. She needed to know that at least Marvin was real. As her embrace tightened about his chest and shoulders, Marvin felt a deep, wrenching spasm shake, almost contort her body. Then the spasm repeated. It shook her even as she trembled, quite unable to stop, unable to do anything about it.

"There, there," he stroked her hair gently. "It's not that bad, surely..."

Marvin was crestfallen. All this work! All this work? Thoughts like needle-sharp daggers cut through his suddenly aching temples.

"It's b... b... be..." was all Jocelyn could manage.

"We'll change it... Tomorrow..." he assured.

"It's be... be..."

"Bad. Bad, I know," he tried to console her.

"Be... Beee... Beautiful!" She blurted out at last, and then could no longer hold back the tears. The front of Marvin's shirt was drenched in an instant.

"B-b-beautiful?"

Marvin took a very deep breath. My God! How he needed to hear that. Two months of tension, of keeping things from

Jocelyn. That was the part that he hated most. She had been the first person in his life from whom he had no secrets. Never again. He swore to himself. Never!

"Come, I have a surprise for you," he said innocently.

"W-w-whaaaaat...? Aaah surprise?" Nothing made sense any more.

Marvin took the bottle and his glass into one hand, made Jocelyn carry her own, and led her back to the downstairs sitting area. Here everything was as before except for a new carpet under the skin rug. He sat her down, gave her a box of facial tissue, and reached into his pocket. From there he took out an envelope. He gave it to her.

"What is it?"

"A surprise," he repeated.

Jocelyn tore the envelope open and took out a crisp sheet of folded paper. Even as she read it, her eyes once again grew wider. The document was a deed of ownership of the building bearing her studio's address. The deed had been made out in her name. Once more the floodgates opened as her exhausted body collapsed in another shudder.

Marvin went to the kitchen in search of a new box of tissues. He took his time. He also felt emotionally exhausted. He had been torn, uncertain. Now, on the last day of his holidays, he merely felt tired. When he returned to Jocelyn, he found her completely recovered. There was even a touch of fresh makeup on her face. She was holding up a glass of Champagne for him. When next she spoke, her eyes gleamed with a naughty sparkle, her lips just a little pouting.

"Marvin?" Her voice was demure.

"Yes, darling?" He wondered what was coming.

"Do you still want to marry me?"

"I am giving it serious consideration." He, too, was beginning to recover.

"How do I know you're not marrying me for my money?"

"You don't know. But it improves your chances..."

"I was afraid of that."

With that, Jocelyn's lips trembled. She reached out for the new box of tissues. Then, holding the whole box against her heaving breast, she fell back against the settee. It was a fair, if slightly exaggerated, imitation of a Victorian swoon.

"You men are all the same!" she whimpered in a deeply hurt voice.

"Maybe. But I am willing to learn new tricks if you let me?" With that, Marvin moved closer to the long-suffering quarry.

"Why, Sir! Well, I never! Do you wish to have your way with me?"

"Yes, you did, and I most certainly aim to try, Scarlett," Marvin replied in his best southern accent.

It was all much too much. Jocelyn snuggled close to Marvin and listened to his heart restoring its normal rhythm. It took time.

"I love you," she whispered.

These were the last words either spoke for a long while.

* * *

23

Freedom

Only two witnesses were present.

The *Palais de Justice* registry office was as inane, bleak and impersonal as only a government office can be. Cold fluorescent lighting underlined the insipid dullness of gray furniture nailed to a gray carpet spanning between severe gray walls. One obligatory colour accent behind the judge's daïs failed to relieve the inherent lassitude. This municipal chamber of joy was presided over by a longhaired, spectacled, dull-faced registrar, hiding in a frayed black robe apparently designed to conceal the dubious sexual affiliation of the wearer. He or she was either a very effeminate man or a very masculine woman.

As Marvin entered the courtroom, he experienced an uncomfortable sensation of *déjà vu*, of something sinister better left forgotten.

Mrs. Prentis bore witness on the side of the bride, John Norwich on the bridegroom's. John, Marvin's senior by some ten years, had joined the City the same year as Marvin. Since Marvin's last promotion, this mature, elegant, confirmed bachelor was the only man who continued addressing Director Clark by his first name.

The marriage ceremony was as close to a burlesque as anything else emanating from any authoritarian source. For the last five minutes, Jocelyn, Marvin, Mrs. Prentis and John Norwich stood at attention waiting for the morose hermaphrodite to hand down the sentence.

"You realize that I repudiate all responsibility for any petulant contention I may be forced to make in the French language!" Jocelyn whispered in Marvin's ear.

Actually she spoke French fluently, and she had whispered a little too loudly. In the presence of Quebec functionaries, one does not joke about anything connected with the Official Languages Act. Language, be it French, *patois* or *franglais*, was a matter of pride, of culture, of heritage, not of jest or reprobate ridicule. As punishment for Jocelyn's folly, they all had to endure a bilingual repetition of all the marital assertions, be they vows or threats, thus stretching the farce even longer.

At long last—the nuptial kiss.

Rudolf Valentino himself would have approved Marvin's arabesque-assisted osculation. This was a new, different, to the two witnesses completely unrecognizable Marvin. John Norwich gasped, Mrs. Prentis gasped twice, Jocelyn giggled with impunity.

Justice accomplished, they all signed the official ledgers and filed outside in quick succession. Once outside the dismal mausoleum, each one breathed a generic sigh of relief.

Nuptials notwithstanding, Jocelyn and Marvin continued to act like perennial teenagers. Or perhaps like... newlyweds? Marvin, donning his debonair suit of lightheartedness, lifted Jocelyn up in his arms and paraded down the long granite stairs toward the awaiting limousine. He accomplished this feat with a perfectly straight, perhaps even somber face. Jocelyn judged Marvin's behaviour as perfectly normal. Mrs. Prentis thought otherwise.

"My God!" She squeezed hard the best man's arm. "Whatever happened to the poor boy?"

By that time Marvin had carefully deposited Jocelyn on the sidewalk, only to perform a quick dance reminiscent of a fandango. His dark hair, deeply suntanned complexion and a thrusting chin combined to accentuate the seriousness of the occasion. Mrs. Prentis's cheeks assumed a dangerous hue.

Neither Jocelyn nor Marvin wanted a marriage ceremony. Neither needed it. Neither wanted to tie, by force or otherwise, another person to themselves by an act of law. Now or ever. They both believed that marriage was an agreement between two free people to help each other grow. Together. To grow as human beings, as individuals and, should it be so destined, to impart those very same sentiments to their children. There was no room in their philosophy for witnesses, for togged functionaries, nor any other officials deriving their authority from a fancy dress or a diploma.

In time, Jocelyn and Marvin would want to invite their friends to join them. Not to celebrate or witness any vows, for none such had been made in earnest, but to share in their joy of sharing each other. To celebrate their newfound freedom to live and support, and to help each other. Freedom to expect nothing, to rejoice in their giving, to celebrate with them the exalted, the divine, the unifying art of loving.

In spite of the banality of the ceremony, or perhaps because of it, Mrs. Prentis had shed a secret tear. It could have been a long-awaited, long-hoped-for tear of joy. Whatever had happened to the poor boy, he did look happy... And Jocelyn? Jocelyn was a miracle worker. Of that Mrs. Prentis was absolutely certain.

The chauffeur took them to a small restaurant where Mrs. Prentis had arranged for a small reception. The fat mushroom corks, once driven in by the *Cuvée Dom Pérignon*, twice ricocheted off the ceiling. They toasted the newlyweds. John poured again and toasted Mrs. Prentis. Mr. and Mrs. Marvin Clark toasted John and Mrs. Prentis together. Then they all toasted each other. By the eleventh toast, John Norwich was beginning to regard Aunt Jenny with a suspiciously promiscuous eye. The luncheon was noisy, tasty and joyful.

At long last, Marvin, who had had his office provide an extra-large limousine for the occasion, had the driver drop them off at the studio and their guests at their respective addresses. *"La commedia è finita!"* Marvin sang in his best Italian, when finally he and Jocelyn were left alone. He then turned to his bride and said: "You are sure you want to marry me?" There was real concern in his voice. Perhaps a touch of incredulity?

"Not if you ever sing again," she sounded very grave.

"I promise. Well?" he insisted.

"I'll think about it." Her brow furrowed in a visible effort of concentration. "The answer is no. Not if we have to go through all that again."

Then Jocelyn smiled with that incredible, spontaneous warmth, which had made Marvin fall in love with her the very instant he had first met her. He again recalled lying at her feet, at the bottom of Aunt Jenny's staircase.

"But I am quite prepared to live with you in sin. The more often the better!" she added with a salacious if contrived wink.

"Can't you ever be serious?" he asked gravely.

"I was. Shall we go upstairs?"

It took all the time Jocelyn could spare to convert the marvelous new space into a living, breathing home. Before, the studio was a workspace with a small part reserved for collapsing from exhaustion. This premise would not work anymore. The new configuration not only offered individual rooms but even defined areas destined for specific uses. The lower ceiling over the sitting area, the mezzanine bridge, the circular stair divided the space into identifiable compartments.

They still had to transport Marvin's stereophonic system and install it upstairs, in his extra large study. Downstairs, Jocelyn's own radio and tape recorder provided the necessary white noise to mask, on occasion, a hammer chopping at hard gypsum plaster. Then there was the new furniture, new curtains, new king-size, voluptuous, multicoloured linen, and new towels for the bathrooms. But what made the biggest difference were the many light fixtures. By having them wired together, Jocelyn could completely change the appearance of the whole mystery garden.

Finally, Delicious Monster was hauled to its new location. First, the myriad liana had been lowered to the floor of the attic. Then, six pairs of very careful hands transferred it to a large station wagon. In its new location, *monstera* was attached to a special latticework on the underside of the bridge, with additional wires spanning up to the edge of the roof light. The two enormous earthenware pots rested at the far end, where the studio space ended and the sitting area began. The Monster looked deliciously happy. Jocelyn looked exhausted.

Marvin? Marvin looked and was flabbergasted.

He had never imagined what Jocelyn's touch could contribute. His intention had been to resolve an irresolvable problem. To find or create a space, any space, in which they could both live together. Jocelyn had started where Marvin had finished. She had created a series of havens overlooking an enchanted garden.

"An Eden. A place that dreams are made of..." He seemed lost in utopia.

"Yes, Adam. Now you can take out the garbage!"

Jocelyn was ready to resume sculpting. She surrounded her worktable with twin rows of pots Marvin had initially supplied. Some of the rubber plants and palms had grown into trees, reaching up almost to the underside of the roof lights. Before, Jocelyn had worked in a conservatory spattered, here and there, with some subtropical flora. Now she would work in a veritable jungle. She felt a bit like a monkey.

Time was also fast coming for a house-warming party.

Initially, the party was intended for Aunt Jenny with lodgers and a few colleagues from Marvin's old department, complemented by the usual contingent from Jocelyn's library. Then dear Aunt Jenny did her usual kind of good-natured meddling. She telephoned her brother. She also announced to

any and all who would listen that the forthcoming party would
be a celebration of nuptials.

Jocelyn and Marvin had once overheard her.

"The innocence of youth, a new bride and her knight..."
Aunt Jenny had whispered conspiratorially.

"New? Wouldn't a bride slightly tarnished be closer to the
mark?" Jocelyn murmured.

"She said new, not young, darling, isn't that a
concession?" Marvin asked.

"Speak for yourself!"

"Would you rather be tarnished?"

"Of course. Very young, brand new, slightly tarnished in
transit. That way you can blame it on the Post Office. Everyone
else does!"

Once the cat had escaped the bag, Mr. & Mrs. Clark
decided they would just as well be hanged for a horse as for a
hare. They invited all, literarily *all* the people involved in the
reconstruction of the studio. Starting with the architects and
engineers, and ending with every single workman who had
taken part in the remodeling, in any manner whatever. Their
wives, if such were in evidence, were also welcome. Next came
the people with whom Marvin had worked most closely of late,
plus some from his more prosaic past in the P&R Department.

Marvin had compiled the guest list with the help of the
irrepressible Miss Gascon who, in the meantime, had become
'slightly' pregnant. He discovered that Miss Gascon had become
a Mrs. in a *very* secret wedding, intended to conceal a slight error
in the timing of a romantic interlude with her paramour, about
four months ago. Marvin was happy for her, though a little
afraid of losing her good services. Then he relaxed.

"I would very much like to come back after the shortest
possible maternity leave, Sir. The moment he'd be due, I mean
her, I mean, well, you know, Sir...?"

"You will be more than welcome, Mrs. ah...?"

"Oh, it's still Gascon, *Monsieur*. It seemed much easier that
way."

Indeed it was. That way.

In the end, neither Marvin nor Jocelyn had any idea how many people came to the "wedding". John Prentis, who stayed with them for three days in Marvin's upstairs study, counted a grand total of sixty-two wedding presents. All that in addition to flowers, some magnum bottles of Champagne and a few oversized boxes of delicious chocolates.

Mr. Prentis had arrived a day early and insisted on picking up the tab for the whole reception. Marvin gave in partially. He allowed him to pay for the food, but absolved him from any costs of alcoholic beverages. Then John Prentis insisted that Marvin address him by his first name.

"There's just no way that you'll call me daddy! Why, I'm young enough to be your...?"

"...brother?" Marvin liked the echo of Jocelyn's smile in her father's eyes.

John's waving arms reduced the question to a matter of no importance. Instead, he resumed his unsuccessful attempts to ascertain Marvin's position at the City Hall.

"You must be doing something right, my boy, if they kept you there that long. Mustn't you?" John's keen eyes searched Marvin's face.

"Not necessarily, John. I do believe that for the first fifteen years they weren't quite sure if I had been there at all," Marvin assured his father-in-law, with a perfectly straight face.

"If you weren't all there?" John Prentis asked over the din of drinking people.

"No, Sir, I mean if I had been there at all," Marvin corrected.

"Isn't that what I just said?"

Mr. Prentis was definitely confused. He also looked a trifle worried. Then he shrugged and went looking for his daughter. Finally he found her hiding in the jungle.

"Is Marvin all there?" he asked her point-blank.

"Good Lord, Daddy, of course not. He never has been!" she assured her father with quiet confidence.

At that precise moment, Mr. Prentis decided that his daughter must know what she was doing, and if she didn't, she looked damned happy doing it. There still was virtue in ignorance, his face indicated.

"I'll have me a little drink and mind my own business," he muttered to himself, in a resigned tone of mutter.

Then came the orders.

During the next hour, fourteen people asked Jocelyn to reserve for them one or the other of her sculptures. Jocelyn was very ambivalent about accepting orders during her wedding party. The men insisted. Most had worked on the alterations and wanted a souvenir of their labours. The cameras were clicking like giant crickets on a summer evening, their flashes like fireflies. Admittedly, the sculptures had been on display. There was no other place to put them. Marvin was tickled pink.

"Don't worry, darling, I paid them enough in overtime alone to cover all your prices!" he whispered to her on the side. But he wasn't mercenary. He looked as proud as punch.

The last guest, not counting Jocelyn's father, left at two o'clock in the morning. The nuptials had been an unqualified success.

Three days of cleaning up later, the newlyweds began to settle into their new routine. Jocelyn continued at the library, working on her sculptures in the evening. Within three weeks, she asked the director of the library if she could reduce her working hours to some sort of part-time arrangement. She wanted to spend more time with Marvin, without sacrificing her creativity. Recently her boss, Director Robinson, had been told to reduce his budget. It all worked out fine. Jocelyn and one other employee, who had made a similar request, had been left to split one full-time job between them. Six half-days, or three days each per week.

In two weeks all had been settled. Jocelyn worked one week Tuesdays through Fridays, and the following week, on Monday, Friday and Saturday. Jocelyn retained her much-needed contact with the 'outside world' while being able to put more hours into her sculpture. Although she took her wifely duties very seriously, her obligations remained quite singularly undefined. Marvin, having lived all his life alone, had few demands on

Jocelyn's time. He had always been steadfastly independent.
Neither of them was particularly gifted in the culinary realm.
They opened cans, ate out, and not less than twice a week visited
Aunt Jenny. Dear Aunty was more than happy to see them.

For Marvin it was like rolling back the time.

For the moment, Marvin's old attic remained unoccupied.
On occasion, while Jocelyn indulged her need for women's talk
with Aunt Jenny, Marvin would don his old, nowadays seldom-
used suit of invisibility, slip out unobserved, and climb the long,
creepy staircase. At the top he would pause, then enter quietly,
almost shyly, and listen to the distant echoes of his past. It was
there, sitting on the narrow sill of the bay window, his foot
dangling to and fro like a metronome counting off those distant
echoes, that Marvin reviewed the last year of his life.

It came to him, over a number of visits, that the seemingly
disjointed events of his life had been arranged and imposed on
his will for a specific reason. They all led toward predetermined
aims. Forces, which remained beyond his comprehension,
guided his every move, even his thoughts, to a particular
purpose. There had been no accidents. No luck. There was only
evidence of an unwavering purpose.

Initially, when Marvin had begun escaping from the
vicissitudes of objective reality, he had not been aware that, by
hiding within the subjective realms, he had abdicated the
privilege of being a cause—cause defined as that which is
responsible for an effect. He had abdicated the responsibility
and thus the growth resulting from being an initiator of events.
Inadvertently, he had become a lax, pliant effect of other
peoples' initiatives. He had become a product, a result—rather
than the creator. It was all the more strange that it took him such
a long time to realize this inherent self-imposed limitation since,
within his inner worlds, within the subjective realities, Marvin had
been the sole architect, the supreme creator of those enchanted
realms. The earliest steps may have been the result of some
deeply rooted subconscious currents, perhaps some repressed
hungers, unrequited desires—but not for long. No matter how
great the inboard computer, sooner or later the ship would have

veered off course, had it not been held firmly by the calm, confident hand of a determined captain.

A captain, a creator. A Master of his universe.

Marvin's subconscious mind was the inboard computer; his conscious awareness—the captain's steadying hand. As he gathered experience, the computer accumulated additional data. The inner realms grew in geometric progression. From buoyant fields of wild flowers, by shifting his attention, his mind could whisk him to the heart of a distant galaxy. The limits seemed defined only by his own ability to absorb what he experienced.

And then his computer must have reached an overload.

Rather than explore ever-widening horizons, Marvin noticed that he was returning repeatedly to his favourite havens. He had drawn a full circle. What began as an escape and had grown into a creative impulse reverted, once more, to an escape from a mundane reality. Marvin no longer challenged new worlds; no longer did he act as a brave explorer. Rather, he began to rely on the inboard computer, on the acquired knowledge, to provide an escape. An escape into realms of stability, of safety. The monotony from which Marvin had been escaping began to invade his inner worlds by a strange, persistent osmosis. It seemed to infect the inboard computer like an invective virus: denying change, challenge, denying vitality. Perhaps denying life itself.

Peace, desire for inner peace, had become Marvin's obsession.

It was about then, a year ago, that Fate threw him into the turbulent waters. His ship plunged into mysterious chasms; it was battered, buffeted, ripped by unknown forces. Marvin had thought that, forewarned, he would know more of what lay ahead. It turned out to be an illusion. Forewarning may have made him more resilient, but it failed to reveal what lay ahead. He had already lost the explorer's instinct. The winter that followed had forced him into facing new currents, into drawing on his innermost resources to keep a steady hand on the difficult, heavy-weather helm of his irrepressible, often unresponsive vessel.

Finally he stopped. He threw in the towel.

Bruised, tired, resigned, Marvin gave up hope of resolving his turmoil by mental processes which had once served him with such practical successes. He stopped analyzing, dissecting, even attempting a synthesis. He reached deeper. He began listening to the dictates of his innermost heart. He began looking forward. He stood up to face the future. A humbling, risky, perhaps a deadly journey, but no other course offered any hope whatever. Then came the first glimpse of a rainbow.

Rather than sating his long-entrenched desires, Marvin directed his efforts at uncovering what had caused them to start with. He refused to remain a mere cork bouncing on turbulent waters. He resolved to become a prime cause—not just of his inner subjective universes, but of the flesh and blood worn on his weary bones. For the first time in his taxing life, Marvin resolved to assume total responsibility for all, yes, for *all* his actions. No longer would he blame arduous fate, or governments, religions, or sways in economic currents for the trials and tribulations of his personal existence. Marvin was ready to reach out for the helm—regardless of the weather.

It was a new beginning.

One such soul-searching evening found Marvin again brooding over some real or imaginary problems. Again he leaned against the darkening window, his leg dangling over the narrow sill. He didn't notice when Jocelyn entered; his old carpet absorbed the sound of her steps. With his back to the window, Marvin's face was in shadow, his facial expression not immediately discernible. Jocelyn sat next to him saying nothing. She had learned to respect her husband's need for moments of silence.

She waited by the windowsill as a summer drizzle began spattering the large panes with elongated tears.

Marvin sighed, gave Jocelyn a noncommittal smile. His mind was still distant, toying with memories, his eyes resting on the piano at the far end of the room. They had left it behind. At least for now. The piano steadfastly refused to repeat the magic that had once spawned the *Poème*. Marvin closed his eyes. The echoes. The long-lasting echoes... A distant gale... snow swirling madly, cold, cold indifference....

Marvin took Jocelyn's hand and pulled her toward him till she leaned her back against his chest.

"Listen," he said. "Close your eyes, let go, and just listen... to my past..."

She heard nothing but a gentle tattoo of raindrops. Then the pattern became superimposed on the steady beat of Marvin's heart. Strong though almost silent, yet as unrelenting as the waves pounding a rock overhanging an ocean. Jocelyn listened to the distant echoes. Then the waves flattened, melted into a bleak, featureless wilderness. A moment of oblivion... She thought she had seen it. She thought she had dreamt of it before...

....indifference dissolving into buoyant waves of springtime: waves of light, golden, victorious, cutting through retreating cloud cover... golden rays, piercing, explosive, passing so quickly, so quickly.... like gossamer haze of a tenacious memory...

....new waves, sweltering, slow, lazy, relaxing.... unhurried buzzing within lethargic beehive, droning over an ocean of wild, wild flowers... all colours, a myriad... a trill of a lark, clear, soaring way up high, contented... flirting with marshmallows, sweet, pink in sunset, suspended, inert, ignoring the gentle breath caressing her face... so gently....

"Once this was my private haven. My own little escape..."

Marvin's voice reached Jocelyn from a great distance. She stirred slowly, unwilling to give up her vision.

"Don't move just yet, darling." Now he sounded much closer. "I'm right here, with you."

As though in a dream, Jocelyn felt his arms around her, her back pressing against his chest, her head resting on his shoulder. An inexplicable joy ran through her body, like a current of pure pleasure. She now held on to her vision, to his arms, to his support. She was willing to stay there forever. Her eyes opened only after she felt a touch of his lips. The contours of her vision trembled, shimmered like an image distorted by hot air rising over a surface saturated with a summer's sunshine, then drifted away, slowly...

"Did you see it too...? What was that...?"

Her eyes closed again in a vain attempt to recapture what was there no more. Marvin could only smile. He could only guess at what it was that Jocelyn had seen or imagined. He'd probably been there, many a time.

"That was my inner kingdom," he said at last.

In a way Jocelyn knew that, but the answer failed to satisfy her. Did Marvin imbue this room with his presence? Had the long years of lonely contemplation impregnated these walls, this space itself, with his dreams, his desires? There was no point in rushing him. If it was his to share, he would—in his own time, when he was ready.

"You're welcome to visit. There are no restrictions," he continued smiling.

"How?" she whispered.

"The same way we did today. It is a secret method. I have no idea what it is..."

"But... but..."

What could he tell her? Years upon years of diligent pursuit....

"You must enter what I call a desireless state of consciousness," he finally answered. He knew that his reply didn't really make sense. "In a way I cannot define. It, then, makes you... receptive?"

"But I want to return there!" Jocelyn rebelled. "The beauty, the serene beauty..."

"That is the whole trouble. To *want* does not open the gates. When you push, you only block the access further. The gates open inward... toward you."

Marvin spoke slowly, as if thinking aloud. How could he tell her that by retreating he soared forward? He had made so many of those inner travels, yet he had never attempted to analyze the methods of entry into his private kingdom. It worked or it didn't. He simply tried again, if need be.

"Oh, why am I so stupid? I just do not understand." The wondrous joy instilled by her vision seemed to dissipate. Her hunger to see, to hear more, again, at will, displaced her previous pleasure. "Please tell me, Marvin."

She looked lost, like a child. Her eyes pleaded more than her words demanded.

"I only wish I could, dear. It is as I said. A state of no desire. When you expect nothing, you possess the kingdom. For as long as you have needs, unfulfilled desires, you just cannot enter... What more can I tell you? Relax, have unbounded faith, ask for nothing, trust and be thankful."

Marvin's eyes closed, his vision turned inward. For an instant he saw six candles burning steadily at the distant altar. Then, years ago, just looking at them had been enough. Just looking. That was how it had all started. Things were so easy when one was a child... So many years. As so often when sitting here, alone, Marvin scanned his years of withdrawal, years hidden behind thick walls of sophistic armor. There had been dangers inherent. There had been years of escape. There had also been great freedom.

"There are no armed guards blocking the way to the inner realm," he said softly. "No one but you can keep you from entering. This whole, endless reality lies exclusively within you."

Sometimes it had been so simple. Sometimes he recalled sitting for hours just hoping...

"You mean, within *you*!"

An accusation was only half hidden in her strangely avid eyes. How well he remembered. The inner kingdom creates an irresistible hunger. He smiled his understanding.

"Some time ago I made a considerable effort to define reality. To set the line between the inner world and the outer. I could not. The nearest I came was to accept that what I do perceive with all my senses is also real, regardless of any objective definitions. Whether there is an independent reality to which we can all gain access, I do not know. I do know that this is the second time that you chose to visit mine. Perhaps love is the key. Perhaps trust. Perhaps it's just an act of faith. I do not know. It might be the combination of all of them. One thing I do know. And that is that if you dictate your conditions of entry, if you push against any barriers, real or imagined—you fail. Relax, trust, be grateful. Be grateful for what you have. For reasons I do not understand, this state of consciousness is the closest to the desireless state I mentioned before. Also, it is the only state of consciousness that offers, affirms and maintains freedom. Freedom from any and all conditions. In any world. In this valley of death or within the inner kingdom. It is really up to us. As always."

"So we do have free will." She remembered their previous discussion.

"From all I can gather, we are only free to oppose our progress toward the ultimate realm of unmitigated freedom. We can delay it, perhaps for millions of years, but we cannot oppose it indefinitely."

As Marvin talked, his voice gained authority. This was his turf. This was where he had spent painful years crawling, then walking, before he'd learned to fly.

"That alone is enough to relax anyone's wrought nerves," Jocelyn mused.

"It should be. But you know, it is quite incredible to what length most people would go to delay their inevitable arrival at the gates of their private heaven. If it weren't so sad, it would be laughable!"

As if to prove his point, Marvin's wry laughter had no mirth in it at all. He was thinking of his own adamant procrastination.

"Will you teach me?" Jocelyn's tone was almost plaintive.

"I don't know that I can—that anyone can. I can tell you what route I took to find the gates, but there are no guarantees. Every human, every being in these countless universes is a unique tiny universe unto themselves. I am the way, but only for myself. You are the way. Your way. I can point to the direction I took—you must see if it works for you, if it gets you anywhere. I can always try to help you, I always shall; but you must do your own walking, running, climbing. Ultimately soaring. There are no shortcuts that I know of."

Marvin looked into her eyes filled with sparks of an iridescent rainbow. He had never been more aware how much he loved this woman. He could tell her that she, in a way, had opened his gates after they had remained closed for a number of months. But would it help?

"It doesn't sound very easy..."

Jocelyn looked a little sad. She looked as if a wonderful toy had been given her and then suddenly withdrawn, without so much as an explanation why.

"Don't be sad. I shall tell you a little-known secret on this eternal journey. Little known, because we seldom look under our feet. The secret is that, once you find the way, it will seem so obvious, so simple, almost easy..."

"Almost?"

"There seems to be a small catch. The way is very narrow. It is extremely easy to fall off the ridge... and the higher you climb, the farther there is to fall. There are no guarantees. Ever!"

"Never? Never is a long time!" Jocelyn couldn't accept that. "Surely once you learn, acquire experience..."

"Never. There is another catch. You may never stop on this journey. It has no end, no beginning. There is always the next step. And the next. And then you realize that today will always remain the eternal now. The sum total of all your yesterdays. The first, always the first day of your eternal future."

"It sounds almost like fun!" Jocelyn said, though her voice did not yet carry much conviction. "It's like living always in the present."

"Precisely," Marvin agreed.

"I love you," she said.

"Now, in the present?"

"I suspect, a bit longer."

"Eternally?" he teased.

"That's quite a long time," she mused.

"I have plenty of that," he assured her.

"Oh, all right then. Have it your way."

"What? Right here? What about Aunt Jenny?"

"I don't know. You can ask her later, if you like!"

And they went on like this, and on and on... Eternity did seem like quite a long time. They just didn't mind anymore.

What really mattered was today.

* * *

24

Being

"Now what?"

Jocelyn was happy. She spent long hours with her fingers, hands, arms up to her elbows in cool yielding clay. Her compositions had grown larger, more commanding, exuding confidence. Dreams made solid. She had spent years running away, or perhaps searching, and now she had found it.

"I have. Haven't I? Is there more than this?"

This was never all there was. Each day brought new insights, new ideas, new challenges. All she had to do was to listen. Relax and listen to her inner voice. Some called it inspiration. She called it humble sedulity.

Jocelyn spent days alone, allowing her mind to wander. Her fingers kneaded, cajoled and caressed the malleable substance. Hour after hour she transmuted the gray, yielding protoplasm into abstract ideas, then solidified them into living forms. Living? Very much so, once she breathed life into them.

Her fingers moved practically of their own volition. The sculpture had already been created. It already existed in her mind. It was up to her hands to bring it out into the open. A dormant entity frozen in time and space. A paradox. By making an idea permanent, she made it transient. The act of birth carried a sentence of death. Irrevocable. Aren't all things physical—transient?

And now what? And what of Marvin?

Marvin returned home daily at the usual time. A hard day in the office? Not really. The usual. It that all there was to it? The usual?

"You know, we had both started by running in search of something in quite opposite directions... only to find it at the bottom of Aunt Jenny's staircase."

"Yes, darling. I love you, too."

Marvin was a little more tired than usual. It was Friday. The last arbitration had dragged on for a month.

And what of Marvin?

For a long time, only Aunt Jenny had known of their particular dilemma. Aunt Jenny's keen perceptions seemed reserved for those willing to stand quietly on the sidelines. But later on, it had been Jocelyn who had caused Marvin to take a sharp, recondite turn on his personal journey. It had been Jocelyn who had awakened him. True, she had stirred in Marvin emotions of latent adolescence. But it had also been she who had shown this dear, once introverted hermit that love could not be secured by reciprocal, only by unconditional giving.

"How's your new creation coming?"

Marvin peeked over her shoulder. Until the sculpture was finished, he could seldom read Jocelyn's intentions. But peeking was fun. He used the opportunity to plant a kiss on her neck.

"It won't be finished if you carry on like that," she rebuked gently.

Jocelyn covered the clay with a wet cloth to protect it from drying. Her hands still dirty, she leaned back on her hard-backed chair. Her eyes were shining, the afterglow of a creative effort.

"People say that art imitates life. That's nonsense." Jocelyn sounded as though she had expected an argument.

"I agree," Marvin smiled; he'd guessed what was coming.

"That it does or it doesn't?"

"That it's nonsense."

Jocelyn sighed with relief. She looked triumphant.

"Right! Surely, art is meant to inspire life, not to imitate it! In a way, it initiates a process of life, or at least participates in the rites of initiation."

"In its highest form," Marvin nodded.

Jocelyn went to wash her hands. She came back with a bottle of wine and two glasses. Tonight they were eating at home. The wine would serve in lieu of cocktails, to wash down the main course and as an after-dinner digestive. A sort of three-in-one trick. She put the tray down on the low table and turned to go back to the kitchen.

"I have a surprise for you," Marvin spoke to her back.

"It will have to wait, darling. It's Friday, remember?"

Marvin went upstairs to put on casual slacks and slippers while Jocelyn disappeared into the kitchen. Friday was Marvin's day off. Off—from the domestic chores. He was not allowed into the kitchen under any circumstances. The same was true of Jocelyn on Mondays. Back downstairs, Marvin picked up a copy of the *St-Onge Herald* and took a sip of cool Chardonnay while waiting.

He found his name mentioned in the *Herald* almost daily. Without the slightest effort on his part, his name became well known to the citizens of St-Onge. A limelight he once tried so hard to avoid. It no longer bothered him. It also gave him no pleasure.

On the other hand, Marvin's unprecedented success in the field of arbitrations had given him a powerful if bemused hold over the City Fathers. Two weeks ago he had presented mayor LeGrand with a proposal. His Worship had completely forgotten Marvin's original letter of appointment. He had refreshed the mayor's memory particularly as regarding one phrase:

"...to *initiate*... new proposals... directed toward establishing a closer and more intimate relationship... (with) ...the general public..."

He had underlined the word *initiate*.

In addition, Marvin had carefully highlighted all the pertinent clauses in the original letter, noting quietly but firmly that there was no any mention of any arbitration. At this, Jean-Paul LeGrand's face had turned a few shades redder. All the same, the mayor had judiciously decided not to argue the merits of Marvin's new proposal.

Marvin had asked for very little.

He had requested that City Hall donate its walls to the young, or the unknown, or the up-and-coming artists who needed wall space protected by a good security system, while offering a good public exposure. The City Hall's extensive corridors qualified on all counts.

The following day, notices announcing the mayor's generosity had appeared in the press. The response had been tremendous. Within the next two weeks, Marvin had discussed the program with eleven other municipalities surrounding the *Ville de Montréal.* All were enthusiastic. This was great P.R. work, they all said.

Marvin was pleased. The groundwork was laid. The formulation of criteria for the selection of artists remained the only outstanding matter.

"So what's the surprise?"

"I need your help." Marvin tried to look contrite.

"That is the surprise?"

Marvin told Jocelyn about the outstanding matter. They agreed to use basic James Joyce criteria as guidelines. If possible. If not...? Jocelyn sounded doubtful.

"Well, we'll see. Beauty's in the eye of the beholder, but art? There seems so little beauty around these days. It must have something to do with the way people live, I suppose."

"Something to do with the time factor?" Marvin mused.

"How come?"

"You cannot measure art in terms of time. Had they told the Egyptians to build the pyramids in a couple of years, or decades, they would never have been erected. One cannot measure art with a yardstick of time. Yet today, if an artist doesn't produce a work of art in a few hours, he doesn't eat."

"I suppose artists would find working on an hourly basis rather demeaning, don't you think? But we went through all that before," Jocelyn reminded him.

"And are no nearer to the solution."

"A talent is a gift. One must repay it. Too many artists seem concerned with their egos rather than with the act of giving..." Jocelyn said. "You either are an artist or you are not. You cannot become one if the gift isn't there. All you can do is be."

They sipped some more wine.

"Aunt Jenny is right," Jocelyn declared out of the blue. As Marvin didn't comment, she continued. "She is, sort of, just being."

"As against becoming?"

"Well, becoming takes time. Being... just is. Anyway, there is a difference." Jocelyn's voice tilted upward, formulating a question.

Marvin thought that, at this rate, one bottle of Chardonnay would not last the evening. He was in no hurry. He needed to take his mind off constant squabbles about matters of little importance. About matters toward which he felt profound indifference. Perhaps that is why he was so good at his work. His success may have been due to his complete emotional detachment. Essentially he dealt with matters of pride, ambition and money or, to be more concise, of human greed. Matters that neither would nor could affect his life.

Jocelyn's words turned Marvin's thoughts to Aunt Jenny's Victorian mansion.

Perhaps only now, perhaps it had always been that way, but within the mansion's dark-red, ponderous walls time appeared to have stood still. His attic had remained empty. Aunt Jenny no longer needed the extra income. She did what she did to be useful and kindly. If in later years she would need any assistance, it would not be financial; rather, she would need some help with the preparation of meals. Those she could no more stop providing than her guests could stop breathing. At least, not until then. Once Aunt Jenny had confessed to Jocelyn that when the time came for her bones to take it easy, she would offer her attic to any girl willing to help her in exchange for free lodgings. Marvin thought Aunt Jenny was a very wise woman.

"Well, she is active, efficient, organized, never in a hurry. She is the source of her lodgers' happiness. She is their hope, their security, their protection. Not a bad way to live. In a way, she is just 'being'. *Par contre*, you and I seem to be in a state of constant becoming," Marvin admitted.

"So who's right?"

"We all are, but she is closer to... She is closer to the theoretical ideal."

"Why didn't you say perfection?" Jocelyn was a mind reader.

"Because perfection doesn't exist. To accept perfection would be to deny becoming. And being, for that matter."

"Oh?"

"That's a little more complicated." Marvin took another sip. "I'd have to venture into realms which ruled my life for quite a long time. As I see it, becoming is a function of advancing on our personal journey by the use of our senses. We do things in order to learn, to acquire experience. We see, smell, feel, touch... whatever."

Jocelyn slid down onto the carpet and leaned against the settee with her elbow on Marvin's knees. Now and again she nodded in agreement or moved her head to one side as though waiting for a further explanation.

"Now with being, that's quite another story. Being defines a state beyond our sensual perceptions. To *be* you must *become* that which commands your attention. Remember what I have said about Aunt Jenny? I didn't say she works or does anything efficiently. No. She *is* efficient. She doesn't make her 'boys' happy. She *is* the source of their happiness, their security and so forth."

Marvin stopped abruptly. His face indicated that he, too, was coming to a new understanding.

"That must be the secret," he said slowly.

"What is?" Jocelyn seemed a tiny step behind his reasoning.

"The fulcrum. The state of balance. The becoming. The freedom. It all fits in!"

Marvin raised Jocelyn to her feet, lowered her onto the settee and started pacing the studio. He seemed intent on holding something intangible, something that might slip from his grasp at any moment. A single phrase, an idea, kept flashing through his mind. What was it? A dream? What... *The two are one.* That was it. But what did it mean? He tried to wrench it out of his mind.

"Being!" He repeated. "It is at this thin razor's edge that we each balance our fate... That thin edge between the tangible and the intangible. There is within us a centre of consciousness, a seed of our self-awareness, a nucleus of our life force..."

"....a soul?" Jocelyn asked.

"Very well, a soul. We, our acumen, our emotional body, our physical senses are its outer instruments for gathering experience." Marvin spun on his heel to face Jocelyn. "We may choose to be passive, like our soul, or active, like our physical consciousness. It is our choice. Do you understand me?"

"I understand that our soul, being eternal, is outside the limits of time and space. That is self-evident. But you are saying that we have the capacity to, sort of, oscillate between the passive and the active states?"

"Yes and no. It is a paradox. In our physical bodies we are in a constant state of becoming. In our inner self, we are static. We are free, with practice, to partake in gathering experience from either standpoint. We never cease to be souls, but on occasion we can shed our physical consciousness and experience life directly."

Marvin sat down. He felt as though he were coming out of a dream. A dream which lasted millions of years. An eternal dreamer... But which is the dream, he asked himself?

"So both states are correct," Jocelyn reasoned.

"Both are necessary. On earth, soul can no more experience colour than a blind man. The conscious self, or soul, is becoming us in order to gain an experience. It sees through our eyes, hears through our ears. It has its being in our bodies!"

There was another moment of silence. What Marvin just said sounded almost like blasphemy. Jocelyn had been taught that soul is immortal and thus perfect, omniscient, all-powerful, akin to Divinity.

"You are soul. You *are* the eternal state of *being*. You can *be* anything you want. You are, even as I am."

Marvin's eyes narrowed, as though still searching for the elusive, the impalpable.

"You mean.... being is an attitude, a point of view..."

"I mean that your consciousness is an attribute of a soul, not of a body."

"In a way that's obvious. But it's hard to think of myself as a soul aware of my body, rather than a body being aware of a soul."

"Are you aware of your soul?" Marvin pressed his point.

"To be quite honest, no."

"Are you aware of your body?"

"Of course!" Then Jocelyn's eyes gleamed with sudden understanding.

"What is it that is aware of your body?"

"Why, my *self*. That's right. My... self. My self gives me awareness..."

"Your self *is* your awareness. That is why you *are* soul!"

It all seemed pretty obvious. Yet Jocelyn still found it hard to treat her physical body with the same detachment as she felt for a dress or a pair of shoes. She said as much.

"Detachment is hard. But so is patience, humility—all the divine attributes. For me, detachment is made possible only by living in the present. That's what *being* is all about. We must be free from any emotional anchors with our past, free from the expectations of results in the future. To live in the eternal present is to reject the limitations of time and space. Freedom is, can be, only in the here and now..."

"What of our physical bodies?" Jocelyn sounded a little skeptical.

"I, soul—gather experience by becoming one with my physical body. I, soul—make use of the attributes of my physical consciousness. I invest my consciousness to experience the process of becoming. Something tells me that it's a never-ending process. Perhaps an ascending spiral."

"I, soul, can gather experience only by becoming the object of my attention, and thus I must become one with my physical body...." Jocelyn nodded slowly as she repeated Marvin's spoken thoughts.

"I couldn't have put it better myself. Right now, I and my body are one."

That was it! *The two are one.* Where have I heard it before, he wondered. Marvin had a strange notion that Jocelyn had known it all along. All along...

"Shall always have bodies?" She was seldom satisfied with just part of the answer. Or part of a question.

"I suppose. After a fashion. But only if we want to advance. To indulge in becoming."

"Perhaps there are moments of rest? In some kind of heaven?" Jocelyn mused.

"Bodiless?" Marvin found the idea amusing.

"I don't think I would like that."

It was evident that, since meeting Marvin, Jocelyn's attachment to her body had grown stronger than ever.

"What, a restful heaven?" Marvin asked.

"No, having you bodiless."

"You'll never change, will you?" Marvin wondered in sheer exasperation.

"You mean I'm not becoming?"

"Ha, ha!"

"Do you want me to change?"

"Not in a million years," Marvin assured her. He seemed horrified at the prospect.

"I might be old and gray by then," she warned.

"Not if you don't change. But even then, I'd leave your grayness behind and just take your soul with me."

"Bodiless?" She fluttered her eyelashes coquettishly.

He reached for her with unaccustomed masculinity.

"Let me go. The potatoes are boiling!"

"So am I. I feel an urge for becoming a..." Marvin emitted a sound halfway between a lecherous dog and a starving lion.

"Another experience for your soul?" Jocelyn did her best to be serious.

"I *am* my soul! Remember?"

"I've never made love to an angel..."

"I have. Since I met you." Of that, Marvin was certain.

"Something tells me that I shall enjoy this business of being."

"That's good. I think you're supposed to."

"I wonder what heaven is like..."

"Come upstairs and I'll show you."

Jocelyn smiled. She still wondered what it was that she so loved about this man. Was it his probing mind? His wavy black hair or his strong arms and body? Or was it his soul? His unique state of being?

There were just a few steps to heaven.

She is still wondering.

Lethargic summer flowed into the red sunsets and the rich golds of Canadian autumn. Then came the rigors of a hard, cold winter. Then followed the fleeting exuberance of springtime, then.... She finds it strange how closely each year resembles the seasons of her soul.

Marvin continues to learn a lot on his inner travels. Sometimes they are lucky: they travel together. Now and then, their being is interrupted by periods of intense becoming. Intense, sometimes trying, always educational. Always bringing them a little closer together. A little closer to the state of freedom. It is all a lot easier now. They are no longer in a hurry.

They both know that they are eternal.

* * *

Epilogue

At the far wall of the sitting area hangs a large, square sculpture. Most of it seems taken up by a nondescript, unexplored background. An area of irregular, concentric waves, coming and going to and from the central whirlpool, which, in turn, appears to gather its strength from the vast, undulating wilderness. From the surrounding space. Those who look at the sculpture say that they are drawn toward the centre of the whirlpool by some strange, almost hypnotic power.

At its very centre the whirlpool holds a single eye. The eye is static, yet it follows you wherever you go. It remains with you.

The sculpture is not for sale. Their friends regard it as a powerful example of abstract design. To Jocelyn it is a portrait of Marvin.

* * * * * * *

Acknowledgments

My profound gratitude to all who read and offered valuable advice during the early stages, before this book first saw the light of day. My particular thanks go to Madeleine Witthoeft, who burned a lot of midnight oil poring over my effort with painstaking commitment, and to Kate Jones, whose diligent editing as well as subsequent proofreading raised this book to acceptable literary standards.

As always, my thanks go to my wife, Bozena Happach, who offered her sculpture to grace the cover of this book, for inspiring my life and offering comments during and after the completion of the first draft. We hope our combined efforts add up to giving you hours of pleasure.

Sincerely,
Stan I.S. Law

To order books please contact
INHOUSEPRESS, MONTREAL, CANADA
email: info@inhousepress.ca

CPSIA information can be obtained at www.ICGtesting.com
Printed in the USA
LVOW071347220313

325519LV00001B/173/P